WITHIN A WAKENING EARTH

THE HYPERBOLIA SERIES

UNDER A DARKENING MOON
WITHIN A WAKENING EARTH
INTO A HEARKENING SKY

WITHIN A WAKENING EARTH

HYPERBOLIA, BOOK TWO

PETER A. HEASLEY

First paperback edition April 2023

Cover image of ammonite by Matt Heaton/FossilEra, used with permission.

ISBN 979-8-9867574-2-1 (hardcover)
ISBN 979-8-9867574-7-6 (paperback)
ISBN 979-8-9867574-3-8 (ebook)

peteraheasley.com

For Tommy and Matt, my brothers

PART ONE

WAKENING BIRTH

1

Mort opened his eyes and closed them again. The blur that had come to him in that glimpse spoke pre-dawn twilight. His muscles were soft and relaxed, and he did not attempt even to twitch a toe or a thumb. This was the most content-ed feeling he had ever had upon waking, and waking had always been more pleasant than being awake or asleep, so he would savor it.

He could hardly feel himself breathing. The air was somehow thicker, a river gently flowing in reverse, into the many branches of his lungs and out again, as slowly as the tide. He floated on this current of serenity.

After a few minutes, finally curling a toe, he realized his legs were tucked upward and off to the right. His girth would normally never have allowed this. He brushed his thigh with his fingers. The skin began to burn a little where his fingers touched, so he stopped.

He kept his eyes closed because they wanted to be, be-cause his body would soon return to sleep. It was Sunday, and he had no need to leave his bed.

Mort pushed down against the blanket with his foot, and the blanket pulled against his head. He was under the chenille blanket, which was why his breath was warm and humid. His arm would not respond easily to pull the blanket off. He might have still been in sleep paralysis. He crawled his hand upward across his body with his fingers. It burned again where his fingertips touched, and his stomach felt hard. He pressed around the edges of some kind of ball in his stomach. He moved both hands across his abdomen, which felt much thinner than it ever had before. He knit his brow and smacked his lips in thought. When he opened his mouth again, he could feel the air rushing in thickly.

The more he bent his fingers and toes, the more energy poured into his limbs. First his forearms, then his thighs, and finally his shoulders and hips took strength. His face felt thinner. He turned his knees upward, which untwisted his abdomen and brought the strange, hard ball in his stomach to the center of his attention. His hands could not find the edge of the blanket behind his head, or anywhere. The harder he pressed down with his feet, the more firmly the blanket pulled against his head.

The surface of the blanket felt smooth, like felt. The air between his body and the blanket felt as thick between his limbs as within his lungs. He opened his eyes again, and all was blurry and brighter.

A memory returned, or a dream, wherein a piece of plaster had fallen on him during the night. There had been many strange dreams that faded from his consciousness as soon as he remembered them, of wind storms and barking dogs and a series of unspecified catastrophes.

His skin burned nearly everywhere. He pressed against

the blanket, but it held him tight. He breathed in heavily, and this burned his lungs, too.

A brighter seam appeared in the blanket, perhaps where it had worn over the years his grandmother had used it. Onto it, he put his fingernails, which he had let grow a little long. She would forgive him, if she could see from wherever she was, for the long fingernails and for what he was about to do. He tore at the bright seam.

The blanket gave way more easily than he had expected, and it tore more like a thick plastic bag than fabric. Light poured in through the tear, and the blanket began to cling to his skin. Mort pulled himself upward, through the tear. Cold air seared his face and shoulders. He winced in pain, and the breath this reaction would have automatically drawn inward did not come.

He could not breathe. Nothing would move in or out. He put his fingers into his mouth to pull out his tongue, but it was in its normal place. His hand flailed a little in his growing panic. His body was covered in some kind of slime. The steely ball in his stomach pulled down on his throat. He pushed his stomach upward, against his lungs, which sparked a brief spasm. This threw open his diaphragm, and he coughed out some of the slime. The great gulp of air he took in singed his lungs, and he expelled more liquid.

Shivering, Mort pulled up his legs through the opening in the blanket and hung them over the side of the bed. Everything was still blurry, but he could feel his feet dripping with the whitish goo. He slid them onto the wooden floor, and he continued sliding off the bed. He pushed upward with his legs and threw his arms out to grab the top edge of his tall dresser, but his legs failed, and his bony hip hit the floor. He shivered and cried, but tears would not come.

After a few minutes on the hard floor, frozen in weakness, and after his bedroom had grown much brighter, Mort felt at once every limb spring to life with some electric charge. His inner organs, too, vibrated as if someone had switched on a circuit. He could see more clearly, especially through the center of his vision. The slime had dried in large pink-white flakes on the skin of his spindly body. He stood up.

The white sac from which he had emerged lay on his bed, resembling a rubber change purse he had had when he was a child. He dipped his finger in a puddle of the slime inside the sac where it had not yet dried. It smelled of newborn babies. As did the whole room, which otherwise looked just like he had left it when he had switched off the lamp the night before. A bit of plaster really had fallen from the ceiling, though. There was no other possible sign of entry for whatever had cocooned him, nothing out of place in this room except for the broken sac and his naked body, thin, frail, and trembling.

Mort put on the only thing that would hold up at his skinny waist, black sweatpants with a drawstring. There was no bulge at his stomach, not while he was standing, but he could feel the weight of whatever had lodged in it. The last thing he had put there was almond boneless chicken, if he remembered correctly. He shuffled to the bathroom.

The hallway smelled mustier than it had before, and the nightlight was out. The only light came up the stairwell and bounced off the faceted glass handle of the bathroom door.

His grip was not strong enough to turn the handle, which had always stuck. He bounced his bony body against the door, but it did not budge. He did not have to go. He only wanted to look at himself in the mirror. His grandmother's door was closed. Instead of struggling with another door, he went toward the light coming from downstairs.

The musty smell grew stronger as Mort approached the stairs. He could see a little dirt sprayed along the floor in the foyer below. The thick handrail held sturdy. The living room had become a jungle. If he had been asleep for a few days, or even weeks, his plants could not have grown across the floor like this. The large front window had broken, and the boxwood was growing into the house. Mort put on the Crocs he had kept in the coat closet at the base of the stairs. Shards of glass broke beneath his steps. The wallpaper was covered in mildew.

Some creature had ransacked the refrigerator, but the kitchen was otherwise cleaner than the living room. No water came from the sink. No water came from the sink of the half bath, either. It was too dark to see his face in the mirror there, but he could see the thin silhouette of his head. He had never kept plastic bottles of water in the house. He was not thirsty anyway, he realized and then thought he should be.

As he walked back from the kitchen to the living room, he passed in front of the image of Jesus that he had always walked past before, careful not to look at His face. *Jezu, ufam tobie*, the painting said. He had kept it hanging on the wall in honor of his *babcia*, who had always kissed it with her hand. After whatever had happened to her house and his body, this painting still hung, and the merciful eyes of God still stung him with judgment.

Mort put his hand on the railing to go back up the stairs, but something caught his attention. He gazed upward, toward the dark hallway above, and some feeling like dread came over him. He raised a foot to take the first step, but something creaked loudly upstairs. Looking around again at the living room, the walls vibrated some alien quality, some danger. He put on a windbreaker from the closet and went out the front door.

His lawn was overgrown, as was everything else on Eveque Street. East English Village had always been leafy, and now it looked like the rest of Detroit. Houses had crumbled. Grass and trees had grown up through the cracks in the street. Cars were rusted, tires deflated. Whatever had happened to his house had happened everywhere. Perhaps the moondark had done this. He looked back toward his garage, which had fallen in a little, just enough to make opening the door look dangerous. His car would not have fared better than anything else on this street.

Mort walked toward Mack Avenue. His regular stroll to the hospital and back usually took him along Chandler Park Drive, but he would have a better chance of finding something, answers, anything, on the commercial street between his house and the hospital. At the next intersection, he looked both ways and saw more of the same: thick vegetation. Closer to Mack, he heard what sounded like thunder behind him. As he turned around, he traced the leafy line of clear, blue sky back toward his house, near which a cloud of dust billowed into the street. He rubbed his stomach back and forth just once, dropped his head in thought, and turned back to make his way to the hospital.

2

Todd sat on the end of the bed, his eyes pressed closed, his mouth wide in a silent scream. Every breath seared his lungs. He knew that if he breathed normally, if he did not hold his breath, each gasp for air would not rush in like a knife. He forced his breath in through his nose, out through his mouth. In and out, like he had often practiced.

Something smelled of a newborn baby, but he was not in the maternity ward. He knew he was in the hospital because he could feel the plastic railings along his bed. It was dark, and his eyes were blurry. He had woken in this position, farther up the bed, naked, with only a dreamlike memory of coughing hard to clear his lungs. His skin was tightening.

"Dear God, I'm sorry," he said, but his voice was no more than the squeak of a weather vane in the wind. "I promised you, and I promise again. Just let me live through this." Todd did not remember what he had done. It had been a long time since he had taken anything that could have led to this.

Todd felt up his arms for the IV, but he was not connected to anything. Flakes of some kind fell off his skin. He opened and closed his eyes repeatedly until his vision returned. Toward his right was a blinded window. To his left, two other patients slept soundly, large lumps of white fabric. There was an empty bed between him and the window. He turned his legs toward this side and, carefully holding the plastic railing, alighted gently to the floor. He nearly fell but did not and reached his other hand for the empty bed.

He opened the blind at the window, and after his eyes adjusted to the searing light, he saw that the adjoining roof was covered in greenery. "I don't remember that," he said, if only to test his voice, which he could now hear. There was no equipment in the room, only sleeping bodies. His bed was a strange mess. He opened the door.

"Hello?" he called. The lights were off in the corridor, but light from some hidden window showed him through. He shuffled along the floor tiles, using the plastic chair rail running along the wall to keep steady. A breeze reminded him he was naked, and he covered his genitals with his free hand.

The nurses' station was empty, dark, and silent. Todd leaned against the high counter. Binders stood in a row or open on the desk. No lights shined on the telephone or from the computer screens. His mind could not reach any conclusions, and he did not feel worried about what he saw, only curious. "Hello?" he called again with more vigor.

The rooms surrounding the nurses' station were empty. He found scrubs stacked neatly on a metal rack, searched for a medium size, and put these on. Dry hospital socks felt better on his feet than the cold vinyl tile, which had felt as dirty as it looked.

Todd did not recognize this hospital. He had been to Belmont many times, for himself or for others. Maybe this was Resurrection. He stopped halfway down some blank corridor. "Oh. Okay. Right, God. I'm dead. That's what this is, isn't it?" The murky gray light surrounding him and the musty smell invading his nose convinced him otherwise. He continued through endless corridors, finding himself, once again, at the nurses' station. "Just go downstairs, Theodore. Face whatever is there."

The first door he found, not far from the nurses' station, warned that the emergency alarm would go off. After thrusting his hip against the panic bar, he heard only the echo of threatening darkness. The door slammed behind him. He reached for the pipe railing he had seen and followed this down with both hands, taking the steps sideways, slowly.

Three or four stories down, his legs aching from all this work and his hands about to lose their grip, Todd followed the railing as it curved into a concrete wall. He felt along the walls and shuffled along the floor until he felt another door and another panic bar. This one opened more easily and let in broad, new light. This was the entry to the hospital, as empty as everywhere he had seen so far. Light poured in at a sharp angle from behind him, and he could see his shadow on the floor. He walked a few steps to his side, and his shadow split, one darkened silhouette following him and one not. Then the other shadow fell in behind him again. Todd's legs froze, and his heart raced. Some kind of strange murmuring came from behind, and before he could process this, he heard a knock on the glass. He breathed in sharply as he turned.

A man stood behind the glass, much taller than he, gangly underneath his black sweatpants, Tigers windbreaker, and green Crocs. His bare, red, splotchy head hovered above his hunched shoulders.

"This could be good, or this could be bad," Todd whispered to himself. The man yanked on the door handle, but it would not open. He pointed to the door handle. "Okay, maybe not a zombie," Todd said and pushed on the door.

The hot, fresh air brought a whiff of the same newborn smell Todd had grown used to in the hospital. The man entered with it, and his eyes searched Todd up and down. "You know what's going on?" the man asked, in a low mumble that Todd took a few seconds to decipher.

"I just woke up to this myself," Todd said.

"Huh." The man looked around, past Todd, into the empty atrium.

"No one else is here, as far as I can tell," Todd said. His throat scratched. "The place is empty. Where are we? I mean, what hospital is this?"

The man looked down at Todd, his eyebrows wondering how he could not know this. "Resurrection."

"Ah. Okay, so...is anyone out there?"

The man shook his head then said, "No. I just walked up Mack. It's all gone."

"Gone? Like—"

"Like, no one's been here for a long time. By my best estimate of the trees growing up through the street, I would say forty or fifty years. But I could be off."

"Well, that can't be, since we're both still here, so.... Maybe we're deceased or something? My name's Todd, by the way."

"Mort." Mort shrugged. "Maybe. Who knows. I don't feel dead."

Todd watched Mort's eyes, which drifted around the room. "Not that we'd know, right?"

Mort did not reply and walked past Todd, deeper into the atrium of the hospital.

"So when you were out there, what did you see? Was it, like, a war zone, or like zombies came through? A bomb? Were we nuked?"

Mort did not turn around and said, "No, it just looks like everyone left all at once, you know, leaving everything to decay."

"Alright, well, I'm sure they're somewhere, you know, all huddled together. We just have to find them."

"I'm kinda tired. It took me over an hour to get here. I just woke up this morning, and my hip hurts."

"Right, you're right. Let's maybe just make a plan, find some clothes, water, whatever we need."

Mort looked around, nodding. "How is this place still standing? Nothing else is. Let's go to the cafeteria." He turned and walked with a decisiveness Todd did not expect.

Todd followed.

***

Mort and Todd sat at a table in the cafeteria of the hospital. Todd studied Mort, who sat hunched over, hands clasped on the table, his eyelids growing heavy. Mort winced at some pain every few minutes.

"It's pretty quiet," Todd said. "Kind of surprising, how quiet the apocalypse is."

Mort nodded heavily.

"Or death, or wherever we are."

Mort nodded again.

"What are we supposed to do next? I don't feel particularly hungry or even thirsty after all this time."

Mort raised his head and rubbed his stomach. "Agh," he winced. "That's it. There is something in my stomach. Like a," he pursed his lips, "ball."

"Maybe some water would help. We should drink something. Hold on. Stay here. Let me see what I can find."

Todd stood up and found that his muscles, too, had begun to relax again. He gripped the edge of the table. "Whoa. Okay, just a minute." Holding the edge of table, he made a few mini squats. "That seems to do it. Maybe, Mort, you should do the same. I know you're tired from your walk, but just to keep from slipping back into sleep, perhaps. Come on. Up and at 'em." Todd grabbed the underside of Mort's arm. "Come on. Let's go. Just keep the blood pumping."

Mort lumbered upward, held the edge of the table, and, with his eyes closed, made a few mini squats. Todd heard a sigh of relief issue from his own mouth and repeated it a few times, as if making exercising noises. He did not want Mort to think he was relieved that he thought his new companion for the apocalypse was already dying, or worse, that he would be difficult to live with.

"You seem to know your way around here. Let's go to the pantry and see if they have any bottles of water," Todd said. Mort straightened his back, taking his height to almost a full head above Todd's eyes. Todd heard him breathing heavily. "Go ahead and put your hand on my shoulder. I think we need to do this, you know, move around. Just tell me where to go."

Mort quietly steered Todd to the pantry. Inside, Todd saw loaves of bread in chewed-up plastic sleeves, gray and hard where they had not been eaten away by rodents. A few large cans of clam juice had burst open. A pallet of bottled water lay on a lower shelf.

"Voilà," Todd said. "We're in business."

"BPA," Mort said, as if moaning. He leaned on the metal rack. "Look. They're all cloudy. It's been too long. We have a better chance with the pop cans. Sugar's a preservative. Grab me a Fanta."

Todd held a water bottle to his face and held it against the light coming through the pantry door. "Okay, so, BPA. Right. That's, like, a chemical, I guess?"

Mort reached down for a can of Fanta, which made no sound of spray when it opened. He tasted a little and slapped his tongue against the roof of his mouth.

"Any good?" Todd asked.

"Flat. Better than nothing."

Todd tried one. "Bleagh. It's so sweet. I never used to drink this stuff." He looked up at Mort, who seemed to be reviving. "Well, let's just sip at it a little, as need be."

Mort looked around then made for something in the kitchen. He held a radio in his hands, still plugged into the wall. There were no batteries inside, and Mort set it heavily back on the upper shelf of the prep station without closing the battery case.

Todd very subtly leaned forward and back again, wanting both to close the radio's battery case and not to offend his only waking companion. "So, yeah," Todd said. "We're not really going to find food in here. Maybe…."

"Let's go walk around and sort out what we know," Mort said. Some new light glimmered in his eyes. Todd grabbed another Fanta for himself and one for Mort.

The two men walked the corridors of the ground floor. Where the halls grew dark, they caressed the wall. Todd thought they would head only toward patches of light, but Mort seemed to see in the darkness.

"I don't think I've ever really been through Resurrection," Todd said. "Been to Belmont plenty of times. They say at Resurrection, that's what the doctors are counting on to save you in the end."

"Belmont. Nice. You from Grosse Pointe?" Mort asked.

Damn, Todd thought. "You really know your way around."

"Been here a lot over the years. My grandma was in and out a lot."

Double damn. "Did she pass away before all this?"

"Yeah. Lung cancer."

"Ooh. Tough one."

"She was. This was actually a pretty good hospital, you know."

"Yes, of course, I know, I was just making a joke, just trying to add a little levity to our, eh, predicament."

"How did you get here anyway?"

Todd breathed in deeply, thinking of a way to make peace with this man. "I don't know, actually. To tell you the truth, I had probably just overdone it. With something."

"I see."

"Actually, I don't know. I don't remember doing anything. I was doing pretty well for a while there."

"You don't think it was the moon?"

"The moon? Why the moon?"

"You remember. All kinds of crazy stuff happened after the moon blew."

"What does that mean, 'the moon blue'? Did the moon turn blue?"

Mort stopped and turned around. With the diffuse light of a large window behind him, he was little more than a silhouette. "The moondark, Todd. Last August. You know, big burst, cloud of light, aurora spreading across the sky? Mass hysteria? Not ringing a bell?"

"You're saying the moon, like, literally blew up?"

"And you're saying you fell asleep before all that? It didn't blow up, it was still there, it just somehow shed all of its light."

"Did, like, maybe you dream all this up? How can the moon do that?"

Mort walked toward the large window near a nurses' station. In clearer light, he turned toward Todd. In a deep monotone, he said, "I don't know, you know? How can any of this happen? People were trying to figure all this out when I fell asleep, which was in November."

"Well, I fell asleep in mid-August. Wait a minute, Mort. When I woke up, there were other people in the room with me. I wonder if they had the same thing happen to them."

***

Mort stood over the hardened lumps in the room where Todd had woken while Todd stared at a white, leathery sac covered with dried goo on the bed he had vacated. He had taken the sac for vomit-soaked sheets before.

"I don't think these two made it, Todd."

"What is this thing, Mort? What, are we, like, pod people now? What is all this? Did aliens do this? Did the government? Mort, what the hell is going on?"

"I don't know. I'm a biologist, or was, and I don't know." He sipped his Fanta and walked over to Todd's sac. "Well, here, look. There's a mark on it. Maybe that will tell us something." Mort held the lower left corner of Todd's sac into the light. "An anchor. What does that mean? Whose company logo is that?"

Todd looked at the shape, green and distended across the white, leathery patch Mort held up. He looked up and down the sac and pressed a finger to some part of it. A sweaty chill washed over his face, and his stomach turned. "Oh, God." He turned toward the empty bed. The light coming through the window warmed his clammy face. His mouth opened for tears but none came from his eyes. "Oh, God, Mort. That's a tattoo I had on my calf. That's my skin. I think that's my skin."

3

Mort's feet hung well beyond the end of the bed in the pediatric ward one floor below the room where Todd had woken. This was the most well-kept room they could find for
rest, free of dust, debris, and human detritus. The multi-col-
ored balloons on the wall were drowning in the deep wash
of red pouring through the west-facing window. Mort had
seen many sunsets on several continents, and this was the
deepest red he had ever seen.

Todd erupted into choking sniffles again. After the initial
shock of seeing his old epidermis lying like a used tissue on
the hospital bed, Todd had briskly walked out of the room.
Mort had followed to keep the man from harming himself,
but he soon found Todd methodically searching through
drawers and shelves for supplies. Todd had changed into a
new set of scrubs, vigorously peeling and rubbing the last
of the dried-up goo from his skin and ordering Mort to do
the same. Over the course of several hours, in which they
navigated every habitable floor, the two had filled canvas
laundry bags with changes of scrubs and socks, face masks,
surgical equipment, bandages, rolls of paper for lighting
fires, an unopened bottle of bleach, and a half-used bottle of

cheap Canadian whisky. Todd's share of the whisky had just reopened the sobbing gates.

"Why am I not actually crying?" Todd said.

"Sounds like it to me," Mort replied.

"It's everything except actual tears. Look."

Mort looked at Todd's puffed, splotchy, and dry face. "Huh."

"Huh, you say. You're taking all this in stride."

"We're alive, right? We'll figure it out." Mort stared up at the ceiling. "Newborns don't actually shed tears for a few months after birth. Maybe that's it."

"Kind of fitting, then, that we're in this room," Todd said. "Newborns. But dealing with a totally shit world outside. What was it really like out on the street? There's no one? Nothing?"

"Like everyone just up and left a generation ago."

"So we're the left behind? Left behind to do what?"

"Beats me. You believe in all that stuff, the rapture or whatever?"

Todd put his hands behind his head. "I mean, I believe in God," Todd said. "Maybe not the rapture, per se."

Mort quietly breathed a sigh of relief and turned back toward the ceiling. "So what does God say we do next?"

Todd was silent.

"Thought so. That's why I say we just figure it out. Everyone's gotta be gathered somewhere. We'll find a working radio."

Todd huffed. "What if we don't really want to find the others? What if it's bad, like, Mad Max out there? I do not feel equipped to handle that."

Mort put his hands over his face. "Right. One day at a time, then. We'll figure it out." He stared up at the ceiling, which grew dim and gray. His eyelids began to fall.

"I wonder where my family is."

Mort pulled open his eyes again.

"Did you have anyone else, Mort? You mentioned your grandma. Are your parents around? Brothers and sisters? Wife, girlfriend? Boyfriend? I still lived at home with my parents. Thirty-one years old and at home. My brother Jake, Jacob Farkas, Jr., mind you, he's ventured out. Still in GP, I mean, but basically on track. My sister Evelyn got her M.R.S. degree, married a diplomat, and is now living in Morocco. I hope. God, I wonder what my shop looks like. I have a hair salon, three chairs. It's not bad. And, yes, I know what you're thinking, so, alright, fine, Dad did fund it, but it's a loan. An interest-free loan but still a loan. And it's going fine. In fact, I think that's where I was when I passed out or fell asleep or whatever, closing up, waiting for Frankie to get out of the bathroom. Frankie rents a chair there. Maya, too, but she wasn't in that day, which is weird, because it was a Saturday—oh, no, that's it, she was at a wedding up in Traverse City. That's big bucks to fly your stylist up for your wedding. God, she must've made a killing. How did we get here? Oh, yeah, right. So did you, like, wake up at home? Was anyone else there?"

Mort waited until his every nerve ending stopped shooting sparks into the boundary layer of air around his body, pulling his skin and his patience tight against his bones, then said, "No."

"No? No one?"

"Just me. I never really knew my parents. Grandma was it for family."

"Oh. That's, um...."

"It's not anything. It is what it is. If you don't mind, Todd, can we just rest now? It feels like summer outside, and the sun just set, so it's got to be around nine or ten o'clock. It's been a rough day."

"Yeah, sure, alright," Todd said. After a few seconds of silence, he added, "But you're not afraid of going back to sleep? Like, not waking up again?"

"At this point, it's all the same to me."

***

Mort woke in the pitch darkness. His heart, by his measure, had woken before him and was beating steadily now. Pulling his head backward, toward the window, he saw one or two stars above the treetops. Todd was not snoring. Anything could have woken him, even a slight breeze over his exposed feet.

Mort tried to recall anything peculiar about the last night he remembered. It had been like many other nights, eating Chinese food in front of the television, sporadic thoughts of where to spend his first Thanksgiving alone breaking through the laughter of the studio audience. The idea had come to him to spend the day helping at a shelter. He might even have smiled at this.

The ball in his stomach pressed heavily against his spine. He had not noticed it during his foraging with Todd. The Fanta and the whisky had seemed to slip right past it—

Someone else was here now. Someone was behind the door just past his feet.

This had woken him, perhaps, his brain interpreting the noise in his sleep. But there was no noise now. There was no light apart from those dim stars, and yet his mind's eye saw the slender figure behind the door. His imagination was inventing this presence, putting together all the dangers, giving them the form of something he could fight. He had felt a similar dread when he had looked up the stairs of his house yesterday morning. His brain was alert to some danger. His house had been about to fall, and his brain had known it.

Mort rubbed his arms against the fabric of the bed. The presence did not flee from this sensory assault and seemed to see him all the more sharply. This, whatever this was, was staring back at him now, through the door, through the black. Mort had measured many feelings through another's gaze, like frustration and pity, but he had never felt hate. This is what it felt like, searing hatred. He pulled his feet up onto the bed, raising his knees.

"Mort?" Todd whispered. He had fear in his voice.

Mort breathed out sharply, not realizing he had been holding his breath. "Yeah?" he whispered. He was trembling.

"Where are you?"

Mort swallowed and breathed. "In bed."

Todd was silent.

"It's alright. Something woke me up, too."

"I still feel it," Todd said. "Behind the door."

"Me, too."

"What do we do? It knows we're here."

"Hold on." Mort reached for the bottle of whisky on the table between the two beds. If the person opened the door, he would chuck it at him. Instead, the air grew hot with the penetrant gaze. The glass bottle began to slip within Mort's sweaty grip. His body flashed cold. He did not know if it was better to keep his eyes open or closed.

REAAAGH

"Whawoowoo!" Todd shrieked.

Mort, sitting upright, pushed air through his mouth. "Okay. It's okay. It's just an owl."

REAAAGH

"Omigod omigod," Todd said. "Omigod omigod."

"It's okay, it's okay, it's okay. Whew. It's okay. That's all it was. Nothing more."

"That's all it was," Todd said. "Just staring through the window."

"Yeah." Mort's shaking hands put the bottle back on the table. He did not sense the presence behind the door anymore.

"But," Todd said, "maybe let's just put something in front of the door. There was, like, a desk over here."

Mort, still full of adrenaline from the owl's screeching, sprang out of bed and bumped into Todd, who was already standing. He was happy to laugh at this, to laugh with Todd. He felt his way to the wall and turned left. The desk was not heavy, but it would provide at least some obstacle to whoever might try to come in. Mort shuffled backward for a few yards and stopped to feel for the door. "Okay. Here we are. This should do it."

Back in their beds, Mort heard Todd alternate between sobs and chuckles. He was doing the same. Sometime during another of Todd's soliloquies, Mort fell asleep.

***

Mort stood with Todd in front of the hospital. The strange purple light that had filled the pediatric room when they had woken lingered more lightly out on the street and gave the world before them enough of an alien hue to make each man wary of stepping out into it. Todd was nudging a wheelchair forward and backward as if it were a stroller and not a makeshift wagon filled with supplies. Mort was glad he had insisted on keeping his Tigers jacket, for it was a little chilly this morning.

"Mack's right here," Mort said.

"It's clearing up, I think, this light."

The two men stood silently, gazing at the houses fallen into their foundations and the trees rising up through the breaks in the road.

"Now or never, right?" Mort said this hoping to jump-start his otherwise energetic companion. His legs would not volunteer the first step.

"Right," Todd said. He pushed the wheelchair forward.

Mort followed. They agreed to head right, southwest on Mack Avenue, until they came to Mort's street, and forage what they could in the stores along the way. A supermarket had caved in. They could not trust the drugs in the pharmacies. A bicycle shop was inaccessible. The cars in the dealers' lots were disintegrating.

A gardening center promised entry. The sky had turned a more natural blue, and the air was clear.

"This place was good," Mort said. "Smaller than the place I worked at but still good."

"I thought you said you were a biologist," Todd said.

"I was. Well, in graduate school anyway. Took some time

off, worked in a garden store for a while. Then Grandma got sick, and here we are."

"I see," Todd said, following Mort through the open fence and into a maze of flowers and ivy. "What should we be looking for, you think?"

"I don't know. Buckets, knives, rope, whatever. Seed, I suppose, if we need to just settle down somewhere and start planting."

"Maybe a real wagon," Todd said. "Ooh. Speaking of...."

After Todd pulled a wire-mesh wagon free of its ivy clutches, Mort set three small paving bricks inside it.

"What's that for?" Todd asked.

"For cooking. Three bricks makes a kitchen."

Todd nodded, and Mort walked into a part of the store that had not collapsed. He stared at a row of shovels, rakes, and hoes. Something attracted him to this display. Some calculation was happening in his brain whose reasons had not yet risen to the surface. He picked up a hand trowel, which was pointed and almost sharp.

Todd came around with the wagon, which was filled with buckets, rope, and cloth. "Oh, that's brilliant." He took the trowel from Mort. "We can shovel our poo into the ground. Better that way. Fewer diseases. I saw that on one of those survivalist shows once. I think I could start a fire if we needed to. I haven't seen any flint or matches, though. Maybe at a camping store, but I haven't seen one. We'll look through houses that are still standing. I mean, you have that stuff at home, right? I'm actually really afraid to see what my house looks like. God, what is this world we're living in?"

Mort slowly jabbed at the open air with another trowel.

Todd's eyes followed the thick blade then dashed to behind Mort, at the long-handled rakes and shovels. Mort turned, and it seemed like the two men were subconsciously calculating the figures still hidden in Mort's head until Todd's hands began scanning the array of tall, wooden-handled tools for shafts onto which the trowel would fit. But the short shaft of the trowel was solid.

"What if we stuck them into the bamboo poles an aisle over?" Todd asked. "Then we'd have spears."

Mort pulled the full wagon along the broken sidewalk, feeling a smile on his face. He would make a spear.

About ten minutes into their walk farther along Mack Avenue, Mort recognized the corner of his street and turned right.

"You live on Eveque?" Todd said.

"Yeah."

"Me, too."

"Really?"

"Yeah, like at the other end of it, on Jefferson. Or a little past, on the water."

"Huh," Mort said. "What a coincidence."

A few minutes later, Mort and Todd stood before the crumbled remains of Mort's house. The second floor had fallen in, almost intact, upon the first floor.

"I'm so sorry, Mort," Todd said. "This was your home."

Mort looked at the house where he had been raised since his early childhood. He summoned many memories, but none of them matched the pile of yellow-brown bricks before him. "Well, I guess that's that." He turned and caught a look of astonishment on Todd's face. He began pulling the wagon in the direction of Todd's house.

"That's that?" Todd asked. "This was your home."

Without turning around, Mort said, "It's where I lived. Now I have to find a new place to live, that's all."

4

Todd stood in the cul-de-sac in front of his house. He had not yet told Mort which house was his, not for dramatic effect, but because he could not believe what he was seeing. He wanted time to think about what he saw before him, to prepare for a reality very different from what he had come to expect on the two-hour-long walk from Mort's house. All along their shared street, when he was able to take his eyes off the broken pavement below him, he saw in the once well-groomed neighborhood broken windows, crumbling roofs, and soot-blackened bricks. City Hall and the police station were in ruins, as was every house they passed. Every house except Todd's.

"I hope it's the one that's all boarded up," Mort said.

"It, in fact, is."

"That's a relief," Mort said. "Well, sir, lead the way."

Todd dropped the wagon's handle and walked toward the front door, which, like every window on every floor, was covered in painted plywood. The lawn was overgrown, and there was a new tree or two, but the roof was intact. He felt the edges of the plywood, wondering how he could get past it.

"What about the garage door?" Mort asked.

Todd walked over to the garage door, which had no handle.

"Hold on," Mort said. "We'll use the trowels."

Todd stared blankly at the trowel in his hand while his brain tried to summon what purpose Mort had in mind. He settled on mirroring Mort's actions, which was to wedge his trowel between one end of the wide door and the concrete pad and lever it upward, put his fingers in the gap, and pull. Daylight poured into a garage empty of cars and lined with shelving Todd had not seen before. He studied the strange new items on the shelves. There were kerosene lamps and matches, freeze-dried food and glass bottles filled with water, strangely shaped flashlights, and one wind-up radio.

"Oh, good," Mort said, picking up the radio. He had brought the wagon into the garage. "Preppers, eh?"

"Not really. This is," he scanned the walls of the garage, "this isn't like them."

"But they must've seen everything going on, you know? They got ready. Who knows, maybe they're inside, asleep like we were."

Todd's arms froze as he clung to a shelf, and he felt his stomach contract around the same kind of heavy ball Mort had mentioned he had, and which Mort thought was an ulcer or tumor. Mort had not spoken about it again but had winced every time he drank the flat Fanta. Todd had known knots of anxiety before, and this was different. He felt afraid even to look at the door going into the house from the garage. This heavy ball in his stomach drew all of his energy and emotion to circle around it like it was a black hole.

"I'm sorry," Mort said. "That was stupid. I'll go first, check things out, you know?"

Todd nodded a little. He heard Mort open the door then felt Mort's arm brush by his head as he returned to grab a flashlight. The flashlight made a noise like a toy pull-back car, which echoed sporadically from within the house, fading as Mort went deeper and higher into the unknown.

When Mort seemed to be in the basement, Todd relaxed his hands and looked around the shelves. This loosened his body's grip on the ball in his stomach. There were containers of clear water and filters and chemicals with which to purify more. With all the windows boarded up, it did not seem that his mother and father had intended to stay here.

"It's alright," Mort said, standing in the doorway. "There's no one inside, not anywhere. It's all neat and clean, too."

Todd brought a lit kerosene lamp into the kitchen. It smelled a bit musty, but everything was clean. The refrigerator had been emptied, cleaned, and unplugged, along with all the other appliances. The furniture in the great room was covered with sheets. A few boxes of instant logs sat next to the fireplace. The computer had been removed from the study, but the shelves were still lined with books, knickknacks, and photographs.

Mort was scanning the house as well, and with his chin stuck out and his hands clasped behind his back, Todd thought he looked like a detective. "Your family have a pet toad?" Mort asked.

"What?"

"I see pictures of each of you in the family on the hearth shelf and one framed photo of a toad."

Todd repressed a smile and walked quickly into the great room. Above the fireplace, in five identical frames of a cheap, drug-store variety, were individual pictures of his mother, father, brother, and sister. Where Todd's picture should have been, there was a picture of a toad.

"All these pictures are new," Todd said. On the back of his mother's frame was her name, date of birth, and other vital information. "The one you think is me is Jake, Jr. That's understandable. We look alike. I'm the toad."

He turned over the toad and read:

Dear ~~Toad~~ Todd:

If you're reading this, you're as smart as I've always thought you are. And you're awake. We left you at Resurrection because that seemed like the safest thing to do. You would be better taken care of than with us. Certain doctors seemed to be interested in your case there. We are going to the diner—you know the place. The moon has fallen into a pattern of almost daily eclipses. Being near Detroit or any other major city doesn't seem wise anymore. I hope that changes. When I get Mom and Dad set up I'll come back and get you.

Love,
Numero Due

Every muscle in Todd's face posed for tears, but none would stream from his eyes. His chest shook, and he moaned his joy at knowing his family had escaped whatever had happened. He felt Mort pull the frame from his hand.

"Toad?" Mort asked.

"You know, Todd, Toad. It was Jake's nickname for me because I have wide shoulders and no hips, no butt. Jake. He's Numero Due. Evelyn was above nicknames. Okay. Wow. So, yeah. My family is out there somewhere. We have a destination."

"A certain diner?"

"This is code, just Jake being funny. The diner the Ram's Horn, which is not actually a diner, well, it's a diner around here, hence the double entendre, but it's also the name of a mountain in Montana, near Big Sky. That's where they are. We had a timeshare."

"Big Sky, Montana," Mort said, handing Todd the frame. "That's pretty far to pull a wagon."

***

Todd sat with Mort on the back terrace, looking out over Lake St. Clair. The water, always silver-blue, began to shimmer gold under the late afternoon sun. This shallow bulge of water, overwhelmed on maps of the Great Lakes, had nevertheless always held the Canadian coastline over the horizon except toward the southeast, near Windsor, where Todd was gazing. But Todd could see the other coast clearly in all directions.

"The air's so much clearer now," Todd said. "I can see much more of Canada than before. One would never realize how deep the horizon goes with such dirty air. The Earth is healing."

"Uh huh."

"Maybe that's what all this is. The Earth has spat us out, is scrubbing herself clean of us filthy humans."

"Todd, come on. I'm trying to listen."

"*Sor*-ry," Todd said.

Mort was scanning the frequencies on the wind-up radio. Its squawk and static disturbed Todd's newfound tranquility, but he agreed with Mort that they should not formulate a plan without all the information they could gather. Todd sipped some whisky, better stuff that his parents had left behind. The shadow of the house enclosed them and grew longer toward the southeast.

He looked over at Mort's ankles, less red and splotchy than they had been, poking through the end of the pants Mort had insisted on taking from a clothing store in the Village this afternoon, green corduroy dotted with pink embroidered whales. Todd had begged him not to wear them, but Mort had said that as long as he was staying in Grosse Pointe, he was going to dress preppy, to which Todd had relayed that no one really dressed that way, except sometimes, and that Todd's own clothes, for instance, were all black.

"Isn't that the standard uniform for a hairstylist?" Mort had asked.

Todd had said no and then realized he had had no real reason for wearing black before. The two men were wearing matching purple polo shirts, their collars popped.

"I've been through it three times, there's nothing on FM," Mort said. "I'm going for the AM now."

Todd wanted to listen as much as Mort, but a thought grew persistent. If, as Mort the biologist and gardener had been saying, a whole generation had passed, forty or as much as eighty years, his family would no longer be alive wherever they were. He would be looking for nieces and nephews or whoever had inherited the cabin. Mort could not be correct, though. No one could sleep for that long. There must be some other explanation for all the growth and decay.

"We can't be the only ones around here, or even the only ones who just woke up," Todd said. "How long was Rumpelstiltskin asleep for?"

"Sh, hold on, I think I've...nope. Who? I don't know. Rip Van Winkle, you mean."

"Here's my plan. We use my house as a base, and we venture out into the city each day in different directions, looking for traces of civilization."

"Not a bad idea." Mort continued turning the dial. "You have fishing gear? We can't keep eating that old dehydrated food your folks stored up."

"Maybe in the garage, I don't know. Dad had some stuff unless he took it with him."

"That's one run through the AM. I'll go over it again."

"Here, let me try."

Mort wound up the radio's generator and handed it to Todd, took a drink, and winced. "I'm gonna go look for fishing gear."

Todd began scrolling through the band. A bird hovering over the lake drew his eyes upward. The shimmering waves, their gentle lapping against the seawall, and the vapors of the whisky overcame the grating, un-patterned noise coming from the radio. Todd's eyelids began to droop. He snapped his head upward just as the radio was about to fall from his hands. Mort was standing in front of him. His thin, Edvard Munch face was pale and shaken.

"What? What's going on?" Todd asked. "You alright?"

"I…. Here, I found a couple of rods and a case full of lures and things."

Todd set the radio on the table and rubbed his face. "You look like you've seen a ghost. How long was I out?"

"About ten minutes, I guess."

"Alright, wow."

"And, yeah, I don't know, something did happen. Sort of like last night. Hard to describe. Nothing, I guess."

"Look around, Mort. Nothing is nothing. I mean, everything is something. You know what I mean."

Mort sat down and opened the case of lures. "Just, you know, the jitters. I mean, look around."

Todd leaned his head in his hand and looked over at Mort. "Let us stick together, though. Who knows what's out there, real and unreal. Alright. Let me get back to this radio." Todd resumed turned the dial.

"You're going too fast," Mort said. "Nice and—"

…oledo…

Both men shot upright. Lures spilled out at Mort's feet. Todd finely tuned the dial. Classical music began playing. Todd looked at Mort, who was smiling back at him. Todd set down the radio, picked up his glass of scotch, and began dancing on the terrace with some large, invisible partner. Mort raised his glass. The men clinked, and Mort joined Todd, bouncing his knees and swaying back and forth.

The music ended, and the deejay returned, educating his audience about the piece and giving station identification: WATT FM in Toledo.

"That's it," Mort said. "All we have to do is get to Toledo."

37

"On our way to Big Sky, of course."

"Of course. We'll find transportation there."

"But how do we get to Toledo? I'm exhausted already. My little body just woke up." Todd sighed. "Plus, I just don't feel equipped to walk through whatever's out there. God, it could be zombies or aliens or who knows what. I mean, I'd maybe feel safer on a boat or something."

Mort looked at Todd. "Right? Why not? Do you have a boat?"

***

"This is totally stealing," Todd said.

They were in his neighbor's shed. Mort looked at the fourteen-foot rowboat in fiberglass made to look like wood, in good condition, and possessed of both oars. "Their house is falling apart, Todd. They're not around."

"This boat is definitely not big enough. I mean, it's a big lake out there."

"We stick close to shore. We could get all the way to Toledo in this."

Todd looked toward his house.

"I know how you're feeling. If my house hadn't fallen down, I'd feel the same way, perhaps. It's safe here, so far. I don't know. But it's probably safer elsewhere."

"Or more dangerous."

"We'll be offshore. If things look crazy from the water, we can just row back here. Downtown'll be just a couple of hours by boat. If it's full of zombies or whatever, we can hide behind Belle Isle on our way back here. They won't be able to track us in the water. That's zombie truth."

Todd leaned his chin in his hand and stared at the boat.

He put his hand to the bow and shook it, as if to test its sturdiness. "Let's just sleep on it. It's getting late anyway."

***

Mort lay in the bed belonging to Todd's father. With approval that Todd had given only with half-lidded eyes, Mort also lay in silk pajamas his father had left behind. Todd knelt by his mother's bed, praying. Mort waited for him to finish and extinguish the kerosene lamp.

"What's with the two beds anyway? Your folks not get along?"

"They said they got along because they were in two beds. They said they actually got the idea from watching some old television show, and when they made fun of it to friends, they were like, they'd totally been doing that for years, sleeping in separate beds. How all that works is a mystery to me."

"Your parents' love life is a mystery? At least you knew yours."

"What happened to your folks, if you don't mind my asking?"

"It's hard to say." Mort pulled his hands behind his head and gripped the top of the pillow. "What I mean, I guess, is that I don't really know. Grandma was always sort of shady about it, her friends, too."

The nervous din of dead air filled Mort's ears.

"You don't have to say, of course," Todd said.

Mort lay his hands on his stomach. "It's like there was always this thing everyone talked around, like some great big invisible elephant in the room. All I know is that there was some kind of legal trouble, maybe even jail, and they either disappeared or are dead. There's nothing online. I know that they were managers at GM. Dad was working in Iran for a while, before the revolution. GM had a thing going there. He brought back all kinds of stuff, rugs and knick-knacks and things. I always wondered if my folks were somehow involved in the revolution back in '78–'79, but that's me just trying to be romantic about the whole thing. *Babcia* was not, just stoic. She ground it out every day. She worked the line in Hamtramck, saved up, and got a place in East English Village. I was born in Warren, but after whatever happened—I was three or four—she took me in."

"What's her name?"

"Renata. Renata Sobieski. My mother's mother. Like the great king who saved Europe from the Ottomans."

"Oh, maybe you've got great warrior blood in you."

"Well, I don't know. Not in that way anyway. No, actually, there was this poster we had, a travel poster, you know, for local tourism in Iran or whatever, another thing Dad had brought back. It was a pleasant scene of some young people at a lake. All the words were in Iranian script, I couldn't read it. But the people in the scene, I don't know, they sort of looked like they could be my neighbors; it didn't seem all that exotic. I know now that we're all Indo-Europeans, but I used to just stare at that poster, as if there was another world out there where I could…I don't know…." Mort's chin fell heavily.

"Where what, Mort?"

Mort felt his eyes swell. He pinched them and tried to mask his heaving breaths.

"Where you might feel at home?" Todd said.

Mort swallowed loudly and heaved a breath outward

then recovered. "That's actually the only thing I miss from that house."

"We'll get you a new one."

"A new poster?"

"A new house. A home. You're right. We can't stay here. We have to get on with these strange new lives of ours. Maybe make new ones."

5

The last fish flies clung to the tower of the red brick church, which told Mort it was late June or July on Lake St. Clair. He and Todd had set out to forage for supplies with which to fill the boat. So far unsuccessful, they'd stopped at this relatively intact church. Even its grounds seemed well kept until recently, but Mort could find no other sign of life around the building. The heavy wooden doors that opened toward the lake were locked, as was every other door to the church, rectory, and school. They were an hour's walk from Todd's house, and this was, so far, the closest they had come to a lingering human presence.

"It's almost like you can feel that people were just here," Todd said.

"That's just our brains processing the evidence of human activity. We give it life. Like yesterday, with whatever fear I felt in the garage. All it takes is a funny noise or a rustle in the grass, and our brains build it into a monster."

He watched Todd lean his spear against the base of the church. Duct tape had served to keep the trowel on the bamboo handle. Todd watched his spear fall, and, instead of picking it up, he continued doing what he had set out to do, feeling the bricks with the palms of his hands.

"How about we head home? I mean, to your place. It's been a long morning."

Todd pressed the side of his face against the bricks. "You're Polish," Todd said. "Are you Catholic? This could be your church."

"I am, I guess, I don't know. I don't think much about it. That was all Grandma. What about you?"

"I go to a nice Lutheran church not far from here. Let's maybe go there now."

Mort tried to suppress a yawn.

"It's on the way home."

***

A few hours later and after a nap, Mort sat on the seawall at Todd's house, fishing. He was not hungry, but logic told him to eat. The ball in his stomach might let only liquid pass by, but he and Todd had to try more solid food than the stale paste that the dehydrated stuff from Todd's garage had become when mixed with water.

After finding Todd's church in disrepair, they had walked up one street and down another. Like in the hospital when they had first met, Todd would not let Mort succumb so easily to fatigue. Their spears had become helpful as walking sticks.

Todd had been proven right. A ruined and pillaged sporting goods store had provided backpacks and an eight-by-eight tent. Most cooking gear had rusted, but they could use the one knife they had found. Plastic water bottles and a pair of hiking boots for Mort's large feet rounded out their find. Clouds had come in to cover the second half of their walk, but Mort had insisted they find headgear of some kind.

From beneath the brim of his new Lions cap, Mort lifted his head from the shallow lake toward a horizon that seemed to tuck itself upward, hiding behind a blanket of clouds.

"I just wish there was actual information coming out of this radio," came Todd's voice from the terrace. "One station playing classical music. It's almost like it's all prerecorded."

A series of large shadows raced silently over the surface of the lake in front of Mort. He turned in their direction, toward the north, and saw two pairs of small aircraft flying high along the lake's edge. They seemed rectangular in shape and without wings but flew so fast he could not make out much about them before they became too small to see. They made no noise.

"Did you see that, Todd?"

"See what?"

"People. Flying. In something very quietly."

Todd sprang upward to see, and his legs almost gave way. He held his face as if he were dizzy and sat down again.

Mort walked over. "It's alright. They're gone anyway. Maybe toward Cass Ridge Air Base. That's closer than Toledo. Way closer. Just about twenty miles north."

"But upstream, right? I do know how the current goes around here. I'm not sure I can muster enough muscle on the boat to get us against the current. We did maybe overdo it today."

"If people are passing by, perhaps we should stay, like you said. We'll take it easy."

"But they made no noise. How will we know they're coming?"

"We build a fire. I'll chop down your neighbor's boat house. I saw an axe in the garage." Mort turned toward the garage.

"Now you have all the energy," Todd said.

Mort turned and shrugged at Todd, and when his eyes faced forward again, his legs stopped so suddenly it was as if he had walked into a glass railing.

Two green eyes pierced the murky depths of vegetation between the garage and a tree. The cougar's fur looked dark, almost black, in the shadows.

"What do we do, Mort?" Todd whispered from behind him.

The cat made a noise like a chuff or a short meow then slunk backward into the wild hedges.

Mort pulsed out a stowed breath. "Nothing."

"What do you mean? We're in his territory."

Without daring to turn around, Mort said, "Her. No. That was some other kind of signal. A warning."

"Well, yeah, she's warning us about being in her territory."

Mort's long limbs loosened up again. "I mean, warning us like we were her cubs." He turned toward the shimmering lake, whose silver-blue light filled his eyes. A waltz from the radio filled the air. "Let's just get to Toledo. We'll float our way down."

6

Todd gripped both sides of the narrow boat at the stern
while Mort lowered himself down a ladder on the seawall,
careful to avoid the rusted rung on which Todd had stepped
and nearly fallen into the lake. The boat was tied to the ladder. Everything else was already in—their bags, the tent, the
fishing gear, their spears, the buckets, and a few instant logs
wrapped in garbage bags.

Sometime during the night, Todd had woken up to the
sound of a helicopter passing overhead. After briefly trying
to wake Mort, he'd decided to race down to the lakeside to
shine a flashlight in the air, but by the time he had found the
flashlight, which he or Mort had knocked under the bed in
his sleep, and reached the back terrace, the helicopter had
been far to the south. Mort had eventually shuffled downstairs, but they could find nothing in the dark with which to
light the neighbor's boat house on fire. When a jet had shot
overhead an hour later, Todd had sighed. When the helicopter had returned from the south, it had been early morning,
and despite his and Mort's best efforts to wave their hands
in the air while pumping generator flashlights, the pilots,

flying near the cloud line, clearly could not see them or their meager beacons.

The boat rocked when Mort stepped in, but he sat down quickly, untied the mooring, pushed off the seawall with an oar, and began rowing. Todd was unsure why he rowed directly out into the lake until Mort nodded back at the house, which had become visible over the seawall. Todd blew a kiss. His eyes became blurry.

"Hey, look," Todd said, wiping his cheek. "Real tears. It's about time."

Mort was looking past him, toward the rear. In his corduroys, polo shirt, and Lions cap, Mort made it look like they were out for a little fun. Todd let his hands rest on his lap.

In just a few minutes and with little talking, they rowed into the Detroit River. Mort rowed gently, as agreed, so as not to grow tired. No signs of life came from the houses on Windmill Pointe or from the marinas farther down. Todd was not sure what to make of what he saw in the Detroit skyline rising above the trees or the housing blocks along the river, what ruin belonged to this new world and what ruin belonged to the Detroit of old. At the Belle Isle Bridge, about two hours into their journey, Todd asked, halfheartedly, if Mort wanted to switch, to take a rest. He said no.

Once past the bridge, Todd could feel his own face screwing tight at what he saw. One of the four shorter towers of the Renaissance Center was leaning against the central tower, and another one had fallen into the river.

"Everything alright?" Mort asked.

Todd pushed his chin forward. "Maybe."

"Maybe? That's your favorite word."

"Okay, now's not the time for that."

"What is it time for?"

"Maybe rowing a little farther from the edge."

Mort turned the boat around to have a look for himself. "That's not good." He pulled the boat alongside the tower that had fallen onto its side and into the river like a jetty. Its blackened steel skeleton loomed overhead. Fragments of glass hung like sharpened teeth. The seawall had caved inward, and the river's current had carved away at the clay beneath the building. Todd reached out for one steel beam, which was now a column.

"This might have fallen recently. Maybe the tunnel collapsed. Tell you what, though, let's go in."

Todd could not summon the courage to say yes or no.

Mort rowed between the upper floors, which rose like walls on their right and left. Carpet tiles had begun to pull loose from the decking. Two or three cubicles still clung to that concrete slab, and a computer monitor dangled from its power cable above him. To Todd's left, the ceiling tiles that had not disintegrated were saturated with river water.

"This would be a great place to fish," Mort said. "Look at them. They can hide from the birds here."

Todd looked into the river, which was clearer than he remembered, and saw a few fish rising closer to the surface and sinking back into the depths. The boat broke out into the daylight at the other end of the building. Breathing freely again, Todd looked back at the tower through which they had just rowed. "This place is getting so surreal."

"Tell me about it," Mort said. "Well, what do you say? Should we go into the city?"

Todd knew that safety was only going to come by facing the unknown. Mort pulled the boat toward some concrete steps and moored the boat to a cable strapped horizontally against the seawall. The broken concrete steps led up to a parking lot. Todd handed Mort both spears then, with his hands gripping the cable, reached his right leg toward the closest step. The boat slipped outward, and his foot missed. Faking an embarrassed smile, he looked over at Mort, who was not laughing.

"You alright?" Mort asked.

With his left foot still in the boat, his right foot soaked in rusting river water, and both hands gripping the horizontal cable, Todd's brain could not tell him which muscle to move next. Mort had not made fun of him.

"You want to switch into the Crocs we found you?" Mort asked.

Todd looked into the boat, into the thicket of supplies beneath the benches.

"Better not, if you don't mind the wet socks," Mort said. "Who knows what we'll be walking on up here."

At these words, Todd's brain unlocked his limbs. He pulled his left leg over, dry, onto the next tread and walked upward, his right foot squishing at each step.

**

Todd stood next to Mort, close enough that the tip of Mort's makeshift spear, held diagonally, shielded Todd's chest from what he saw before him. Todd, too, was gripping his spear, whose base blocked Mort's knee.

A thin layer of dust and soil blew in swirls across the city pavement where weeds and trees had not broken upward through the cracks. Ivy hung from the elevated tracks of the People Mover, where it crossed Woodward. Joe Louis's fist struck the ground. The wind whistled through the urban canyon before him.

Todd jumped. A couple of birds flew from the upper story of one building to another.

"This does not look promising," Mort said in his monotone voice.

"Look at the cars, Mort," Todd said. He heard his own voice shaking. "Just like elsewhere. They're stopped in the middle of the street. This is really like the rapture, like everyone just disappeared at once."

Todd could hear Mort pushing a breath through his nose. "What do you say? I-75 and back? It's about a mile each way. Piece of cake."

"Let's walk down the middle of the street. No zombie surprises."

"There's no way zombies survived in Detroit, not with all its firepower."

Todd laughed a little, which loosened his limbs. "Right. Let's go."

Woodward Avenue had become a gorge in a jungle. Trees grew thick through the meridian, and the vines had followed their limbs to the second and third floors of the buildings above, forming a kind of trellis in places. An unseen pair of creatures frolicked in an empty trolley car.

"You know what eases my mind a little, Mort? I don't see any bodies."

"You're right."

"There were none in the hospital, either, except for the two in the room with me. So we're not talking about a pandemic. Or zombies."

"That does leave mass alien abduction."

"That it does, Mort, thank you."

"Just doing my job."

The two men walked on.

"You're humming, by the way," Mort said. "You hum when you get nervous."

Todd sighed. "Sorry. Dad used to complain about that, too. I don't even notice."

"You know what, though, keep it up. It might be keeping the wolves and monkeys away."

"Wolves?"

Mort was silent for a moment then said, "Just a figure of speech."

Todd tried to hum again but found he could not do it on command.

The two men reached the end of downtown Detroit. Northbound I-75 had become a trickle of water. The parking lots in front of Comerica Park had become an array of grassy veils growing up through the pavement. They pushed their way through until they reached the stadium. Without a word, they walked through an open gate. They assumed positions on the field.

Todd batted with his spear as Miguel Cabrera; Mort pitched as Justin Verlander. The home runs ran into the dozens, the two-foot-tall Kentucky bluegrass unsuitable for running the bases. Three large chunks of the stadium that had fallen near center-left served as hapless outfielders.

The two men switched, and Mort now batted as Lou Whitaker. Todd, ten years younger than Mort, could not think of a pitcher's name from that era, and Mort did not seem to care so long as he cheered Mort on in a long and low "Lou." Todd obliged, and when he finished, he heard his droning cheer echo strangely off the empty stadium walls. Mort swung at his first pitch and homered, naturally. The groaning cheer resumed but not from Todd. Mort squinted toward the outfield then pulled his head back.

"Todd," he said in a low voice. He waved Todd forward with his hand. Todd began looking behind him. "Don't make eye contact, just walk forward, slowly."

Todd walked forward. His heart beat faster. He heard rustling in the grass behind him.

Mort's face began quivering. "Don't run, Todd. But come on."

Todd's knees began to buckle, and he felt frustration at his progress as a sensation in his groin.

Mort grabbed his free arm and pulled him. "Let's go to the dugout. Nice and easy, now."

Without daring to look back, Todd followed Mort into the visitor's dugout. Safely behind the steel pipe railing, he looked out over the field. A large, hairy animal with horns like a rhinoceros was plodding its way directly toward them.

"It looks like a rhino," Todd said.

"Uh huh," Mort replied. "A male. The other two are fe-males."

"Two?"

The male rhinoceros walked to a few paces before the dugout. He sniffed and huffed heavily, turning his head right and left to see the men out of each eye. The females had followed from a distance.

"He's hairier than I remember rhinos being," Todd said. "They must be from the zoo."

"No," Mort said.

"No?"

"No. We need to leave now."

The male raised himself on his hind legs and stomped the ground.

"Oh, God," Todd said. "Okay, um….." He looked around.

"We hop into the stands. Come on."

When Mort turned, the male walked forward and poked his horn between the railings. He held there for a moment and swung his horn from side to side, then pulled out again. At this, Todd scrambled past the beast toward Mort, moving faster than he could think. Without knowing how, he was up in the stands with Mort, looking down at the grass. The male was already back with the two females, chewing the grass.

"Just like that," Mort said, trembling. "Just like that, they're back to normal. As if there'd been no danger. And I'm still shaking. Oh, God, Todd, this is bad. This is really bad."

"It's alright, Mort. We made it out."

Todd had never seen eyes like those that Mort made. This was a special kind of fear.

Todd followed Mort's brisk pace back to the boat. Mort said nothing. The overgrown city seemed so much safer than where they had just been, but Mort swung his arms and his spear angrily through the walls of grass rising up from the road. When Todd stopped to untangle Mort from a vine, he could see that Mort was ready to cry or scream. Todd insisted on rowing and did not notice that he had stepped through the water to enter the boat. He did see Mort's white-knuckle grip on its sides. His head hung in front of his shoulders. Only when Todd had rowed about a hundred yards from the river's edge did Mort look up and turn around.

"What's so wrong?" Todd asked.

"That was a wooly rhino, Todd."

"Okay…."

"They've been extinct for twelve thousand years. And they lived in Eurasia."

"Okay, so maybe they're still around?"

"No, Todd, that's not how it works. That's not how it works. I don't know where we are, Todd. There are people around us we can't reach and animals that shouldn't be here. I don't know what this is. I don't know what this place is."

As Todd rowed downriver, he looked back at the crumbling, overgrown city above and his trembling, angry friend below. The fallen tower grew smaller in his sight and looked more like the scaffolding of a half-built bridge. He did not feel whatever fear Mort was feeling because he did not really know what kinds of animals should be living in this world. He only grew afraid for his friend and wondered what to do to keep him well.

Ex cursus

Billy tried to turn the engine over again without success. He sat in the new Volare, hands and head on the wheel. If he couldn't make this run, he couldn't go to work tomorrow. If he couldn't go to work...he did not know what came next.

"Pour a little gas in the carburetor, Billy," said a familiar voice coming up from behind the car.

Billy looked in the side mirror and jumped out. "Uncle Frank! Long time no see! When did you get here? I didn't hear you pull up. Are you staying? Mom's away for a few days."

"Good to see you, boy. Come on. Let's have a look."

"This thing's a piece of crap. Almost brand new, and it won't start." Billy leaned on the driver's side door then pushed himself off. In front of him was a 1979 Plymouth Volare Road Runner in spitfire orange. His father had boasted about the car and its color and all that he had been doing for his family and for his people. His father had run off, and now the car would not start.

"I've heard about these," Uncle Frank said. "A lot of them have problems. Come on. Let me show you an old trick."

The car soon started, and with it running, Frank led

Billy through a diagnostic. After about an hour, with the sun settling down into lazy late afternoon, they finished their work, satisfied. They went into the trailer to relax.

"You have to work?" Frank called to Billy in the kitchen.

"Tomorrow," Billy said. "I had to be sure that thing was working first." He brought out a couple of pops. They sat in the living room, where Billy's little sister, Lola, lay on her stomach watching cartoons. Billy took off his shoes.

"That's smart," Frank said. "Take all of the assurances you can get in this life."

"Are you staying here, Uncle Frank? You're welcome to use my bed. How did you get here, by the way? Did you walk from Crow?" asked Billy.

"I just came by to give you a message," said Frank. Francis Little Rock kept mostly to himself and was noted for precisely this kind of behavior, delivering cryptic messages from unknown parties that, nevertheless, bore out grave consequence for their recipients.

"What, uh, message is that, Uncle Frank?" asked Billy.

"Run."

"Run?" Billy laughed uncomfortably. "Run where?"

"Run now," Uncle Frank said, rose, and turned off the television. Lola turned and complained, but Billy could hear the cars coming down the road. He peeked through the window, saw them, and sighed. Each of the black Broncos had a dirt bike strapped to the tailgate.

"Hide, Lola. Hide under the house like last time," Billy said. "Use the trap door."

"Do as he says," said Uncle Frank, kissing her on the head.

Billy was out the door. As the thin metal door slammed against the frame, Billy's bare feet landed on the dusty ground. He paused for a split second, enough to gaze through the windshield of that first truck, now turning up the long driveway. He knew who was inside, felt he made eye contact, but it didn't matter. He ran.

Billy ran as fast as he could through the grass of southern Montana, following a trail he had kept over the years. In a short while, he heard the bikes start, their demon-pitched voices screeching from afar. Billy could run long and fast but not that fast. He would hide in the ravine.

Billy ran. He ran through the tall, gray-green grass under a goldening sky. He ran between patches of pines and hills. He knew every rock and crevice and made a path to draw those bikes into them as he ran.

As the ravine opened up to him, an image flashed before Billy's eyes, something from the old cartoons Lola watched. That makes no sense, he thought. Impossible. But his uncle's voice thundered within him: "Run!"

The bikes gained on Billy, and so did fear. Every breath now carried a brief shout. Again, the cartoon flashed in his mind, but with it, his uncle's eyes blazed: "Run!"

Billy searched for the path down the slope. Should he turn now and try to outrun them there? Should he turn last minute and risk their catching him on the angle? The fear grew, and Billy's legs burned. Somewhere in his mind, a cougar roared. The fear turned into fire.

Billy turned for the path down at the bend in the ravine. They would be over him, above, and he'd find shelter in the pines like before. But those bikes were gaining too quickly. The knobby rubber tires nipped at his heels just as the ground began to give way. But as that ground dipped, Billy did not fall with it.

Billy was running on air. He looked down in harrowed confusion mixed with fiery fear. That cartoon image flashed again; cartoon characters only fell when they looked down. Yes, he was now running on a cushion of air. Yes, he would keep running. Yes, the bikes had stopped to look up at him. Yes, he had turned their attention from Lola. His face widened with happy anger.

Billy ran as the ravine fell away below him. He ran on a sheet of air. Every exhale became a shout of victory. Each hammered breath forged fear into fire. That fire blazed into holy terror. The image of Saint Peter on the waves flashed before him. He would not falter. He would not fear, though he flew on his feet thirty fathoms above the floor. The pines rising up from the ravine were like seaweed over which he swam. Billy ran and shouted and ran.

As he ran across the ravine, the roar of the bikes behind him became the confused echo of some wounded animal.

He reached the far side of the ravine. As the ground rose up to meet him, as his feet felt the earth again, he began to trip. Billy ran, falling forward until he stumbled atop some low rise and down the other side of it. He landed on all fours, hands on the ground, head down, panting.

As Billy gasped for air, every breath carried a moan full of terrified tears. The wave of holy terror on which he had ridden over that ravine crashed upon him. He brought his face into two fistfuls of grass, tears streaming down his cheeks. He moaned and coughed as his breath slowly returned to him.

After a few minutes, Billy saw two beaded moccasins appear just below him. Two familiar, fingerless gloves grasped him by the arms and attempted to pull him up. Uncle Frank stared at him intensely.

"Uncle Frank...how?"

"Not how, why. Why explains how."

"Wha—Why?"

"To make you feel the terror within you. To make them feel that terror when they see you. Do you feel it now, White Wolf? That is your name from now on."

"Agh!" Billy moaned in terror. "O-o-oh!" he coughed out.

"I came to tell you to run. Next time, you will not need to run at all."

"Uncle Fra—" Billy began, but his uncle had vanished.

PART TWO

NIGHTS AND DAYS

8

Mort opened his eyes to see Todd's sleeping face filling his field of vision. He jerked backward against the side of the tent. He pushed himself upward, squeezing the heavy ball in his stomach. The way his stomach pulled as he twisted and rose, that weight seemed tied to the Earth.

During the day, on their way out of Detroit, many more helicopters had come and gone, presumably between Toledo and someplace north like Cass Ridge. No one aboard would have made out the two men in their little boat on the river. Mort and Todd had decided not to waste their instant logs on fire signals. They would reach Toledo soon enough.

Outside the tent this morning, the terrible purple light of dawn contradicted the cool, refreshing air that Mort breathed, which shook his skin awake. In this light, the river was black. Grass surrounded him on this tip of an island neither he nor Todd was totally sure was Grosse Ile. They had rowed into a canal and pulled the boat ashore. Todd had rowed almost all the way here from downtown. Perhaps his new friend was right that he had misjudged the rhinoceros he had seen. Perhaps he had wanted to be frightened, finally to put a face on the lurking threat. Perhaps the wooly rhino, too, had been asleep all these years and had woken to a world in which he and his harem could live freely. The animal had woken to an ancient threat, his old foe, a man with a spear.

Mort relieved himself behind a tree. The light was already clearing, and he saw, through a thicket, the frozen eyes of a deer. He returned to the tent and saw Todd's bleary, confused face poking through the flap. "You look like a baby who's not sure he wants to be born," Mort said.

Todd nodded then went back inside. He reemerged a minute later, fully dressed, and began folding his mylar sleeping bag. Mort had given up on his during the night, preferring a slight chill to the sweat and the constant crinkling noise.

"We have some more friends," Mort said. "A little less threatening this time."

Todd looked around, eventually fixing his gaze on a herd of two or three deer hiding behind some trees.

"What do you say? We could try our spears on them. Venison would be better than the salty paste we've been slurping down."

Todd looked over at Mort through half-lidded eyes.

"What, are you a vegan or something?"

"No," Todd said. "I've hunted before. With a bow and arrow, even. Not that I hit anything."

"Alright, then."

Todd turned to face Mort, his hands on his hips. With one hand he gestured toward the deer. "Good luck."

On this tiny tip of an island, itself an island made by the channel, it took Mort about an hour to corner the deer within what he thought was his range for chucking the spear. Todd joined him, either out of curiosity or to prove a point. With Todd's lazy stance and his spear hung horizontally below his waist, elbows and knees locked, he certainly was not there to help. With one cervine rump finally facing him, Mort leaned back and heaved his makeshift spear. Even had the deer not bounded away as soon as the missile sliced noisily through the air, Mort would have missed widely.

"Okay?" Todd said.

"What? I got the distance."

Todd turned away.

"Oh, and you're some kind of expert in spear hunting?" Mort said. Unlike every other Michigander he had known, Mort had never been hunting. His family had no cabin up north. He had had no father, uncle, or friend to show him how.

"You think it was just that easy for our ancestors?" Todd said. "Haven't you ever watched how the bushmen of Africa do it? It's going to take another hour for you just to find a good position again. Come on. We're burning daylight, as Dad would say."

***

Mort rowed through the narrow channel of the Detroit River, which really meant riding the gentle current and using the paddles just enough to keep a few dozen yards from land. His thin muscles quivered from time to time, as if they were still yawning and stretching their way out of sleep. Only his long legs wanted more room among the many things filling the small boat.

Gray clouds blanketed the sky. Every sign of human

habitation, the houses and marinas built along the river-bank, told of absence and decay. The bridges were passable, at least at certain points. Todd played the radio in the hope that the music would echo off the water into someone's sympathetic ear ashore. Over a couple of hours, they rowed the length of Grosse Ile that way, two men channeling the hope that, somewhere, someone else had made a home around here in this new order of nature. They did not know how much farther Toledo was by boat.

Mort knew he was reaching the end of the island when Todd's eyes widened to match the mouth of the river. He turned the boat to look for himself. His stomach quivered a little, and the heavy ball within it floated weightlessly for a moment. The river was now several miles wide and would soon open up into Lake Erie. This was the shallowest of the Great Lakes and almost the smallest, two facts that did not help Mort or Todd take in the vastness of the water all around them. Mort did not know what to say. Their boat felt suddenly very small.

"I'm starting to get hungry in a real way," Todd said. "The ball in my stomach is not as big, maybe, or it dissolved since the one time I really felt it."

"I'm starting to wonder if the ball we each have isn't a yolk sac of some kind, like certain fish are born with until they can feed on their own. But that just doesn't explain how either of us could have fed on ourselves for all this time."

"Um, yeah," Todd said.

"Maybe it is time for a break, you know?" Mort replied, happy to land someplace and let his mind wrap around what he was seeing. They rowed between two ends of a breakwater into a manmade cove with ragged rocks formed into straight edges. They pulled the boat onto a gravel path that protected the marsh behind them from the lake before them. That marsh, stretching for miles inland, admitted few trees, and a wind blew mild but constant. Mort stretched, and Todd imitated him automatically. They stared off across the endless silver mirror of the lake.

"This should be fine if we just keep close to the coast," Mort said.

Todd cleared his throat. "The shore, you mean."

"Lakes have coasts."

"Seas have coasts, and oceans. Lakes have shores."

"Seas have shores, you know, the 'seashore'? Lakes and oceans have both shores and coasts. It's interchangeable terminology."

Todd huffed through his nose.

Mort was glad for a little levity, but the abyss before him soon swallowed it up again. "Alright. Let's fish," he said. He was glad for this, too, for fishing was a thing he did know how to do. He set up both reels, and, sitting on the outer rocks, the two men cast their lines.

"Are you even hungry for real food yet?" Todd asked. "Is that ball still blocking things up?"

"I'm helping you. Two lines are better than one. Just like you helped me this morning with the deer." Mort did not look over to see Todd's reaction to this.

After they cast their lines, Mort let his head hang down for a moment. The water lapped gently over the open mouths of the mussels clinging to the rock. Mort's chest and shoulders swelled with joy. "Look at this, Todd. Look at these things. Look how immense this lake is. It goes on for hundreds of miles. Whole naval battles were once fought here. All of this laps gently against the rocks. And these little guys, and the moss, they cling to this edge. They have no idea how much power is out there, against them, how much energy is stored up in this lake, how much a storm could discharge against them. Here they are, clinging to life wherever it can be found. These mussels have no idea how far they've come, stored in the ballasts of ships and let out here, thousands of miles from their native habitat. They just take in a little water at a time, grabbing whatever nourishment comes their way."

Todd looked over at Mort then downward, between his feet.

"How much is out there, Todd?" Mort looked out over the lake again, careful to keep his eye on the bobber. "Our minds, we're like these mussels. The more we study the world, the universe, everything in it, the bigger it becomes. We can only take in little gulps of water, hoping to catch a little food for our thoughts. Imagine the great abyss of knowledge out there, Todd."

"Yeah, totally," Todd said.

Mort sighed. He watched the bobber bounce between the waves.

Todd said, "You told me about your work before, Mort. What was it again? Extremo...?"

"Extremophiles. Lichens in Antarctica. There, too, imagine it. Miles of ice pressing down above you, blocking out all the light. And you, little lichen, you find a source of heat, some sulfur. Somehow, after millions of years, life finds its way. God! Life will find its way everywhere. That's what moved me to study biology. Life will cling to anything. No matter what the situation, life will find a way. It may take time, so much time, so much change, but life will cling to every little shore set against the vastness of death."

"Kind of like us now, I guess."

Mort breathed long, in and out. "Yeah. Kinda like us."

"But not our lures. There is no life clinging to our lures."

"No, there is not."

"If you don't consider it a sacrilege, maybe we could just boil up some of these mussels?"

"Not a good idea. Zebra mussels eat garbage, toxins. Not much meat in them anyway. We just have to wait it out with the fish."

***

Mort lay on the gravel path a little ahead of where Todd was cooking his fish. Mort had caught and gutted it, but he was not hungry, not even with the smell of its roasted flesh wafting into his nose. He was hungry for knowledge, specific knowledge of what rose above him.

It had taken all afternoon to catch a fish big enough to eat, and in that time, the two men had decided they had rowed enough for one day. Excitement for what they had thought they would see in Detroit and fear for what they really had seen had driven them on yesterday. On this stretch of gravel, far out of range of any haunted city, and with helicopters coming fewer and farther between, their bodies' claims for rest echoed strongly among the lapping waves, flapping wings, and croaking frogs.

The clouds had covered them while they fished and had

been unfurling for the past couple of hours to reveal a field of stars. Mort had tried to explain again why every night would be a moonless night. He could not explain, though, the new shape the sky had taken.

Where the sun had set, to the west, the ground was broad and flat enough to show what they had not yet seen in the city—that the sun, rather than falling behind the Earth, seemed rather to glow redder and smaller, finally disappearing upward behind a line of blackening sky. The horizon as a whole turned red with the sun as it smiled upward behind some invisible sphere that spanned the visible Earth. In the dark of night, the stars clustered at the edges of this great sphere all around, west, north, and south. Mort, lying on the gravel, waited for the clouds to reveal the eastern edge of the Earth and the starry cluster he predicted should be there.

"I'm no astronomer," Mort said. "But am I wrong about this? That the sky looks strange?"

"You're not wrong," Todd replied. "I've seen many a night sky, and this is unique. It's like looking through a magnifying glass."

"That's exactly what it looks like, Todd. Good analogy." Mort did not turn back to see Todd's reaction to his compliment.

"Maybe that's your moon," Todd said. "You said it went dark. Maybe now it's transparent."

Mort could not tell if Todd was being sarcastic. "The moon never filled the sky like this. This doesn't bother you?"

"It doesn't sound like it's really bothering you."

"You're right. It is fascinating, though."

"I'm breathing, so everything's alright. And now I'm eating. You sure you're not hungry?"

"Yeah. And I'm sort of glad. I mean, maybe it's this heavy ball in my stomach, an ulcer or whatever it is, but I'm glad I'm not tempted to eat. I ate too much before. I was, how do you say, a bit hefty."

"Hefty? What are we talking here?"

A smile stole its way onto Mort's face. "Three-eighty. I think my old skin bag was a bit roomier than yours, at least from side to side."

"Gross."

Mort pressed his fingers against his ribs and sides. "I feel happier talking about it now, with the weight gone, than when it was obvious to everyone and everyone was trying to help."

Todd was silent.

Mort looked backward to see Todd's face, glowing with the last flames of his little fire. His eyes stared into somewhere else, and his mouth, remembering every few seconds to chew the fish within it, hung sad. Mort wondered what he had said. He looked forward again, down the length of his lanky body, toward the eastern horizon. The clouds were pulling back, finally, to reveal a crescent of sparkling light, a scimitar of stars.

9

Todd stood next to Mort, studying the house before them, a small Cape Cod in gray shingles and a pink door, almost fully intact. They were a few hours' guided float southward this morning and had reached a sharp spit of land lined with houses. This house was not on the shore but just inland, across a narrow street. Todd rubbed the side of his neck with his hand, knowing what Mort was about to say.

"The only two houses we've seen in this condition have belonged to us," Mort said. "Somehow, my being asleep inside kept my house upright. Your house had been well-sealed against the elements. This one has not been boarded up. So you know what I'm thinking."

"We are definitely going to knock first. No creepy surprises."

"Of course."

Todd waited.

Mort threw a hand forward, inviting him to do the knocking. "If no one answers, I'll go in first. Fair?"

Todd huffed, walked to the pink door, and knocked. "Hello?" he called out, the word squeaking and broken. He tried again more firmly. "Hello?" He jumped at a hand on his shoulder. It was Mort.

Mort opened the door, which was unlocked. Todd followed him inside. Woven into the heavy odor of dust and mildew was a fine thread of the newborn smell that he and Mort had finally shed after days of rowing. There might be someone like them here.

In the living room, everything was in order, and framed pictures still leaned on bookcases. The ground floor comprised no more than the living room, the kitchen, and a half bath. There was no basement. Todd stared into Mort's back as he followed him upstairs. The landing was no bigger than their two bodies. Three closed doors surrounded them.

Mort knocked on the right-hand door then opened it. Sunlight poured in through a window. From what Todd could see, this was a small guest room, but there were signs that a teenager or a young man had come through from time to time. The bed was neat and dry.

Mort opened the left-hand door. An open window let a breeze into the room, which smelled heavily of a sleeping sac. The bed was unmade and stained with what Todd took to be the goo. This room was well decorated and clearly lived in. The otherwise clean carpet had wet marks in the shape of footprints.

At the center door, Todd put up his hand. "It's alright. I can do it this time." He did not bother to knock, figuring that the person had left already. The doorknob turned, but the door pushed back at him. "It's a little stuck on something." He pushed on the door a couple more times, to little effect. Mort's hand came down on his shoulder, and his eyes adopted a look Todd had not yet seen, some kind of condescending wisdom. Todd looked at Mort's hand and again at his face. "What?" Todd asked.

"Todd."

"What?" Todd wriggled his shoulder free of Mort's hand.

"Maybe I should handle this."

"Handle wha—No. No no no." Todd grimaced. "No no no no no."

He saw Mort wedge himself between the door and the jamb. A light was on inside, or it came through a window. "Yep," he heard. Mort made sounds of struggling to lift the body. A strange gurgling sound echoed off the tile walls of the bathroom and into the horror chamber that the small house had become. "Whoa," he heard Mort say.

"Oh, God, is it bad? I don't want to know. Tell me."

"Go get some clean sheets from her bedroom."

"Clean sheets...clean sheets," Todd repeated. He searched through the closet until he found folded sheets. When he passed through the bedroom door again, he saw Mort's thin, white forearms clamping a Black woman's body upright. Her limbs hung loose, and her head rested on Mort's shoulder. Dried flakes of clear-white goo fell from the body, and Todd nearly fainted.

"Come on. Lay the sheets out in her bedroom."

Todd found himself obeying this without a thought. He spread one sheet easily with a flick of the wrists. Mort barreled through, and Todd could feel the woman's body pressing against him. He stared down at the naked body, lying on the sheet. Todd chastised himself for thinking she looked like a crushed grape. Some phrase he had heard once in church came into his mind: *The enemy has pursued me; he has crushed my soul against the earth.* Todd burst into tears and fell on his hands and knees. He felt the other bedsheet graze his face as Mort lay it on top of the woman.

"We should bury her," Mort said.

Todd recovered enough to say, "With what, our spears?"

"I think if we get her downstairs, the house will take care of the rest, you know, fall on her like my house fell after I woke up. I think she died just a few hours ago. She was still a little warm and flexible."

Todd threw up.

***

Todd stood next to Mort in the living room at the dead woman's feet, which poked through the sheets. They were gray, the only color he could find. He had helped Mort carry her body downstairs. While he had been cleaning up the mess he had made in her bedroom, Mort had found the skeleton of a cat, named Loftus on the tag still around its neck, and laid it next to her. From the pictures in her living room and some mail lying around, they determined that her name was Charlaine Jackson and that she had a grown son named Niles.

"Todd, will you do the honors?"

"Why me? You found her."

"You're more of the praying type."

"This is true. Okay. Dear God, we just want to commend to you Charlaine. Please receive her soul into your loving arms. We pray for her son Niles, wherever he may be." The house creaked loudly in a few places. Todd caught

Mort looking around with uncertainty. "Lord, we just pray for peace in this world and for your guidance." The house creaked again.

"Time to go," Mort muttered.

"Um, amen." Todd said.

"Amen," Mort echoed and flicked the sign of the cross across his face.

The house creaked loudly. The front door stuck a little as Mort tried to pull it open, and the wall around it visibly shifted as he walked through. Todd pressed his hand into Mort's back as they raced through the doorway. The two men walked speedily down the paved path to the street and each jumped when they heard the first timbers snap.

Once on the street, they turned around. The small one-and-a-half-story house twisted a little where the roof met the wall then collapsed. A cloud of dust wafted toward the two men, carrying with it the scent of plaster and mildew.

"She had dumped her sac and the dirty sheets in the tub," Mort said. "They were still wet. If we had got to her a few hours earlier, I don't know, maybe we could have saved her, you know, from whatever got her, choking or starving or shock."

Todd, with his hands on his hips, caught himself beginning to shrug and turned his shoulders one way, then another. Glad he had escaped the falling house and sorry for Charlaine's fate, he did not know which feeling to feel. His head fell, and he turned toward Mort, who interpreted this by bringing his arm around and tugging Todd toward him. He heard a slight gurgle in Mort's stomach and smelled his breath.

"Are you feeling alright?" Todd asked.

"I don't know," Mort said. "I think lifting up Charlaine tore something loose in my stomach."

"Yeah, your breath smells like you have giardia. Have you been drinking untreated water?"

"No, just the stuff we've been treating." Mort's intestines gurgled again. He turned around and began walking stiffly toward the boat.

10

Mort lay on his side, his knees pulled up, a rainbow-striped inflatable pool tube serving as a pillow. He watched Todd, who was grilling fish in a small barbecue he had found in a nearby garage. Todd had found the pool tube and inflated it for him. Todd had walked through every passable door in this small neighborhood jutting into Lake Erie looking for a change of pants for Mort and had found cargo pants that were almost long enough. Todd had then fished for what he was now cooking.

Mort had spent most of the afternoon squatting behind a fence, watching thick black bile ooze down between his feet. The wretched stench had threatened to make him vomit many times, but there was nothing in his stomach, which stung with emptiness. The heavy ball had broken open. Mort studied the ooze as best he could, thinking that his body had been feeding on it for some time. It had the color and consistency of used motor oil and smelled of sulfur.

Todd had kept bringing water to Mort, but it washed out separately from the bile. Todd brought the only fruit he could find to supply some fiber, crab apples. From the moment he first bit into one, Mort knew it would help, for he devoured the rest of it savagely as his body craved more. Todd gave a subtle *hmpf* of approval and brought back three more, instructing his charge to eat slowly and carefully. Mort heard Todd biting into a crap apple, and this time the grunt was not of approval.

Mort was exhausted. His stomach felt like a balloon in a vacuum, ready to burst from being pulled outward in every direction. His anus burned. In between, he had no word for how his intestines felt except for "mud" and "a river of mud." He lived only for the gentle breeze that came from the lake every few minutes.

Todd brought Mort a little fish on a ceramic plate absconded from a house. Mort let each tiny morsel dissolve in his mouth as much as it could before he attempted to swallow it. Whatever spice Todd had found in one of the houses—oregano, perhaps—could not help dissolve the green cloud of nausea that had immobilized Mort's esophageal muscles. At some point, after it had grown a little darker, Mort watched Todd pull away the plate of uneaten fish and replace it with crab apple slices.

Before bed, Mort mustered enough energy to help Todd with the tent. The two men then pulled together a couple of wooden pallets to make a bed for Mort, softened with a foam pool float. Mort would sleep outside, in case he had to make another emergency squat. It was a warm night anyway, and Mort could stare up at the stars in the swirling marble that englobed them. He clung to his spear like a child would a stuffed animal.

***

Mort woke gazing upward at the stars. The spear had

rolled onto the ground. His hip and shoulder bones dug against the wood pallet when he moved, even through the foam. So he tried not to move. Tonight could be like when he first woke up, just a few days ago, already a lifetime. His stomach felt less ill at ease than it had earlier though his intestines still felt steeped in mud.

Todd snored a little inside the tent, which was just out of arm's reach. The stars above shined silently. Mort had noticed a zone in the sky, halfway between the center and the edge, where the constellations had not been completely reconfigured by whatever the moon had done to the sky. Perseus was chasing Andromeda, or the other way around. A gentle breeze blew across him from the lake, and he rested his ears on the lapping of its waves against the seawall below him, counterpoint to Todd's snoring.

Mort heard some activity in the water below, perhaps a bird bathing or fish jumping above the surface. The breeze also picked up a sound, a sort of low, metallic moaning. Todd had stopped snoring at some point, and this low moaning, along with the playful splashing in the water, was all Mort could hear. He focused on these sounds, which, for reasons he could not understand, began to make him uneasy. The moaning of the wind took on, if he was not imagining it, a sultry laugh. The air grew humid, almost thick. His heart raced, and Mort stretched out his body, making sure he was not curling back into the placental sac in which he had woken just a few days ago.

As the air grew thicker, the stars grew dimmer and the moaning wind became a discernible voice. It—she, he could say now—said, "Mort" and snickered alluringly. Mort had never heard a woman's voice draw him like this except from behind a computer screen. "Mortimer," she called. This could not be real. If only for the sake of ensuring that he not curl up again into a coma, he sat up.

As Mort sat up, the air grew thicker. He could see almost nothing now and rubbed his hands up and down his sore, skinny torso. He stood, and the darkness was complete. The voice and the breeze and the splashing and the lapping of the water were all gone. He could not even feel his feet on the grass. His arms did not fall quickly when he dropped them, and he felt himself floating. He took a step toward where he knew the tent was, and this thickened the air. He took a step backward, and the gooey, muddy air swirled around him.

Mort felt the viscous air in his lungs. It did not choke him outright. He was not drowning. Instead, he felt his consciousness leaving him, something like what happens on the way to sleep. With the last words that would form in his head, he knew his mind was leaving him.

The dumb, hang-jawed animal that Mort's body had become could only wonder at where he was without words. If his eyes were open or closed, he could not say. He was a thing in the midst of some other thing, but that boundary was dissolving. The mud inside was the mud outside. He was mud. All mud. All nothing.

Some swift current came through, and something hit his face. He felt himself. He felt pain where he was hit. He felt pain in whatever had hit him. This was his hand, he knew. He moved this hand and hit himself in different places. He jerked his arms and flailed his legs, and these hit something hard. The ground. He drew deep breaths, and whatever he was breathing seared his lungs. He savored this new pain because he could feel himself alive inside. He breathed and moaned, and he could almost hear this moaning. Yes, he could hear it, and he began to grunt and scream. This burned his throat, and he smiled at the pain of being alive.

All at once, the light of the stars returned. If a curtain had been lifted, it had been pulled out from his throat like a magician's handkerchief from his wand. Mort felt the cool grass beneath his feet. Todd snored gently inside the tent. The waves lapped against the seawall. A gurgling sound emanated from his belly.

Mort squatted over the seawall and expelled the rest of whatever had been in his intestines. He heard rustling in the tent.

"Mort, you alright?" Todd said.

"Yep."

"Thought I heard yell...." Todd's voice drifted off.

"No, just here, shitting on the mermaids."

"Alr...."

Mort looked up at the stars, and Andromeda was now above him, somewhat stretched and distorted, like the woman had broken her chains. A little to the southwest, he could see, just above the Earth's horizon and below the sphere of stars, in the hazy, black band that separated them, something glowing. If it was city lights or a bonfire, he could not tell. Lying on his bed again, he gazed downward between his feet, toward that fire, and fell asleep.

**

Mort woke in the clear sunshine. Todd had somehow mowed the patch of grass they had made their camp, a small triangle of land between the seawall, a garage, and a stream trickling into the lake. Mort spotted an old manual push mower leaning against the garage. He was hungry.

Mort stood and stretched. There was no heavy ball in his stomach pushing back. Somehow that thing had nourished him for the generation in which he had been asleep. Todd thought his had probably dissolved naturally. Mort walked toward the stream, on whose bank the boat was moored, looking for his fishing gear.

Todd was in the stream, holding down a child's soccer net. Mort followed his friend's logic and nodded. Todd, catching him out of the corner of his eye, turned his gaze toward a bucket, nodded boastfully, and returned to his work. In the bucket was a one-pound channel catfish.

"Nice work," Mort said.

"Sleep well?" Todd asked. "You feeling better?"

"I'm hungry, which is a good thing. Like a normal person again."

"Good. But we're not going anywhere today. We're not taking any chances with your gastrointestinal tract."

"I see you mowed."

"There's nothing wrong with a little civilization as we go, maybe even re-civilizing this world. This is a small neighborhood. We could forage today and set off again tomorrow."

"Yes, sir."

Todd walked over to the bucket, another small catfish in his hands. "You'll do the honors?" Todd prepared the fire while Mort gutted the fish. "You were talking in your sleep last night," Todd said. "Something about mermaids."

"No, I was very much awake. The breeze or the stream somehow sounded like mermaids. I stood up to check it out, which dislodged the rest of it."

"I thought there was yelling, too. Any funny business, let's share it. The last thing we need is more of whatever horror we got that first night."

***

That night, Mort lay in the tent with Todd, their spears between them. They had spent the rest of the day foraging in whatever houses were safe enough to enter. In addition to pliers and playing cards, they found a wind-up alarm clock. They let it run at what they determined, by the shadows, to be noon. The small stash of popcorn kernels they had found was for emergency use only. Mort felt content with a belly full of the catfish Todd had caught. He laughed a little at the image of Todd, standing in the stream, holding the creature up to his face and contemplating the animal as if it were a friendly alien coming to visit. In his reverie, Mort did not think much of the movement against the side of the tent and drifted into sleep.

Mort woke to one of the spears digging into his shin. He thought Todd had rolled over onto them again and meant to push him away, but Todd, still on his back, had not disturbed the spears. Still, the spear would not push away. There was a long lump at the center of the tent, beneath it.

"Didn't mow everything," Mort said in a barely audible murmur.

The lump moved. Mort jerked his hand back. He poked at it with his finger, and it slithered away.

"Just a snake," Mort murmured. When his heart stopped racing, he drifted off to sleep again.

Mort woke up sharply. Todd had been shaking him. "It's just a snake," Mort said.

"Yeah, well, fine, but it's like all around the tent."

"What?"

Todd poked at the walls of the tent. The snake was wrapped around three of the four walls, including the side that opened.

Mort did a calculation. "That's at least twenty-four feet long. Not possible around here unless someone had a python or an anaconda for a pet."

"Let's not talk about possibilities, Mortimer, and face reality." The walls of the tent pulled inward. "Omigod omigod. It's going to choke us to death."

"That means this thing is over thirty feet. It's not going to get a good grip. It would need to coil a couple of times around us."

"Are you not worried about being killed by a massive snake? These things eat deer whole. I will not be swallowed whole."

"It's going to give up soon. But if it makes you feel better, let's give it a couple of pokes with our spears. Just up the zipper a bit."

"I am not putting my hand near that thing."

"Alright then hold the spear. I'm telling you, you watch too many movies. A snake like this is not going to be venomous. You ready?"

Todd picked up a spear. "Ready. Just count to three, and I'll jab." His voice shook.

"No, I will open the flap in a calm manner, then, when my hand is free and clear, I will tell you to strike in a swift yet calm manner. Alright?"

"Alright."

Mort pulled open the zipper about a foot and held the flap back. Under the starlight, he could distinguish nothing of the snake. "Go."

Todd struck at the opening repeatedly. The snake released its grip and slithered away. "Woohoo!" Todd pulsed out excited breaths.

"You see? Nothing to worry about. Now it knows that this tent is a dangerous animal. You are a serpent slayer. A dragon slayer."

"Theodore Broderick Farkas, Dragon Slayer. I like the sound of that."

Mort zipped the tent closed and lay down.

"Aren't you curious about it?" Todd asked.

"There's nothing to see out there. It's long gone by now. It was someone's pet python gone wild."

As Mort lay, he listened contentedly to Todd's occasional chuckling, coming down from his adventure. His eyes grew heavy, but he began to perceive a glow outside the front of the tent, casting his feet in silhouette. The smell of the fire reached his nostrils. "Our cooking fire reignited," he said. "That might be more dangerous than the snake."

Todd held a spear toward the zipper, ready to defend Mort in his mission. Mort unzipped the flap all the way and peeked out. He did not see the snake, but rising from the smoldering fire was a thin beam of white light about ten feet tall. "You ever see anything like this?" he asked.

A minute later, Mort stood next to Todd outside of the tent, spear pointed downward. The thin beam of light seemed to be swirling inward, like a vortex.

"Okay, we're back in spook city," Todd said.

"Yeah."

A few seconds after saying this, during which they simply stared at the strange light, two diamond shapes rose just above the pot of catfish stew, catching them like eyes. Before either man could react, it reached upward to about three or four feet, and the light showed the snake clearly.

The snake's head reached forward gently. Mort and Todd each backed away, stepping on the tent and raising their spears. But the snake twisted around the beam of light, as if using it like a branch to warm itself over the fire. The reptile's scaly skin glistened white from the light of the beam within its coil and red with the flame below. It pulled itself upward, wrapping its thirty- or forty-foot length around the column of light, and hung this way above the pot. Its tail flapped a little, and the diamond eyes, now four or five feet above Mort's head, glared down at him.

"Now we are in a bad situation," Mort said. "Shuffle very slowly sideways."

Mort had not landed a single step when he felt a burst of air at his side, like someone had flicked a sheet. Ash from the fire began swirling upward as a wind picked up. The serpent seemed bothered by this and turned its head this way and that, looking for someplace to strike. The ash multiplied and became a tornado enveloping the snake. As the diamond eyes fell behind the gray whirlwind, it began to shriek. The shriek grew louder and higher-pitched as the animal thrashed within the vortex of ash. The wind bellowed the fire brighter and taller until it consumed the tornado of ash, which grew whiter. All at once, the fire died down and the ash dissipated, leaving empty air where the column of light and the snake had been. Mort gripped his spear, feeling the wood, testing reality. He looked over at Todd, who was not blinking.

After a minute of staring warily at the fire, Mort heard Todd say, "How long before we can get on our way?"

11

Todd sat next to Mort in the tent, cross-legged, spear in hand, listening to the clock tick. Neither man had said much after the snake and the whirlwind that had taken it away. Both men had determined to stay awake until first light, at which point they would pack up and start rowing. By the clock, that would be three hours from now, around six. Neither man had recalled at what time their encounter began, so they could not really say that a great deal more time had passed in the experience than both men had felt.

Todd replayed the image in his mind of the snake, as thick as a leg, coiled upward around that column of light. He could still see the scales, dark gray or blue, glistening red from below and white from above. It was not the flexing, undulating motion beneath those scales that bothered him, or even the eyes sparkling above. Nothing in the physicality of the scene or its strangeness made him afraid, then or now. It was a feeling, rather: undefined, unnamable, sickening and horrid, hateful and angry. Something in what he saw made his blood grow sticky, and Todd feared it would stop coursing through his veins.

At the slightest hint of purple light soaking through the

walls of their tent, Todd and Mort did just what they had planned. They packed up their tent, took down their stove, and put everything in the boat, where they made room for the small soccer nets. By the time they finished, there was enough light to see everything clearly. The light in the direction of Toledo, which Mort had first seen a night earlier, still burned brightly.

They had not spoken about what they had seen the rest of the night, as if by tacit agreement not to invite anything further and to listen for the slightest uninvited rustling in the grass. Todd rowed out from the seawall about twenty yards and breathed as if he had not done so all night. Mort nodded toward the east, and Todd turned his head. Over the endless lake, the sun was rising. More accurately, it looked like it was slipping downward from behind the sphere of the sky above, into a line of haze, some misty canyon between the Earth and sky. Todd rowed slowly while he contemplated this mystery with Mort.

Todd turned back and saw the sun on Mort's face, but some movement on land caught his attention. He jumped in his seat when he saw a human form standing where their camp had just been. Mort turned to look, and Todd yawed the boat so both could see. It was a Black woman wearing a white linen dress. The dress radiated in the rising sun, and her dark brown skin glowed to a golden hue. She did not smile, and yet her face spoke of confident, contented joy.

"It's Charlaine," Mort said.

Todd studied her features. "Are you sure?"

"Who else would be sending us off like this? Besides, I got a better look at her than you did."

"Should we go back? Maybe she can guide us, give us answers."

"I don't know. Maybe this is how it goes, you know?"

At that moment, Charlaine began to disappear, beginning at her feet. It was not like she was dissolving into the air or fading into some special ghost light, but like an invisible blanket were wrapping around her. This continued slowly until just her head and shoulders remained visible. She brought her hand up to her face, palm out in greeting. Todd put up his hand. She then turned her hand and made a slight jerking motion toward her face. Mort, who had been waving goodbye to her, pulled his hand back as if uncertain about what she had done. As her hand fell again, the invisible blanket closed around her, and she was gone.

"What was that move she made?" Todd asked. "With the hand, I mean."

"I don't know."

Both men were silent.

After a minute, Mort said, "Well, what do you say? Should we go?"

Todd began to row but stopped as tears fell. "I'm sorry, I just…. That was so moving. I mean, you think maybe she was protecting us?"

"Yeah, maybe, I don't know."

Todd slouched on his bench, oars in his hands, tears falling freely.

"Tell you what, Todd. Just row. I'll be your eyes. Let it all out."

Todd began to row weakly and felt like he was just slapping the oars against the surface. "Aren't you moved by this? We've just seen the spirit of a woman we buried, and she protected us from that snake, and now she's going up to heav—" Todd burst into sobs.

"I *am* moved," Mort said. "Very much. But also confused. In any case, it takes a lot to get tears out of me. I don't think I've cried since I was a child."

As he wept, Todd turned his focus to grateful prayer. He had no words, only calling to mind God's presence. Then, all at once, he stopped crying and started rowing. He saw Mort, gazing over the lake toward the emerging sun, with a look he thought troubled: lips pulled slightly down, head tilted a little forward, brow like a closed gate, eyes focused on the other side of the Earth. He wondered what made Mort react so dully to the danger of the snake around their tent and so coolly to Charlaine's appearance. He had been annoyed by Mort's droning monotone before. Todd felt shut out and was offended by this, that after five days together, his saturnine companion for the apocalypse should share nothing with him, express nothing, have no real feelings about anything except a wooly rhino.

***

After six hours of rowing and fishing, Todd sat next to Mort at land's end, a tiny spit of land pointing south, across a bay, toward Toledo. Toledo was burning. The light that Mort had first seen at night and whose smoke Todd could smell before he saw it was the city ablaze.

"That must be where all the planes and copters were going," Todd said.

"But then they stopped."

"Maybe they got everyone out?"

"If so, is there anyone still there? It's a whole city, there's got to be."

"There's no more music on the Toledo radio," Todd said.

Mort hung his hands from his head and sighed. "We've got a good vantage point. Let's cook up the fish we caught earlier and see what we see in the meantime."

"Okay," Todd said once Mort had a fire going under the fish. "Before we venture into the hot unknown, I would like to share my theory as to what is happening. It affects us. That is, we affect it. Are you ready?"

"Mm-hm."

"Okay. So. You got all freaked out by a wooly rhinoceros. That's something that only you could know about. I would have seen them and said that they had escaped from the zoo and thought nothing more of it. You were not affected by the presence of a forty-foot snake around our tent. I was. That is because I know something, or I think I know something, about the snake. What I mean is, its real significance. Why it showed up at all."

"Okay. . .."

"And it's this: I'm not a great hairstylist."

Mort sighed.

"No, listen. That shape that the snake took around the light pole, it made itself into a barber's pole. Red, white, and blue. Red light from the fire below, white from the light within, and blue. . .sort of the color of the scales. Are you following me?"

"Yep."

"So I think that whatever we're facing is a manifestation of our conscience, whatever we feel guilty about."

"You feel guilty about being a bad barber?" Mort asked.

"No, but the truth is, and this is what I feel I need to get out now, is that while the shop is set up to provide for my creative outlet, et cetera," Todd waited for a rush of guilty tears, which did not come, "Frankie and Maya are the real talent. They rent chairs in the salon, and I live off that. I mean, I do have clients, mostly older ladies who come in too often for conversation. I am good at that, which you probably disagree with, but that's a function of your personality."

"My personality?"

"Yes. You maybe mope a lot."

Mort breathed in heavily.

"Anyway, this isn't about that. We're talking about my issues and how to resolve them before we get ourselves into more trouble. I make money off of other people's talent. That's what the snake represented. That's why I was afraid. So. There."

Todd waited. He had just made his confession. He should receive his penance from Mort and absolution from the Earth, which was acting as God's minister. He wanted to hear something clear and definitive.

Mort flipped both fish fillets in the pan. "Huh."

"Huh?" Todd resisted the urge to smack Mort in the face with the spatula. Maybe that was the motion Charlaine had made toward him.

"I don't know. I guess I'd have to think about it," Mort said.

"In terms of what?"

"Like, you want me to confess, too, or something?"

"We're talking about me right now. Tell me what to do."

Todd leaned with his hands behind him on the grass and turned his gaze toward Toledo. The fire no longer looked as intense as it had an hour earlier.

"Well, in that case, let's see. What you're saying would be true of anyone in the ownership class, I suppose. What you did all kinds of people do, movie producers, agents, bankers. There are people who are talented, and then there are people who scout for talent and make money off it. Did your dad help you hire these people on? Frankie and Maya?"

Todd struggled to remember the precise order of events. "He was somewhat involved, yes."

"So it seems that Jacob Farkas, Sr., found a way to bring his other son into the investment business."

Todd brought his hands forward, between his crossed legs, and pulled at some dry grass. He had expected Mort's analysis to feel like a sharp rebuke. Instead, he felt a warm, tingling wave wash down his body. His father had known him better than Todd had given him credit for, and Todd did not know if he was angry about this or pleased.

"Let me ask you this," Mort said, plating the fish and handing one to Todd.

"Hm?"

"If you had thought your father saw right through you, would you have agreed to your 'interest-free loan'?"

Todd picked at his fish with a fork.

"As for me, the story is simple. I was scooped. Sort of. I was doing work on lichens that took a lot of fieldwork. I was happy about that, going to Antarctica. And I knew it would take time. But this other guy comes along. Others had been drilling core samples in the ice and broke through into a subglacial lake. Lots of material there. He starts publishing like crazy on crustaceans. I'm still trudging along like moss on a rock. I get back to U of M, and, I don't know, I'm just looking around at the lab, at everything. It's like, all at once, every ounce of energy I had, all the enthusiasm, just drained out of me. I could hardly get myself to write up reports. I thought some time off would help. It didn't. Eight years went by, and there I was, living with Grandma, working for minimum wage at a gardening center with no desire to do anything else."

"Eight years?" Todd asked.

"A rut's a rut. Eight years and a hundred and eighty pounds. Tell me how you get out of that rut. All of this is terrifying, Todd, and maybe I don't express myself with the enthusiasm you require, but I feel like I have a new life now. The wooly rhino.... I don't know. Because it's going to take it all out of me, everything I am, to survive in this place."

Todd looked up at Toledo, where a few thin fingers of black smoke curled as if to beckon him. He sighed and took a bite of fish. He had hoped Toledo would be the end of this journey. He had hoped his confession would serve as the moral climax to the story. He took another bite of fish. The way Mort had just expressed things, each man still had a long way to go.

12

Mort took the oars first in the morning. It was more than a mile westward across the bay, and the more he rowed, the smaller he felt as the finger of land on which they had camped fell away into the vast lake behind it. Southward, to his right, a sliver of land, the Ohio shoreline, lay several miles away. Todd seemed to revel in the scenery. Mort's heart began to pound. Todd looked unconcerned, but he could see where they were going. The waves felt bigger, and one or two of them splashed into the boat. Todd answered Mort's questions with placid half-sentences: "We're fine"; "Just keep going"; "Almost there."

Something knocked on the hull of the boat. Mort jumped. Given everything they had experienced, the presence in the hospital and in the house, the cougar and the wooly rhino, the coiling serpent and Charlaine's serene gesture, this would be a good time for a sea monster to wrap them up and take them under.

"Bessie!" Mort said.

"It was just my foot," Todd said.

"No, that's what we saw last night. Bessie."

Todd appeared to consider this.

"It fits the bill: forty feet long, Lake Erie, a sea monster."

"Yeah, but we were on land. And it definitely looked like a snake."

"Maybe Bessie's an old dinosaur. A plesiosaur."

"Don't even start with dinosaurs," Todd said. "I do not want any terrordactyls up in the skies. Haven't you seen *Jurassic Park*? When the terrordactyls started picking off people from above? No way. No more talk about dinosaurs."

"Did you say 'terror-dactyl'?" Mort felt relieved already to talk within his domain.

Todd huffed. "Did I say something wrong? Row to your right some more. Good."

"It's called a pterodactyl. Pteranodon, actually. It has a silent P."

"And how would we know that?"

"What?"

"That its pee was silent."

Mort laughed a little, forgetting to answer. He rowed onward with occasional fits of laughter. He did not know if Todd had joked to make him feel better or not, and he did not care, for it had worked. After about ten minutes of this, half an hour into their journey, Todd finally told Mort to turn the boat southward. When he did, a large and dilapidated marina came into view on his left.

They had agreed to keep rowing until they came as close as they could to the fire, which had dwindled to a few thin lines of black smoke. Another hour of rowing took them past shorefront houses and a long breakwater, into the mouth of a river whose name escaped both Mort and Todd. Soon, to his left, Mort saw something that made him smile.

"Look, Todd. The Coast Guard."

Todd turned to look and studied the scene.

"The Coast Guard, Todd. I guess we're on a coast after all."

"Fine, you win. But, um, doesn't it maybe look like there've been people there? Somehow?"

***

After turning into the marina on which the Coast Guard station sat and mooring the boat, Todd took his turn surveying the scene. A few small red-brick buildings comprised the station. Surrounding these, the asphalt parking lot had broken and crumbled, but the grass growing between the cracks had recently been mowed. A long wooden boardwalk in decent shape lined the seawall, and on this lay a pair of large pontoon-style paddleboats.

"God, if we only had these before," Todd said. "Alright. Shall we try the doors?"

"Center door first this time," Mort said, and he pulled on the door. It opened. "Okay, wow, okay. Hello?"

"Hello?" Todd echoed.

They each took a step inside.

"Hello?" Mort called.

Their sonar greeting pinged off the walls of the station as they walked, timidly, deeper into the small building.

"No one's here," Todd said. "And it's dark, and we don't have the flashlight."

"We'll try the other buildings, then. Before we do, if you don't mind, I'm going to use the bathroom. My pee will not be silenced."

Todd walked outside and over to one of the paddleboats. For all his years living on a lake, he had never seen a design like this: about twenty feet long, it had two matching cockpits near the stern, with just enough room behind the pilot seats for a Naugahyde bench that spanned the seven- or eight-foot width of the boat. Between the twin cockpits was a gap that led onto a large flat platform running all the way to a square bow. The two dashboards were filled with modern gauges and switches, and the two wheels looked like they belonged to an airplane. The boat looked suited to something the Coast Guard might have except for the push pedals beneath the dashboards and the absence of any insignia on the hull.

Outside, the twin hulls of each boat lay directly on a carpet whose edges did not show. The more he looked, the more it seemed that the carpet was connected by chrome bars to a mechanism between the hulls, and he wondered if the pedals made the carpet move. Todd had never seen this kind of propulsion. He had also never seen a small boat with a solid gunwale, and he noticed that on each side of the cabin, between the bench seat and the pilot chairs, the gunwale folded down to provide stairs upward. He stood and scratched his head.

Mort made a sipping noise behind him.

Todd turned and saw Mort drinking something out of a coffee mug.

"What, you find coffee or something?"

"Yes," Mort said, almost singing.

"Wait. Really?"

Mort pulled from behind his back another mug of black coffee. Todd tasted it. It was cold and probably a few days old. Todd closed his eyes and sighed the relief of a soul that had just entered paradise.

"You found this inside?" Todd asked. "So this means that human beings have been here recently. Maybe they're all over there, putting out the fire. What do you think?"

Inside the station, every drawer was locked, and on the one piece of paper left on the one occupied desk, paper that had the feel of finely woven plastic, they could make out a few cryptic handwritten notes:

OMCG Toledo Relay. Scan Report I-75 Lima Corridor. Date: GE+27.166. Time: 15:00.

No sleepers sighted from scan corridor. No penetration at ConCen's. Followed trail of non-migratory flight of deer back to origin, nul finding. Spotted unbroken roof in Findlay, foliage too thick. Rec ground penetration.

The other notes read nearly the same for other interstate corridors and different dates and times.

"Are we living in 'GE+27'?" Todd asked. "What does that even mean?"

"I don't know. Twenty-seven years since the apocalypse, I guess. I could see that."

"And they, like, find no one from here to wherever?"

"Guess not." Mort picked up a blue cookie tin that had sat on the desk. "Maybe there's some sewing supplies in here." He struggled to open it, and when he did, its contents flew out onto the desk.

"Cookies!" Todd said. "Omigod, cookies. Omigod."

Todd continued his exclamations as he stuffed a cookie into his mouth. They were peanut butter. He almost cried.

***

Mort sat on the wide Naugahyde bench of one of the boats, eating cookies and drinking coffee. Todd sat in the pilot's chair ahead of him to the right, looking at the dials.

"You know, I have driven many boats," Todd said. "But there are some things here I do not understand. Like, for starters, there is no accelerator handle. Two, its depth gauge, which I've never seen in non-electronic form, is divided into two parts at two different scales, feet and tens of feet. Third, the whole thing looks kind of slapdash. And I don't even know why battery life is shown in...I can't even read it. GrEV(M). And then there are these pedals, like it's a toy boat." Todd lowered the chair and began pedaling.

Mort heard something moving just beneath the floor. He walked forward and sat in the other chair. His pedals were not moving with Todd's. He looked over at the wisps of smoke coming from some inland part of Toledo. "We've got to walk over there, I guess." He fell back against the chair and lazily lifted his hand to touch a dial. "Altitude in meters. Weird. It's not a gauge, this one. Let's see." He turned the dial a little above the line marked *Brake*. The boat heaved upward a few inches. He pulled both hands away from the dashboard like a criminal stopped by the police.

"What did you just do?" Todd asked.

Mort turned the dial back to *Brake*. The boat slowly came to rest on the boardwalk.

In a low, searching, unsteady voice, Todd said, "Maybe it is a toy, you know, on a pole?"

102

Mort looked at the professional-grade materials and gauges, however provisorily they had been put together. He left the boat and stood behind the stern. "Todd, keeping pedaling and turn that knob again. Just a little. Just a tiny bit."

Todd followed orders, and the boat rose a few inches. Mort could see the carpet between the twin hulls lift with the boat and undulate slowly. He came to his knees and bent over. Nothing but daylight held the boat aloft.

"Uh, Todd, I think, yeah. The boat is floating on air."

"Oh, God, let me see." Todd turned the dial, and the boat slowly sank. Mort took the other chair while Todd hopped out of the boat. "I'm ready," Todd said.

Mort pedaled and turned the altitude dial. The boat rose a few inches. He turned the dial a little higher.

"Oh…my…Lord," he heard Todd say. "Owwowwow! Ouch. That hurts."

"What? What is it?"

"It burns if you wave your hand between the magic carpet thingy and the ground. Like heavy-duty static electricity."

Todd sat next to Mort in the boat, rubbing his hand. Mort looked at the different switches and dials. "You ready?" Mort asked. "Here goes nothin'."

"Wait. There are no seatbelts."

Mort stopped. Todd had a point. "We'll go low. There is a guard rail."

"Gunwale," Todd said.

Mort began pedaling. "I can feel it now. There's a big flywheel below us, giving our pedaling momentum. Now, up." He turned the dial, and soon they were above the level of the roof of the building behind them. Mort turned the steering wheel, which made the boat yaw. "Now, how to go forward?"

Todd flipped every switch he saw. A radio came on, then a searchlight on the bar above them. Finally, the dashboards seemed to glow. Todd's steering wheel was linked to Mort's though the pedals were not. Todd pressed a button next to the steering column, and it fell forward, toward him. "Oh. Whoops."

"Maybe not whoops," Mort said. He pressed the same button on his steering column, and it, too, fell forward. He grabbed the steering wheel and pushed it ahead. The boat inched forward. "We have forward acceleration, my friend."

But Mort began trembling. Everything about the boat felt suddenly foreign. He shifted in his seat to remind himself he was not strapped in, taken prisoner. His stomach fluttered, and his throat began to close.

"Are you alright?" Todd asked. "Just relax. Let me play with it for a while."

Right before they hit a tree, Todd took control of the boat. Mort pedaled to feel useful and in some sort of control, and after a few minutes of awkward maneuvering, Todd seemed to have a full grasp of the flying boat's mechanics. They sailed a few stories above the treetops. The boat moved forward like an aircraft but did not roll when it turned, sliding instead like an automobile on ice. In fact, just a few feet above the bay, Todd tried to roll the boat, but it would not lose its horizontal attitude. To slow the boat, Todd learned to pitch the bow upward and release the pedals, letting the flywheel and the undulating rug bleed energy toward the horizon. Todd landed on the boardwalk and clapped.

Mort smiled for Todd then turned, gripped the steering wheel, and leaned his forehead against it. "A flying boat. These are what I saw from your house before the copters came down. Nothing about this world is going to feel normal, is it?" he asked. The sound of his own voice bouncing off the dashboard made him feel less alone in his wonderment.

"I guess not," Todd said. "I mean, look how we woke up."

Mort turned his head to see the smoke still rising from somewhere in the heart of Toledo. "And what are we going to find in there? Do you feel equipped for that?"

"I don't know. Maybe. We've come this far, Mort. Let's just see how far God lets us go."

Mort traced his finger through the condensation he had breathed onto the center of the steering wheel. He turned his head and looked out toward the expanse of Lake Erie.

"Look. Caterpillars become butterflies, right?" Todd said.

Mort looked down at his skinny body. He nodded, and his stomach fluttered.

13

Todd stood on the bow deck of the flying boat, receiving things from Mort as he handed them upward: their camping bags and the tent, the soccer nets and fishing gear, the three bricks and the instant logs that had been serving as their stove. Floor panels had revealed a large flywheel and other strange equipment they had dared not touch.

"This is the last of it," Mort said, as he handed the spears up to Todd. "This is totally stealing."

"What choice do we have?" Todd said. "If we get in trouble, we'll just explain our situation."

"I'm sure they have some kind of GPS tracker on this thing."

"All the better, right? Then they'll come find us." Todd turned and laid the spears in the gap between the cockpits then latched closed the folding windshield between them.

Todd piloted the flying boat up the river, toward downtown Toledo, at an altitude of five hundred feet. Mort made the conversion from meters for Todd, who could not handle mental math very well, especially when a decimal was involved. Calling a meter a big yard did not help, especially where altitude was involved. Todd insisted Mort say nothing about kilometers, whose pronunciation Mort nevertheless corrected.

The two men looked out, left and right, and saw what they had seen in Detroit and in every other neighborhood they had passed along the lake shore: ruined houses, office buildings, and factories, some burnt to the ground, others covered with vines. A pack of dogs wandered the streets. They reached a decrepit old downtown area and saw that it was not here from which the smoke rose, but behind it.

They turned west just past downtown, past another grassy ballpark, and soon saw an interstate freeway cutting through the earth before them. To the right of this, in the distance, was where the lingering smoke rose. Soon they saw, built atop the berm of the freeway, a tall concrete wall.

The wall seemed to enclose a whole neighborhood, which stretched to the north. Closer to the freeway was a large building surrounded by parks. North of this, for exactly 2.00 kilometers, the wall enclosed several blocks of old Victorian houses. This area had not been ruined by time, though much of it had recently burned. The smoke and its odor began to irritate their noses. Without asking Mort, Todd brought the boat to rest on the street in front of a church.

"Doors are locked," Mort said.

"I know, I just thought that maybe people might be gathered here." Prayer would not come in words, so Todd looked upward and sighed, hoping the soaring Gothic spires would carry his breath upward to heaven. He heard a jingling sound. He looked around. "Do you hear that?"

"What?" Mort asked. "Yeah. There it is. A dog. Let's be careful."

Todd looked where Mort had pointed and saw a healthy-looking German shepherd with a black coat and tan legs. It barked. "Maybe let's just—"

"Yeah."

The two men stood in the boat and watched as the dog approached. It wore a red collar, and when it sat on its haunches, they could see its tags. It barked in a way Todd thought might be friendly, but he had little experience with dogs, as his father had displayed little tolerance for disorder.

"Is there something wrong with its back legs? They're spread out like a frog."

"That might be bred into them, not sure. He seems friendly. What do you say?"

"I've never had a dog before."

"Well, you do now." Mort opened a stern stair, and the dog hopped onto the boat with a gentle tug from Mort on the collar. Mort pet the dog, which received this happily.

Todd stood straight and reached out his hand, which the dog licked. "Oh," he said, reflexively bringing his hand up to his shoulder and pointing with his index finger at the sky. He had seen his father make this gesture of rebuke many times. Correcting himself, he bent forward again and pet the dog on the head.

"What's your name, boy?" Mort said. "His tag says Sir Bear."

"Sir Bear? That sounds like the name of a stuffed animal."

"We could change it. How about Rin Tin Tin? You like that? Yeah?"

"You're naming him after the boy in the kids' books? I believe the dog's name was Milou. I read all those. They helped me learn French."

Mort looked up at Todd quizzically. "Rin Tin Tin is a dog actor from the old days. You're thinking of something else."

"Okay. So what do we do? I mean, if he poos or whatever. How do we even feed Sir Bear?"

"First things first. Our friend here is going to help us sniff out some live bodies. Aren't you, boy? Yeah. That's right."

Todd winced as Mort let the dog lick his face.

***

Todd took the boat a few feet above the debris through the streets of what he and Mort had come to learn from signs was the Old West End. Sir Bear was in the bow, walking along the gunwale with his head poking over, to follow some interesting scent or another. The three living creatures, none of whom seemed eager to leave the safe confines of the flying boat, found no one this way. Most houses had burned but not all of them, and of those still standing, some looked like they had not been lived in at all. It was clear that some configuration of humanity had chosen this neighborhood in which to gather and to wall it off. Some conflagration had recently razed it. None of its inhabitants responded to calls or woofs.

At the end of their run down the last of the long streets, Todd set the boat down on a stepped plaza leading to the large building they had first seen, an institution of some kind. Standing on the well-maintained pavers, he felt Mort nudge something against his back. He turned and took his spear.

"This looks legit," Todd said.

"Yeah," Mort said in the monotone Todd knew signaled uncertainty.

"Well, shall we?"

"Slowly, I guess. I mean, this could be Planet of the Apes or something. You coming, boy?"

Sir Bear made no effort to leave the boat.

"What's up with you, Mort? You're normally the one to go in first, to nudge me forward."

"Yeah, I don't know. Got a funny feeling."

"You had a funny feeling out in the bay, too, but that was just nerves. Come on. We're burning daylight out here."

In the dark glass doors, Todd saw his and Mort's wavy reflections. Apart from their modern clothes, with their baby-bald heads and spears they looked like warriors on the march. Todd was first to open the door. Right away, even as the cool air flowed past his face from inside, he could tell that this was a museum.

"Oh, it's the Toledo art museum. Don't you remember coming here on field trips in school?"

"No. No, I do not. But it looks like offices now."

The two men walked through the galleries, still filled with classics of Western art. Some rooms were brighter than others, lit by skylights or windows. Every room, though undamaged by fire, smelled of smoke. In many, they saw desks and cabinets, piled on top of which were stacks of the plasticky paper.

Todd took the squeeze flashlight from Mort and began rummaging through the papers. He found more of the cryptic shorthand in reports of sleepers, budgets for scouting activities, and receipts for the acquisition of building materials. He arced his head over the array of desks and filing cabinets. It would take hours or days to discover who was here and where they might have gone.

Todd turned around to see Mort staring at a painting awash with daylight from a skylight above. He came forward and read, "Lot and His Daughters. Artemisia Gentileschi. 1635-1638." In the painting, Lot sat in obscurity like a beggar between his two daughters, who, wrapped in pale skin and bright clothing, almost seemed like the heroes of the painting.

"Tell me, Todd. You're a religious guy. What is the moral of this story?"

Todd suddenly felt like the dark air between him and Mort risked becoming some infinite chasm. He almost said something flippant like, "Don't get drunk, or your daughters will take advantage of you," but thought better of it. To him, this was another of the strange Old Testament stories with which he did not really have to contend. He did not want to contend with it now that it had sparked something within Mort. "I don't know. But, hey, let's go find a kitchen. They've got to have one if people are working here. Come on." He tried to peel Mort away from the painting. "Let's go."

They found a kitchen down a flight of steps. By flashlight, they searched through the cabinets. When they opened the full-size refrigerator, the light inside turned on. Todd walked over to the door and felt around for a light switch. When he pressed it, the ceiling lit up.

"Of course, they have electricity," Todd said, still adjusting to the light. "Alleluia, of course. Thank God. I bet this whole place is lit up. Ah. We just stay here until they come back."

Mort nodded.

Todd pulled out of one cabinet an unlabeled mason jar, opened it, and sniffed. "Peanut butter, of the natural variety." He set this on the counter and pulled out another jar. "Preserves, of an unknown species." He poked his finger inside, pulled out a little of the dark fruit, tasted it, and said, "And still unknown, but tasty."

Mort walked over to Todd, reached behind him, and opened a wooden box sitting on the counter behind the mason jars. Inside was three quarters of a loaf of unsliced bread. "It's peanut butter jelly time," he said in a deep, deadpan voice.

Todd, for whom Mort's monotone stripped away the meaning of the words he spoke, had just begun to open his mouth in comprehension when Mort, managing something like a smile, pulled out from a drawer a long serrated bread knife. Todd then marched around the table in the kitchen, thrusting each mason jar in the air like a baton and singing, "Peanut butter jelly time, peanut butter jelly time/We're here, we're fine/Peanut butter jelly time."

Mort joined in the march.

***

"Peanut butter is heavy," Todd said.

Both men sat hunched over, their elbows on the table in the staff kitchen.

"It is," Mort said with a weary voice.

"It's been nine days, awake, alone with whatever's out there."

"Eating only fish and rehydrated food paste, until now. And we still don't know what's out there."

Todd put his head down on the table.

"But here we finally have electricity, plumbing, and peanut butter," Mort replied, barely enunciating his words. "And jelly. And bread. Don't forget the cookies and the flying boat."

"We still have a ways to go, don't we?"

"I'm afraid so. These people, whoever was here, they left in a hurry. Maybe they got spooked by something."

"Don't say that. Let's just have a nice, comfortable night in a warm, dry place. Maybe two or three nights. We could take our flying boat out and scan the area. Besides, people are coming back here soon."

"You know what will help digest this peanut butter?"

"Mm?"

"Whisky."

"Amen."

Mort's chair scraped against the vinyl tile floor as he rose. As he stretched, his long arms pushed upward an acoustic ceiling tile, and his shirt rose above his belly button. For the first time in the week and half they had spent together, Mort looked like a grown man to Todd.

As they made their way upstairs, they turned on every light switch they could find. The gallery lights were probably controlled at some console somewhere. They were walking through a large storage room full of glass objects when Todd could hear the dog barking.

"What do you think?" Todd said.

"Dogs bark. It's because we're away."

They made their way through another storage room full of glassware. Todd stopped and admired a pair of glass candlesticks. The dog's barking grew higher in pitch. "Are you sure he's alright?"

"Actually, no. That sounds a little desperate now."

Mort and Todd walked briskly back to the entrance to the museum. Sir Bear, from the boat, was barking at two other men in the plaza. One stood rather stiffly, staring at the dog. The other man, also standing stiffly, turned his head left and right, taking in the entrance to the museum. Their clothing was bright and strange, like old European military coats above knee-length skirts.

"Omigod, people!" Todd said. He set down the canvas bag he had taken from the kitchen with the peanut butter, jelly, and bread and rushed toward the door. Mort yanked him backward at the collar. "Whawhat?"

"Sh." Mort's hand still gripped Todd's collar and was shaking.

Todd tried to understand what the men were saying to each other. They spoke in short bursts of words that were muffled by the glass doors. A third man walked up the steps of the plaza toward the other two. His gait was very stiff. His knees rose a little too high, and each footfall looked calculated and approved.

Mort whispered in Todd's ear, "Do those look like human beings to you?"

Todd tried to shake off Mort's suggestion, but the more he studied the men, the more artificial, the more programmed each gesture seemed. And when they stood next to each other, they moved in imitation of each other. Todd's legs weakened, and his stomach fluttered.

The third supposed humanoid took his place next to the second, gazing at the glass doors of the museum. The second one pointed directly ahead of him, well to the right of Mort and Todd. The third one did the same.

"Todd," Mort whispered. "The glass is like a mirror. I don't think they know that, these robots."

"I think you're right."

Todd watched the three humanoids. The one staring at the dog came over and joined the other two.

Mort continued, "I bet we don't have too long, though, before they figure out who's who and open that door in front of them. We can go out here and arc around them to get to the boat."

"If this door is even open." Todd was trembling all over.

"Take the pb and j. If they come after us, chuck it at them. And hold on to your spear."

"Oh, God, Mort."

"Come on. We knew we'd have to face something like this someday."

"On the count of three. One…two…three."

The door burst outward. Mort pushed Todd through. The three humanoids turned their heads in unison. Todd felt like his intestines were being pulled out. Mort pulled him forward by the handle of the canvas bag. Todd followed Mort across the plaza and around the stern of the boat, to the portside stair, which they had left open. Sir Bear was still inside. Todd slipped on the stairs. He did not know if and where he was hurt. The three humanoids were marching in step toward the boat. Todd was in his pilot's chair, gripping the wheel. Mort was already pedaling. Todd saw the three faces of the humanoids just over the gunwale, right next to him, as the boat soared upward, above the museum.

Mort yawed the boat, and Todd could see more humanoids walking toward the plaza, half a dozen or so. Their voices gave off some kind of radio squawk as they spoke. The machines made to look human stared upward, and some pointed at the boat, which drifted backward. Mort yawed the boat again, and all Todd could focus on was Lake Erie, spreading wide before him.

Sicut cervus

White Wolf looked out over the water. The aspens, on the other side, shone yellow and white through the green pines. Their reflections quivered on the gently rippled lake below. All of these aspen trees were one creature, joined at the root. He closed his eyes for a moment to take in the autumn breeze. What kind of creature would hide its wholeness beneath the dirt? He opened his eyes to taste anew this irenic scene. In this little corner of Arizona, he could be home again. In Montana, though, he would not have to drive through hours of deadly desert to savor this oasis.

"Ranger DeSoto?" a voice asked.

White Wolf turned around. Lieutenant Devor was standing with Mr. and Mrs. Kim. This was why he was here and not retired. With a brief glance at their faces, he knew he had a real case before him. If Mrs. Kim had been trembling and shaking before, as Devor had said, she was pale and rigid now.

"Thank you for coming out to Kaibab," Devor said. "You've already read Mr. and Mrs. Kim's statements?"

White Wolf nodded. He addressed the couple. "How do you do?"

Mrs. Kim looked around fifty, Lola's age had she still been alive, and about the same height. Mr. Kim was a bit older, in his early sixties, White Wolf's age.

Mr. Kim translated for his wife into Korean. She bowed and spoke, her husband translated, and the introductions concluded.

"Mr. and Mrs. Kim," Devor said, "Ranger DeSoto is a special investigator with the Navajo Rangers. He has developed a particular expertise in dealing with these kinds of cases."

The four sat at a picnic table. White Wolf did not take notes but watched the woman's gestures as she spoke. Her delicate fingers made the shape of the thing she had seen better than her husband could describe. The jerking motions of her arms, head, and mouth breaking through the bonds of her trained demeanor told him that the vision had threatened more violence than perhaps even Mrs. Kim had realized. When the interview concluded, the four stood up.

"Do you believe us?" Mr. Kim asked.

"I see that your experience was real," White Wolf replied.

"Do you believe in these things?" Mr. Kim asked.

"I believe in God," White Wolf said. "Everything else can be measured."

"How will you measure it?" Mr. Kim asked.

"I will sit and wait. It might take hours or days, but I will become invisible to it."

It took only a night and a morning. White Wolf sat in the forest, not at the precise spot of their encounter but nearby, in a lightweight folding chair. The sun, about a hand above the horizon, pierced the haze between the trees. It was here that the shimmer was hiding, in the folds of sunlight, amidst the columns of thin trees. White Wolf did not move his eyes or even blink. If a moving object blurred in a still photograph, in White Wolf's gaze the shimmer grew sharper as everything in the background, trees and leaves and critters, vibrated into a haze.

Still, he waited. All of the phenomena that the Navajo Rangers investigated, UFOs and Bigfoot and skin-walkers, these left traces that they could measure, imprints and residue. Seeing the thing was to make it disappear. White Wolf's way was to disappear, to lure the unknown into view. He had done this with not a few criminals as a police officer in Billings and Las Vegas. He, himself, had become the shadow into which they lurked. Many men retired in order to sit in silence on their porch. White Wolf had done what the desert fathers had done in Egypt, in that barren desert, all those centuries ago. They went out into the desert to make combat with the devil. That combat was to sit still long enough to lure the other out of hiding. A night and a morning was all it took for whatever had haunted Mr. and Mrs. Kim in Kaibab National Forest, this oasis in Arizona.

The shimmer split into two vertical lines, or hardly lines—rather, folds of air. One went to his right and the other to his left, each just inside the edge of his vision. If this thing had seen him, it also wanted him, or else it would have disappeared. It might be testing whether someone was present or not, as the human eye pulls whatever is new into the center of its sight. White Wolf did not twitch a muscle. He had learned to see with his whole eye.

The air between the two folds began to pull, taking on

horizontal folds like stretched fabric. The trees and the light behind bent with it like a reflection on a lake. The fishing would begin.

Dark forms floated behind the curtain of air like fish in a clear lake. As soon as White Wolf looked, he would give them some singular form and some way of harming him. That is what Mrs. Kim and many others like her had done. Her startled mind had given that thing some frightening form. White Wolf would let these float. He would make them reveal more of themselves. He would learn what they really were.

The forms came together. A bulky body stood on two spindly legs. A long, conical neck rose from its rounded shoulders. The head was no wider than the neck, and long, pointed ears reached outward. A pair of thin hands spread open at the top of its head, their skeletal fingers spreading upward and sharpening into points. The head bent downward, and those fingers reached toward White Wolf.

All at once, the wavy scroll on which this scene was being written burst into butterfly fragments, and the two vertical shimmers flew away. White Wolf looked around and cleared his throat. He heard footfall behind him, then a grunt. A mule deer buck walked forward into view. White Wolf sighed then reached under his chair and pulled out a thermos of coffee. He drank and watched the deer, whose breath fogged in the chilly air. The buck grunted again.

"You in a rut, too, my friend?" White Wolf asked. To the old man's surprise, the deer did not bound away but turned its head slowly toward him. He looked into the animal's black eyes and thought he saw something like intelligence.

"You're right," White Wolf said. "That's close enough for one day."

The deer turned its head toward something behind White Wolf. He folded up his chair and strapped it over his shoulders. When he turned, he saw a man with a rifle. Startled a little, he said, "Excuse me, sir, the season doesn't open for another week or so." Looking into the man's black eyes, he saw blank animal stupidity. He walked across the man's field of vision without turning his head again.

"Very clever, Billy," the man said.

White Wolf did not turn to look at the man again and walked down the path he had taken up, out of sight.

PART THREE

CHOSEN PATH

15

Mort woke up the next morning in the forward deck of the flying boat he and Todd had stolen from the Coast Guard, and in which the two men and their adopted dog, Sir Bear, had fled a robot-infested inferno. A thick, white mist filled the morning sky near Cass Ridge Air National Guard Base, a two-hour flight from Toledo, back over the Detroit Metropolitan Wasteland, and into another conflagration. Who had carried the spark to whom, Mort did not know, and when he and Todd had arrived yesterday evening, the last of the helicopters were chopping their way westward. They had set down on what had become the kind of place they felt safest, a tongue of land surrounded by water, this one jutting into Lake St. Clair a mile or two from the airbase. In the morning mist, Mort could not tell how far away the pulsing orbs of orange flames were. Sir Bear was within arm's reach on the deck.

The forward deck was the doghouse to which Todd had assigned Mort last night after a conversation Mort remembered going something like this:

"Okay. Time to regroup," Mort had said.

"You keep saying that."

"I am going to repeat myself until you settle down so we can discuss the matter."

Todd, who had been setting up the tent, had stomped over. "Okay. Fine. We've got killer robots out there. That's our apocalypse. For that, I have no plan of action."

"Those eyes," Mort had said, and he lost himself in the memory again this morning. "One was blue, one was red. Like one part of them was angry and part was sad, but they didn't know how to be either one. Like they were alive, but not."

"Maybe they suck the souls out of humans. Maybe they feed on us. I am not equipped to deal with this. I will *not* be food."

Mort had bent over to push a tent spike into the ground and said, "We'll all be food someday. For creatures we can't even see with our naked eye."

"Yes, well, until that day comes, I'm going to keep my bones within my skin."

"It was too late for that day one," Mort had said, regretting it last night and again this morning.

In response, Todd had made one long, wailing moan and told Mort he needed space to talk to God.

Mort had then lain in the flying boat.

He rubbed his face this morning. He had found it refreshing to sleep in the open like this.

A horse sighed somewhere.

Mort sat upright and looked around. Sir Bear did not budge. Mort stood and stretched.

Over a line of tall bushes, he saw a dapple-gray horse sipping from the lake.

Where are your friends? Mort asked in the quiet of his mind, not daring to shatter the stillness with a spoken word. The answer came. A woman walked up to the horse.

She was tall, of medium complexion, with long dark hair banded or loosely braided, and some of it fell in front of her shoulders. She wore a full-length linen dress, and her strong, bare arms worked freely.

Mort felt his knees give way a little. He did not know what to do. He wanted to call out to her, to meet a fellow human, to be saved. But she was perfect, too perfect. If she were another mirage or the dangerous imitation of everything he had ever wanted, he should say nothing. If she were real, she was too perfect, and she would not want him. Mort felt a familiar sadness well up within him. He sat down again and waited to see how long this illusion would last. It would be better to make an experiment out of this and not to know heartbreak again.

The horse turned its head, and Mort could see a long cone reaching skyward from between its eyes and ears. "Ah," Mort said softly. This was a unicorn. A mythical creature had become real, and so the woman with it was safely out of reach.

The woman turned in his direction as if she had heard him. She squinted in his direction. This was a human gesture, a sign she was not omnipotent.

Mort waved, and she waved back. "Todd," he yelled.

She pulled her head back.

Sir Bear sprang to attention and barked over the gunwale.

The woman seemed startled. She turned and bent down

behind the unicorn, lifted something off the ground, and fastened it on the creature like a saddle. It was bigger than a saddle, though. She mounted, and something like wings unfurled and flapped. The mist had hidden these before. The woman and her unicorn galloped a few paces and flew upward, disappearing into the mist.

"What was that all about?" Todd asked, his eyes following her into the milky sky.

"Nothing, I guess. Maybe it's all mind tricks, you know: you with barber-pole serpents, me with beautiful women riding unicorns."

"This one could have been worse."

"Yeah," Mort said, rubbing his face and neck. "At least she was pleasant to look at."

"To each his own," Todd said, in a dull tone Mort was not used to, and which he thought was his proprietary trait on this adventure.

Mort did not press Todd on this.

***

When the mist cleared, Mort and Todd explored Cass Ridge, which had never been a large air base and which had become mostly overgrown, its one runway included. There was no one to prevent them from entering and no one to explain what had happened. One personnel helicopter was smoldering on its side, the only thing that really seemed to have burned. Another pair of flying boats, similar to the one they had been operating but with clear Navy markings, seemed long-ago abandoned.

The only office building not overcome by nature's greedy fingers was locked.

"We could break in," Todd said.

"These people are coming back, I'm sure," Mort said.

"Are you, though?"

Mort was not.

Todd shined his flashlight through a window. "A few papers on a desk, filing cabinets, big map on the wall."

"Why do the flying boats over there have Navy markings? This was an Air National Guard base."

"You are asking the wrong person, Mortimer. Okay, so the map has a big wavy line cutting through the United States. We are in what looks like they are calling the 'Secure Zone.'"

Mort looked at the smoking helicopter. "This cannot be the safe zone."

"'Secure Zone,' just to be precise."

Mort looked over Todd's head, through the window, at a map of North America illumined by rings of lens flare from a squeeze flashlight. A dashed line wended a southeasterly way from the Pacific Northwest to well below Michigan and the Great Lakes before hitting the Atlantic coast somewhere near southern New Jersey.

"It almost looks like the edge of the ice sheet at the Last Glacial Maximum."

"Meaning...?"

"Meaning there have never been wooly rhinos around here. All this was once under thousands of feet of ice."

The flashlight died down, and instead of pumping it back to life, Todd pulled away from between Mort and the window. He gave Mort the flashlight, turned toward the crashed helicopter, and put his hands on his hips. "I almost have an idea, Mort."

"I'm all ears."

"That all this once being under ice, I don't know, maybe affects it in some way today?"

"I don't see how, at least as far as our current predicament goes. But look: the choppers we saw last night were headed west. Your family is out west, inside the Secure Zone. So why don't we lay out a plan, then? We can get pretty far in this magic carpet of a boat. We'll aim for Chicago and see what we see then keep going if necessary."

***

Two nights later, Todd lay in the tent, on a cushion of earth north of Chicago, on a windswept plain of low grass and sandy soil not far from Lake Michigan, filled with the pleasant sound of chirping crickets. They had followed the interstates from city to city—Lansing, Kalamazoo, Gary, Chicago—at what seemed to be the most efficient speed and altitude for them, forty knots at four hundred feet. They would only stop for food, rest, and the most obvious signs of human life. Between the peanut butter and jelly, popcorn, and fishing poles, there had been plenty of food. The deck of the boat was a comfortable place for one of them to stretch out his legs while the other pedaled, but, with their muscles still growing again from what must have been years in a coma, they could not go too far at once. Food and rest became the only things to make them stop since they had seen no one.

"Not a soul," Todd said. "All of these cities. The farms. No one."

"Agree with me, though, that it looks like someone nuked Chicago."

"I can't disagree, but maybe that's where the asteroid hit. Or the moon, as you've been saying."

"An asteroid would have left a crater. The moon would have torn the Earth inside out. Only a nuke could have torn a hole that size in downtown Chicago."

"It is possible people are hiding away. I mean, would we have ever seen that one neighborhood in Toledo, or Cass Ridge, from the sky? It's like the old needle in a haystack. We might as well head south," Todd said.

"What about your family?"

"Let's face it, Mort. They're gone."

Sir Bear perked up at something.

"We don't know that," Mort said. "And we don't know what we'll find going south, or east, or anywhere. If we get to Big Sky without finding anything, we'll go down to Mexico. We'll set up shop on the beach somewhere. Like in *Shawshank*."

Todd listened to the chirping crickets. What made it hard to keep pursuing something when it took just as much energy to turn aside?

"I'm starting to wonder if that woman weren't real," Mort said.

"Riding a unicorn near an air base? Maybe she's the Valkyrie that torched it in the first place. Don't make it real in your mind, what can't really exist for you."

"Fair enough."

The crickets wove their winged song through the night air. Todd turned all of his thoughts toward the single sensation of their sound. A low groan emerged from somewhere, far from the tent.

"What kind of animal is that, Mort?"

"I do not know. It's not a rhinoceros of any kind, as far as I can tell."

"That's a relief."

The groan seemed to grow louder. So did the crickets. Sir Bear began barking. Todd squeezed the flashlight. Mort put his hand on the dog's back, but Sir Bear turned and growled at him. The two men sat up. Mort was making motions with his mouth, as if he was talking, and he might have been, but Todd could hear nothing but the groan of that creature, as if it were trying to overcome the crickets and could not, as if it were some behemoth being eaten alive by a million little crickets.

All at once, the noise stopped.

Todd could hear himself breathing. He could hear the creak of wood in his hands—he had picked up his spear without knowing when—and the rub of the polyester tent beneath Sir Bear's paws.

"Todd?"

Todd had to swallow in order to respond. "Yeah."

"What was that?"

"You're asking me?"

"Alright, then. I'm also formulating a thought."

Todd's shoulders fell from his ears, and he put down the spear. "I'm all ears."

"You remember the owl, the first night?"

"Yes."

"And the cougar, who I still say was warning us about something?"

"Go on."

"And now these crickets?"

"I see where you're going with this."

"Charlaine swooped in and defended us against the worst manifestation of what's out there, but the animals have been, too. I know this doesn't sound like me to say, but I think something is at war on the Earth. At war with us, in it. That's where everyone else went. Maybe it couldn't get us because we were sleeping. But now that we're awake, good ol' Mother Earth, she's sending her best weapons to protect us, her animals."

"Like the swine on the shore of Galilee," Todd said.

16

Todd, on all fours, poked his head through the tent zipper into a bright, fresh morning. He waited there for a moment, his head pounding, while his body decided what to do with the contents of his stomach. He and Mort had finished the bottle of scotch last night.

As his eyes adjusted, he could see Mort's lanky body bent over at the edge of the field. Sir Bear's head and tail bounced upward through the grass in various places in between. Todd laughed a little, thinking Mort was suffering the same fate he was, but saw him scratch his chin and squat to take a closer look at something.

Todd took courage from his companions and stepped out of the tent. The low morning sun warmed the back of Todd's head and neck. He ran a free hand through the downy tuft of hair regrowing everywhere except his crown. A generation of stress-free sleep could not cure androgenetic alopecia. He should not stress now. He was alive, free, in the sunshine, not alone, and whatever fearsome thing was out there, the Earth was here to protect him. He closed his eyes, as if this alone could cure his hangover.

"Hey, Todd," Mort called.

Without opening his eyes, Todd held up his index finger. "I think these are dinosaur tracks."

The same spasm of muscles that heaved laughter out of Todd's chest sent a spray of brown vomitus into the clear air.

***

During the next hour, while Mort cooked popcorn for breakfast and Todd sat in his chair on the boat, sipping water and leaning against the gunwale, Todd learned, or at least heard, a great deal about dinosaurs. The tracks Mort had seen would have come from a large sauropod like *Apatosaurus*, *Brachiosaurus*, or *Diplodocus*.

When Todd asked if scientists had deliberately placed them at the front of the alphabet, Mort lost track of his thoughts.

The tracks, themselves, disappeared as abruptly as they had appeared, from one wooded grove to another about a mile away.

When Mort eventually gave up on following them and the boat stopped swaying to every excited jerk of Mort's steering, Todd asked, "So this is like another wooly rhino situation, right? I mean, how did a dinosaur get here from Africa?"

"Todd."

"What?"

"All of those dinos I mentioned were native to North America a hundred million years ago."

"That leads to my next question. How are there still tracks around? Wouldn't the rain wash them away after all this time?"

"Not always. We have many examples of fossilized footprints. But these were not them."

"Okay.... Wait. What?"

"I think that groan we heard last night was a dinosaur."

"False. You're saying that just to scare me."

"Think about it, Theodore. Don't you see this world becoming whatever we want to make of it?"

"In a limited sense, I suppose."

"We could still be asleep, for all we know." Mort breathed a deep breath of satisfaction and almost smiled. "I feel good. Don't you see? What this is all about?"

"I guess I don't."

"We're not here to run from anything. We're going to Big Sky, and we're going dinosaur hunting along the way. It's going to happen. It's inevitable. Because we're here to make it happen."

Todd glanced toward the bow at Sir Bear, whose tongue flapped in the breeze. A smile forced its way onto his own face. He would enjoy whatever Mort was up to, as long as it took them west. He had never really had a friend and was beginning to suspect Mort had not either. And his friend was finally happy.

17

A day's pedaling a boat through the air, broken only by a stop for fishing in the Mississippi—where Mort had pretended he had also read *The Adventures of Tom Sawyer*—brought him, Todd, and Sir Bear to southern Minnesota, where a thunderstorm began to cast the sky in hues of charcoal. Mort saw something on the ground below that signaled as well as anything else a place to land for the night.

Mort stood on the ground with his hands on his hips, staring proudly upward at the giant green man dressed in a leafy toga, his head about fifty or sixty feet above him. He looked over at Todd, who seemed less sure. Sir Bear was somewhere sniffing around.

"Please tell me this is a human thing," Todd said. "Please don't let this be the religion of the skirt-wearing humanoids we saw in Toledo."

"Ho-ho-ho," Mort said.

"This is not Santa Claus. Is this what Santa Claus is like in Minnesota, like, some Swedish version? If this town is called Blue Earth, why is the statue green?"

"Because he's selling frozen vegetables, Todd. Don't you remember the commercials?" He remembered that Todd was ten years younger than he. "No, I suppose not. It's the Jolly Green Giant."

"Right. Because, of course, human beings would put up something like this. Because someone like you would stop here."

"Well, aren't you a party pooper."

"I'm just tired. Long day. I went from hangover to dinosaurs in about ten minutes and, having caught nothing in the Mississippi, am surviving on popcorn and jelly."

"Fair enough. As it turns out, we may have to shelter here." Mort pointed to a small barn not far away. "Let's see about it before it gets too dark."

"Good. Maybe Swedish Santa Claus will protect us. No. Forget I said that. Are you listening, Mother Earth? I did not say that. No green giants. Just normalcy. A good night's sleep, for God's sake and mine. Thank you."

"Is that how you pray?" Mort said. "I was always taught to be nice to God."

***

The barn was not leak proof, and Mort, Todd, and Sir Bear were not the only ones seeking shelter from the rain. While the two humans warmed themselves at the small fire they had made in a barrel, Sir Bear carried on protracted negotiations with a raccoon in the corner. The two animals spoke the language they shared, a string of subtle growls, hisses, and sighs.

"They can be cute, eh?" Mort said. "I wonder why we never made pets out of raccoons."

Todd looked over and grimaced. "Because maybe they pick through the garbage, and are gross, and look like little bandits. There has to be an exchange of some kind. They have to want something we have and have to offer something we want. Dogs help us in our duties. Cats eat mice. Raccoons do nothing but eat our garbage."

"That's a service, isn't it? We could invite them in, eat out of bowls, and so on. And they could lay around looking cute in the house."

"Cute? Have you seen their weird paws? They're like little hands. Like, little troll hands."

"Well, since we're sharing the barn with this one, let's call him Rocky. Like from the song."

Todd smiled and sighed at Mort. "I don't know what song you're talking about, but how about Rebecca? Because this is a girl raccoon. A mother. She's got her litter right behind her."

Mort noticed the small balls of fur scurrying behind the creature, who grew angry at the flashlight being shined upon her. "Becky, then. Becky Raccoon."

"Nope. It's Rebecca. Trust me on this one. I see it in her. She's a Rebecca. She used to let the guys who pass by the garbage cans call her Becky, but now she's got a litter of her own to take care of, which she does with fierce generosity. She goes by Rebecca now. Rebecca Raccoon, Registered Nurse."

"Rebecca Raccoon. So be it. You should write a children's book about Rebecca. Warn girls about hanging out at the garbage cans. You know, Beatrix Potter was a mycologist before she got into writing children's books."

Todd stared at the raccoons.

"Just something to look forward to, is all I'm saying. I can do the drawings."

Todd leaned his chin onto his folded hands. "Maybe I will write a book. If we ever get back to humanity."

***

Water trickled across the unfinished barn floor, so Mort and Todd slept sitting on plastic milk crates and leaning against a thick wooden post. The boat would not fit inside, so they had snapped its cover into place. Todd woke to catch his sagging head several times and would have leaned it against Mort's shoulder, but Mort was slumped forward. Frustrated, Todd looked around the room still dimly lit by the rusted glow of the fire burning in the barrel. The storm had passed, and some water still dripped in the corner of the barn to Todd's left, away from Mort, Sir Bear, and Rebecca, who had taken off anyway. Sir Bear, in fact, was lying on the floor in front of the baby raccoons, boxing them in between shelving units. "Rebecca, you old slut," Todd said in a whisper.

He turned back to the dripping water in the corner. Lightning, flashing dimly from the distance, shined through a window. That corner did not light up with the rest of the room. Todd, curious, pointed the flashlight. The light did not reflect off the form in the corner. Water dripped onto it and fell down the side, as if down a man wearing a raincoat.

Growing afraid, Todd began to reason with himself, deducing that the hooded form was a hanging robe or sheet or blanket. It took him some time to summon the courage to add a scrap of wood to the fire. He removed his hand from the opening of the barrel and turned away from the flames to see them reflecting off Mort, now leaning back against the post.

But Mort was somehow more distant than before. Though he had been just six feet from the fire, now he seemed across the room. Todd began to walk back to his seat, but the more he walked, the farther away the wooden post became. He turned back around to face the fire, but this, too, was out of arm's reach. His stomach quivered, and he felt his breath leaving him.

"Sir Bear," he called weakly, but the dog was fast asleep, as were all the baby raccoons behind him.

Todd tried everything in his power not to turn back to that corner, but he felt that blackened robe beckoning him. Every time he turned his head to the fire, to Sir Bear, and to Mort, each of those familiar forms grew more distant until they were no more than blurs of light in a vast field of darkness.

"Jesus," he sobbed. He closed his eyes and reached out left and right, but nothing remained within reach. "Jesus, please don't do this to me. Please help me."

Slowly, hesitatingly, he opened his eyes. Mort, Sir Bear, and the furnace were like distant stars in the night sky. The form was right behind him. He could feel it. It was not hot or cold, angry or hateful. It was simply there, which was the most terrifying thing it could be.

Choking on his halting breath, Todd slowly turned. *Okay, Jesus, let me face this.* He saw nothing there. He looked left and right and saw no one though he felt its presence. It was behind him again. Todd turned and saw the three lights he had come to know, the fire and his two companions, held together in the void. The void shimmered and took shape, a solid flame of black. The three familiar lights bounced and multiplied in the folds of the iridescent form. Todd began to see a collage of shapes and colors. None of it was fearful or grotesque, and none of it formed a whole image. It seemed like his own memories laid out before him in little mirrors.

Those memories took shape. He saw himself in various guises over the years: a little-league uniform, a ski outfit, and a captain's hat; a choir robe and an angel costume at a nativity play; a tuxedo dusted with cocaine. Black lips and moonlit skin. Hospital gowns in blue and green. These memories looked back at him like strangers. They studied him and each other, and no one knew how they all fit together.

The fabric holding these fragments tore apart. A hundred little mirrors spread out like stars in the night sky but formed no constellation. They simply flew away, a billion miles away from each other in the deepening black.

Todd tried harder to hold them together, to read them like a book or a building, but he could not find what held them together. Each fragment of his former life flew away with its own personality, its own history, its own future. Todd began to breathe heavily then held his breath. He grew frustrated and cried out to see himself as a whole but could not.

The space between his memories grew wider and darker. Blackness flowed like a river between islands of moving images but seemed to go nowhere. Those islands fell away from each other like boats on the sea, a flotilla lost in the fog, distant stars in an ever-expanding universe.

He could no longer breathe or remember how to breathe. He slapped his hands against his chest in his panic. He did not know how to move the air in or out. He pried open his mouth with his hands and tried to pull out his tongue, but this was not the problem. He smiled tearfully and looked up, ready to die.

Todd did the only thing that came to him to do, and he exercised his jaw up and down, forming A's and O's with his mouth. He tried to say, "Ow," moving from A to O. This seemed to have some effect, as he began to hear himself whisper, "Ah-oo." He kept on, his voice becoming surer and surer. Rejoicing in this, he continued until he heard a wolf howling from within him, "Ah-oo," loudly and clearly. His breath returned, and he laughed.

He saw the three stars he knew appear again from behind the distant fragments of his life, which now dissolved into obscurity. Those three lights began to move together and grow larger and eventually merged. Todd continued to howl like a wolf, beckoning them to him like the full moon.

Those three lights became one and grew bright, then the figure reemerged. It blocked out the light of the stars as it moved toward him, eclipsing them. It drew near and reached out its shadowy arms. Todd howled all the louder at this form to defy it. It grabbed him with strong, cold hands, and he pulled away, howling in disdain, "Ah-oo."

"Todd," the form said. "Todd." The form shook him. "Todd, wake up!"

Todd, no longer howling, began to make out Mort's face.

"Todd," he said more calmly. "Are you alright? Are you there?"

Todd stood still, no longer wrestling himself away.

"Todd," Mort said, rubbing his hands up and down Todd's arms. "Hey."

"H-Hey," Todd said in a whisper. He looked around and saw himself back in the barn. Sir Bear looked up from his protective place, concerned. Seeing he was now safe, Todd began to cry a little. Mort held Todd by his shoulders at arm's length. Sir Bear lay his head down again.

Todd wriggled free and tried to talk, hiccupping as he did. "I-guh, I-guh, I've never been a whole person. I've only ever done what I could do to make others keep me around. I've made myself into everything and have become nothing. I'm nothing! I'm nothing!"

Mort grabbed him by both shoulders again. "Listen to me," he said firmly. "You're all I've got. You're everything to me right now. You got that? You're whole. You are a whole person. Maybe a wolf, too, I'm not sure. But definitely a whole person. I'm alive because of you."

Todd nodded. He heard Mort's words, but the only way he could believe them would be to feel them as Mort felt them, and this was where Todd doubted that Mort had really meant them.

A few minutes later, sitting on his milk crate again, leaning against the wooden post, Todd shined the flashlight. The corner was empty, just a heavy post dripping with water.

18

Mort pedaled first the next morning to let Todd sleep off his terrible encounter. A light drizzle fell through the warm air blanketing the Great Plains, an endless array of abandoned farms, the sleepiest land Mort had seen so far. But Todd was unable to stay asleep for long.

"What are we really facing, Mort?"

"Like I said, whatever we want to face."

"I did not want to face what I saw last night."

"Alright. I emend my statement, then. We are facing what we need to face. As for the cities we've seen, and compared with the tree growth, which I estimate now at between thirty and forty years, it just doesn't seem like the buildings should have deteriorated so much so quickly. It's almost like they've suffered some severe weather, like a long period of torrential rains or heavy snow. That's certainly possible and might explain why we don't see people around, you know, like they actually just moved away. All of this could just be some climate event. Maybe they are all down south, and we're going west, and that's why we haven't seen anyone. What they're calling the 'Secure Zone' just means everyone's moved out, the military's secured it.

"As for us, we, in our own unique solo journey through it all, are facing what we need to face. In that light, it's also quite possible that, since it's all been very personal so far, we are, in fact, no longer alive. This is…whatever. Preparation. Purgatory."

Todd sighed. "I don't know. I feel like God would be a bit clearer about all that. Especially to someone like myself, who prays."

"Maybe I'm here just to muddle things up for you."

"Well, then let me ask you. If we are dead, what's the point in chasing down a dinosaur? It seemed to both of us the other night that the crickets were attacking it, if it was even there at all."

"I'm a biologist, Todd. What better way to finish out life than by encountering one of its greatest mysteries?"

Todd raised his head off the gunwale, knit his brow, and studied Mort for a moment. Just as soon, Todd's face fell, telling Mort that whatever train of thought Todd had seen coming had passed the station. Todd leaned against the gunwale again, closed his eyes, and said, "It's like the whole Earth is some place between waking and sleeping."

***

Todd worked alongside Mort at a makeshift workbench, the open rear hatch of a red Chevy truck, improving their spears. They had found a place to rest for a few days just east of the Missouri, a spit of land jutting into a lake. This small peninsula had come complete with a barn that had weathered the decades well and which was large enough to house the flying boat. The house was dry and intact but, as best as they could tell, free of sleepers. The garage was full of tools, including an old hand drill Todd was using to drill through the pole and into a folded seam of metal on the shaft of the garden trowel to keep it from turning inside the hollow of the bamboo.

"I can't keep the drill bit from spiraling off the pole," Todd said.

"Poke a hole in it first."

"Poke a hole before I drill a hole? With what do you suggest I do that, exactly?"

Mort handed Todd a Phillips-head screwdriver. Todd cast umbrageous eyes at him. Mort shrugged. "What? It's just a suggestion."

"So you're the scientist. Why don't you go fix the truck battery?"

Mort looked ahead. "Damnit, Jim, I'm a biologist, not an electrician."

Todd, turning the screwdriver into the end grains, huffed, smiled, and nodded. The wide drill bit then went in straight. Todd turned a few screws through the holes in the wood and into the longitudinal seam of the trowel shaft.

When Mort's spear was refinished in the same way, the two men admired their craft.

"How are you going to take down a dinosaur with this?" Todd asked. "Or even a wooly rhino? You saw how you did with the deer."

"It's not only about dinosaurs. That was just one thing. Who knows, I could hunt down a woman, the one I saw back in Michigan. The world's whatever we make of it now. Maybe I could make her real, you know?"

***

The next morning, with their spears more confidently planted next to them in the earth, Todd fished with Mort at the edge of the small lake near their acquisitioned farmhouse. With his shoes off, pants rolled up, and feet covered in the cool mud of the shore, Todd closed his eyes serenely.

When he opened them a few seconds later, he saw an animal poking its head between the trees across the lake a hundred yards away. As it reached its head down to drink from its side of the lake, Todd could see small ribs or spikes running down its long neck. The head itself resembled that of a turtle, with a colorful sac above its nose like that of a rooster, but it was impossibly large. Another of its kind, but smaller, came up next to it and began to drink, though a bit more timidly, and Todd thought this must be the juvenile.

Todd turned to Mort. "Is that...?"

"Sh." Mort stood stiff. "*Camarasaurus.*"

"Camaro-saurus?" Todd whispered. "Because it has a mullet on its nose?"

Mort's head made a slow, mechanical turn toward Todd, and his wide eyes shined with some kind of black fire Todd had never seen in his friend. Mort's head swiveled back into place while a smile that seemed more menacing than delighted slipped upward. Mort began carefully putting away his fishing gear.

Sir Bear seemed unmoved by the sight.

"Let's watch from the boat," Mort said. "In case he moves. We're too close for comfort anyway."

The mud slurped as Todd freed his bare feet.

The juvenile *Camarasaurus* pulled back into the trees.

The older one raised its head to thirty or forty feet and huffed through its nose.

Sir Bear crouched into a ready stand, wagged his tail, and barked.

The older dinosaur also ducked into the trees.

"Come on, Todd. Now."

Todd turned too quickly and, with one foot still stuck in the mud, fell on his face.

***

"I'm sorry," Todd said.

Mort was sitting in the garage with him, angrily sharpening his spear with a metal file.

"None of us could know how fast a *Camarasaurus* could run."

"Or how silently," Mort said and flashed his eyes up at Todd.

"Oh, I'm supposed to be quiet now?"

Mort stopped filing and sat hunched over his work. "No. You're right. Look what we did find: the dinosaur knew enough to use a paved road to hide his tracks. That is brilliant. I could write a whole thesis just on that encounter. Doctorates have been made from less."

"The *dinosaur*, Mortimer." Todd spread his hands. "Can we take this for what it is for one moment? We saw a living *dinosaur*. Not in the movies. In real life. And you're already thinking about doctorates."

Mort resumed his filing at an easier rhythm. "Again, you're right. I'm sure whoever else lives in this world has already got the scoop on dinosaurs."

Todd sighed but slowly enough not to let Mort hear. The

man could not even see a place for himself in the apocalypse while he was in the middle of it.

Sir Bear lay his head on Mort's lap but quickly turned toward some sound only he could hear.

"What is it, boy?" Mort said. "Did Timmy fall down the well?"

Todd heard a flock of ducks take flight off the water. Mort seemed to notice this, too. Sir Bear held himself in fidgeting stillness while his masters listened for what he could already hear. A deep groan carried over the water.

Todd looked at Mort and whispered, "Who says there are no second chances?"

The corners of Mort's mouth curled upward as he shook his head.

Another groan throbbed through the air. Todd looked around at the garage. It was sturdy. They could hide in the cab of the truck. Their spears would do no good.

A third, louder groan resonated with the bed of the truck, and some nails shook in place. The dinosaur's footfall sent no vibrations. Sir Bear tucked his tail between his legs and looked upward for answers.

"Mort," Todd said, the word drowned out by a groan right outside the barn. Heavy breathing followed.

Mort opened his mouth to answer when the garage shook around them. Dust fell from the top of the open rafters. The behemoth was rubbing its side along the wall of the garage. Todd clung to the truck. Mort seemed dazed and confused. The rubbing stopped. All was silent for a few seconds. One heavy thud came from outside the garage, behind

Todd. Mort regained his composure and gave Todd a look he did not understand.

"Come on," Mort whispered.

"Come on, what?"

"Let's go look."

Todd shook his head and crossed his arms. Mort, with eager face, grabbed his shoulder. Todd's finger went up in the air without his thinking about it, brushing off Mort's hand. Mort grabbed his spear.

"No," Todd said. "If we go out there, it's without weapons. I don't want to be seen as a threat. Can we not look on from the boat?"

"The boat's in the barn, in the other direction. Come on. This thing is big, too big to be a theropod. It's our *Camarasaurus*. It'll be friendly. It sounds like it's lying down right now."

"If am I crushed to death by its big elephant paw, I will resurrect in this weird world into the most God-forsaken monster you have ever seen and follow you into your nightmares."

"Deal."

Todd followed Mort out the door, along the outside edge of the garage. Mort peeked around the corner and watched for a few seconds then continued. Todd closed his eyes briefly and walked forward.

The *Camarasaurus* seemed bigger than the two he had encountered before, but he had not seen their bulk or length. It lay on its side, the long tail running back along the length of the garage. He could not see its head. A weak groan came, followed by a dusty snort.

"Is it sick?" Todd asked.

"I don't know." Mort turned his head around the next corner, as if to catch the length of the tail, and snapped backward. "There's another one coming."

Todd heard a few heavy puffs of breath. The head appeared from behind the garage and began sniffing at the base of the other's tail. The one lying down pulled its upper rear leg forward, exposing its genitals.

"Oh, God." Todd put his hand to his forehead and closed his eyes.

"Theodore Broderick Farkas, you and I are about to witness one of the greatest mysteries in biological paleontology unveil itself before us."

At the word "unveil," Todd tucked his face against the wall of the garage.

Mort continued as if Todd were not actively blocking him out. "It is hypothesized that dinosaurs, like modern birds and lizards, used the same orifice for mating and defecating, the cloaca. That's what you see there. The male comes up and rubs his cloaca against hers. It's called the 'cloacal kiss.'"

"How romantic," Todd said. He looked for Sir Bear, who was not with them.

"Now we get to see how it works in dinosaurs. Come on. I order you not to miss this."

Todd turned. He squinted and screwed his lips into a tight squiggle. He did not know what was more revolting, what he was about to see or the eagerness with which Mort wanted to see it.

The male walked forward. His belly rubbed along hers. He lowered his pelvis, and his tail covered the action.

Mort's face began stiffening, as if his smile were freezing into pain. Todd turned back to the couple. Waves of fat rolled forward toward her neck. Mort was slowly sitting down. After a long minute, the male grunted, sniffed at the female's head, and walked away.

"That wasn't so bad," Todd said. He looked down at Mort, who had his hands on his knees. His face was frozen, red with strain. Suddenly, his mouth opened wide, and his eyes closed, like a child about to cry. His hands came near his face and held there, shaking. Mort wailed loudly in short bursts. "Omigod," Todd said.

Todd knelt down next to Mort and wrapped his arms around him, rocking Mort side to side. His body was trembling. Todd looked back at the female, still lying prone just a few yards away. "I know, Mort. It's very exciting."

"They're right in front of me," Mort cried out.

"Maybe too much excitement for one day. Or one life."

"*Babcia*," Mort said.

Todd pulled his head back in confusion.

"Grandma, get them away from me. They're right on top of me."

Todd looked at the female dinosaur, whose length, as she lay, almost filled his field of vision. Some kind of image flashed in his mind's eye, a voice calling from within a hollow Earth to a dark hollow in Todd's own body, where his stomach ball had once been, and he understood.

They had not just been too close today. This was more than emotional excitement. This was a world of Mort and

Todd's own making, and Mort was making it from things to which he had perhaps been too close, too soon, and had forgotten. Todd remembered what Mort had said about his parents' disappearing into the penal system, and he burst into tears. He pressed his lips against the top of Mort's head and held him there, gently rocking him.

19

Todd cooked popcorn over a fire just outside the barn door and sat so he could keep an eye on Mort. Mort had not said much. After consoling him for ten or twenty minutes, Todd watched as some shield went back up over Mort. He had politely but firmly pushed Todd away and said, "It's alright. It's okay. I'm fine." Mort had stood up and walked inside the garage. Since then, a few hours ago, Mort had resumed sharpening his spear with a metal file.

Todd figured that this required the popcorn. Mort would taste it and feel at home again. Sir Bear seemed to know at least the smell of popcorn and wagged his tail with happy impatience. Todd did not want to leave Mort alone by fishing in the lake. He did not know how to speak to him. Sir Bear nudged his nose into the arm that held Mort's spear in place, and Mort ignored him. Popcorn was the only medicine Todd could think of, popcorn and booze. In his careful search of the decrepit house, Todd had found bourbon in a plastic bottle.

"Lunch is ready," Todd said, pouring the hot popcorn into a plastic bowl from the house. Sir Bear lunged at it, and Todd gently smacked him on the nose, thrusting his finger into the air. He then put his hand down on Sir Bear's head to pet him. He had assumed Sir Bear had been eating on his own and did not realize how hungry the dog must have been.

Mort calmly laid aside his spear and dug his two hands into the bowl, pulling out his portion. Todd grimaced at this and poured some out on the ground for Sir Bear. Mort buried his face between his laden hands, covering his nose with oil and salt. Todd picked up a few pieces at a time. When Mort finished, he licked the oil off fingers already streaked with metal and resumed his filing. Todd looked around and saw the plastic bottle of bourbon. He held it out to Mort, who refused with a simple upturn of his palm and a polite nod.

"It's five o'clock somewhere," Todd said, taking a swig. "Oh, God, what pooschwaggle is this?" He rinsed his mouth out with water.

Todd then picked up an atlas they had found to study it. It was another six hundred miles to Big Sky. At forty miles per hour, that was fifteen hours in the air, two whole days, and he did not know how constant Mort's feet would be or how steady his hands. They could spend the night after this in northeast Wyoming. Todd looked more closely. "Devils Tower. How wonderfully ironic." Todd kept studying the area, looking for some more obvious sign. "Mort," he called.

Mort did not answer and kept filing his spear.

"We are going to stop at Mount Rushmore tomorrow," Todd said.

"Cool."

Todd tried again. "It's almost halfway to Big Sky. If we're tired, we can just sleep on George Washington's head."

"Hm," was all Mort offered.

Todd looked at Sir Bear, who seemed to take this as an invitation to more food. "Come on, Sir Bear. Let's go fishing."

***

Todd, Mort, and Sir Bear lay in the bow deck of the boat that night. Todd had insisted that the spears, both of which Mort had sharpened in near total silence, remain in the stern for fear of slicing someone in his sleep. That was Todd's least worry now. A gentle rain had found them. Todd had prided himself, as a stylist, on making his customers open up to him. Now he realized that, in their world, he was one of the few whom they knew would listen to them. He was their confessor in a world in which pastors took part in their politics. Todd had nothing to gain from their weakness except a hefty tip. They might have known his parents and his story and felt at home in his weakness. Todd had not made that impression on Mort yet. Mort did not seem the kind to open up to a bartender either. Todd doubted that Mort's grandmother had shown much toleration for emotion. Based on what Mort had said, she had borne the heaviest of it, whatever Mort's parents had been involved with, which Todd suspected and which he could not bring himself to name even within the safety of his own skull.

Todd's stomach growled. He had not caught any fish this afternoon. They had run out of peanut butter and jelly. He could have made more popcorn, but they should ration what they had. Mort had not complained. Sir Bear had made a halfhearted effort to snag a duck. They had survived this long against Mother Nature and all of the surrealities she had summoned simply by dwelling within her. This might not go on forever, not without help.

Big Sky was not a promise and began to look like less than a feeble hope. It was their chosen path, the only thing they could have chosen in their near-total ignorance of the world around them. Jake had not come back for him because Jake was no longer in this world. Jake had not survived this. They should have stayed in Detroit, at Todd's house, opened the shutters, mowed the lawn, and used the boat to scan every square mile of the city. They could have made a radius of hundreds of miles using only day trips. Todd had studied this in the road atlas. Pittsburgh, Cincinnati, Toronto, Buffalo, and everywhere in between were all within range of their winged feet.

They had not done this because it had not occurred to them to do this. They had chosen a path and taken it. They had reached Chicago and been spooked by nuclear holocaust and the impossible revival of dinosaurs. They had not turned back because they had mistaken fear for wonder. They had become entranced by what their minds could produce on this planet and its strange new sky, relishing even the attention paid to them by waking nightmares.

Maybe that was all that had happened to Mort. He had simply woken to the reality that this world was a living nightmare. He had done what any healthy person should do. He had gone back to sleep.

20

Between an endless gray sky and the earth that folded up beyond it, the wind lashed Mort's face. It beat against him, tightening and reddening, browning and hardening. He did not know how leather was made, but this method would suffice. The soft, doughy scientist was becoming a road warrior. He had known all his life that beneath a fatty mound of undigested anger lay the bark-wrapped skeleton that now squinted over the Badlands. There had been no man in between that soft skin and those grizzled bones, no pleasant medium through which he could summon the spirit of humanity.

Todd and people like him had made their way through with good humor and a dozen delectable weaknesses. He felt sorry for Todd in this place. Todd would feel more at home among those who knew how to give and receive.

"Do you want to talk about it?" Todd suddenly asked.

Mort did not know how. "No." He owed Todd more than that. "Not now. Too windy." Mort really did not know what had happened, why he had reacted the way he had. He had seen what every biologist yearns to see. It did not disgust him. He had seen that many times among many species, including his own, at least on film. Perhaps that was just it. He had come too close. It had surrounded him with no television frame to hold it back.

Todd put his hand to the altitude dial and began turning it. They had been flying at no more than four or five hundred feet above the ground at forty miles per hour since Cass Ridge. This altitude and speed had been the most energy-efficient. Todd turned the dial and pedaled faster.

Their altitude rose quickly for the little extra energy Todd put into pedaling. At a thousand feet, Mort helped. At two thousand, the hills began to flatten. At five thousand feet, the men disappeared into the stratocumulus.

When they broke above the clouds a few hundred feet higher, the sun cast a regal array across its hidden kingdom. All was brilliant white and blue. Behind them marched great columns, cumulonimbus flashing their swords, knights on horseback opening their purses upon the parched ground, priests in golden vestments making swift and refreshing peace between heaven and Earth.

Ahead of them, the promise of the impossible smiled with snowy teeth. In the far distance, where the horizon should have fallen, the Rocky Mountains rose, row behind row. At ten thousand feet, they could see their world clearly. Earth had become a bowl. Even Sir Bear turned his head in wide-eyed wonder.

Mort's heart beat against his bark-hardened chest, and he would have remained up here forever, but his legs grew tired. He nodded in Todd's direction. Todd understood and turned the altitude dial downward.

When they fell below the clouds again, Mort said the

first thing that came into his mind. "What did you mean about the woman in Cass Ridge? I thought she was beautiful, but you did not."

Todd pulled his head back a little as if surprised by this question and turned to Mort. "That's what's bothering you? No, I mean, maybe I didn't get a good look at her. I just meant that if she was some temptress or goddess, they could have done better, that's all."

Mort, who had been replaying that scene to drive away the dinosaurs, wondered what it was he had missed about her or what qualities he had misplaced. "Yeah, I guess I do that."

"What?"

"Put them on pedestals."

"We all do. Here, come on. Let's land in this little town down here. My legs are tired, and so are yours. It's about lunchtime anyway."

They landed on a main street filled with parked cars, which had been long abandoned. Once out of the boat, Mort stretched. "Oh, God, what weird place have our winged feet brought us to now?" The style of all the buildings was Old West, and on one side was a place for which Mort had seen signs all along the road below him, Wall Drug. "We cut upward between clouds and stars for a few minutes and land in the Old West." He grabbed both spears and handed Todd his, admiring his handiwork.

Once he saw that Todd was ready, they walked toward the big green drugstore, which for some reason also boasted a museum and a chapel. Sir Bear ran on ahead but stopped, looked at something they could not see, and turned to the humans for help.

"What is it, boy?" Mort asked.

There, behind a minivan, hitched to a lamppost, was the woman's dapple-gray unicorn.

Mort walked up to the unicorn. He heard Todd say something like, "Be careful," but his brain did not register the meaning of the words. The horn was not natural and was strapped on, as were the wings. The material of the wings was a lot like the carpet that had been lifting the boat on which he and Todd had been flying but much thinner, almost translucent. Some sort of cabling ran from the stirrups to the wings, and wiring ran back down from the horn. It was a normal horse made up into a flying unicorn.

Todd must have said something, maybe just Mort's name, for Mort turned unthinkingly toward Wall Drug. Standing half-hidden behind a thick wooden post was the woman. She looked much paler in the gray and green light than she had when the white mist had lapped against her on the promontory of the lake shore. She did not move or even blink, and if a slight breeze had not stirred the tresses of her hair and the folds of her white linen dress, which was a little dirty at the cuffs, she would have resembled a marble statue.

Mort's stomach began to quiver. The horse stepped sideways and gently knocked Mort toward the minivan. The woman jumped a little and clung to the wooden post with long, elegant fingers.

"Hello?" Mort said.

"Be careful," Todd whispered. "We don't know what this is."

The woman seemed to hear this and pulled her head back a little.

This gave Mort courage to face the vision. "Do you speak, or am I supposed to interpret your silence? Is that the trick?"

"Are you sleepers?" she asked. "Or scavengers?"

Her voice fell a note or two into tenor range. She was becoming perfection for Mort, and he began to recede into his skull.

"And who are you?" Todd asked.

"My name is Cici," she said.

"I'm Mort. Mortimer."

"Mortimer," Cici echoed softly. Mort imagined she was savoring every syllable. "Did I see you both a few days ago?"

"Don't answer that," Todd muttered to Mort.

Mort forgot what she had said anyway. The only thing between him and the drugstore that moved was the swaying of the horse's tail at the bottom of his field of vision.

"I understand if you two are scared," Cici said. "You look like you just woke up. Where are you going?"

"Where is everyone?" Todd asked. "Are we the last survivors of humanity?"

Cici seemed to resist rolling her eyes and smirking. "Yes. Us and about a billion other people. But they're mostly down south."

Mort heard Todd repeat the words, "a billion," but they meant nothing to him. She and he were the only two souls in the universe.

"If there are a billion people," Todd said, "why have we seen no one?"

"You were at Cass Ridge," Cici said. "There were dozens of people there."

Mort recovered enough to say, "We must have got there too late from Toledo."

"So you were also in Toledo?" Cici said. "Why are you asking *me* where everyone is? Why didn't you just go down to Cincinnati or St. Louis?"

"A map said this was the Secure Zone," Todd said.

Mort, who was now contemplating Cici's long fingers clinging to the post, saw in his mind the framed picture of his grandmother's Divine Mercy, the one he had tried to ignore the first morning he had woken, and imagined Jesus almost smiling.

"You know how the Navy talks," Cici said. "Everything a euphemism. Maybe you don't know how the Navy talks. The only thing making the northern latitudes secure is the absence of people."

"And why are they absent?" Todd kept up his interrogative tone.

"Polar drift," she said and did not explain more.

Todd turned to Mort. "What is polar drift?"

"I don't know."

"And why are you up here?" Todd asked. Mort knew why Todd was being so defensive, but he wanted to enjoy this fantasy for a little while.

"To train my horse to fly."

Todd did not seem able to respond to this.

This fit with the reality they had been experiencing in their flying boat. Either she was real, or it was all fantasy.

Words escaped from Mort's mouth. "And how is that going for you?"

She sighed. "I've hit a snag."

"What snag?" Mort asked.

"He got spooked. It turns out horses do not like to fly. I tied him up just a few minutes before you got here."

Todd turned to Mort again. "Did we spook the horse?"

"I don't know, Todd."

"What do you think? Is she maybe actually real?"

"I don't know." The thought of her being real frightened Mort more than fantasy.

Todd appeared to think for a moment and turned back to the woman. "Miss Cici, would you kindly explain to us what kind of world we're living in?"

She stepped out from behind the post and held her hands at her waist. "When did you guys fall asleep?"

"That's irrelevant," Todd said. Turning to Mort, he whispered, "Let's not feed her any information."

"What I mean is," Cici said, "it helps to know where to start. You saw the moondark?"

"Yes," Mort said.

"And the Great Eclipse?" she asked.

"No," Mort said.

Todd twitched.

"So," she said, "the general thinking goes that soon after syzygy, the moondark expanded or gave the illusion of expansion. During the darkness, many people disappeared. After that, the climate went sort of wonky, and those who remained moved into the middle latitudes."

"The climate went wonky?" Todd asked. "How many years ago was this?"

She grimaced. "That depends on your definition of a year."

Sir Bear started barking fiercely, and Mort recognized the same tone he had heard outside the museum in Toledo. He held his spear with both hands, turning his eyes toward where Sir Bear was looking and back to the woman. She seemed concerned, but this could be a trick, the trap into which she had led them.

From around the corner of Wall Drug, a dinosaur appeared, a large raptor whose lurking head met Mort's height. It was covered with brown and gray feathers, which grew longer along the tail and arms. It was alone.

"Did you guys bring that?" Cici said. She clung to the post again.

Between Sir Bear's barks, Mort heard Todd whimpering.

The raptor, a *Dakotaraptor* if Mort remembered correctly, lurked forward.

"The boat," Todd said.

Mort could not think. The minivan blocked his view of the boat, which felt a half a mile away. The raptor had spied the horse and seemed to be moving slowly, if only to study the two other creatures standing behind it. Mort could hear its large talons clicking on the pavement. "Todd, let's back away. Around the van, go behind."

Todd stepped backward with Mort. When Mort reached the horse's front legs, the tip of his spear grazed its ribs. The horse leapt forward, still tied to the lamppost, and bucked its way around to the other side. This knocked Todd against the minivan, and he fell to the ground. Mort heard Cici shriek.

The raptor ran toward Mort and stopped just twenty feet away. Mort stood with his back to the lamppost and the horse with Todd at its feet. The *Dakotaraptor* bared its teeth and chirped. Mort did not know if this was meant to frighten him or to call its friends. The ancient animal might not know what to do with what it saw.

Mort did not know what to do either. He felt frozen with as much indecision as fear. Todd was awake and seemed to be thinking about pulling himself under the van. Mort dug his palms into the spear, heavy duct tape at the end near the trowel point, blistering fragments of bamboo at the other end, where it had worn down against dirt and pavement.

He felt his muscles soften and sadness wash downward, as if nature had spoken to make of him a gift of prey to predator.

Charlaine appeared somewhere in his mind, casting the fierce eyes of a mother cougar at him.

Mort breathed. He forced long, seething breaths between his clenched teeth. His chest heaved, and his hands fell forward and back, pendula of a clock or a child's swing. He groaned. With each new breath, his groan grew louder and became a growl. The raptor chirped, and Sir Bear barked behind it. This dual aural assault seemed to distract the raptor. Mort saw this and growled louder. His lips curled upward, and his bared teeth opened wide to let out a new sound. What animal lent him this voice, the cougar or something else, Mort did not know. He ground the spear into his palms.

The raptor tapped its talons on the concrete. Mort turned his eyes to those keratin scimitars. This was enough to make the raptor leap.

In an instant, Mort's field of vision was filled with the *Dakotaraptor's* chiseled maw. Mort found the tip end of the spear buried deep in the monster's throat. His left arm was in there, too, wrapped in moist muscle. His right hand was pinned between the end of the spear and the metal lamppost. The animal did not move, but dim embers of hate glowed in the animal's eye.

Mort reasoned, for a brief moment, that some part of him should be in great pain. He felt nothing. He may have severed the dino's spinal cord. He wanted some assurance before he attempted to move, but none would come. Todd was not there. Cici had vanished. Sir Bear was barking.

Mort used his right hand as a fulcrum to push the heavy dinosaur downward with his left arm, still hidden in a gaping tomb of teeth. Lightning shot through his right hand. When the raptor finally lay on the ground, Mort found himself astride its neck, staring down its open jaws. His left arm was free, and with it, he thrust down on the end of the spear. Slivers of the spear had sliced through his right hand. From the *Dakotaraptor's* throat, blood welled up between pink folds of flesh.

He had slayed a dragon.

White fabric flicked before Mort's face, carrying a whiff of pleasant perfume. Cici had walked past and was untying her horse.

"Get away before the other two come," she said. "I'll go find my uncle Billy."

Mort's brain did not register the meaning of these words or the other sounds that Cici made. He pulled his spear out from the raptor's throat. Something pulled at him from behind.

"Mort, let's go let's go let's go," Todd was saying.

Mort followed Todd back to the boat. The spear was still stuck in his right hand. Sir Bear was in the bow already or had followed them in. The boat began to rise, and Mort saw two other *Dakotaraptors* rounding the corner of Wall Drug. He turned and saw Cici galloping away behind him. The raptors chased after the horse, slipping a little on the concrete street. They ran right underneath the boat and stumbled on the other side. The waving carpet that held the boat aloft had stunned them with electric shock, just as it had done to Todd in Toledo. The boat yawed, and Mort could see Cici and the horse flying upward and away.

At around a hundred feet in the air, Todd paused to catch his breath. Mort looked down at the dead dinosaur. He had just done that.

His right hand throbbed, and he was about to vomit. He did not know if he had asked Todd to do so, but Todd, with one great jerk, pulled the flayed spear free from his right hand.

"A bit of bone came out with it," Todd began to say before Mort passed out.

Vicinti sumus

Todd pedaled toward the setting sun. He knew the general direction of Devils Tower, as it was on the line they had been following since Chicago. Mort held the atlas weakly with his left hand. His right was swelling larger every hour. No saturation of the sun's golden rays could mask the clammy nausea Todd knew Mort felt.

Todd saw only the talon when he closed his eyes. Though it had been well past his feet, he remembered it larger than his head, clicking right next to him on the concrete. He knew he had seen the demon bird come around the corner, but the only memory that would stick was that talon ticking down to death. If some supernatural force had pulled him under the van, it had done so because he had desired it more than anything in the world and had not had a single shred of strength to accomplish it. When he had found himself standing behind Mort, beckoned by something Cici had said, he'd had to study the scene, to assure himself Mort was really on top, that the world had not turned upside down to devour him. Mort was alive, next to him, right now. Todd turned to look, to reassure himself again. The dinosaur was dead.

Cici had told them to go to Devils Tower. Todd had heard this, and Mort had not. Mort remembered other things about the event that Todd did not, but Todd could not be sure Mort was not delirious. Todd thought that Cici was going to meet them at Devils Tower, but Mort had heard something about an uncle Billy. At some point, they could put together their stories. He hoped Mort could share the pedaling now, but Todd did not want to make things worse for his hand. Todd was no expert in stab wounds; he did not know how bad it was that the bamboo had splintered into six knives as it had pierced Mort's hand. If Cici and Billy did not show up, he did not know what he could do to save his friend.

He had a friend to save. He had known he had a friend all this fortnight but felt it especially now, at the threat of loss. He pedaled onward, making each thrust his prayer.

***

Todd woke up under a dull gray sky. A slight breeze blew across his body, and he relished this peace. He did not remember, for the moment, from what battle he had fled. He knew he was atop Devils Tower, nine hundred feet above danger. Sir Bear scratched. Todd remembered Mort and turned quickly to the side. Mort was awake, lying on his side, looking sick, and staring toward something. The infection in his hand had swollen past his wrist. Mort motioned with his other hand to remain low and to be quiet.

Todd pulled himself upward. An old man was sitting about thirty feet away, cross-legged, his eyes closed. He was dressed like a Native American, in frilled leather pants, bare chest, and feathers all around. Todd looked to Sir Bear for some sixth doggy sense about this, but Sir Bear seemed not to notice the man.

The man opened his eyes as if sensing the attention Mort and Todd were paying him. He gave a small, serene smile. "What bear are you fleeing from, that finds you up here?"

"Excuse me?" Todd asked, sitting up on the bow deck.

"The locals—the Lakota, the Cheyenne, the Crow— they share a legend about this rock, that it lifted up to save young girls from a bear. You can still see today where the bear scratched the side to climb upward."

"Did the bear get them?" Todd asked.

"Of course, not. We would not have the story if the girls had not lived to tell it."

"Are you Billy?"

The man pondered this for a second and said, "That is one name people know."

"Okay, Mister Billy," Todd said. "My friend is injured. Where should we go? We just woke up, sleepers I guess you call us. I mean, there are hospitals and things?"

"Yes, of course," the man said. "You would find such things directly south of here, in Denver and environs."

Mort muttered something to Todd, which he eventually interpreted as, "Cici said everyone went south."

"Do you want to come with us?" Todd asked the man. "How did you even get up here?"

"Where the bear scratched, it made it easy for man to climb. Isn't that the way of nature? The big animals softened the soil for man." The man looked outward, around at the landscape. "What a soft and gentle world man has inherited.

If you think about it, though, it's all the digested remains of earlier generations. And this generation will be returned to the Earth, to soften it for the next. If you'll allow the expression, man has made his home on a layer of shit."

"Well," Todd said, "that shit has come back to bite us." He wondered how long he would have to endure this conversation to gain safe passage to Denver. Philosophical monologues could be the rule in this Thunderdome. He did not want to offend the man. "Would it be easy enough for us to get down to Denver?"

"Certainly. But then what?" the man said.

"Then safety," Todd said. "Fellow humans, houses, society. We've been on our own for a couple of weeks now."

"And bravo to you for surviving so long in nature's gauntlet. Don't you feel more alive out here, on the brink of death at every turn?"

Todd could not deny this feeling. "Are we really awake?"

"Is one ever?" the man said. "What could convince you that you were alive and awake? What kind of knowledge would that take?"

Todd looked at Mort's swollen hand and drooping eyes. "A doctor would. You know, machines, electrodes, brainwaves, antibiotics."

"You run into a problem there, my friend," the man said. "It's almost like begging the question. If you make the machine in your dream, will it not tell you that you're awake? That's like all your science. It's all one big machine you've built in a dream to convince you that you're awake when, in reality, you can see only by colors and shadows."

"Okay," Todd said. He rubbed his face. "Do you have

maybe some traditional medicine or something? My friend has an infection."

The man closed his eyes for a moment. Todd knew the expression on his face, especially when he reopened his eyes with a smile. This was utter rage. "Maybe your friend is the infection."

Todd walked his fingers across the deck, looking for his spear.

The man continued, "What I mean is, you people have not stopped moving across this planet from the beginning, not since you were kicked out of the garden. Every time you move, you grow. You move because you feel fenced in, but you move and grow and make the rest of this land a prison for those who live in it, caged in by highways and power lines. You don't see how crafting a world to your liking shapes the world into a little hell for everyone else who has to live here."

Todd saw that the man had nothing else with him but these words, but he looked strong and had somehow climbed this rock on his own. Sir Bear might help if the man became dangerous. Todd began to pull his feet under him.

"Why not die right here and die painfully?" the man said. "You'll die someday anyway, and some other creature will swallow you and shit you out. Enjoy the pain. It's the reminder that you're alive and not some machine. In fact, the everlasting pain of hell is a gift to the damned. It's the only way they remember they exist at all."

The man's face grew stern as his eyes followed something behind Todd. Before Todd could turn to look, another man walked along the boat. He looked older than the one sitting and perhaps also Native American. He wore blue jeans and a Carhart jacket. He pulled a large plastic case over the side of the boat, laid it on the bow dock, and opened it. Todd looked back at the man sitting cross-legged.

"*Háu*," the first man said.

The second man did not acknowledge this.

"*Haáahe*," the first man said. "*Kahée*. We need to help our friends here. Encourage them to try the remedy for pain that nature has provided."

The second man pulled a modern, compound bow out of the case and set it to the side. He took off his coat to reveal a gray, pocketed t-shirt. His leathery forearms showed vigor. The old man picked an arrow shaft from the case and turned it upside down, screwing it into a tip he seemed very careful not to touch.

"Is this your remedy, apple?" the first man said. "What good is an apple going to do these men? Are you going to shoot one off my head?" He kept sitting. "Huh, apple?"

The second man strung the arrow into the bow and pointed it at the first man. Todd looked at Mort, who barely registered his confusion through drooping eyes.

The first man began to squirm a little but did not stand up. "You've got it backward, apple. You shoot the arrow at the apple. Give me the bow, and I'll show you."

The second man fired his arrow at the first man. Todd jerked. The first man caught the arrow in his hand, just inches from his face. The second man turned to Todd and said, "That will keep him busy for a while."

Todd stared at the first man while the second man walked into the boat at the stern. The second man walked forward, knelt down next to Mort, and looked at his hand. He slapped Todd's shoulder. "Come on. Clock's ticking for your friend here. Does this old Wind Scout work?"

Todd nodded. He rose and looked down at the first man, still struggling against the arrow, the sharp, metallic point nearly at his nose.

"Go on, *glonni,*" the first man said, seething. "Remember, all of you: you are shit, and to shit you shall return."

Todd sat in his pilot's chair and started pedaling. The second man sat in Mort's seat.

"Just ignore it," the second man said. "My name is White Wolf, by the way. William DeSoto White Wolf."

Todd did not know what he was supposed to say. They hovered a few feet above the tower.

"Did that thing tell you to go anywhere?" White Wolf asked.

"Um…." Todd swallowed to lubricate his throat. "Denver."

"I see," White Wolf said. "That would normally be a good suggestion. In this case, though, it means we should think of something else. Oh, you have an atlas. That'll help. Here. Point us west by northwest. How fast does this thing go?"

Todd did as White Wolf said. The case for the compound bow slid across the bow deck. Sir Bear observed everything with nonchalance. Todd could not see what state Mort was in. The old man next to him had put his jacket back on. He was barefoot.

***

Mort stared upward at the dull gray sky. His eyes closed

and reopened, and he was not sure how much time had passed in between. He did not know if what he had just seen was real or a dream, but he heard the old man clearing his throat from time to time. He studied the folds of the light gray clouds above him. Those were real. Everything else— Cici in the mist, the mating *Camarasaurus*, Cici in town, the *Dakotaraptor*, and now this old man, who had just shot another old man—all of that belonged to a dream. But his hand was ready to burst. He reached out with his left hand to pet Sir Bear, who came and lay next to him. Mort closed his eyes.

Mort opened his eyes again to find himself walking out of the boat toward a large cabin resting on a hill above the open plain. Its windows glowed warm light, a lighthouse above endless waves of hills.

He found himself inside, lying on a couch. The old man muttered a few words in a combination of English and some Native tongue.

The face of an old woman hovered above him. Mort could not tell if she were smiling, not by her mouth, and her eyes sprung sweetly from under long, heavy lids that clung with crow's feet to high cheekbones. The golden raisin of her face, humming something gently, studied him and his hand. She was someone's grandmother, he knew, because she had already adopted him, had already absorbed his cares. She was his grandmother now. Mort felt his lips curl up a little at the edges. She smiled, too, and Mort fell asleep.

PART FOUR

WAKEN TO YOUR WORLD

22

Mort woke up on the couch in the cabin, warmly lit by the low morning sun. A metal cooking ladle served as a cast, his hand taped around the bowl and his forearm to the long handle. The swelling had gone down but not completely.

An image of the Sacred Heart gazed at him, awash in shades of green. Jesus' subtle smile lost its usual severity behind two large photographs, each of a Native American woman. They looked nearly identical, and because one photograph seemed much older, he took them to be mother and daughter. A well-used candle sat in front of each, and other Native artifacts in shapes and materials Mort could not describe hung around this little prayer corner, anchored by a statue of the Blessed Mother in a style Mort had seen many times before and could not name.

Todd slurped something out of a mug. He was sitting in an armchair behind Mort, his feet up on a padded footrest, and wore a white bathrobe. Todd was studying the contents of a large book of black-and-white photographs. "Good morning, sleepy head," Todd said without looking up.

"Morning." Mort sat up and found himself dizzy. "How long was I out?"

"Not counting the trip up here? Since yesterday, midday. Mr. White Wolf taped your arm up and said he was going to Denver to see about a doctor after he found Cici. He is her uncle Billy. To be honest, I don't know how to address him, and he seemed a bit too distracted to answer any question directly. His mother, Marigold, has been taking good care of us, more so me because I've had the benefit of her rabbit stew and, at this moment, her homemade blueberry muffins." Todd stuffed a muffin into his mouth, smiling with his eyes.

"I am hungry," Mort said.

"Hold on." Todd went into the kitchen and brought back a mug of coffee and a muffin.

"Thank you, Marigold," Mort said, looking around at the open-plan cabin. "Where is she now?"

"I don't know."

Mort's body melted as he bit into the warm muffin, and he felt a surge of something like tears fill his face. He knit his brow. "His mother? How old is Marigold?"

"Ah, now you're asking the right questions," Todd said. "She is one hundred and twenty years old."

Mort had seen pictures and videos of centenarians before. "She didn't look much older than eighty. How old does that make Uncle Billy?"

"Ninety."

"They have good genes, I guess."

"Nope. Not the issue, it seems."

Mort looked up at Todd and stuffed a piece of muffin into his mouth, to tell Todd he was not going to play this question-and-answer game.

"Alright," Todd said. "Here's the deal. It's way weirder than even we thought it could be but also not. All this happened twenty-seven years ago. The moon went dark, like you described, people freaked out, and then the moon fell into this thing with the sun, you know, where there's always an eclipse. It went scissor-y, as they say."

"Syzygy."

"Whatever. So come New Year's Day, boom, the eclipse encircles the whole globe, darkness for a few days, which feels like only a few minutes to most people who lived through it, then everything's back to normal, except that exactly eight ninths of the population is gone."

"Eight ninths?"

"A third of a third remain. It's almost a billion people. That's not the weird part. We still have countries and technology and things, but it's all sort of chaotic, as everybody moved south to escape the hard winters."

"What's made the winters hard?"

"Okay, this is where I get confused, and Marigold doesn't really seem to understand it either. Something to the effect of the seasons don't go according to Earth's rotation but the moon's, like the Earth moves like the moon now, or the Earth doesn't move at all, but the sun and planets do, according to the way the moon did, and there's still no moon in the sky. That's where she sort of just threw her hands up in the air. Anyway, summer and winter come and go like before, but a more severe winter is traveling the globe. It was really bad in North America for, like, the first decade, which is why everyone had moved out of the Secure Zone. It's like a mini-ice age in Europe right now. Oh, and I almost forgot: the sea level fell by four hundred feet during those three days and is still falling. But no one really goes to the coasts except scientists and the military."

"So it *is* a climate event. It's like the Younger Dryas all over again. That would explain wooly rhinos but not dinosaurs. God, this muffin's good."

"Right. So all the stuff with the animals, she said, is the Earth waking up and remembering her dreams. She then said, and I quote, 'If you want the science-y mumbo jumbo, ask the people Billy hangs out with. But you don't have to be a scientist to know when someone is waking up.'"

Mort rubbed his face. "What about the humanoids? Are they past, present, or future?"

"Hm?" Todd said. "Oh, yeah. Marigold had no idea what I was talking about with those."

"Did you ask her what puts all of this together? Like, what causes all of these disparate things to happen at once?"

"It's all a preparation," came Marigold's voice. She had appeared close enough to Mort to stroke his short hair and smiled at him. He smiled back defenselessly. "How about some bacon and eggs?"

"Yes, please," Mort said.

She walked away, toward the kitchen. "Oh, you two. All the way from Detroit in a flying paddleboat. There's a joke in there somewhere, I'm sure. Bet you scared Cici. I hope my Billy finds her soon."

"Wait," Todd said. "When we last saw her, she said she was going to find her uncle Billy. Did she not find him first? How else could he have known where we were?"

She was silent for a moment as pots and pans came out

of the cabinets. "A wolf can smell for miles, much farther than it can see."

***

Mort and Todd sat in the living room of Marigold's house after a pleasant dinner. She had gently asked them to leave Sir Bear outside. They had learned that Marigold was once a dancer in Las Vegas. They had learned little else about her, her family, or the world in which they were living. Every question about the fate of humankind, the changing of the seasons, and cohabitation with long-extinct mammals on land that might or might not have been part of a reservation met with stories about kicking her legs up as one of Cleopatra's ladies-in-waiting or about her favorite performers of the era, with a special fondness expressed for the ever-congenial Louis Prima. Mort could not tell if she had dementia or was deliberately avoiding his topics.

Todd had begun doing the dishes when Marigold slapped his hand and shooed him and Mort into the living room.

Mort looked at Todd. "How long do we stay here? I mean, how long should we stay? You know, out of politeness and all."

Todd shrugged.

"Did Marigold say anything to you?"

"Only what one is supposed to say, like, 'Stay as long as you need.' But we really shouldn't go anywhere until a doctor sees your hand, and Billy White Wolf said he was going to see about that in Denver."

"I feel like I'm imposing. Should we...do you have any of that pooschwaggle?"

Todd huffed. "Are you really just bored? We should maybe start writing down our adventures."

Mort leaned forward and rummaged through the pile of old magazines, recent newspapers, and books of nature photography. He pulled out a DVD in a sleeve and read the title aloud to Todd. *"Waken to Your World: An Orientation for Sleepers*, by the Department of the Navy and the OSS." Mort looked around for a television and found none.

Todd plucked the DVD from Mort's hand and walked into the kitchen. A few minutes later, Todd and Marigold walked into the living room.

Twenty minutes later, Todd and Marigold were asleep on armchairs. Mort struggled to keep his eyelids open as he watched a man race through confusing diagrams of celestial dynamics and climatology in a dreary tone made drier by poor audio quality. The Earth had somehow captured or absorbed some of the moon's orbital dynamics. The Earth day had become twenty-four hours and fifty minutes long. The north and south poles were drifting along what used to be the Arctic and Antarctic circles every 18.6 years, as if the Earth were spinning like a top. The new Arctic circle reached as far south as New York and as far north as the old North Pole, depending on the where Earth was in the two-hundred-and-thirty-month lunar year. There were Earth-year seasons of summer and winter, like before, but also lunar-year seasons of summer and winter, leading to long periods of intense cold and freezing then warmth and melting. This, combined with slightly modified ocean currents from the drop in sea level, led to the greening of the

Sahara and the melting of Antarctica. Mort barely registered those last three words before he fell asleep.

***

Mort woke up sometime later. The DVD menu cycled silently through images of well-lit cities, tranquil plains, and government seals. Mort closed his eyes, and when he re-opened them, a figure stood before the television—a blackened silhouette, arms and legs spread slightly as if ready for a fight. After half a second of stiffened calculation, Mort sprang up from the couch and reached for his spear, which was not there. The metal ladle taped to his arm hit a lamp, and after the brief moment it took his body to react, Mort yelped with pain.

Todd sprang up, saying, "What? What?"

Indistinct words issued from the shadow's gravelly voice.

A lamp came on. Marigold looked around bleary-eyed. White Wolf was standing in front of the television. Mort and Todd caught their breaths. Mort held his arm. White Wolf reached toward Todd for the remote control, and Todd jumped back a little. White Wolf's silhouetted pose had been one of searching for the button on the television itself.

"Whoa, you guys are jumpy," White Wolf said.

"Sorry," Mort said, "it's been that kind of trip. What about a doctor? Did you find Cici? Are we going to Denver?"

"One thing at a time, Mortimer," White Wolf said. "What, were you guys watching this old video? No wonder you were asleep. At least you don't have to endure three days of orientation in Denver. If it weren't for the breakfast buffet, people would curl right back up again into a coma. You'd think the government could hire an actor or something to do these things. Or even a real writer."

"You're the government, Billy," Marigold said, rubbing his cheek. She shuffled to her room.

"Where's my spear?" Mort asked.

"Where it can't deep fry anyone," the old man said.

"What does that even mean?" Mort said.

"What my friend means," Todd said, "is thank you for saving us and letting us stay here. We owe you a debt of gratitude."

White Wolf's eyes flicked back and forth from Mort to Todd. "Don't thank me yet. Why don't you guys go hunker down in the loft for the night? Wepwawet will be coming up in the morning. They're bringing a doctor, of course. But they'll want to know about your particular experiences."

"Who is Wepwawet?" Mort asked.

White Wolf weakly pointed to himself with his hand and said, "The new OSS. The Office of Special Science."

23

The next morning, Mort was outside working on left-hand-ed dexterity by tossing sticks for Sir Bear when he saw a pair of vehicles ascending the long driveway. A white van bounced from side to side in the ruts and potholes while a black car, in front of it, rolled up smoothly. He tossed the stick again and hit a tree. Todd was somewhere inside the house.

When the black car arrived, Mort noticed that it was hovering, like the boat but with much more control. The white van was on rubber tires. The cross on the outside told him it was his medical team. No one came out of either vehicle for a few minutes while Mort stared. Sir Bear, sitting next to him, gave a requisite bark.

White Wolf came from around the house and stood next to Mort. "What are they waiting for?"

"Beats me," Mort said.

White Wolf gestured toward the car, walked to the rear passenger window, and peered in. The window rolled down, and he spoke with someone inside. White Wolf looked at the medical van then turned to Mort and rolled his eyes. He walked up to Mort, looked down at Sir Bear, and asked, "Is the dog real?"

"He growls and farts, that's all I know," Mort said.

"Let me take him around the house. You go on inside. Come on, Bear. Come on, pooch." White Wolf walked away, clapping for the dog to follow. Sir Bear seemed unsure and looked to Mort, so Mort walked with them.

When Mort came in through the back deck, he found a small middle-aged woman in dark blue khakis and a plaid vest clearing Marigold's coffee table. She straightened and cast her eyes first on Mort's makeshift splint.

"Is that painful?" she asked.

"Not with whisky," Mort said, without realizing he had not had a drop since the encounter.

"You're on no medication for that?" she asked.

"If they gave me something two days ago, I am not aware. My name is Mortimer, by the way, but you probably knew that. Mortimer Sowinski."

"Dr. Doris Huntsman," she said, reaching out her hand. Mort took it with his left. "Please excuse our behavior with regard to your dog. Some members of our team were not comfortable with his presence."

"Because he's real or because they thought he was not real?"

She smiled and approved his question with narrowed eyes. "Is Mr. Farkas here?"

"He is, uh, in negotiations with Montezuma at the moment over a certain revenge contract." Mort liked smart women, as they brought out his sense of humor.

She did not wince or roll her eyes at his joke.

"I see," she said. "In that case, it's best we start by looking at your hand."

***

Mort sat with Todd, White Wolf, and Huntsman at the kitchen table. He looked at his new cast, which he would wear for three weeks to a month for puncture wounds, two broken metacarpals, and severe bruising on the palm. Todd had wandered into the medical van asking for Imodium, which had given Mort an opening to ask the nurse if she had an associate named Rebecca Raccoon. Todd had smiled, and when the nurse had replied that it sounded like the name of a cartoon character, Mort had been relieved. He could communicate with the people of this new world. The aura of formal but not unfriendly reserve that surrounded Doris Huntsman's slightly graying hairs was unique to her.

"Mr. Sowinski, Mr. Farkas, thank you for being so accommodating," Huntsman said. "And thank you, Mr. DeSoto, for hosting them here. This gives us a particular advantage."

White Wolf leaned back. "You all can thank my mother. Speaking of, if you guys are going to stay here, and you're very welcome to, could we just get you to sign off on these, uh, insurance documents? It's so we can take care of any special need you might have."

Mort looked at several pages of dense typeface printed on the kind of woven plastic paper he had seen in Toledo, then at Todd. Huntsman and White Wolf were glaring impatiently. Todd shrugged a little. Mort invented a new signature with his left hand. White Wolf retrieved the signed documents.

"Gentlemen," Huntsman continued, "I know you have a lot of questions about the state of the world, and I know you've learned quite a bit about it from your experiences on the road and from the DVD you watched last night. Undoubtedly, you want to get back to civilization and lead your lives as best you can. Particular aspects of your adventure, however, require us to ask you to remain apart from the cities, at least for a time."

She stopped, as if to invite Mort and Todd to ask about these "particular aspects," so Mort did.

Huntsman replied, "The most immediate issue is dinosaurs. You may have thought that dinosaurs were a reality here, but they are not. Wooly mammoths, saber-toothed cats, giant sloths, yes. But not dinosaurs. They are unique, or nearly unique, to your experience."

Mort remembered that Cici was surprised by the *Dakotaraptor*. "So how exactly—"

"Mr. Sowinski," Huntsman said, "the word 'exactly' is not helpful to us here. The Office of Special Science does not deal with chemistry or physics. We grew out of Naval Intelligence. Consider us more of an office of special reconnaissance."

"I still like plain old Wepwawet," White Wolf said.

"What I mean is this," Huntsman continued. "The two of you are carrying around some kind of heavy weaponry. And shielding, it seems, of a psychical nature. This takes us to another particular aspect: how you traveled from Detroit, through Toledo and Cass Ridge, and all the way to South Dakota without encountering another human soul."

Mort rubbed his chin. "We did see Cici in Cass Ridge, very briefly."

"She was at Cass Ridge?" White Wolf asked, with the slightly accusatory tone of a protective uncle.

"Well, I wasn't sure she was real at first, being that her horse looked like a unicorn in the mist and all."

White Wolf made as if to pound the table with his fist and looked at Huntsman, who sighed. He said, "She's gonna get herself killed on that thing." He rose and walked toward Marigold's room.

Huntsman opened a notebook. "Could you describe for me the path you took? Please understand that my questions are in no way judgments on your decision-making. We simply want to understand the when, the where, and the why, as it were."

Mort saw, or imagined he saw, Huntsman suppressing a giggle at her sound play.

Todd sat back, which Mort took as an invitation. "I woke up at home, and when I went outside, I saw how ruined everything was, so I went to the hospital, hoping to pass someone along the way. I found Todd there in the same state I was in. We went to Todd's house, which was in much better condition than anyone else's, as his brother Jake had boarded the whole place up and absconded with their parents to Big Sky. We were weak and tired, and when it seemed like none of the helicopters or Wind Scouts going back and forth between Toledo and Cass Ridge were going to see us, we commandeered our neighbor's boat and rode the current. Detroit was infested with wooly rhinos, down-river with deadly snakes and mermaids, and Toledo with humanoids. What are those things, by the way? Where did they come from?"

Huntsman inhaled deeply and said, "In time, Mr. Sowinski."

"And flying boat technology, with its magic carpet?"

"That is also an artifact of time," she replied.

Todd leaned forward. "Wait. Is there something going on with time? Is that how we were able to be asleep for twenty-seven years and how White Wolf is ninety and Marigold is a hundred and twenty and you are...."

Huntsman raised her eyebrows.

Mort would save Huntsman from Todd's curiosity. "So the humanoids, were they attacking us in Toledo or not? Are they like flying boats and cars, things we picked up from another time?" He surely wanted to know how old Huntsman was more than Todd, and he might gain her favor this way.

"Like I said, in time."

White Wolf shuffled back into the kitchen, his swinging arms clutching a folded road map and a yardstick. He slapped the yardstick on one end of the kitchen table and began unfolding the map. Todd helped unfold his end of the map, which showed the whole continental United States as it had been before the Great Eclipse, and smoothed out the creases. Huntsman looked for a place to put her notepad, eventually settling on Florida. White Wolf slapped the yardstick on the map and began to draw a pencil line from wherever they were in south central Montana to Chicago. Todd raised his finger and asked if he could nudge the yardstick north of Chicago. White Wolf sat back while Todd drew the path they had taken, all the way back to Detroit, writing asterisks where they had slept and exclamation marks where they had had strange encounters. White Wolf looked at Mort, and his eyes seemed to ask if this was what Mort had been enduring for two weeks. Mort pressed his lips inward and nodded.

White Wolf side-eyed Todd. "Is it my turn? Alright." He took the pencil from Todd and began making other markings, circles and squares and triangles, at points not too far from their chosen path. One circle was north of Detroit. He thrust his finger at it. "That is Cass Ridge, where about two dozen naval militiamen have been retrofitting personnel choppers with hover tech. And where a certain someone was getting her unicorn worked on. The way the story has got to us out here, when Toledo was radio-hacked, their militia coast guard sent Wind Scouts in all directions. Cass Ridge sent a crew, saved some, but one of the old machines crashed. You saw that. You guys showed up in Toledo and Cass Ridge within windows of a few hours when no one was there. Toledo's under control now. Someone's probably looking for Sir Bear."

Mort's shoulders fell.

White Wolf continued, "You took an old Navy scout reconnaissance prototype given to the Ohio Militia Coast Guard and went straight into the flames that these guys would not have entered without a hundred armed soldiers in formation."

Todd put his hands against his face and tried to repress successive bursts of laughter.

Huntsman, with her arms crossed, gave him the side-eye.

Todd looked at Mort, who said, "Peanut butter jelly time."

Todd covered his face again and began shaking.

White Wolf continued enumerating the installations and minor population centers that Mort and Todd had just barely missed or flown directly over.

Mort could not tell if Todd was laughing or crying.

"Then," White Wolf said, "you landed here, met our little Cici, and made dinosaur city."

Mort did not hear whatever the old man said after that. He stared at the thin pencil line in the shape of a shallow ladle. This was the constellation of stars that had led him to that wonderful, mysterious woman. Without willing it, he looked up toward the image of the Sacred Heart in the living room. From where he sat, though, he could see only the photograph of Marigold's granddaughter, Melody. She seemed to look at him through living eyes.

"Do you see why I express my wonderment?" White Wolf asked.

Mort nodded. "Statistically—"

"Statistics explain the forces we cannot see at work," Huntsman said, "like in quantum mechanics and the social sciences. In a world where the invisible is becoming visible, we have no more recourse to statistics and probabilities. And believe me, Mr. Sowinski, I'm not making a religious argument, like God's hand has been at work. We have too many devils to face first. Are you beginning to understand why we want to know how you slipped through a thousand miles of civilization undetected, seeing and manifesting things that very few people have?"

Todd pulled his face free of his hands. His eyes were bloodshot, his cheeks were wet, and he was smiling.

Huntsman laid her hands on her lap and in a calm tone said, "I know you two have been through a lot. Like I said, we're not here to judge the decisions you made. We are, rather, fascinated by the result. We will help you complete your journey to Big Sky, and eventually to resettle. But we want to be sure that whatever ability it is that you have to manifest dangerous entities is under control, or...." She looked at White Wolf with slight resignation. "Your manifestations, and the clarity of your path, might be indicative of another set of special circumstances. We would like you to help us test this...," she looked at White Wolf again, "hypothesis."

"And how will we do that?" Mort asked.

"By going to Yellowstone."

24

Doris Huntsman would let Mort and Todd waste no time. After lunch with Marigold, they were on their way to Big Sky. In Huntsman's flying car, this trip took less than an hour.

Todd was looking gloomy, nibbling on a thumb between his teeth and staring out the window at the mountains whizzing by. Mort thought he could distract him by posing questions to Huntsman about hover technology. Huntsman said it was a matter of applying discoveries in metallurgy to textile science; the driver clarified: "The rug that keeps your boat aloft is woven metal and wool. That's an early model. This old Buick has for wheels what you'll see at Yellowstone, devonium coils." Todd's breath was fogging the glass.

"Who made these discoveries?" Mort said. "You'd think science would take a back seat during the apocalypse."

Todd turned away from the window. "Don't you know what the word 'apocalypse' means, Mortimer? It means 'unveiling.' Everything's being revealed."

"Especially what's on the continental shelf," the driver said.

The resort area of Big Sky had not endured the long

winters well and had been completely abandoned. After the initial shock, which he felt come even from Huntsman, Mort watched Todd's eyes dart rapidly, studying every detail. Todd sat up and directed the driver. His family's cabin was a little south of town, on a narrow road that ran up toward Ramshorn Peak, the mountain named, Todd's family had joked, for the Detroit-area diner. The modest, timber-frame house, in a cul-de-sac with a few others, had held up relatively well but was clearly not occupied by the living.

Huntsman gave a few quick instructions. Todd was to stay in his seat. The driver pointed the car at the house, tapped a tablet, made a comment under his breath, and pressed a button on the dashboard. The car hummed a deep electric hum, and Mort's body vibrated very pleasantly. The driver pressed another button, and after a heavy pulse, the vibration ended. He tapped the tablet, made another comment under his breath, and walked out with some kind of weapon in his hand. He tested the handle on the front door, which opened. Mort took this as a bad sign. Todd was tapping his thumb against his teeth. The driver disappeared into the house behind the broad beam of a flashlight. Mort had done this for Todd once before. He did not know what result he hoped for now but that it was definitive.

After a very long minute, the driver returned and walked to Huntsman's window. Mort could barely hear what they were saying just a few feet ahead of him. Huntsman turned around to Todd.

"There's no one inside, Mr. Farkas. It's a bit disorderly, and there are signs that no one has been there for a long time. Do you wish to go in?"

Todd nodded.

The driver brought Mort to the back of the car, opened the trunk, and pulled out a shield made of metal cage. "Mr. Sowinski," he said, "I will walk in first with Mr. Farkas behind me. You will follow. In the event, and only in the event, that something unsightly approaches us, you are to press this button here." He showed him a button where the cage met the handle. "That will energize the devonium shield. Do not, and I repeat, do not touch the element to anything except what should not be present with us. Do you read me?"

Mort studied the strange weapon and nodded. "I read you."

Mort looked at Todd, who was distracted by the empty house he was about to enter. "Doesn't Todd get one, too?"

"Not today," the driver said.

The house bore the scent of several species of animals and the debris from many years of wind and rain. Todd directed the driver where to go and studied everything carefully. Mort saw a ceramic toad on the mantel shelf. Todd picked up the anuran coin bank. Even after pulling the plastic plug on the bottom, he could not pull out the paper stuffed inside. Todd threw it against the floor. It did not break.

Mort looked at the driver and made a crushing motion with his shield. "Should I?"

The driver waved his free hand. "No no no no no. Don't even joke about that. Really."

Todd took a glass snow globe and smashed it against the toad. He read the paper aloud:

Dear Evie, Jake, and Todd:

Your mother and I have decided to go on to Denver, where everyone seems to be gathering after that strange eclipse and the darkness. Jake, whether you have come back with Todd or not, come meet us there. We won't know exactly where to go. We're leaving with a caravan of people coming out of Big Sky. The phones are not working, and the radios are full of strange sounds. You'll just have to look for us. May God bring us all back together soon.

Love,

Dad

"Well, that's good news," the driver said. "They survived the Great Eclipse. It means they're on Earth somewhere, or at least in it."

At those last four words, the eyes of Mort and Todd fixed on the driver, whose face showed immediate regret.

They were not back in the car long before Huntsman directed the driver to gain altitude and give Mort and Todd "the view." After cruising not far above the broken roads between the mountains, the car soared to several thousand feet. Through the window, Mort could see a kidney-bean-shaped depression twenty miles long and almost as wide. Near the southwestern end, he saw a series of spirals that looked made of rock in a somewhat neat array, around a hundred in total.

"Welcome to Yellowstone National Park," the driver said.

"Um," Todd said. "So I've been here before. I mean, not from above. Where's the lake?"

"Gone," Huntsman said. "You've both certainly heard that Yellowstone was a vast caldera, a supervolcano ready to blow."

"Omigod, that's what destroyed everything?" Todd said.

Mort wished he would just listen.

"No," Huntsman said. "Instead of blowing out, it caved in. The lakes, the magma, everything has sunk."

"Grand Prismatic Spring? Old Faithful?"

"Gone," Huntsman said.

Mort sensed she was enjoying the drama. "So it just sank into the ground? I'm no geologist, but it seems something would have to make room for those reservoirs of magma to disappear from near the surface. Where did they go?"

Huntsman turned around in her seat and looked at both men. "That's what we want you to tell us."

***

On the ground, Mort could see little of what had impressed and saddened him from above. The car hovered before an imposing gate of chain link and barbed wire covered with signs warning intruders and welcoming guests to the facility with clearly defined protocol. The guards at the gate had bayonets on their guns encased in metal cages, and Mort thought that whenever the smoky mountain sunlight caught them just right, they glowed blue like bug zappers. Repeated questions about the humanoids he had seen in Toledo met once again with silence.

"Look at all the horses, Mort," Todd said as they passed through the gate.

"Yeah."

"Is there a reason all the soldiers are on horseback?" Todd asked.

"It's rough terrain," Huntsman said.

"Why doesn't everyone just use hovercars?"

"They're expensive."

In a few minutes, they exited the car at a circular fence about one hundred yards in diameter. All around the muddy plain, trees leaned and lay on the ground, the result, Mort guessed, of the caldera's sinking. The fence had no barbed wire on top and was of a thicker gauge material woven into a diamond-shaped pattern not denser than chain link but certainly sturdier. This was not to keep man and beast in or out. This fence was part of the device they were entering.

"Can you tell us what we're doing now?" Mort asked.

"Yes," Huntsman said. "We are asking you simply to ride down a shaft we have dug and to report what you see."

"Is there a particular reason that Todd and I are more qualified to do this than the hundreds of armed men and women we have passed? Or drones, for that matter?"

"There is, we hope," she said. "As for drones, we can only control them by line of laser sight. Radio frequencies are unstable. As for other humans...they can be unstable, too."

"And because Todd and I survived a fortnight on our own, we can survive whatever is down there? Is it hell?"

"It is not hell. It's certainly not hot enough."

A shelf-jawed military commander approached Huntsman. They spoke in muted tones. The commander waved over a subordinate holding a clipboard, but Huntsman said something to which the commander replied, "They don't even have IDs yet, do they? And one guy's in a cast."

"IDs are coming down tomorrow morning with White Wolf, who will explain why we're moving so quickly with these two."

The commander shuttered his eyes. "And the other two?"

Huntsman replied, "We're seeing who's available. We want these guys in alone at first."

"I need backup before we do this again," the commander said.

"The Belly's on the East Coast. The Hands are tied down at the moment in Denver."

"Mort—" Todd began.

"Sh."

"Not before one of them gets here," the commander said.

"Fine," Huntsman said. "It's late anyway, and they need training on the dervish."

After a few more muted words, Huntsman walked back to Mort and Todd.

"Answers," Todd said. "Now."

Mort looked at Todd, who was as angry as he had ever seen him.

"If you would please bear with us," Huntsman said. "Your ignorance of the situation will mean greater safety for you and a clearer lens for us to see what is happening."

"What does that mean?" Each word escaped from Todd like the clip of heavy shears.

"This little experiment," Mort said, "has this been going on since before the moondark? Were Todd and I experimented on? Is that why we fell asleep and woke up in skin bags? Have you been working on this all this time?"

Huntsman held her hands in her vest sleeves and spread her elbows a little. "The answer to all of those questions is no. There are hundreds of thousands of people who have woken up just like you did, in all kinds of situations, and many, like the woman you met, who died soon after. Both of you woke up at the same time and within a mile of each other. We're hoping that whatever sort of bond that this and your waking experiences have formed will help you, and us, down there. That's it. When you come back up—"

"If we come back up," Todd said.

"*When* you come back up," Huntsman continued, "we will debrief you on everything else. For now, your ignorance is—"

"Yes, a lens, we get it," Todd said.

"We'll stay here tonight," she said.

As they followed Huntsman to a trailer, Mort said, "We should've brought Sir Bear."

At this, Huntsman's head jerked back, as if she had not accounted for the dog in their adventures.

25

Todd lay on the upper bunk in a small room at one end of a double-wide office trailer made into guest lodgings. A flood of light from the fixtures along the fence outside fought its way through the plastic blinds at the window past Todd's feet. When the metal mesh of Mort's bunk below him stopped squeaking, finally, Mort took to brushing the wall with the fingernails of his broken hand.

"Mortimer. Please stop."

"It's soothing, the little vibration. Healing through vibrations. Sounds like something you'd be into."

Todd huffed. "Well, I'm not. We need to do a reality check here."

"Agreed."

"I'll begin. Where are we?"

"Yellowstone National Park."

"Which is now a gigantic crater."

"So they say."

"Into which they have drilled a hole."

"They would say 'bored,' but yes."

"And into which bored hole they want us to go."

"So they say."

"Is this not more made-up stuff? Think about it. The devil-man on Devils Tower tells us to go to Denver, but he's obviously mean, so we do the opposite, heading straight into his trap. All these people, Cici included, work for him. She led us to him. Are we even here? Or is this all the product of our minds? Do these people seem real to you?"

"As real as anyone did before we fell asleep. Marigold is nice. The pain in my hand is real."

"It's almost too perfect. You miss your grandmother, and so Mother Earth Dreamland gives you a new one, complete with fantasy woman and Indian guide. And what do I get?"

"Well, alright, let's play this game. Let's pretend it's all fake. If I've got everything I want—and don't forget, I'm also a dragon slayer—then this is the end of the road for me, this hole. You're still on the hunt for your family. Your adventure continues."

Todd's lips swelled with the thought of loss. "Don't say that."

"Don't say what?"

"That this is the end of the road for you. I can't live by myself in this world." Todd wiggled his feet in front of the glowing window blinds. "I couldn't do it before, either."

"No one can, Theodore. Trust me. I love my grandma, but at the end, she pretty much left me alone to make a mess of myself. I get it. Three nights ago, we were out on the plain, surrounded by dinosaurs. Now we're surrounded by humans who don't get how alone we've been out there and who want to make lab rats out of us. We shouldn't even be doing this, but what else is there?"

"We could've maybe just taken the boat to Denver."

"Stolen government property."

"We're strong enough to walk now."

"Maybe," Mort said. "But...I don't know. Something tells me to trust White Wolf and Huntsman."

Todd ran his knuckles along the angled ceiling. "What's that?"

"Despite White Wolf's uncanny ability to have reached us where only flying things can go, and Doris Huntsman's buttoned-up demeanor, they don't seem to have it all together. They're partly guessing."

Todd felt as if someone had wrung his innards like a wet towel. "Oh, God, Mort."

"Sorry, wrong words. What I mean is, they're like us, and that's why they want us. Hey, I know: it's like our spears. It's like the four of us, and whoever the other two are the commander was talking about, we're like the tip of a spear. Sharp, powerful. We're just need securing to the right shaft. Not bamboo, that's for sure."

"So then what? Whose hands are these spears going into?"

Mort sighed. "I don't know. Why don't you ask God for us?"

26

At breakfast in a small mess hall, where none of the soldiers or scientists paid any attention to Mort or Todd, Huntsman rose from her place across from them and met White Wolf at the door. Mort trained his ear in their direction, hearing something about Cici in Denver with her dad, words more valuable than gold, for he now knew where she lived. White Wolf made a brief wave to Mort and Todd. When Huntsman returned, she handed the two men identification cards from the State of Absarokee.

"Okay," Mort said. "Don't we have to be Crow Indians to be residents of Absarokee?"

"Don't you remember being adopted into the tribe?" Huntsman asked.

Todd looked up at Mort, who said, "No, not really."

"Not in the form of an insurance waiver, yesterday morning?"

"What, why?" Todd said. "Why tell us this now?"

"You'll find our bureaucracy as inefficient as it was before. Maybe worse. Local government is much better at things like this these days. And maybe that's to our advantage," Huntsman said. "The government in St. Louis will take a while to catch up." She drilled her dark eyes into Mort.

Mort looked outside at a pair of large earth-moving machines.

Todd said, "Wait. Is all of this, what, some private project? Not exactly legal?"

Huntsman smiled. "One hundred precent legal, Mr. Farkas. Just not exactly well-publicized. And we'd like to keep it that way."

"Oh, I see," Todd said. "It's to your advantage, then, to keep us locked up like prisoners until you can use us in your weird experiment, where we're going to disappear with our new IDs, and, poof, it's like we never existed. I see. I get it now. Good ol' government back to its old tricks. You take advantage of our vulnerability as newly awakened sleepers, make us feel at home with Squanto, experiment on us, and bring us here to be fed to the Earth dragon so that he doesn't wipe out another third of humanity."

At this, Mort saw a soldier turn around and chuckle.

"If all this is White Wolf's idea, as it seems, why isn't he staying here with us?" Mort said.

"He has to run. Commander Headley wants assurances. White Wolf is trying to ascertain them."

***

Inside a dimly lit hangar, Mort saw a small array of the underground exploration machines Huntsman had called the "dervish": what looked like large, round gumball machines, globes of glass over gray metal flanges.

"Why are they called dervishes?" he asked.

"Ah," came a voice from behind. A well-groomed man

in gray coveralls walked forward. "Because of how they achieve lift. Behind the metal cowl holding up the cockpit are a series of woven skirts made of wool and metal alloy. They spin to create the same wave action you saw in the Wind Scout, only much more efficiently. We get a hundred times more graviton-volts per square inch this way."

"I see," Mort said, and he rubbed his neck. "You drill with these things, too?"

"We remove rock with a version of them. Our drillers look like teardrops. They burrow downward, leaving pulverized rock behind for the dervishes to scoop up. But that's become less necessary lately."

"Oh?" Todd said.

"Doris?" the engineer said.

Huntsman took her cue. "As I was starting to say at breakfast, we don't have to go too far down before the crust opens up into a series of empty chambers. At the time of the Great Eclipse, there was a very rapid evacuation of liquid magma from the caldera, leaving behind what appears to be a large section of sponge-like crust."

"And mantle," the engineer said.

"So you need us to...what, exactly?" Mort said.

The engineer smiled and nodded at Huntsman. "Let me do a final run-through on their dervish." He walked briskly away.

Huntsman clasped her hands at her waist. "You two appear to have an enhanced capacity for maintaining rational thought in the face of dangers both real and perceived."

The neatly branched tree from which Mort normally

plucked his responses turned into a tangled grove. Todd spoke Mort's thoughts:

"I can assure you, Ms. Huntsman, that no one has ever said that to me in my entire life."

"Me, neither," Mort said. "I wouldn't call our response to whatever's out there strictly rational. On the contrary, uh, we had help."

"Help?"

"From the animals," Todd said. "And Charlaine."

"That is White Wolf's hypothesis, as well," she said. "Shall we put it to the test?"

They began walking toward a dervish.

"Wait a minute," Mort said. "Are you saying people go crazy down there?"

"I'm saying that we are certain you will not."

Todd's eyes grew wide, and Mort put his hand on his shoulder.

Mort let the engineer help him up a small ladder and into the dervish. Part of the glass globe had been pulled back. Inside were two seats and two sets of controls, just like on the Wind Scout, but in a much more cramped environment. Todd seemed to sit comfortably. Mort's knees pressed against a fiberglass dashboard arrayed in glowing buttons and lights.

"Don't worry about all those," the engineer said. "Our first run will be remote-controlled. We just want you to get a feel for how the dervish flies. We have all day and maybe then some to teach you the rest."

Mort looked around for a second and said, "You people are all pretty nonchalant about this."

"Mr. Sowinski, many checks and double checks have been made. The machine is foolproof. Mother Earth, on the other hand, she admits no fools."

"That's the best compliment I've been paid yet," Todd said.

Huntsman said, "Mr. Farkas, if you simply do this, there will be many more compliments to come. We're going to send you out now. Don't be scared to look down into the hole."

The capsule closed, and the machine inched forward. Even outside the hangar, in the overcast light, the dervish did not move very quickly. Mort said so.

A voice came through the radio: "The dervish is built for underground, for precision, not speed."

"How is it your radio works?" Mort said.

"Line-of-sight laser," came the engineer's voice.

"So when we're down there, out of sight?"

"We have relays planted, but that's a dimension of things we have to work with."

"Okay," Todd said. "What about this hole you've dug?"

"Why don't you take the controls, Mr. Farkas? Give it a whirl."

"Yeah, Buzz Lightyear," Mort said.

Todd grabbed the flight controls and said in a muted tone, "To infinity and beyond."

Just as quickly as he had gained control over the Wind Scout in Toledo, Todd mastered the dervish. After finding and circling around the borehole, he buzzed the hangar with a devilish grin. Mort was glad for this.

***

Mort and Todd spent all day learning the dervish. Since Mort, in his cast, could not adequately control the machine, he set out to learn all the buttons, lights, and displays. Todd discovered, to the audible horror of everyone on the ground, that the dervish was capable of an acrobatic loop. After Mort determined that his lunch was not going to leave him, an image flashed in his mind of Huntsman looking up from the ground, arms folded, with an air of self-satisfaction. She had found her men. But they had not been underground yet.

"Are you two Chuck Yeagers ready yet?" the engineer said.

Mort looked to his side, at the hole in the ground. "So soon?"

Huntsman came on the laser-line radio. "Commander Headley's been called away for a few hours."

"When the cat's away...." Mort said.

"That's the spirit," the engineer said. "Don't worry. We've got a pre-programmed path for you to take. Just relax and enjoy the ride."

An orange light came on by itself, indicating autopilot. They hovered slowly toward the hole.

"Mort," said the engineer, "just go ahead and turn on the heads-up display and voice scroll. You'll be out of contact soon. We want a record."

Mort pressed the buttons marked HUD and VS. He saw little in the daylight and looked over the edge of the capsule into the unending black. His heart beat against the glass bubble. Before he could speak, his stomach rose into his lungs. The lip of the hole rose above him. The heads-up display, an orange grid in the shape of the hole into which they were descending, showed more clearly. At minus thirty feet, the mouth of the cave narrowed into a throat that, with what little light remained, glistened with rocky mucosa. Mort swallowed hard.

He could hear Todd whispering some prayers.

"Well, maybe it's time to start recording what we see. Hey, look, Todd, it's translating my words to text on the screen."

Todd made the raspberries, which became a string of consonants.

"Nice, Todd. Let's just do this and get on with our lives."

"Easy for you to say."

"Easy for you to say. Your family might be in Denver, for all we know."

"It's been twenty-seven years, Mort. I should be fifty-eight. Mom and Dad would be on either side of ninety."

"Yeah, but you see how Huntsman looks at fifty or however old she is."

"You like how Huntsman looks?"

Mort looked at the screen, which recorded every word. "Erase that," he commanded the screen.

The words "erase that" appeared.

"Delete previous entry."

"Delete previous entry" typed itself on screen.

"Shit."

A series of asterisks appeared. Mort looked over at Todd, who was biting his fist in laughter. "I've missed this," Mort said. "Alright. Status update. We are at minus one thousand feet. Damn. That's deep. And counting. No visual contact.

The lidar grid shows the shaft at, what does that look like, Todd? Is that a scale? Ten feet in diameter?"

Todd playacted the part of a serious pilot. "Affirm ten-foot diameter. Minus one four double zero altitude."

"Is that how you say that?"

"Beats me. If they want to send a hair stylist and a biologist in a bubblegum stand down into the bowels of hell, they'll get the quality of reporting they deserve."

"Minus sixteen hundred."

"Minus eighteen hundred."

The two men counted at irregular intervals while the dervish descended to ten thousand feet. At around thirteen thousand feet, a symbol appeared on the screen that congratulated the occupants of the dervish on surpassing the previous record of deepest mine on Earth. Todd commented that they were in the domain of science fiction.

"Have we not been in the domain of science fiction since we woke up in our own skin bags?" Mort asked.

"You know what I mean. Here we are again."

"But there's nothing going on. We just keep going down this tunnel. Wait, no, now something is happening."

At around sixteen thousand feet, the tunnel opened up into a chamber several hundred feet in diameter. A label in the corner of the lidar screen indicated Magma Chamber 1.

"Magma Chamber One?" Mort said aloud. "Where's the magma? Alright. Yeah. Now we're back in sci-fi land. Do we...what do we do?"

"The orange light is still on. I guess we keep going down."

The dervish passed through the lower wall of Magma

Chamber 1 and into Shaft Section 2. This went down for only a hundred feet before they passed into Magma Chamber 2a, inside of which the capsule automatically made a lateral translation and descent into Magma Chamber 2b.

"All of this is mapped out," Todd said. "We're definitely not the first ones to get this far."

"The outside temperature reads fifty-five degrees. I'm guessing it should be way hotter by now. There should be molten rock around us by now."

"They should have put a bathroom on this thing."

"Maybe they put a porta potty down in Chamber Thirty-Three, where the little people have a party waiting for us."

"Little people?"

"Or whoever lives down here. You gotta know that's why they're interested. It's either resources or alliances. Do you really have to go, Todd?"

"I thought we'd get a break before we went down. I'll try to hold it."

The two men passed through larger and larger magma chambers, most of which were no longer connected by artificial shafts but by natural, spongiform openings. Once inside Magma Chamber 27, at a depth of one hundred and thirty-three thousand feet below the surface, the orange light turned off.

"I guess this is it, Todd."

"Guess so."

"What do we do now?"

"We go exploring."

"Why do you think the others never made it this far?"

"Beats me. I feel fine. Except I really do have to pee."

"Is there a water bottle or something you could use?" Mort asked.

"With you right next to me?"

"I will turn away."

Todd landed the dervish at the bottom of the chamber.

Mort turned on the exterior lights and used a toggle to point one at various parts of the chamber floor. It was all glistening gray rock except for one small lump a few dozen feet away. When he heard Todd screwing the top back on the water bottle, he said, "Let's go see what this thing is."

Todd flew the dervish laterally until Mort told him to stop.

It was a human body in gray coveralls, lying face down. Mort remembered how Todd had handled seeing Charlaine's body, but he would be in trouble with Huntsman if he did not report what he had seen. He was sure he could not handle the controls with one hand. He could tell Todd to steer back to where the autopilot had mapped. He scanned the floor with the exterior light. The rock crept upward into an unmapped area. This body might have rolled down from there, the way the arms and legs were splayed.

He spoke to the machine. "This is Mortimer Sowinski, reporting at a depth of one hundred and forty-three thousand feet on the floor of Magma Chamber Twenty-Seven. This is the largest chamber we have entered, coming in at a maximum height of eleven thousand feet. It is elongated from southeast to northwest, eight hundred feet at its widest and seven thousand feet at its longest. We have not used the lidar yet to see if this chamber empties into another at either of the long ends. We will use the dervish to map the rest of this chamber. What do you say, Todd?"

"Sounds good."

The southeastern end of the chamber, which was closest, was sealed into a tight crevice from bottom to top. They passed their point of entry as they headed for the northwestern end. The rock began to rise as the walls narrowed. Near the end, Mort noted another object. He could not hide this from Todd.

Carefully watching Todd's hands next to him and his reflection in the glass canopy, and when he was sure that Todd was seeing another dervish, he said, "Mortimer Sowinski here. Theodore Farkas and I note a crashed dervish at the northwest end of MC Twenty-Seven. Marking this as Location B."

"What was Location A?" Todd said.

"The first object I saw."

Todd began to breathe heavily but said, "It's okay. We sort of expected this, didn't we? We knew this was why they were sending us down here." Todd's breathing mellowed. "You're right, Mort. Let's keep going. Fear lives in ignorance."

Fear lives in ignorance. That had been a mantra of Mort's all the way through schooling. After suspending his doctoral studies, he had stopped saying it and thinking it. He must have said it at some point in his adventures with Todd, or Todd had learned it on his own.

"Just a bit more, I think, Todd. Past the capsule."

The two men hovered upward in humid silence.

"And here we have the other body," Mort said. "Marking

Location C. It appears that the person was headed for what looks like a small opening. The bodies are not decomposed. We can maneuver our capsule to look at the opening, but it is too small to pass through." Mort looked at Todd, whose eyes gazed emptily a thousand miles ahead. "What do you say, Todd?"

Todd nodded weakly and positioned the dervish in front of the narrow opening, a slit the shape of a cat's eye. He thought they might just squeeze through.

Todd put his hand on Mort's arm. "That's probably what these people said."

"What?"

"That we might just squeeze through the cat's eye."

"How do you know what I was thinking?"

"Because you said it."

"I did not."

Todd was silent a moment, looking at the screen. "Well, maybe I could just tell what you were thinking."

"Yeah, but you used the exact words I had in my mind. Let's get out of here. We've done enough for today."

"I agree," Todd said and yawed the machine.

In the headlights, Mort saw that the glass on the fallen capsule was cracked on its outer edges, as if its two occupants had tried to ram their way through the narrow hole, drawn into it or away from something else by force of madness. Mort checked his own thoughts and found them stable. He pressed the autopilot button, and the dervish whirred upward, from chamber to chamber, while he and Todd said nothing.

27

Todd stared at a large chocolate cake on which was written, in blue icing, *Congratulations, Mort and Todd.* Men and women in lab coats, coveralls, and camouflage clapped all around him and Mort. He felt so removed from the scene that he wondered if this was what a circus animal experienced. Mort's distant eyes spoke of the same sensation. A couple of scientists or administrators poured liquor into coffee mugs. Finding Huntsman and studying her face, Todd wondered if they were not clapping in relief. Finally, he heard someone mutter, "Look at them. I told her the cake was out of touch."

Huntsman cleared her throat and spoke. "Mr. Sowinski, Mr. Farkas, thank you for your efforts today. You have opened for us a new vista, taken us all a step further. I should say that, in so doing, you now hold the record for deepest Earth dive at 144,072 feet."

Todd pulled his head back a little, searching for a way to respond. Mort looked lost between a smile and sadness. "Um," Todd said, "thank you. Maybe, however, that distinction should go to the two guys we found in the chamber? I'm sorry. Just, this whole thing is really strange."

"Yeah," Mort said with more force than Todd was used to.

Someone coughed nervously.

Huntsman spoke softly. "Yes, you're right. It, uh, it means a great deal to us, as it would have to those men, that you made it so far and back...successfully."

"Jesus, Doris," someone muttered.

She continued, "Perhaps it is time to explain things to you."

Someone whispered in her ear, and she nodded.

"We'll cut up the cake," she announced. "You two have a seat, grab a coffee or whatever you like, and we'll explain everything."

Todd sat on a metal folding chair next to Mort. The plate holding his cake and the cup holding his coffee were thicker than he expected for an office party, of some kind of plastic that imitated ceramic. While he waited for Huntsman to try to convince someone else to come with her, he noticed that everyone had cloth napkins as well.

"Gentlemen," Huntsman said, sitting across from them, "please eat your cake while I explain what's going on. And I apologize if the gesture seems obtuse. We're all of us very proud at what you've accomplished. Let me explain.

"The two men you found were the last we sent in. They were trained Navy Seals. Physically, mentally, the best. But they grew as confused as everyone else who's descended more than one thirty-three. Others never even got that far. The Earth, as you have experienced, or some entity operating through the Earth, has shown itself able to manipulate human beings' mental state. The closer to sea level we get, and especially below, the more astringent this becomes. But you traveled across the North American Secure Zone with little problem. We thought we could send you a little deeper than we have so far managed to go. Had there been any problem, the Voice Scroll would have picked it up and triggered an automatic return to the surface."

Todd watched Mort swallow some cake and said, "So you're saying we could've died like them, or gone crazy like the others? I'm, like, not even angry right now, I'm so confused and sad. What is this really about?"

"Hold on a second," Mort said. "The autopilot turned off when we got to one thirty-three. Most of that chamber was not mapped at all."

Huntsman knit her brow.

"I told you, Todd. These people have only got things half figured out. But that's no reason to trust them now." Mort stood up. "Take us to Denver. Take us to Todd's family. You can't keep us like this. No one was there for us when we woke up, and we made it all this way by ourselves. We did the thing you asked of us even though you hid a lot of very important information from us. We're alive, you're happy. As far as I'm concerned, we leave on equitable terms." He thrust out his left hand to shake.

"Mr. Sowinski, Mortimer," she said. "Mr. Farkas, I would like to share with you information you're not going to get in Denver. If you would sit and stay for a moment, even if you decide to leave, you're owed at least this much."

Mort huffed through his nose. "Even if we decide to leave?"

"Yes," she said.

He looked at Todd, who was drawing lines in the icing on his plate with his fork. "I just want to see my family."

"You will, Theodore," Huntsman said. "Please just give me ten more minutes."

Todd put a bite of cake into his mouth.

Mort sat down.

"Alright, gentlemen," she said. "I'm going to lay out for you a series of events, as they happened, and then explain our theories as to how the universe is currently constructed."

Todd coughed out a brief laugh.

Mort turned a grim stare from Huntsman to Todd. "You want to go, Todd? We don't even have to listen to this."

Todd waved his fork in the air. "No, by all means, Doris, tell us how the 'universe is currently constructed.' God knows we've seen some weird stuff. Why not a little more? Hell, we've been deeper inside the Earth's crust than anyone ever. Let's hear how the 'universe is currently constructed.'"

Huntsman evened out the folds on her pants. "I'll begin. You are both familiar with the moondark."

"I saw it," Mort said. "Told Todd all about it. He was already asleep."

"And many people did fall asleep at that moment, and after. Some people who remained awake began exhibiting powers like you two have shown, a certain kind of porosity or transparency vis-a-vis a world hidden from us by time or some other quality, which I will not call the 'supernatural' or 'paranormal' world. I was deeply involved in several of those cases without realizing that the less successful I became in measuring these abilities and the more rigors I put these people through, the more prepared they became for facing what occurred during the Great Eclipse.

"You were both asleep for the three days of the Great Eclipse, but those who were awake experienced them very quickly. I did not. I was fully conscious for those seventy hours of darkness but saw nothing and heard nothing. I was safe on a boat, sucked out far from shore by the rapidly receding ocean.

"The water had protected me just like the water protected you on your journey. By some instinct, you two kept close to the water. Things only got really bad for you when you went inland, but what you could have experienced farther south, what we call specters or spectral events, and which I'll explain later, was mitigated by the reality of the Secure Zone. The fact that it was once under miles of ice means something still today."

Todd looked at Mort. "Didn't I say that in Cass Ridge?"

Mort locked his arms on his knees and hung his head. "You want to put us through the same rigors as those people."

"The stakes were high then, and they are higher today. Let me explain. At the moondark, the natural moon became, essentially, an idealized form, so perfect it could reflect no light or energy. Then, at the Great Eclipse, it became something more. It has become a boundary between our world and the rest of the universe. The moon did not expand in size. It fully assumed its function as an organizing boundary, a portal, if you will. We call this current property of the moon the 'moonshock.' You noticed how the horizon seems to fall upward now instead of downward. This is because, at the very least, the moonshock is acting like a lens, distorting all that we can see, bending everything around it.

"It is more than that, though. It is a hard boundary between us and the rest of the universe. We cannot penetrate the moonshock with satellites, spacecraft, missiles, or anything. The sun, planets, and stars are all inside, like they were locked in a snow globe."

"So someone built a shield around the Earth, is that it?" Mort said. "A transparent shield?"

"That is one theory and the easiest for most of us to comprehend, given how images of alien ships and Dyson spheres have saturated our society. It may not be a bad theory, but it does not account for everything."

Todd said, "That would explain where eight ninths of the population went, into some alien ship."

"Yes, possibly."

"And humanoids to rule over us," Mort said.

Huntsman laughed a little. "Those things can hardly walk straight without careful programming. They require constant human instruction. They were most likely made by human beings."

"Were?" Mort said. "When?"

Huntsman drew a deep breath. "*When* seems to have become a question of *where*, lately. But, if it's alright, I'd like to hold off on that story for another time."

"Right," Todd said. "We still want to know how what's going on up in space has to do with us going down into the Earth."

"Yes, indeed," Huntsman said. "As I alluded, not everyone is convinced we are surrounded by a megastructure of any kind. Some of us, White Wolf included, have directly experienced another kind of reality, a mathematical reality, that accounts for much more of what we measure today. This is called 'hyperbolic space.' Have you heard of it?"

Mort shook his head.

Todd said, "You don't mean, like, in Star Wars or anything, where they—"

"Ah, no. Not warp speed or teleportation or anything like that." Huntsman grabbed a clean plate from the table behind her. "Imagine, if you will, that we live at the edge of this plate. You want to travel to the other side, across the plate. But space bends more and more the closer you get to the center, like in a whirlpool or black hole. It would take you forever to get across the plate. You would get sucked into an infinity of space. Instead, the shortest distance between any two points on the edge is along the edge itself. Are you following?"

Mort rubbed his face. "I'm a biologist, not a mathematician."

"Well," Todd said, "I'm not sure I get what you're saying scientifically, but it's sort of like people. You learn this by cutting hair. Or just by being human. If you want to get at what's really bothering someone, you can't shoot straight for the center. Your words will get lost. Most people can't even see inside themselves that way. Like we're all infinite inside. I mean, how else does God dwell in us, right? Like we're each a big infinite hole. So you take another approach, you talk about superficial things, and you slowly work your way to the center."

"I'm not sure I follow, Mr. Farkas."

"That's what all this is about in the end, isn't it? That there's some connection between the shape of the universe and the shape of each person? That's why certain people have changed because of the way the universe has changed. Am I right?"

Mort gazed at Todd. He was as confused as he was proud, and all the prouder because, out of the corner of his eye, he watched Huntsman at a loss for words.

Huntsman finally cleared her throat. "You may not be wrong, Mr. Farkas."

Todd gave the slightest gloated grin and took another bite of cake.

"So here is the conjecture, you two: that the Earth itself is now inverted around the moonshock. Flipped inside out, literally, physically. It's like the surface of the Earth is painted on the inside of a snow globe, with the whole universe inside."

"What's on the outside, then?" Mort asked.

"That's what we want you to help us find."

Todd scraped at the icing on his plate. "We're going to need a bigger capsule, then. One with a bathroom."

28

Todd stepped out of Huntsman's car in Douglas, Wyoming, and into a blast of hot August air. While still in chilly Yellowstone that morning, he had imagined reading the names of the dead etched in black granite under a heavy mist that dripped tears of ice. Instead, the bronze plaque spoke directly and economically:

Names of Those Slain from the East Rockies Caravan in Douglas, Wyoming, Fifteen Days after the Great Eclipse.

Huntsman had found his parents' names in a government database. Todd had hoped it had been a mistake. He saw their names inscribed:

Farkas, Jacob

Fisher-Farkas, Marissa

Based on the instructions he found posted on the wall, Todd knew their bodies were in a common grave a mile away, outside the city's perimeter fence. He also knew he could register as a relation inside the post office to which the plaque was attached. Rubbing their names with his thumb would be the only caress he could give them. They were lost in a sudden whirlwind of death with so many other millions.

In the post office, Todd watched as a clerk read his name

off his ID card and typed it into a computer. "Is anyone else registered as a relation?" he asked.

The clerk slowly pried her head from the screen. "Doesn't look like it, love."

"Would it be possible to make a correction to the plaque?"

She looked wearily at him.

"All I mean is to put 'Sr.' after Jacob Farkas. His other son is still out there somewhere. And daughter."

She clicked and typed a little more. "Yes, I'm sure he is, Mr. Farkas. I can emend it in the online directory at least." She turned and again smiled and patted his hand, a gesture made not without genuine sympathy.

Todd walked out with an envelope containing his parents' personal belongings and returned to the plaque. He held up his father's pocket watch, which Jacob Farkas, Sr., had inherited from his grandfather. Todd had expected to feel more and did not. He could only summon enough sadness to say that they had almost made it.

He turned and saw Mort seated on a bench, holding Sir Bear by a leash. White Wolf was leaning against the car. Huntsman had stayed in Yellowstone.

"I guess we need to get going," Todd said.

"Take all the time you need," White Wolf said.

"No, that's it. This is all it's going to be."

***

From Douglas, Huntsman's car hovered effortlessly along the eastern edge of the Rocky Mountains toward Denver, which, while not the capital, was the working center of the United States. The driver said very little. Mort said nothing except to point out markers of civilization, which became more frequent as they made their way into Colorado. At one hundred and eighty miles an hour, Todd found it hard to focus on anything except the distant mountains.

A Faraday fence like the one that had protected the site in Yellowstone from specters ran along the freeway in Cheyenne, and once they reached Fort Collins, it followed them uninterruptedly to Denver. At the northern end of the city, they passed through a gate, after which the fence hemmed them in on both sides of the freeway. As they drew closer to downtown, Todd lost count of the gates that opened more quickly for them in their OSS hover car than for the wheeled cars slowly bouncing forward.

They ascended a ramp and turned onto a narrow street whose leafy ruffles already glowed yellow and orange. The car jerked a little as its rubber tires made contact with the pavement. "City ordinance even for tier-one government vehicles," the driver said. Contact with the road, he continued, was meant not just to keep passing cars below eyesight but also to make them brake more quickly. Before they reached another avenue, the car turned into the parking deck of a large building Todd could barely see.

Light gray walls, empty white bookshelves, floor-length vertical blinds, and a faux maple floor sucked the life out of Todd's soul. This was his new home with Mort and, he presumed, Sir Bear.

Todd had grown up with a well-curated mess: expensive rugs and fresh floral arrangements, books falling over themselves, skis standing in the corner. He would have called it shabby chic if his mother had not made sure it was all dusted, if she had not put a finger to everything every day. Athletes and musicians developed styles of delightful imperfection only after they had mastered their craft. Marissa Farkas had been eminent in the field of interior decoration, devoted to one client, herself. It would take Todd years to bring this two-bedroom apartment to such standards. And Huntsman had left him and Mort with three hundred dollars each.

"I know what you mean," Mort said.

Todd did not recall saying anything.

"It's not the way our old homes were. It even felt more natural being out there in a tent. But this is what we were looking for, civilization, a safe home."

"It was a good idea to tell Huntsman to wait until your cast came off before we do anything else with her. *If* we do anything else with her."

White Wolf cleared his throat behind them. He had finally made it up the stairs, declaring his dislike for elevators.

"Nothing's free in this world," the old man said.

"Meaning what?" Mort said.

"Meaning we put out or get out," Todd said. "Hey, are those our spears?" Todd had seen the two spears leaning in the corner of the dining area. Metal mesh encased the tips. "Not a bad way to start decorating."

Mort picked up his spear. The broken and bloodied end had been sawed off. A piece of paper dangled off the shaft by a string. "Not so fast, my friend. Check this out."

Todd examined an etched plaque at the tip end of the shaft. "A licensed spear?"

"Complete with paperwork."

"Those aren't decorations," White Wolf said. "But this

place could sure use some. Let me explain that spear to you. You've seen some action, you deserve that much." The old man brought the tip to his eye and spun the shaft in his fingers. "Yep. This was a steel garden trowel that you very slightly magnetized when you sharpened it. When you struck the *Dakotaraptor*, you completed a circuit: severed dinosaur spinal cord to left hand, right hand to grounded metal lamp post. All it took to charge the metal was to take life from a first-gen resurrect. This will be a good weapon for you to have. Todd, we charged yours ourselves. It's quite a versatile and dangerous metal now. Don't touch it to anything except what you intend to kill."

"What about Sir Bear?" Mort asked.

White Wolf shrugged. "Don't touch it to Sir Bear either."

"I mean, can Sir Bear stay here with us?"

The old man looked around the living room. "You'll have to ask your landlord."

"You're the landlord," Todd said. "Doesn't the OSS own this place?"

White Wolf's eyes fell. "I will have to show you its organizational chart some time." He shuffled into the kitchen. "I saw it once myself." He began opening cabinets and drawers. "You have utensils, at least. You know, there are plenty of scavenger shops in LoDo where you could find some real decorations. It's a nice summer evening. Come on, I'll show you where to get almond croissants. My treat."

"Do we take our spears?" Todd asked. Mort was already gripping his.

White Wolf raised a wary eye toward Mort. "Not if you don't want people asking questions about them. Do your best not to let people sniff at you too closely. They'll know you just woke up by looking at you. Maybe play more naive than you are."

In the elevator, standing behind Mort and White Wolf, Todd caught himself humming nervously, the first time in over a month.

***

Todd sat with Mort, White Wolf, and Sir Bear at a café a few blocks from their apartment. The place could have passed for any in the old world. The streets coursed with people and cars though everyone was quieter than he remembered. The walls of the café hung heavily with the remains of old Earth, knickknacks and pictures from coastal skylines now sunk or fallen. Powdered sugar fell from Todd's pastry onto his pants. At least it was not ringing his mouth like it was for Mort, who stared at the walls. Todd spied someone with an open laptop. He inhaled to ask about the Internet and stopped, wondering if life might not be better without it.

"Huntsman only left us a few hundred dollars," Mort said. "How are we otherwise going to support ourselves? I figure we should get a computer, get hooked in, figure out where things are."

This was the second time in an hour that Mort had read Todd's mind. Or they had spent so much time together over the past three weeks that they thought the same thoughts. Todd looked intently at a small stage for live music and asked in his mind when a performer might come. He waited for Mort's response.

Mort licked a napkin and wiped his mouth.

"You're right," White Wolf said. "We should get you a computer. You'll find the Internet more purely functional than it used to be. Social media's mostly people looking for lost loved ones and sharing conspiracy theories. Then there's the news, and so on. The rest is fairly PG-rated, if you catch my drift."

Todd watched Mort knit his brow, pretending to notice something new on the wall.

"Speaking of," White Wolf said, "the pope is coming to town in a few weeks."

"Which pope is that?" Mort asked, pulling himself upright and obviously happy to have a different conversation.

The corners of the old man's mouth curled upward, and Todd's smile followed automatically. "The same one as before."

Mort nodded.

"Sylvester III," Todd said. "He's still alive?"

"Alive as ever. Aren't you Catholic, Mort?" White Wolf said.

"Nominally," Todd said. "Here I am, the evangelical Lutheran, telling the Catholic who the pope is."

"Enough, alright?" Mort tossed his napkin on the table. "Todd here does enough praying for the two of us."

White Wolf winked at Todd and said, "You'd better get some religion if you want to land a preacher's daughter."

"Who said anything about a preacher's daughter?" Mort said. He looked up and away, sticking his chin out in anger.

A heavy alarm blared briefly. Todd grabbed the edge of the table and looked around. Mort sprang from his seat.

White Wolf grumbled. Sir Bear yawned. No one else in the café seemed to notice.

"That's a perimeter alarm," White Wolf said. "One blast means the metro perimeter. At two, people will start wondering. At three, they'll roll down the gates of the café. At four, you'd better have your spear in hand and be ready to meet God. You guys are both jittery. Let's get you an aperitif." White Wolf waved for the waiter.

"Okay, so what are these fences actually protecting us against? The spirits that came after us—"

"You're no longer in the Secure Zone. You haven't met Casper the unfriendly ghost yet. That's right. You guys haven't had a proper orientation. We live in a world of specters."

"Huntsman started to tell us about those," Todd said. "Devils and humanoids and dinosaurs and specters, oh my."

"They're all of a kit," White Wolf said. "We used to think specters were some kind of entity, but now we know that they're actually like what Huntsman was talking about with respect to the universe. Swirling concentrations of space-time. Specters are conduits for the bad stuff. If you see a humanoid, it got here through a specter. You'll hardly see the specter before...." His face fell. "Just listen for the sirens, and keep your eyes peeled for a glint of light that shouldn't be there."

Todd was warm with cognac when he heard the barista begin to speak loudly with a customer.

—*You believe this? Pteranodons at Cherry Creek.*

—*Dinosaurs? That hasn't happened in years. Decades.*

—*What kind of mindfreak gave us those? It's gonna take weeks to get those things out of the skies.*

—Maybe those long beaks'll take care of the pigeon problem in the meantime.

Todd found Mort looking at him with an expression of sympathy mixed with apology. He opened his throat to the rest of the cognac.

***

Mort lay awake in his bedroom that night. It was the first time he had slept in his own room in three weeks, which had felt like three years.

This was the first time he had slept in his own room since he had met Todd. Todd had become a friend, a true friend, the only friend he had really ever had. But Todd had teased him about Cici in front of her uncle tonight. He had not known what White Wolf had meant by a "preacher's daughter"; he had been angry because he had thought that the whole Yellowstone camp had read the Voice Scroll in which he had talked about Huntsman. Huntsman was no preacher's daughter. Preacher's daughters were either wholesome or rebellious. He did not know what kind of woman Doris Huntsman was, but he could see, especially from White Wolf's words about her unicorn, that Cici had a rebellious streak. She was the preacher's daughter, and in a way he had hoped would not carry over into this new world, another man was making fun of his desire.

Mort had thought they would turn aside from the topic, but while they shopped for groceries after their afternoon snack, Todd would not let up, either, full of spirits. White Wolf had gone home, leaving Todd free to make Mort doubt Cici's qualities. Mort had noticed her sculpted arms, Todd her armpit hair. Mort had claimed, honestly, that it did not bother him. Todd had said the point was that she hoped it would. Mort had said that she should be all the more pleased that a man would look past that to her many other fine qualities. Todd had asked him to consider what kind of woman had nurtured the ability to equip a horse with hardware for flying. Mort had insisted: a genius and an Amazonian goddess. Perhaps Todd was acting jealously.

Mort kept his hands behind his head, gripping the underside of the pillow. He could hear the screech of the Pteranodons in the skies above him. He jumped when one of them clung to the metal bars on his window.

He walked over to the window to study the ancient specimen, lit under a floodlight. What a ghost he must seem to the creature, a shadow lurking in the dark. The Pteranodon tapped the glass with its beak. Maybe it thought Mort was a fish under the water. It tapped again and cracked the glass. There was no way Todd could deal with this animal so close to him. These things might have emerged from Mort's mind. Every time he drew close to Cici, in his mind or in reality, a dinosaur emerged. He was the mindfreak. Todd should not have to suffer the consequences.

Mort took his spear from the corner of his room. He twisted the collar of the metal cage counterclockwise, as instructed, and the cage opened like a flower. He pulled open the window, and the long beak poked into the dark room. "You've waited eighty million years, my friend, and all you get is this. Sorry." He thrust at the three-foot beak, and a few sparks burst into the room.

The animal seemed frozen, clinging to the bars of the window. Mort poked at its body again to no special effect;

the thing was dead. It fell four stories to the ground. Mort closed the cage of the spear and set it back in the corner. The breeze coming through the window felt good, and he lay back in bed.

Beneath the din of late-night city life and through the thin wall that separated their rooms, Mort thought he heard Todd crying. He had drunk cognac and teased Mort this afternoon to drown his feelings. Todd's parents were dead. No one knew where Jake and Evelyn were. It would be a lifetime in this place to find them. Mort had no one to look for except a preacher's daughter.

PART FIVE

WAKE THEM TO YOUR WORLD

29

The next afternoon, Mort was grilling marinated mastodon steaks in the kitchen. This had been, by far, the least expensive meat they could find in the grocery store last night, as the herds roamed about in abundance in the Secure Zone, relatively safe from specters. Mort had almost learned from the meat aisle alone what his new world was like, full of ancient fauna. When Todd, still tipsy from cognac, had asked the butcher whether they should not try giant sloth instead, the half-shaved woman behind the counter grew a smirk and said, "Takes too long to cook."

Todd, at the computer White Wolf had brought over this morning, yawned loudly. "How are we going to get through twenty-five-hour days without coffee?"

This was another reality, the lack of coffee, having to do with the world's ports being hundreds of feet above sea level since the Great Eclipse.

"How did we even do it for those two weeks?" Todd continued.

"Adrenaline. And booze."

After another minute of Todd's clunky, untrained typing, Mort heard, "There are a lot of churches in the Denver area."

Mort flipped the steaks. "Don't you have your own denomination?"

"Mortimer."

Mort waited. Todd wanted a response. "What?"

"I'm doing this for you. You said you overheard Uncle Billy say he was taking Cici down to Denver. He also said she was a preacher's daughter. I'm compiling a list from the most to least likely churches, by neighborhood."

Mort poked at the steaks. Mastodon meat had nice marbling.

Todd continued, "William White Wolf is not going to give up his niece that easily. He wants you to prove yourself. You've got to pound the pavement if you want to fulfill your fantasy."

Mort looked at the cast on his right hand. "She fell into my life once already."

"But she won't again. I guarantee it. Time to share the heavy lifting."

"You, too. Come drain the potatoes for mashing."

A knock came at the door.

Todd rose from his chair, and, instead of answering the door, he grabbed the pot of potatoes.

Mort put the mastodon steaks on a plate to rest them.

As he walked to the door, he heard Todd say something about the steaks to Sir Bear, who growled, and Mort knew Todd's finger was in the air.

At the door were two police officers in slightly more modern uniforms than he was used to.

"Good afternoon, officers. How can I help you?"

One of the officers spoke. "Yes, hi, we're here investigating a possible Pteranodon attack. Any of you folks here have any encounters lately?"

Mort, who had always felt he was doing something criminal whenever he passed a police cruiser on the road or left a store without buying anything, spoke automatically. "Oh, yeah. We had one try to break in here last night. I got him with my spear."

The two officers looked at each other. "You mind if we come in?"

"Yeah, sure. I'll show you. It cracked the window with its beak." Mort looked at Todd, who was standing frozen at the kitchen sink. In his bedroom, Mort pointed to the cracked pane of glass. "You see? He was clinging to the bars."

The lead officer held his belt with both hands, dug his chin into his neck, swayed forward a little on his feet, and said, "Could we, uh, see this so-called spear?"

Mort swallowed. "Of course." He looked at the spear as if for the last time and held it out for the officer. "It's licensed, you know."

His mouth hanging open, the officer studied the weapon, a garden trowel driven into a bamboo shaft that still bore residue of duct tape, all wrapped in modern Faraday mesh. "What in the world is this?"

"I made it," Mort said. "Right after I woke up."

"Let's go back into the living room." The lead officer turned to his partner. "Lopez, would you run this license tag?"

Mort looked for the lead officer's own tag, which read

Flannigan. Todd had not moved from the counter and was only pretending to mash potatoes. Mort shrugged at him.

Officer Lopez called someone from the landline phone hanging on the wall.

Flannigan said, "You guys got ID?"

Todd pulled out of his pocket the Absarokee ID that Huntsman had given him at Yellowstone. Mort slapped his pockets, thinking. His was next to the computer, behind Flannigan. Mort ducked a little and pointed until Flannigan side-stepped to let him through.

Flannigan studied both cards. "Class A-2? How long you guys been awake?"

"A month," Todd said. "Or so."

"Hey, Flannigan," Lopez said, jerking his head toward the phone. With his hand over the receiver, he whispered to Flannigan, casting his eyes toward Mort.

"Shit," Flannigan said. He quickly handed the ID cards back. "Alright, guys. Just a little FYI. It is illegal to de-animate a protected species without clear evidence of danger. You got bars on the window. The creature was not coming in. And I don't know what kind of training OSS gave you guys, but discharging a devonium rod indoors is a major fire hazard. Just look up what happened to Toledo. Have a nice day." He opened the door and left.

"Have a nice day," Lopez echoed. He handed Mort his spear and closed the door behind him.

Mort rubbed his palms into the wood of the spear, another victory.

"Yeah, Mort," Todd said. "You should look up Toledo on the Internet. I wonder what happened there."

Mort chortled, set down the spear, and told Todd to mash the potatoes while he looked up devonium on the Internet.

***

There were two hundred and fifty churches on Todd's list. A dashed line on each page separated the most likely, Protestant and Evangelical, from the least likely, Black Baptist and Hispanic Pentecostalist. Neat bubble handwriting gave the names, addresses, and office hours.

Mort had spent three consecutive mornings walking door to door. Todd would not let him call. Mort had hoped the pastors all knew each other well enough to tell him where to go to find Cici. This had not been the case. He sat on a bench in a small park, eating a sandwich. His feet swelled against his shoes. A Pteranodon hovered in the air. Mort tossed the last crust of bread at the pigeons on the ground. "Looks like the last meal for you, fellas. Any requests?"

A large bell sounded.

Mort nodded and walked toward the Catholic cathedral a block away. He would light a candle for his *babcia*, only because that was what she would have done for him.

As he entered the church, Mort caught the smell of newborn babies and looked around. A small group of newly woken sleepers was in the cathedral, presumably on the kind of orientation White Wolf had talked about. A priest was speaking to them. As he passed the group, Mort gave one sleeper a sympathetic glance, whose thin, red arms clung to the pew ahead of him. Mort met a face full of confusion and fear, and he smiled, hoping to show what confidence a month awake in this world could give.

Mort turned and stopped suddenly before an image of Our Lady of Czestochowa. He knew that name and this image because Renata Sobieski had seared it into his soul as a child. He liked this picture because there was no fake smile on Mary's stern face. He lit a candle for his grandmother. The flame itself would be his prayer.

Mort sensed someone walking toward him, and when he did not pass by, he turned. It was a priest in a long cassock, the one he had seen speaking to the group of sleepers, leaning on a cane. The taut, lined face, holding its years serenely, studied Mort. Mort searched his memory for what made him so familiar.

"It's good to see you here, Mortimer," the priest said. "My name is Father Joseph."

Mort held out his right hand automatically, forgetting about his cast. "It's nice to meet you, Father. How do you know my name?"

Father Joseph took the cast in his free hand, gazed at it, and turned it gently one way and the other. "So this is the price of admission you paid."

Mort looked at the priest's cane. "Admission to what?"

"Come with me, Mr. Sowinski."

Father Joseph turned and hobbled away on his cane. Mort followed.

***

Mort sat in Father Joseph's office, across a formidable ark of a desk on top of which a dozen picture frames stood sentry with their backs to him, sharp black uniforms leaning on single legs. Only a strange cookie jar welcomed him, a portly Black man or woman wearing a red sash over a white robe.

The priest leaned back in his chair and took two snifters from a bookshelf at his side. "Care for a drink?"

"Sure," Mort said.

Mort watched the priest swivel a little in his chair. His Internet research had revealed him as Joseph Conque, one of the suspected sources of devonium. He asked.

"Yes, it's true," Father Joseph said. "I was sitting with my nephew, Devon, on the porch of my new house near Cheyenne Mountain a few months after the Eclipse. I had the hood scoop of my old Trans Am hanging on the wall, and he was admiring it, wearing it like a shield in one hand, when out of nowhere these specters show up. He must have seen them first or had turned instinctively to shield himself from them. Sparks everywhere, and the hood scoop is glowing blue and copper. His face turns green, and he vomits seawater onto the thing, which seems to neutralize it for a few minutes, long enough to put it somewhere safe. And there you have it. Just like with your spear. Only the question is still out there as to whether or not the whole car had already become a devonium rod when I crashed it."

Father Joseph swiveled in his chair, gazing at Mort.

Mort looked at the androgynous cookie jar. "Is that the pope?"

"Some would like to have her that way. Here." He handed Mort two fingers of whisky. "No, the pope's in town in a few weeks, actually."

"I heard. You don't see much hubbub in the papers or anything."

"That's the way he likes it. He's usually here pleading for the Sahara. I say let him. He's done the impossible in getting the Touaregs, Berbers, and Arabs to welcome all those refugees from Europe. Many from here, too. Europe's under a thin sheet of ice right now. You've learned about the long winters, no doubt."

"Yes, and I also know that it means long summers as well."

"But you know people. They focus on the negative." Father Joseph leaned forward. "Are you religious, Mortimer?"

Mort sat back. "Um, not really, Father, no. I mean, nothing against it and all, I just...it's never done much for me."

Father Joseph clicked his tongue. "You're a real dragon slayer, you know."

"It was a *Dakotaraptor*. Not a mythical beast. And maybe that's all the dragon ever was, something unknown but eventually knowable to science."

"'Eventually knowable to science,'" Father Joseph echoed. He leaned back and looked up at the ceiling. "How long is science going to play catch-up with religion?" He looked down again at Mort. "I'm a computer scientist, Mortimer. I've helped launch satellites into space. Human science is a process for arriving at sharable knowledge of what is given so that we can imitate and manipulate reality. What happens when something upends the order of things, turns the world inside out? Our science plays catch-up. And, along the way, we learn we belong to a bigger order of things." Father Joseph's gaze returned to the heavens, or, at least, the acoustic tile ceiling of his office. "An order that is capable of healing the wounds in this one, fixing what this order cannot fix on its own, even using the weaknesses of this world as its strengths."

Mort looked at the priest's hands, held together at his modest belly. "What does that have to do with me?"

Father Joseph leaned forward. "Look to the way you killed that dragon. How did it happen? You did not take the action to spear it in the throat. It slew itself against you. It went after your weakness, and that's what did it in."

Mort looked to the side. "Alright, sure. That is how it happened. So...."

"So don't expect to get anywhere in this weird new world by your strength. You will find, Mortimer, that whatever special abilities you possess come through your place of greatest weakness."

Mort looked down at his own hands.

"I bet it's not there, Mortimer. Think about what else was going on that day."

"I don't have any special powers," Mort said.

Father Joseph coughed. "That's not what Dr. Huntsman has proven."

Mort raised his eyebrows. Even by his own measure, his experiences with Todd had been remarkable. "So, what, does Doris Huntsman just sort of collect people like us? What are your special powers?"

"It's not exactly like that with her."

The door to Father Joseph's office opened behind Mort. Father Joseph looked up and subtly gestured to give him a minute then knit his brow and nodded toward Mort. "I'll be out in a second, Claire Bear."

Mort turned.

Clinging to the door was Cici. She wore loose, kha-ki-colored pants and a light blue shirt. Tresses of her hair fell around her shoulders like he remembered, and her scent softened every one of his sinews. A cast covered her wrist and forearm, too.

"Cici," Mort said. He stood and knocked his chair to the side. "I, uh, I'm glad to see you. It's Mort, Mortimer, from the Wall Drug, you know, with the raptor, where I killed the *Dakotaraptor*, if you remember. I mean, of course, you do. Todd and I, he was the other guy, we've been hanging out with the guy you call Uncle Billy, and his mother, and Dr. Huntsman, but we've been moved down here to Denver to work with the OSS—am I allowed to say that?—and I was just passing through to light a candle for my own grand-mother when Father Joseph here pulled me aside. Listen to me—I'm sounding like Todd right now. Actually, tell you the truth, I was sort of going around to different churches to try to find you, you know, maybe thank you, and so on. Billy said you were a preacher's daughter. You wouldn't be-lieve how many churches there are in Denver. I think I've knocked on about a hundred different doors over the past few days just looking for you."

"Have you now?" came Father Joseph's voice.

The butterflies in Mort's stomach fluttered up around his face and burst into red-hot flames. He could not read the expression on Cici's face. Perhaps it was strained calculation.

"So," Mort said, his searing face now swelling with sad embarrassment, "what brings you around here?"

Cici's eyes darted around the room.

"She is a preacher's daughter," Father Joseph said.

Mort turned to the man in full-length cassock and back to Cici. "Oh. How...?"

"Claire, sweetie, you're right, I do need to get back to our guests before Sister Bethany lulls them back to sleep. Maybe you could show Mortimer out? It sounds like you two have some catching up to do."

Cici's eyes clung to her father as she stepped out of the office. Mortimer made a clumsy bow and followed Father Joseph's extended hand toward the door. He closed the door behind him and found Cici standing halfway down the hallway. She turned, and he raced to catch up with her.

"So it's Claire?" he asked.

"Claire Conque," she said with practiced politeness.

Mort feared that White Wolf had already spoken to her about him. "And your mother?"

Cici opened a door that led into the nave of the cathedral. She slowed her pace. "She's asleep, like you were."

"I'm sorry to hear that," Mort said. Walking behind her meant the benefit of savoring her scent. She did carry herself a bit stiffly, he had to admit.

Cici stopped at the narthex. She studied Mort's face. His confidence returned. He would have stood like a statue for eternity if it meant her gaze upon him. She looked down and away. "I have very few memories of her. Almost none." She walked through one of the large doors out into the bright gray daylight.

Mort followed, and she stopped again on the patio of the church. "I know the feeling, Cici. Both of my parents disappeared when I was very young. As of now, I have no family but Todd." Mort swallowed his breath. "And, uh, perhaps we could get together some time, you know, trade notes on this crazy world."

Cici stuck out her chin a little. "Well, I'm a bit tied up in Boulder at the moment. But, uh...." She looked away.

"How did you break your wrist?" he asked. Mort had long practice in saving women from their excuses not to see him.

"I fell off my unicorn." She pulled a strand of hair behind her ear.

Mort searched his experience for this gesture and had no response. "I suppose that's a small price of admission to pay."

"Admission to what, Mortimer?"

He loved how she said his name. He had to raise a drunken eyebrow to say, "A new world, I guess."

Cici seemed to spy something behind Mort and stuck out her cast-covered hand. "If you're going to be working with my father, then perhaps we should be friends."

Mort shook her hand, fingertips to fingertips. He imagined some occult electricity was passing between them in that tickling sensation. He watched her walk back into the church. All of his inner organs, his bones, maybe even his muscles became like wooden scaffolding that was coming down, leaving only an outer shell of painted plaster. He stared blankly at the city street below him, afraid a breath would break that brittle shell.

Someone slapped him on the shoulder.

"Hey, there," White Wolf said. "Looks like you just had a big meeting."

"Yeah," Mort said. He could summon only one dull tone.

"Well, come on. Huntsman wants you and Todd back in Montana while your hand heals. A month or two in the fresh air will do you guys and Denver a little good. She thinks you two might actually be responsible for the Pteranodons."

Mort looked up at an empty gray sky.

30

Todd walked alongside Mort on a narrow path through the tall grass, down a gentle slope into a pleasant depression. He did not know if it was large enough to be called a valley or steep enough to be a canyon. Even after many summers in Big Sky, he did not know his western geography. He played in his throat with words like *glen, gully, gulch,* and *gorge.* What the Earth was starting to do in Montana she would complete in Yellowstone when Mort healed: curling up around them, closing off heaven, and swallowing them.

White Wolf shuffled ahead of them. Sir Bear ran between Todd's legs. White Wolf had promised a half-mile walk. They had walked much longer than this, but he could see a little cabin now near a creek. As they curved along the hillside, a conical structure began to emerge from the trees.

"Ah, what's this?" White Wolf asked, with evident fore-knowledge. "Maybe you guys want to stay in a tipi?"

Todd prided himself on picking apart nuances of tone, and in the voice of the ninety-year-old Native American, he heard both the genuine enthusiasm of paternal instruction and the coded sarcasm of postcolonial contempt.

Mort said, "I don't know, let's take a look. Do we do anything special to prepare?"

"No, you just go in and lie down," the old man said. "You'll need the kitchen and toilet in the cabin, though."

The cabin was musty but livable. The one bedroom had a bunk bed, and Todd knew that because of Mort's hand, he himself would have to take the top. The tipi began to look tempting.

"What's the large bird on the tipi?" Todd asked.

"The thunderbird. The protector of our people."

"Oh."

"But she is not without need of defense herself. There's a story of the time the thunderbird asked a man to help defend her chicks against the water monster. He fed burning stones into its mouth, which is bad enough, and then poured water inside. That really got him. Boom."

"This is Crow country?" Mort asked. "Is this the reservation?"

"The reservation still exists as a legal entity," White Wolf said. "It shrunk over the years as we sold it off. Now, things are a bit more fluid. You are in the once and future State of Absarokee, an experiment in relative self-sufficiency. But let me assure you that the State of Montana still exists, at least nominally. Some people have kept up herding cattle up here, though I don't know why, given that mastodons and bison seem to spring up out of the soil. Justice demands rent from herders as they pass through. Sometimes they pay, sometimes they don't.

"Anyway, we Crow arrived here from out east, maybe Wisconsin, when the French and British started arming our neighbors. We walked for a hundred years from there to Utah, back to Missouri and up again, on the promise of good land. This is it. And it is good land. We developed the buffalo jump."

Todd leaned against the knotty pine frame of the cabin's bedroom door, feeling the warmth of an old man telling stories.

"Other Native tribes called us the people of the sharp-beaked bird, hence crow or raven, which meant we were smart. Some French explorers called us the Beaux-hommes, good-looking. The first impression we make is of being smart and good-looking. You would agree, right?"

Mort said, "Based on the pictures of your sister and niece, yes."

White Wolf smiled broadly. "Good answer. So this is Crow country, a land prophesied to us. We got hit as hard as any other population after the eclipse, just a few thousand up here now. But we're sticking with it, the hard winters and everything. Besides, the old woman won't let us leave."

"Marigold?" Todd asked.

"*Káalixaalia*. That is the Crow word for 'old woman.' It also means 'Mother Earth.' It is also a name for the moon. Ponder that for a while. The moon and the Earth share a name."

Todd tried to ponder this.

Mort beat him to it. "The moon is taken from the Earth, originally. A Mars-sized planet slammed into Earth. The moon is the result."

"And now," White Wolf said, closing his eyes, "and now,

the Earth is somehow wrapped around the moon and follows her days and seasons."

"If Earth is the mother, who is the father?" Todd asked.

"That's an interesting question," White Wolf said. "Fathers have a way of making themselves not seen, at times."

***

Mort lay awake. By the look of the sky through the ears of the tipi above and the sound of the fauna outside, it was early morning. A horse snorted in the distance. Todd snored softly on the other side of the tipi, twenty feet away. The tipi proved more comfortable than Mort had expected, especially once White Wolf started a small fire in the center and broke out a bottle of whisky and a shopping bag full of ingredients for s'mores. White Wolf had spent much of the evening talking up the great horsemanship of the Crows and his own exploits in the annual August fair as a young man.

This morning, Mort walked through the flap and turned to face the open valley to the north. A thin purple line illumined the horizon. He stretched his long limbs. Some distance away, a horse walked down the gentle eastern slope, across the valley, and up the western slope. Mort admired this and the small, swirling cloud of dust or pollen following in the horse's hoofsteps. He took in a long breath of the big Montana sky. Denver had felt like the world in which he had fallen asleep. He could stay awake here, until his cast came off and he and Todd went deeper into the Earth.

The morning brightened, and another horse, or the same one, walked from west to east, down the valley and up again, somewhat closer this time. Perhaps it was dew that

the horse was shaking loose because the animal was not going fast enough through the grass to kick up anything else.

After embarrassing himself with Cici, or Claire, or
whatever he should call her, Denver had very quickly started
to feel like the world into which he had retreated before he
had fallen asleep.

He could smell the horse, which now walked from east
to west across the valley, taking about five minutes to do so.
The horse was all black. The faint, gently swirling cloud of
dew behind it had some kind of lensing effect, and Mort
searched his mind for knowledge of why that should be, why
the horse had kicked up anything at so slow a pace.

Mort then spent some time thinking of nothing in particular, which he always found a great relief. The sun would
rise above the valley soon, and White Wolf had some work
planned. He turned to go back into the tipi to dress.

Looking into a grove of trees on the western slope, he
felt a presence gazing at him. The black horse burst out of
the shadows and ran right past him, across the stream and
up the eastern slope. The pollenated dew cloud that followed stung his eyes, and when he opened them, he had a
strange sensation of vertigo or of looking at the landscape
through a funhouse mirror. The tipi was briefly very far
away, and when the horse had passed beyond it, the tipi
quickly snapped back toward him. Mort flinched and nearly
fell backward, swinging his arms to keep upright. When he
recovered, he thought of walking out to see where the horse
had gone, but after all he had experienced in this new world,
he thought better of it and went inside.

31

Todd adjusted his tie in the mirror and brushed imagined dandruff off his shoulder. Mort mimicked his actions behind him, standing in the doorway of the one tiny bathroom on the bus. The bus was an OSS mobile office, well-appointed in the style of an RV but always cold.

A quick fortnight had passed in Crow country while Mort waited for his cast to come off. A second, swifter set of weeks passed while Mort and Todd practiced on the dervish, chasing down herds of mastodon on the open plains and slipping through the forests to spy out the still-elusive saber-toothed cat. No dinosaurs emerged from Mother Earth, from the mud where she stored her memory.

They had just descended in St. Louis for a meeting with some government officials. If Denver was where most of the work was being done, St. Louis had become something of a spiritual capital in addition to the actual location of Congress and the Supreme Court. They were going to neither building today.

"Listen carefully," Huntsman said to them in the living room of the bus. "Please be on your best behavior. Not that you've never not been. I don't mean this about you. What

I mean is, word of your success has reached the vice president, and he's the kind of person who wants assurances, especially with our work, the OSS. To be frank, the people you are about to meet have taken on a particular...vision with respect to everything that has been going on the past twenty-seven years."

"Have we ever behaved abnormally?" Todd said.

"Not you, no, Mr. Farkas. Or you, Mr. Sowinski, for that matter. You know what it is we are about to see. All I'm asking is that you act as if this were the most perfectly normal thing there is. The...environment around it...."

Todd had never seen Huntsman at a loss for precise words and looked at Mort.

"I guess just do like you say I always do, you know?" Mort said. "Maintain a dead-eyed gaze. No reaction."

From the outside, the New White House looked no stranger than any other modernist monument Todd had seen in his many travels. Marking the four corners of the complex were three-story office blocks in brilliant white designed to match, to some degree, the original White House, which still stood in a state of minimal maintenance in Washington. Between these blocks, rising as a broad dome in the center of the square they formed, was the Hall of Watchers. This was the unofficial term given to the concrete, circular edifice that housed, Todd had been told, thousands of sleepers. Chief among them was President Deborah Palmer.

Todd, with Mort, Huntsman, and White Wolf, crossed the busy avenue that lined the eastern face of the complex, passed through a handsomely decorated Faraday fence, and walked into the space between two office blocks. All trivial noise dissipated. In the space between the square and the circle, a serene garden absorbed all sound except that of water gently trickling from small artificial springs.

Young men and women in sharp suits milled about slowly, some engaged in quiet conversation, some sitting in still contemplation. It reminded Todd of seeing Salt Lake City full of Mormons or what he imagined the place all the Jehovah's Witnesses lived.

"Do we live in a theocracy?" Todd whispered.

Huntsman turned and glared at him, clenching her lips for him to be quiet.

Todd tucked himself a little behind Mort and Huntsman. He did not notice that he had started humming until White Wolf very subtly cleared his throat.

The entrance to the somnolent mausoleum was simple and spare. The vestibule was colonnaded with quiet, courteous staff. Todd walked through a mechanical gateway he did not realize was an x-ray machine until on the other side.

The first corridor they followed was much taller than it was wide, and nooks with sleepers lined only the ground level. The glass doors leading to each nook were smoked but not so dark he could not make out the rubbery egg shapes inside. It was not quite the Matrix he had imagined.

After passing some way around the circle, Huntsman led them left into an inner, concentric corridor. This second corridor was lower and darker. The pattern showed itself clearly, a labyrinth like the fencing in Yellowstone. Todd was not surprised when, a little while later, they turned into a third concentric corridor, lower than the second and lit just as gravely. The pattern of lowered ceilings hinted at a stadium-like space above them. Sometimes Todd made out another body inside a nook, a silhouette bending over a beloved sleeper. They arrived at another well-guarded vestibule, presumably the end of their journey.

"Excuse me, may I ask a question?" Todd said.

Huntsman's face pleaded for Todd not to say anything, but he could not contain himself any longer.

"Is it called the Hall of Watchers because of the sleepers or because of those who watch over them?"

Huntsman seemed to be preparing a studied answer when a voice escaped from some shadow of the small vestibule. "Ah, that is a philosophical question."

Todd turned to see a well-groomed man in a dark suit.

"Good to see you, Doris," the man continued. "Mr. DeSoto," he nodded to White Wolf. He then stretched out his hands. "And these must be our intrepid voyagers. It is an honor to meet you. I am Senator James Hendel. Yes, quite a problem you pose, Mr. Farkas. Certainly, in the light of recent circumstances, we have reached the limit of our speculative science. But reason remains, and I think it would not be irreligious to propose that, with our sleepers, it is a mutual gaze of protection we afford each other. It is not one or the other first. This whole place, bringing our beloved sleepers together, amplifies their protection over us and gives us a place to come together as a people, to unite us in loving watchfulness. Come, let us go in and see her."

Senator Hendel hooked his arm around Todd's and led him forward. Todd tried his best to hide his grimace.

Two guards opened a pair of doors, and brilliant white light burst through. When his eyes adjusted, Todd found himself in what looked like an amphitheater. The light was mostly natural, from a large skylight at the center of the low dome, and bounced freely off the white walls. Hundreds, maybe a thousand sleeper pods sat in the open upon decks cascading down to the center of the amphitheater, where a single pod lay still. Two torches stood sentry on either side of President Palmer. Smaller torches lined each upper level, one per several bodies lying dormant in sacs of their own skin.

Todd's mouth was agape, and he could feel his lower lip tremble freely. He said nothing, knowing that any word would either be complete gibberish or an unguarded curse. The sight of half a dozen men and women in tailored suits sitting meditatively on benches around President Palmer did nothing to ease his anxiety.

Senator Hendel coughed politely. One by one, the suits turned and rose serenely to greet Huntsman and her team. One by one, Hendel introduced them: congressmen, military leaders, and scientists. One man stood patiently until he was introduced. "And this, as you surely recognize, is Vice President Noah Philips."

"How do you do?" Todd said, taking the vice president's extended hand. He kept his silver curls pulled back with heavy product. "This is all really spectacular."

The vice president smiled. "They call it Noah's Ark, but I can't say that it is really my brainchild. I am glad for it, though. It has been for us," he spread his hands wide to include the others, "leading our country, and I dare say the world, through these tremendously tumultuous times, a place of repose and tranquility. She is certainly still leading us. I simply stand in her place until she wakes. As for the others asleep here, well, they are not all necessarily prominent in the way we think of prominence, though many are—leading lights of science, statesmen, and so on—and perhaps now is a time to rethink earthly prominence. You two, for instance. You came out of nowhere and made your way unseen across this great continent. That is a special kind of prominence, the work of the unsung hero, those chosen providentially to stand guard unseen. It's a shame that Dr. Huntsman did not make you more well known after your successful first run, but I think we understand her methods. Always the exacting scientist." He shook a proud fist in her direction.

She did not flinch.

Philips continued, "Well, we are very glad to meet you before your big return to Yellowstone, where we hope for even greater success. I'm sure that Dr. Huntsman has told you that we're not the only ones pursuing such a course. Let's not let the Russkies or Chinese get the upper hand on us. Though, of course, we are all at the service of world peace now. Come, perhaps just spend a little time with her before you go." Philips gestured with his arms for Todd and Mort to take a seat on one of the benches surrounding Palmer.

Huntsman subtly nodded for them to do as asked.

Todd sat next to Mort on the cold basalt bench. Philips, Hendel, and the others sat down as well, looking on Palmer's placental presence with eerie reverence. It was the kind of practiced calm he occasionally spied on other faces in church. Mort's eyes were closed, and his shoulders were hunched as he gripped the stone bench.

Not knowing how long he would have to sit there made the time pass all the more slowly for Todd. He looked at Palmer, whose body was barely visible through her thin shell. Once or twice she gently stirred, which seemed to draw a little admiration from the others.

Todd prayed. It had been a long journey full of surreal moments, some of them dangerous. He decided, or God had revealed to him, he was not sure, that compared to serpents, dinosaurs, and lurking shadows of hate, this was the most insidious threat he had encountered. He was ready to leap into whatever lay within the empty caldera.

After quarter of an hour, White Wolf began to snore. Huntsman rubbed his back and pinched his arm, apologizing to Philips and the others. Philips made a gesture to suggest it was fine to leave and asked where they were staying. As everyone stood, Todd met White Wolf's face behind Huntsman's back; the old man winked.

The foursome walked briskly and quietly through the circular corridors of the Hall of Watchers, across the busy avenue. Todd noticed that the top of the Gateway Arch was missing; it looked like two fingers slightly curled toward each other. Once the door of the OSS mobile office closed behind him, Todd's inner hounds broke loose, meeting their master just returned home, and he wanted to yell, "Omigod omigod omigod," but he buried his hands in his face.

"Yeah, what the f—" he heard Mort say.

Todd looked up to see Huntsman and White Wolf gazing at them with unveiled faces. He grabbed Huntsman's arms, and she took his. She looked at him almost tenderly, and for the first time, maybe even for her, she felt like a mother to him. As Todd began to speak, he choked back a brief spasm of sobs and said, "Thank God we found you before they found us. Thank you, Jake, wherever you are, for sending us west."

32

A week later, Mort and Todd hovered in front of the Cat's Eye.

They had come down to Magma Chamber 27 several times since returning to Yellowstone via St. Louis, learning to lay laser-line communications hubs. This was important today because they needed the live voices of engineers in their helmets. They had practiced drilling maneuvers above ground and were now on their own. Their dervish had been fitted with a cone-shaped drill head atop the round glass capsule and was fittingly nicknamed the Garden Gnome.

"Are you locked on the center of the eye?" the chief engineer asked.

"Affirmative," Mort said. He could see Todd's eyebrow rise in its reflection on the glass.

"Yaw one hundred and eighty degrees," the engineer said.

Mort did this.

"Now here's the tricky part. After you get the drill spinning, you have to tilt the dervish backward. As you tilt, you're going to lose vertical thrust, so make two motions at once, tilting backward and thrusting forward. Just like we practiced. Just like diving backward into the pool."

Diving *forward* into the pool had been terrifying enough for Mort. He looked at Todd, who had demonstrated much more aptitude with this maneuver during practice. But Huntsman, for reasons known only to her and whatever God she worshipped, insisted that Mort therefore take the controls.

With one swift motion, Mort tilted backward and thrust against the wall opposite the Cat's Eye. The dervish bounced from side to side as the conical drill head settled into the center of the hole, and Mort knew enough to keep thrusting so as not to bounce out again and fall on the floor. The vibrations soon evened out. Mort breathed. It would take no less than an hour to widen the forty-foot-thick walls of the Cat's Eye.

The vibrations grew smooth and soothing. Mort found his eyelids falling. "Did we bring coffee?" he asked. "Oh, wait. No coffee anymore."

"Is there a bathroom in here?" Todd replied.

"There are urine bags."

"That should do away with your appetite. Or are you drifting into sleep, too?"

"No. Maybe."

The Gnome cleared the Cat's Eye in an hour and seven minutes and drifted forward while Mort righted the capsule. The headlights faded into darkness on a road of dust still gently falling from the drill head above them.

"This is Mort. We're reading a cavity in excess of ten thousand feet in every horizontal direction. Downward is another story. The lidar's having a tough time picking up the floor. Todd, do you concur?"

"I concur that I can't tell what it is."

"Do you gentlemen feel secure going forward into a comms shadow?" the instructor asked.

"What do you say, Todd?"

"We've come this far with no problem."

"Affirmative," Mort said.

"Remember," came Huntsman's voice, "check-ins at the Cat's Eye every ten minutes."

"Roger that," Todd said.

Mort mumbled, "It's not so much a Cat's Eye anymore."

Magma Chamber 28 grew larger the farther they descended. They scanned along the southern wall, which had a series of deep vertical ribs running westward for ten miles. Mort thought to himself that it looked like they were in the rib cage of a monster.

"Of Monstro the Whale," Todd said.

Mort breathed in and smiled. "Here we are again, Todd. Of one mind."

"Where's Pinocchio?"

"With the other humanoids, trying to become a real boy."

Eleven minutes had passed, and they returned to the Cat's Eye to check in with Huntsman, who, after a stern rebuke for tardiness, told them to keep going.

Back at the western end of the wall, the lidar produced a blurry image.

"You're probably right," Mort said. He wasn't sure if Todd had spoken out loud or not.

"What?"

"That it looks like a waterfall. Let's put some lights on it."

Water poured out near the top of the western wall of the chamber, fanning outward on its way down as waterfalls do, but never sending up any spray.

"It just falls too far," Mort said. "We still don't know how deep this chamber goes."

He returned to the Cat's Eye.

"We're showing your battery at nineteen percent," the engineer said. "Can you confirm?"

"Confirmed," Mort said. "The heavy drill bit's been draining us."

"Come on back up," the engineer said. "We've got a surprise for you anyway."

***

As soon as Mort broke free of the Earth's surface and saw Claire standing next to her father, his arm around her, Mort realized that a "surprise for you" was intended in the second-person singular. The whole world, including those inside this collapsed caldera tucked away in the Rocky Mountains, knew Mort liked Claire. He waited for another raptor, or maybe a T-rex this time, to come and swallow him and his shame whole.

In the hangar while Mort waited for the technicians to remove the drill head so he could open the glass capsule, Todd turned off the Voice Scroll. "I want to tell you something, Mortimer. You don't know this yet, but you don't need her. If you can at least maybe act that way, you'll eventually realize it's true."

Mort felt his lips already swelling with the sadness of defeat. "Just play it cool, right? Too late for that."

In the hours that followed, Mort made every effort to speak with everyone except Cici, whose image, nevertheless, burned in his peripheral vision. She seemed to have a special touch with Sir Bear, though, and just as Mort, using this as his entry, was ready to recite some casual line he had been practicing since he had landed, Commander Headley called everyone together on the muddy driveway in front of the main office.

"We're all very glad that Claire Conque and her father are finally able to join us. Claire is providing us with the very latest communications drones Scimitech has to offer."

"Hot off the press," Claire said.

Mort was not sure that was the right expression.

Claire approached Commander Headley and pulled out of what looked like a bowling ball bag what looked like a black and green bowling ball. "Ladies and gentlemen," she said, "this is the DD-1026, which we are affectionately calling the Marvin. Like the previous models we've used to scan the boreholes and magma chambers, this one transmits lidar imaging and atmospheric data, but it contains one very special new feature." She handed the spherical drone to Commander Headley. "Would you do the honors? Just toss it in the air."

Headley narrowed his eyes at Claire and handed off the drone to a younger subordinate. Mort was almost glad to see Claire put down; this feeling quickly ended when the drone, spinning chaotically at some thirty feet in the air, emitted jets of air, righted itself, and gently landed in Claire's arms. Hums of approval rose from the crowd.

"We keep going deeper and deeper," Claire continued, "and our tools should become more and more stable. We'll soon send a drone to the center of the Earth."

Todd elbowed Mort.

Mort wanted to hear what Todd had in mind, but no words came. His stomach quavered where that ball of black bile had once been, and he walked forward almost without willing it. He grabbed the Marvin from Claire and said loudly, for everyone to hear, "This is great. I think I just found the perfect hole to put it in."

***

"It doesn't matter what you meant," Todd said. He was in another fully charged dervish with Mort less than an hour later. He had not yet turned on the Voice Scroll. "It's the way everyone heard it. It's also the way Headley's chin bounced up and down like a diving board, trying not to laugh. My God, Mort, even Huntsman chuckled."

"I can do nothing right with her." Mort's chin hung down.

"It's just the circumstances. Everyone here is wound up tight."

"Her father was furious. I've been sent to detention."

"It's called saving face. For you and Claire. She's more embarrassed than you are. Trust me. It's late in the day, but the quicker we drop her drones into MC Twenty-Eight, the sooner she's applauded, et cetera."

Two hours later, Mort and Todd had reached MC 28. Todd was piloting this time. They attached a communications hub to the roof of the chamber and checked and double-checked its connection to the laser line zigzagging its way to the surface. They had three of Scimitech's new Marvin drones strapped to the outside of the dervish's metal cowl.

The lidar image still showed the waterfall at the western end of the chamber, the ribbed southern wall, and no bottom in sight.

"Ready?" Todd said.

Mort nodded.

"I need you ready, Mortimer."

Mort squared his shoulders. "Ready, sir."

"Bomb's away." Todd pressed the release button.

The first Marvin fell for over three minutes, sending back the image of an ever-slightly tightening tunnel.

"O-kay," Mort said. "That's six hundred and sixty thousand feet before we lose contact. That is, my God, Todd, over three times as far as we've already descended. One hundred and sixteen miles."

"The boundary of the lithosphere," Todd said.

"How would you know that?"

"Aren't you reading the things Huntsman's given us to read?"

"Yeah, but…."

"But there's no clear reading of the bottom." Todd stared at the lidar screen. "The waterfall seems to keep going."

"That must be where all the oceans are falling to." Mort let his face grow brighter. "Todd, how many discoveries have we just made?"

Todd leaned forward and stared again at the lidar map.

"Um. ..." He was not the scientist, but the instinct he had developed in the great wide open of the Secure Zone was trying to tell him something in the deep, dark Earth. There had been times when Mort had seen danger and times when Todd had. Mort saw nothing wrong now. Todd could almost see something moving down there.

"I think there's something down there."

"Remember what I said once, Todd?" Mort said. "We create things out of our fear. We're not alone now. We have Claire's drones. Let's let her have a look before our eyes give shape to anything."

Todd sat back and let out a long breath with a hum.

"It's my turn now."

Todd nodded.

Mort reached for the second Marvin's release button and said, "Geronimo-o-o."

"White Wolf will read this, you know," Todd said, a rebuke uttered in a distracted monotone.

"White Wolf walks on air."

The drone fell for one hundred and eighty-seven seconds. A few squiggles of orange lidar lines filled in the bottom of the seemingly infinite well.

Mort coughed. "Well, maybe there is a bottom, you know?"

Todd played with his thumbs.

"What if we just go down there?" Mort said. "We've got plenty of battery and active comms. Surface, requesting permission to descend."

The engineer's voice came back. "Permission granted. Hang close to the eastern wall, away from the waterfall."

Todd grabbed the control wheel. "I have a bad feeling about this."

"Come on. We'll show how valuable Claire's new drones are."

Now we're vindicating you, Todd thought.

I heard that, Mort replied without speaking a word.

The two men descended in a straight line, facing the waterfall at a distance of several miles. The hole beneath them did not become any clearer, but the image of the waterfall began taking on a cascading shape.

Mort said, "But the walls behind it are not stepping forward. The waterfall couldn't be cascading on rocks unless it was following some thin ridge behind it."

Todd huffed. "We are also descending more slowly than we should be."

"Why would that be?"

Todd pulled an empty urine bag from behind Mort's seat. He held up to the top of the cockpit glass and let it fall. It fell slowly.

"Because we're also falling," Mort said. "No, I correct that. We're not accelerating. That thing should fall normally. Yes. You know what? There's a lot more Earth above us than there was before. The farther we go down, the less gravity there will be."

Todd shifted in his seat. "And the less graviton-volts we can use to steer the dervish with. Mort, tell me if I'm wrong here, but is the waterfall not maybe cascading on itself, like piling up because the lower parts are slowing down?"

"How far down are we now?"

"Four hundred and three thousand feet and counting."

"And no sign of a bottom?"

"None. No squiggly lines or anything."

The engineer's voice came through. "We're hearing you guys. Release the last Marvin, and commence your ascent."

"Go ahead, Mort."

The Marvin fell for two minutes. A series of lines like ripples appeared on the lidar screen where the bottom should have been.

"It splashed into water, Todd. Naturally. The waterfall is filling something up."

The ripples subtly rearranged themselves. Todd knew what he was seeing and began the ascent.

"You don't want to wait another minute?" Mort asked.

"Not one more second. Those aren't ripples in water. That's a coiled serpent." Todd glanced at the lidar screen again. A pair of lines shot straight toward the eastern wall.

"Omigod. I think it—"

"Yes, it did. At the same time Claire's probe cut out. It snapped and swallowed the probe."

"Todd, get us out of here."

"I'm doing all the getting I can."

"There's mist rising now. From the waterfall."

"Confirm that," came Huntsman's voice.

Todd looked over the edge. "I confirm. Visually. I can see it. There is a red glow."

Headley's voice hammered through. "A red glow?"

"I also see it," Mort said.

"Get your asses out of there," Headley said.

Todd began to seethe, but there was little his anger could accomplish. His hands had no purpose. Autopilot was still the fastest and safest way out of the cave they had created for themselves.

"Do you remember *Jurassic Park*, Mort?" He was not asking to distract himself.

"Which sequel this time?"

"The original, I think, where the guy says that the T-rex can only see when something moves."

"You think something down there saw us?"

"No. I think we only saw *it* when it moved."

"Claire's probes made it move."

"Maybe," came an unfamiliar female voice.

"Who's that?" Mort said.

"A tongue of lava is rising up toward you," the woman continued. "That's what made the devil wiggle down there. Dollars to donuts the lava's been sent up to protect you."

Huntsman's voice came back on. "Is it gaining on you?"

Todd checked the lidar. "No, it's not."

***

Two hours later, with the lava making no progress against them, daylight finally began to fight back. Mort saw that the evening was beginning to soak the sky in charcoal hues. Emergency lights were flashing all along the fence top. Sirens blared in pulses of four. Everyone was outside the Faraday fence except Father Joseph and Sir Bear. Mort and Todd landed the dervish in the hangar.

Mort walked to the opening of the hangar, where Headley's steel hand held his shoulder back. Huntsman very subtly swayed back and forth. Claire had her face half tucked against White Wolf's chest. Mort did not know what her father was doing out there, or Sir Bear, for that matter.

"What...?" he began before he realized that no one could hear him over the sirens.

A strong wind blew a whirlwind of leaves and dust around the entrance to the borehole inside the Faraday fence. Father Joseph stood serenely with his hands crossed. In place of his cane, Mort saw some kind of brace sticking out the bottom of his cassock on his right leg. Sir Bear began to growl.

The sirens stopped.

The whirlwind increased.

Father Joseph released his hands and held them loosely by his sides. His face was stern, though, and some special glint of metal took over his eyes.

Sir Bear pointed his nose and bared his teeth at something Mort could not see. The only sound that dared ride the wave of this evil air clawed out of Sir Bear's throat as a thousand jagged knives while the promise of death dripped from his naked fangs. The ancient wolf inched out of him, slowly forward. Sir Bear sprang upon the air, and when he hit the ground again, his jaws ripped upward. Mort knew at once that it was a humanoid lying on the ground. Dark, alien flesh hung from Sir Bear's jowls.

Sir Bear then stepped toward another humanoid, whom Mort had not seen arrive. The dog's growling began low, and as he rounded the borehole to meet his second kill, Father Joseph hobbled forward. The humanoid responded to the gaunt priest with a hard military step, which Mort realized was a sign of obedience when it stood still. Once within reach, Father Joseph grabbed the machine-man by both shoulders. Its eyes burst, and it fell to its knees. Sir

Bear jerked back at this and studied Father Joseph. When the humanoid finally fell over, Sir Bear sniffed and growled all around it until he was satisfied the threat was gone.

"Okay, everyone, it's all over," came Headley's voice in Mort's ear.

No one moved. A small surge of thin, red-hot lava bubbled just over the rim of the borehole and stopped.

"What was that?" Todd said.

Mort looked toward Claire. White Wolf was rubbing her arms to console her. Mort turned back to Todd and saw, standing behind him, a tall, pale woman with a dry broom of red hair.

Huntsman stood her small body between them and said, "Mr. Sowinski, Mr. Farkas, meet Lucy MacDuff."

Lucy smiled wryly and said, "The Belly of Boulder, at your service. Welcome to your world, gentlemen."

33

Todd leaned against the wooden porch railing at Marigold's house, staring blankly at a flock of orange dots on a far hilltop and scraping his fingernails against the wood grain. Those were mastodons, he knew. He knew a lot of things now he had never known before. He had seen many things no one in his old waking world could ever have dreamed of seeing. Since he had stepped back into Huntsman's car in Douglas, Wyoming, he had made it farther than his parents ever had in this life.

Behind him was what already felt like a new family: Mort, his friend and adopted brother, White Wolf, Huntsman, Father Joseph, Claire, and Lucy. She was the one who had spoken to them while they were deep in the Earth, calming him and Mort, convincing them the Earth had sent a tongue of lava to protect them from the serpent they had stirred. She was right. It had taken only a small move by Father Joseph back then to ensure everyone's safety. And one large leap by Sir Bear, who was now running through the Montana grass somewhere.

"Oh, I have a question," Todd said, turning around. The others were sitting on lounge chairs or leaning against the railing. No one acknowledged him. "Um, anyway, why didn't Sir Bear do to the humanoids in Toledo what he did in Yellowstone?" No one answered. "Anyone?"

Marigold shuffled onto the porch and said, "Because you and Mort weren't in place yet. You weren't safe. The pack wolf in him was calling for you, first." She set down a pitcher of iced tea.

Mort left the wall against which he had been leaning and poured himself a glass. "So what do we do now?"

This was the fifth or sixth time someone had said this since they had left Yellowstone this morning. No one had found the answer yet.

Lucy said, "I can't really believe you people don't have more holes dug somewhere."

"Who is 'you people'?" Claire said. "You're 'you people,' too, you know."

Todd had sensed that Claire and Lucy were not on the best of terms, and White Wolf had said something to the effect that Claire blamed Lucy for sending her mother into sleep but that there was nothing more salacious than that.

"I'm on my own now," Lucy said. "I stopped digging holes for other people to climb through years ago. My son will see us through. Up, not down."

Everyone except Mort and Todd shifted in their seats and grumbled at this.

"Well, I'm going back to Boulder," Claire said. "The Marvin gave us a lot of good insight. Uncle Danny and I have our work cut out for us."

Huntsman stood up. "Claire's right. There's no use in moping around here. Besides, I have reports to fill out.

Everything must be accounted for. You have no idea, Lucy, how expensive this experiment has been. There's no backup rocket this time, no extra hole in the Earth. Not of ours anyway. Mr. Farkas, do you and Mr. Sowinski want me to take you back to your apartment?"

"I do," Todd said. "I mean, we can maybe start a life now, right? What do you say, Mort?"

Todd saw Mort turn his head a little toward the horizon. Father Joseph seemed to notice this, too, and said, "Come on, Claire. I'll fly you back. Lucy?"

Without another word, Father Joseph left with Claire and Lucy. Todd's new family was already splitting up.

"Mr. Sowinski?" Huntsman said. "Mortimer?"

He turned. "I, uh, I don't know, you know? Can I stay up here for a while? Is that alright with Marigold, White Wolf?"

Mort looked at everything but Todd.

White Wolf tossed his gaze upward through heavy eyelids and said, "Yeah, that's alright. Doris, let's go pack up those dossiers."

"Dossiers?" Huntsman said. Her face then flashed with understanding, and she went inside the house with the old man.

Todd stood next to Mort. Both men leaned against the railing.

"You know what this is about, Todd."

Todd scraped against the wood grain.

"Denver is Boulder, and Boulder is Claire. And when it's not Claire, it'll be someone else. I'm the mindfreak, and my pain will only ever be everyone else's terror, whether that means devils or dinosaurs. I'm forty-one years old and living in a new world, but otherwise I'm the same as I've always been. And if I've got to live another hundred or two hundred years in this God-forsaken terror dome we still call Earth, I'm going to do it safely away, up here, or I don't know where, where I can eventually forget I have any desires at all."

"And dig a garden around Grandma's house again."

Mort squatted down and held the vertical slats of the railing like prison bars.

Todd did not feel sorry.

"You think you're the only one who's had to snuff out his desire," Todd said.

Mort shook his head. He was crying.

"Maybe you're right, Mort. But maybe it's not you. Maybe it's the both of us, together. We're the mindfreak. We woke up at the same time, we grew up at two ends of the same street, you on the park, me on the water. Well...." Todd thought he would cry, too, but didn't. "Fine. You try it out here. I'll try it out in Denver. If it doesn't work apart, we won't be too proud. We'll figure something else out. We'll move to Mexico or the Sahara and fight for space and status with the other billion people in the world." Todd looked up to the gray sky.

Mort stood up. In his face, splotchy-red from tears, Todd saw again the frail man who had first knocked on the hospital door a few months ago. Todd held out his hand. Mort wrapped his arms around him.

34

White Wolf stood outside the door leading to Pope Sylvester's accommodations at the cathedral. He tightened his
bolo tie and breathed deliberately. The door opened before
his knuckles reached the heavy wood. A scarlet-trimmed
monsignor ushered him into an office, where the pope was
sitting, chatting with a couple of secretaries. Sylvester's
smiling African eyes disarmed the old man. White Wolf did
not notice that the pope had stood up until the secretaries
brushed past him. He kissed the pope's ring and sat down,
automatically following the pope's extended arm to a chair.

"Thank you for the honor of inviting me to see you,"
White Wolf said, the only lines he had practiced.

"On the contrary, Mr. Wolf, your reputation precedes
you. Is that how one should address you?"

"However you wish, Holy Father, but Mr. DeSoto would
be fine. That is my father's name. White Wolf does not appear on any legal document. It's a sort of honorific."

"And who gave you this honor?"

"My uncle, my mother's uncle, in fact."

"Does it have a particular meaning?"

"He never explained it, but based on the way my life has

gone, it makes sense. In my culture, the Crow people, in the old days anyway, our scouts were called wolves. So I suppose I've been a scout for a certain kind of person, mostly white."

The pope made the slightest heave of a chuckle. "The Crow people wandered around your continent for many years, did they not? And you fought on all sides for many years to defend the land promised to you. And when the white man came, you sided with him against your enemies. The white man, in return, gave you nothing and took everything else away from you."

White Wolf gazed into the eyes of the man once named Dieudonné Dackouo, looking for a hint as to how to answer this statement. He found only dark mirrors. "I suppose, Holy Father, that we're all in this together now."

"Perhaps." The pope laid his hands flat on his lap. "But do not lose what belongs to you and your people uniquely. It's that special thing that will help all of us. Think, for a moment, son of the clever bird. You certainly know about another wandering people. Why did God set them apart? Why preserve them and test them and whittle them down nearly to nothing? Was it to blend in with everyone else, or was it not to preserve some precious memory, some truth?"

White Wolf stared at the thick brown hands lying ceremoniously on folds of white wool.

"What is it you want right now, White Wolf?"

White Wolf matched the pope's steady gaze. "I have two men whom I believe must stay together. They have been reawakened to complete each other's thoughts and fill each other's hearts and stand at each end of a long bridge, to hold that bridge up for the rest of us to cross."

"What does this have to do with *you*, scout?"

White Wolf let his face fall toward the pope's black shoes.

Sylvester continued, "Tell me, wolf scout: what is it that your people possess for which you were led away from your land for so many years and so mistreated? What truth has God preserved through you, that this was the only way He could protect it? Land is good, but truth is better. Then, as now, the land exists to preserve the truth."

White Wolf inched his eyes upward to meet Sylvester's. This was a man with two names from a people not unlike his own, who had wandered among their own kind until fenced in by those who had forgotten how fluid their own borders had once been. The obsidian mirrors of his eyes almost pleaded with him now.

"Wake your men up to a bigger world, William White Wolf. Wake them up to your world, the world you have lived in from your youth."

***

Mort leaned on his spear outside a stable a few hundred yards across the road from Marigold's house, waiting for some young Crow men whom White Wolf had said would take him horseback riding. Mort had never expressed this desire. He was not opposed to it, either, but hoped that the two times he had ever been riding in his life, once in the eighth grade on a school field trip and once in Argentina while waiting for the weather to clear in Antarctica, would be enough to allow him to keep up with these guys. They were young, experienced, and likely cocky. Mort rubbed the back of his neck. He hoped he would not fall and break it. Learning the Wind Scout in Toledo had made him uncomfortable at first, but he had managed. Learning the dervish in Yellowstone had been much easier, as it was a subtle and precise machine. A horse had its own will. It needed to be trained. White Wolf might have told the men to take it easy. The old man probably had not.

Mort heard someone stirring inside the stable. The men were here. A woman walked out. He had not seen her before. She wore blue jeans and a tucked-in white t-shirt. Brilliant black hair ran nearly to her waist. She disappeared around the corner of the stable.

It was an hour past the time the men were supposed to have come. Mort's watch read 12:73. What remained of world governments after the Great Eclipse had decided to keep the hour the same length as before except the noon and midnight hours, which ran eighty-five minutes each. When the men had said "around noon," perhaps they had meant "somewhere in that eighty-five-minute window."

"Welcome to your world, Mort," he said to himself.

The woman walked back into view and was wearing a sort of woolen poncho, sparingly decorated with Native designs. She disappeared into the stable. Mort had seen very few women other than Marigold on White Wolf's property and did not know who she was. He had started toward the stable to ask her where the men were when she walked out again. She looked at him and smiled then quickly disappeared behind the stable. Mort had taken just a few steps when she reappeared, carrying a saddle.

"Hello," Mort said.

She did not answer or even look but walked into the stable.

Mort followed her inside and found the two men leaning against a stall, Joe Curly, Jr., and his cousin Gray Swan.

"There you are," Joe said. "It's about time."

"I was waiting for you outside. Did you just show up with the woman?"

The two men stood straight. "What woman?" they said in unison.

"The one who just walked in here with a saddle."

The men looked at each other. Gray Swan said, "There's a woman around here? I'd like to know about this. Let's go find her. When the Wolf's away, the men will play."

"Where is he anyway?" Mort asked.

Gray Swan adopted a stereotyped tone and grandiose gestures. "He go to mountain, make vision quest."

"Is that a metaphor for something?" Mort asked.

"No," Joe said. "That's really what he's doing."

"Okay...anyway, is this my horse?" Mort indicated the black horse in the stall next to him, already saddled.

The men walked forward. "What horse?" Gray Swan said.

Mort made an elaborate gesture with his arms.

The two men knit their brow and looked at each other. "Whose horse is this?" Joe asked.

"Maybe this is the one the woman was saddling," Mort said. "She just came in here. You had to have seen her."

The horse walked toward Mort and turned its head and ears toward him.

"She likes you," Joe said. "Here. It's part of your Crow warrior training to steal a horse."

"I don't want to steal that woman's horse. I'm not a thief."

"No, no," Gray Swan said, "it's traditional warfare, you see. You steal the horse, then she chases after you. And then you've got both a horse and a woman. All's fair in love and war."

Mort's mouth broke free of its shackles and curled upward. He eyed the men, opened the stall, and grabbed the reins. The horse walked forward willingly. "You boys better get saddled up," he said, more cockily than he could have anticipated.

The two men took Mort on an easy trot across the Montana grassland. He quickly found riding natural, and the well-trained horse below him seemed to anticipate his needs. Having the five-foot spear slung across his back kept him from slouching. The two men had much shorter anti-specter weapons in rifle scabbards on their saddles.

They came to a promontory and looked out over the sun-bleached land gently folding down before them. At the horizon, the land dissolved upward into a band of atmospheric haze.

"How is it you guys can live out here without fences like they have down in the cities?" Mort asked. "Can't the specters come out of nowhere?"

"You lived up here for a month, Mort. You should know this," Joe said. "Herds of animals rise up to help us."

"I like this way," Gray Swan said. "It means we follow the animals once again. Let everyone else live in cages."

"Speaking of animals," Joe said, "someone spotted a herd of mastodon a few miles north of here. Let's see if Mort and Black Beauty here can pick up the pace. Iyya!"

At a gallop, the black beauty gave Mort every confidence.

He raced alongside the two men on a long, level stretch of soft earth. Whenever one of the two others edged ahead, Mort's mare caught up quickly. His own happy mouth took in miles of fresh air.

The ground began to drop, and the men slowed. Mort's horse did not relent so easily, and he was not sure what he was doing wrong with the reins. Gray Swan ran alongside him to grab the reins for him, but the mare shot into a full sprint.

Mort held on stiffly, knowing that a horse could not gallop so quickly for very long. Something had spooked her. She would certainly see the ground giving way below her. Mort tried to look back toward the men but began to lose his balance. The horse would have to keep him on her until she finished her race.

She raced faster the steeper the land fell. Mort clenched her ribs with his legs. The wind began to burn his face. The grass became a blur. He turned his face from side to side to keep the wind from searing dry his eyes. He did not know how fast this meant the horse was going—faster than forty miles per hour, which he had done in the Wind Scout.

Mort remembered his unease when he had first taken the reins of the Wind Scout. He had felt it again when drilling the Gnome into the Cat's Eye. He had learned both times. Mastering the machine had meant learning his own body. Now he was mated to a mare.

With his eyes closed, Mort felt her muscles roll between his legs. He felt the rhythm of her run. Her mane lashed gently against his arms. He relaxed his shoulders and matched his motions to hers. His mouth opened again, and the wind blew his cheeks wide.

Soon Mort felt no resistance from the ground at all. Even the air had let go of its frictional grip. The horse snorted.

He opened his eyes unto the dim light of a pine forest. It was chilly in here, and he could see the horse's steaming breath, though she barely panted from her sprint. Mort dismounted.

He held the reins and looked at the horse, who turned her head and ears toward him. She followed him to the low branch of a tree, to which he tied the reins. He put his hands behind his neck and breathed long, looking out at the trees, away from the horse.

Mort turned around again and jumped backward. The woman was there, wearing the woolen poncho and holding the saddle over one shoulder. Her other hand held the branch to which he had tied the horse. She smiled.

"Who are you?" Mort asked.

She set down the saddle and squatted, spreading leaves with both hands. She picked up a snail and held it out for Mort. A love dart poked into the soft, slimy slug.

"Mort?" the men called.

"Here," Mort replied. "I'm in the forest."

The woman walked around the trunk of the tree. Mort followed, but she had disappeared.

"Mort, are you alright?" Joe asked. "What happened?"

Mort looked at the snail in his hand. It had retreated into its shell. "The woman stole her horse back. All's fair, right?" He put the snail into his shirt pocket and walked past the astonished faces of Joe Curly, Jr., and Gray Swan. A timid smile broke across his own face as he walked home.

***

Todd sat down at a table in a café, carefully balancing his tray of tea and cookies in one hand so that he could keep a hold on Sir Bear's leash with the other. It had been two weeks since he'd left Mort in Crow country. No one born since the Great Eclipse had any patience for talk about the trivial things of the old world or stories of his adventures in the wild. Fellow sleepers were not as easy to meet as he had thought, and many of them simply gazed at him through some kind of mental fog. He and Mort had been rather unique in how quickly they had come to and survived. After two weeks in Denver, this pet-friendly café had been the easiest place to be alone.

In a corner, behind the dusty rays of golden afternoon, a man tuned a stand-up bass. A tiny woman with bleach-blond hair strummed a sort of miniature harp, a lyre if Todd remembered correctly. The music would start soon. When the music started, and everyone's eyes turned toward the singing voices, Todd would no longer have to pretend he was looking for an affirming glance.

A silhouette passed through the door, tall and lean, and turned his eyes around the room. It grew quiet for a moment, like crowded rooms sometimes do all at once. The look on the barista's face was that of a child caught out too late at night by her father. Todd turned back to the man at the door. His green eyes blazed in his direction. Todd straightened in his chair.

The man walked toward Todd's table with a solemn

grace that said gravity was a mere suggestion. He smiled with everything except his lips. His face was not as young as it had looked from a few feet farther back, or it had merely aged with each minute it spent on this alien planet. Todd's veins pulsed with electric current as if his skin were forming its own Faraday fence. "May I join you?" the man asked.

The café was crowded. This could be better than no company. "If you don't mind my dog, sir."

"Of course, not," he said. Reaching a hand loosely toward Sir Bear, he said, "Hello, little guy."

Sir Bear looked up quizzically at Todd.

As soon as the man sat down, the barista brought him a tray of tea. He must have signaled when he'd walked in, but Todd thought he had caught everything.

"My name is Av," he said and dipped the infuser into the glass carafe.

"I'm Todd."

The man gazed at Todd, who tried not to turn away. The more Todd let Av look at him, the more Todd realized there was no desire on the other man's part. He was, though, penetrating Todd's soul with some paternal power.

"There's going to be some music in a few minutes," Todd said. He broke off a piece of peanut butter cookie but did not dare eat it. "The songs are all different now."

"The world is different now," Av said. He unlocked his gaze from Todd's.

Todd stuffed the cookie into his mouth.

"Someday, though," Av continued, "everyone will forget why they're singing these songs. Not this generation or the one after, but when all is settled again, when things are orderly, when the last of us wakes up, perhaps, we'll have forgotten what had made us live the way we do."

Todd sipped his tea. None of the man's words made sense. "It's already a peaceful world, in some ways. I don't find people as rude or threatening as they were."

"Ah," Av said. "Because we have a common enemy. We are engaged in mutual defense, from table to table in this café, from country to country on this planet."

Todd tried to make sense of Av's clothes. His linen shirt and loose pants were like some futuristic version of feudal Europe. "So some good has come out of the whole thing. Whatever this thing is."

"Let me ask you, Theodore."

Todd tried to remember how he had introduced himself.

Av continued, "Where did man ever learn to fight in wars?"

"Maybe from when we were apes. I don't know."

Av looked out toward the window. Todd noticed a scar on his neck. "Or they learned it from us. Our scientists think we can see without being seen." Av turned his face back to Todd. "But a simple gaze is enough to teach an animal to raise its claws. Tell me, Todd: how would you teach another creature not to kill?"

Todd looked down at Sir Bear. "By feeding him, I suppose. Isn't that how we made pets out of cats and dogs?"

Av reached into a wallet at his hip and handed Todd a business card that read, *Av L. Adamson. Pastoralist.*

"You're going to do fine, Theodore." Av turned his chair to face the musicians. "Let's hear their new song."

The bassist played a drone with his bow. The woman strummed her lyre and sang:

In the darkened night above
All the stars are gathered for a ball
Winter rolls on here below
Fires light the cave the Earth's become

Sleep, my son, sleep, my little daughter
Sleep, my dreaming star
Tell me when you wake, my love, about
Your fate among the stars

Todd looked at every head hanging low in the café, which remembered those they had lost. He thought of his own parents and of Evie and Jake, whose fate he did not know.

Battles fought and dragons slain
Airless dungeons of our own design
Who's alert and who's awake
Watching with a dreaming God within?

Sleep, my love, sleep, my warrior bride
Sleep, my blazing star
Tell me when you wake, my love, about
Your battles near and far

Av's eyes seemed to look elsewhere, into some realm

where he was fighting terrible battles. Todd wondered what kind of heart it took to wear a scar.

A few minutes later, the song ended. Av stood up and said, "Imagine, Todd, if God had taught us all to wage war from the beginning. Maybe that's where we learned it, from the Lord of Hosts."

Todd lost himself in Av's green eyes, forgetting to respond.

Av continued, "How would you teach another not to raise his shield against God when He sends down His gaze?"

While Todd searched for a response, Av paid his bill at the counter and left. Todd finished his tea and cookies while he listened to a few more songs, happier ones. When he asked for his check, the barista told him Av had already paid.

Todd studied the calling card Av had given him. On the back, in elegant script, Av had written:

Wake, Theodore, wake from summer
Wake to winter's chill
Live to wake a world in slumber
Watch over them, still

In limum profundi

William DeSoto White Wolf sat on a bare rock overlooking a leafy gorge in the Wolf Mountains. A vinyl pup tent lay pinned to the ground a few yards away, near the ashen remains of last night's fire. His head bobbed as he drifted in and out of sleep, and the rustle of his heavy coat reminded him to wake. This was the fourth day without food or water. He had not moved from here, the place he had chosen to end his hike, the place he would begin his quest, the place where he had seen an eagle circling in the sky.

This was the end of his fourth day seeking counsel in a vision. He had prayed much as a Christian these four days, calling especially on Joseph the dreamer. No one less than the pope had told him to seek the special truth his people had long held. He sought it in the way his people had done it before. Perhaps he had been wrong to do it this way and this day would close with nothing.

White Wolf looked up at the gray sky. It had stopped spinning with dizzy hunger a few days ago, when his body had learned to draw more deeply from its wells of energy. It was drinking the muddy dregs now, and he could barely stay awake. If he slept the night again, his ninety-year-old body might not wake. If he returned home now, he might not ever know the saving truth: where his people, the human race, might wander on, and how he might lead them there.

As the oceans drained, deadly specters spilled onto the land. Winters ground down the cities of the northern latitudes. A billion people, confined between forty degrees north and south, would eventually become twice that number, and twice again. Blocking an escape into deep space was an invisible, impenetrable sphere where the moon had once stood. Locking the other way out, through the dry sponge of the mantle, was an air of subtle ether that made men mad. Only two people had made it into the mantle, and Earth had rejected them as a pair.

A slight breeze blew, rousing White Wolf just enough to grab his knife. He held the sharp blade to the soft tip of his pinky finger. He would let a little river of blood drip onto the stone to break down the last resistance of his body against spiritual truth and to pose his question to the Earth, which had sent a rivulet of hot lava against his chosen men.

He turned the blade to slice when a pair of warm, soft hands covered his own. Slowly summoning his wits, he studied those hands. Maybe they should be there, maybe they should not. He did not know.

White Wolf followed the arms up to their shoulders. Once there, he saw her face. "Lola," he whispered weakly.

"Billy," she said. She took his face in her hands.

White Wolf put down his knife and held the back of her hands. His sister looked and felt and smelled just as she had before she had died almost sixty years ago. He wanted to fill her palms with tears, but they would not come. He looked up at her. "Am I dreaming or dying?"

"Oh, Billy." She stroked his hair. "You know very well that neither one is possible for you anymore in this world. Come on. Up you go." She pulled his arms.

"I'm so weak. I can barely...."

"Good. You're exactly where you need to be. Up."

White Wolf struggled upward. "Where is Melanie?"

Lola pulled her head back in correction. "Melody Black Mare is minding her own affairs." She held her brother's hand and pulled him along.

White Wolf did not walk forward and pulled her back to himself. "I'm sorry," he said.

"For what?"

"I'm sorry I could not protect you from them."

Lola held his shoulders. "But you did, Billy. I lived long enough to give you Melody. You could not have kept the blood from bursting in my brain as I gave birth."

"But maybe they did that to your brain in the first place. I thought that if I joined them, I could protect Melody, but then they found a way to her heart." White Wolf released a brief spasm of tears.

Lola poked her finger at her brother's heart. "You gave up a life of your own for us, and you wore no holes in your moccasin. Melody's with us, and you know very well how she has been protecting you and your company since. Now those others are gone, and you're still here. Come, Billy. I will introduce you to the ones you should really be afraid of."

Hand in hand with Lola, White Wolf stepped forward, placing a bare foot sturdily upon the open air. Brother and sister walked this way over the wooded gorge, above the darkness encroaching upon the life below.

White Wolf arrived at a tall, wide tipi, a lodge imprinted with a version of the Thunderbird he did not immediately recognize but which he eventually took to be a human-like figure with wings. Lola let go of White Wolf's hand and walked ahead of him. She stopped at the side of the entrance. He could not find a way to open the flap. She nodded a little to what hung above the door.

White Wolf took the pipe a chief would hang at the entrance to his lodge from above the flap, just as a visitor should do, and found himself standing inside. He could make out very little at first as his eyes adjusted to the darkness. He knew only that Lola had entered with him and that there were any number of unknown people sitting around the crackling fire.

One of those figures stood and walked toward him.

"Uncle Frank?" White Wolf asked. His great-uncle looked much younger than he had ever known him, and his eyes glowed with delicate veins of dark green vigor.

Francis Little Rock put a hand to White Wolf's shoulder. White Wolf's heart settled back into his chest at the consoling sight of his uncle. "Come, warm yourself by the fire," Frank said.

White Wolf sat with the entrance to his right and the chief's seat, opposite the entrance, to his left. He began to distinguish several figures in front of him on the other side of the central fire and figured there were more behind him. Frank handed him a wooden bowl filled with a dark liquid whose ripples sparkled when he took it. He drank the warm liquid. His muscles unknotted into soft, childlike strands.

"This looks like a starry night and tastes like pure love," White Wolf said. "What is in it?"

Frank laughed a little. "You have just defined it by its more noble qualities, and yet you want to know its lesser components? That's too much the science of modern man."

White Wolf grinned over the celestial broth, closed his eyes, and drank deeply. When he opened his eyes again, he saw the figures across from him more distinctly. They were men and women exquisitely dressed in skins, quills, and beads. Where their limbs were exposed, he saw, glistening in the firelight, strong arms that had wielded heavy bows and calves that had walked many miles. At the upper reach of each noble repose, sculpted necks served as thrones for faces full of fierce welcome: full lips stretched like lambs upon chins carved like altars, Gothic cheekbones arched upward to eyes opening deep within their vaults upon dark heavens of unutterable truth. White Wolf looked down at his crossed skinny legs, the leather pouch holding his belly together, and the hairless heap of his once-powerful chest. Except for a breechcloth, he was naked. He looked for the bowl of broth, but Frank had taken it away.

After imitating the pose of the noble figures across from him, White Wolf looked left and right. Lola was sitting by the entrance, but the seat across the entrance from her was empty, as was the chief's seat. "I do not see the chief in his place, or his woman."

"And yet they are here," Frank said. "In the tent and in the warm air."

White Wolf pulled the pipe from around his neck. "To whom should I pass this, then?"

"Wait a moment," Frank said. "Wait for your eyes to adjust to the darkness. Wait until you can see what the impatient cannot see. This takes time. Then you will see everyone. Have you not waited four days for this moment? Wait four more minutes, son."

White Wolf gazed into the fire. Its kaleidoscope of yellow, orange, red, and blue played across his brown body. Frank adjusted a log, and sparks danced about the ashen stubble.

White Wolf looked up to see that the bodies across from him were arranged in ranks. Three sat nearest the fire. Behind them was a row of four, and these were dressed like ordinary men and women from different walks of life though they appeared as dignified as the three in front. White Wolf had thought that those in front must have had a higher rank, and now he was not as sure, since another group behind the row of four, an uncountable array of humanity, wore feather headdresses. White Wolf looked up toward the smoke hole, which resembled the old, dusty moon. He looked down again to gauge the size of the lodge, which did not seem capable of holding so many souls. The white feather headdresses wafted back and forth like the grass of an unending prairie.

"Thank you for bringing me here," White Wolf said.

"Now you are speaking sensibly," Frank said. "Do you know those whom you see?"

"I do not."

"And yet you have walked within their realms every day,

young Billy. The three in front and the three behind you are the six corners of the Earth."

White Wolf waited then asked, "And the others?"

"What others, Billy? Did I forget some?"

"There is a row of four, which I suppose make eight if they are behind me as well."

Frank paused, and White Wolf did not know if Frank could see them or not. "What do you think, Billy, about the number eight?"

White Wolf recited from his catechism, "I know of eight Beatitudes."

Frank waited silently.

White Wolf searched his mind for other meaningful eights. "That is two times four, a number of completion for us Absarokee."

"How about this: are there not eight continents?" Frank said.

White Wolf counted on his fingers. "I only know of seven."

"And yet the oceans are falling as we speak."

Electric tremors troubled White Wolf's belly. "I know that Antarctica is melting under the longer summers."

Frank gazed severely at his pupil.

White Wolf suppressed a smirk as he nodded toward his uncle. "You don't mean Atlantis or anything, right?"

"That's the more recent name for it."

White Wolf turned back toward the fire, trying not to laugh, wanting not to offend those present. He looked up toward the row of four. Two of them wore clothes he did not recognize. "That's where we found the technology for hovering, isn't it?"

"And you will find more. Do not worry about what you will call Atlantis, though. It will merely become the haunt of archaeologists and a distraction from real danger. Worry about the last continent, the one locked in ice long before the oceans claimed Atlantis. That is the haunt of a much more ancient sorcery than your so-called science."

"What about my men? How will they build a bridge for us?"

"That is for them to decide."

"How does it work for them?"

"When you first walked on air, William White Wolf, what did I say?"

White Wolf gazed at the fire. He felt himself slouching and sat erect. "Why explains how."

"Do not seek a complex explanation when a simple one presents itself. Do not seek a lesser element when a greater one presents itself. Let me show you what will become of the elements of this universe. Hand me the pipe." With the pipe in his hand, Frank took from a pouch hanging at his neck what looked like seeds and placed them in the pipe. He gave the pipe back to White Wolf. "Put the pipe in the fire."

White Wolf put the pipe in the fire. Only the wood burned at first. Once the flames found the seeds, thick smoke billowed out. White Wolf began to cough. No one else moved, but they seemed to inhale the acrid smoke willingly. The thickening gray filled his lungs with boiling sap. He slapped his hands against his knees in pain, which was all he could do to resist running through the door. Lola sat as calmly as the others. The hot plasma wafting in the air seared White Wolf's eyes and everything it touched. He felt it reach within, slipping through his intestines, gripping his sinews, and boiling his marrow. His lips stretched out against his face to expose more pain to the salve, but every atom of air had become an acid bullet. He pulled his lips back in to imitate the celestial calm of some virtue across from him. His only confidence came from knowing he was not dead.

Once every nerve had failed and every sense faded dull, he felt a blast of fire burst outward from the pipe. He opened his eyes, or they were simply restored. When he felt his feet floating freely below him, he tried to make sense of what he saw.

The dark walls of the lodge shined with a trillion stars. In front of these, the headdresses of the men and women fluoresced with brilliant blue, purple, green, and many other colors he had not known existed. Their faces glowed translucent gold. In place of the rows of three and four, a row of seven radiant bodies appeared like clouds made of precious stone, green and red and gold. The fire had gone out, or, rather, there was only a tiny dot of light at the center of this serene space. The onyx wall of the cosmos began to blaze deep blue from this light, and White Wolf began to fear what he would see if he stayed.

Something marred the scene. White Wolf began to make out large splotches of deep red in different parts of the lodge's walls and was glad for this imperfection, for they made him feel at home. "What are these?" he asked out loud, not sure if Frank was still there. "Are you my home?"

He appealed to these ruddy ponds to take him in, away from the ecstasy that threatened to end his life.

Lola took his hand. Her eyes glistened with love. "They are the Earth's great wounds. That is where she will let you in. Go to the greatest wound you can find, where our people first parted ways with the others to claim our own land, and there enthrone your men."

White Wolf turned from her to look upon the iridescent spirits inhabiting the stars. "I'm looking at you and our ancestors. You are all so strong. I've lived a soft life. You are stone and starlight. I am mud."

Lola smiled at him. "Then become mud." She kissed him on the forehead. He closed his eyes.

White Wolf woke up in a cold, dark tipi, lying on a damp rug, shivering. The fire at the center had not been used for many days. Naked but for his breechcloth, he stepped outside, looked down the small valley, and saw that he was at home.

***

White Wolf sat with Huntsman, Mort, and Marigold at her kitchen table. He had just recounted his dream to them. Huntsman's calm, ponderous gaze comforted him. Mort was stealing glances at the picture of Black Mare. Marigold's eyes danced in the imagined scene.

"How do you interpret this dream, William?" Huntsman asked. "Or is that for someone else to do?"

He looked at his mother, still lost in reverie. "Most of it I understand, and some of it I know I'll only understand when I need to. But I think we need to decide what the wounds are."

Huntsman turned to address everyone. "The large red areas, the wounds, they would seem to suggest a geological condition, empty magma chambers like we've tried to follow in Yellowstone. Perhaps Lucy can help us better identify—"

"This is a biological problem," Mort said. "If I've learned anything in this weird world, it's that life is what's at stake, not silicon. Yellowstone has had massive output in the past, but there are other parts of the globe, other eruptions and impact sites, that have led to much greater loss of life. It should be one of those we're looking for."

White Wolf sighed within himself.

"We could go down to the Yucatan," Huntsman said. "The impact crater there killed the dinosaurs, and we've seen many of those."

"But that's not the worst mass extinction event," Mort said. "Or the first. For that, we would have to go to the Siberian Traps. A mantle plume there caused millions of years of eruptions and the Permian-Triassic extinction event. Anywhere from three-quarters to ninety percent of all life on Earth disappeared. We call it the Great Dying."

Huntsman sat back and crossed her arms. "You heard Vice President Philips. The Russians have been working on something there," she said and put her hand up to her face.

White Wolf cleared his throat. He had hoped his dream might draw some more mystical insight from Doris and Mort. But these were the people he knew. They were the ones appointed to interpret his dream. "But that doesn't match what Lola told me," he said, "to go where our people split off to claim our own land. Are there more traps like this, or a crater, in North America, in the Dakotas?"

Marigold smiled, leaned forward, and patted her son's hands. White Wolf knew this gesture, and he waited. "And yet your uncle Frank spoke to you about continents, did he not?"

White Wolf sat back, drawing his hands across the table, out of his mother's grip. He knit his brow and looked at Huntsman and Mort. A sudden spasm stung his stomach. "Yes. That is where we split off from the rest of humanity."

Mort raised his eyebrows.

"Thank you, Mom," White Wolf said with an irrepressible grin. "It looks like we're going to Siberia."

Huntsman looked away and whispered a curse.

PART SIX

MUD AND STARS

36

Mort sat in the pleasantly lit waiting area outside of a conference room at the OSS Mountain West office in Denver. With him was what was beginning to feel like a family: Father Joseph and Lucy, White Wolf and Huntsman, Claire and Todd. Huntsman was in the conference room at the moment with the director of the OSS and Senator Hendel, both in from St. Louis.

Todd had been cordial with Mort but little more. Every time Mort began to feel down about this, which was often, he remembered that all he had shared with the man were their adventures. They had little else in common.

"So," Mort said, trying to start a conversation after an hour and thirty-five minutes of mostly silent waiting, "how come we didn't have to go to St. Louis? How'd we get the top brass out here?"

Father Joseph, resting both hands on the cane between his legs, said, "To give her a sense of control."

Mort said, "The feeling I got at the Hall of Watchers was that *they* wanted to be in control. Or Philips, at least."

"It's different now. If Philips is going to approach the

Russians about this, he wants his representative to feel in control."

Mort glanced at Claire to see if she was as impressed as he was by her father's analysis. She simply stared into space with another bowling ball bag on her lap and another Marvin inside of it.

The door opened, and an aide dashed out to talk to a secretary. While the two murmured about something, Mort said to Todd, "What's it look like inside the door?"

"Just walls," Todd said. He leaned to the side. "And a memorial plaque to," he squinted, "I don't know."

"Eric Lees," White Wolf said. He was standing by the water cooler.

The aide rushed back into the conference room and shut the door.

Todd leaned forward and ran his fingers along a fossil on the coffee table.

"Ammonite," Mort said. "That's a few hundred million years old. They could've pulled that deep out of the Earth at Yellowstone."

"Not likely," Lucy said. She did not explain about the ammonite any further, as if the mere fact that she was a volcanologist should suffice for him and Todd. Or boredom had sapped her energy.

"Ammonite is named for Amun," Father Joseph said. "He is the Egyptian deity associated with the ram's horn, which takes this shape."

Todd raised his eyebrows. "The ram's horn, you say?"

"That's making me hungry," Mort said.

Todd laughed a little.

Mort's heart lifted.

"Amun was a king who regained control of his country against the foreign Hyksos," Father Joseph continued. "To enshrine his success, he becomes a king, Amun-Ra."

White Wolf poured himself another glass of water, drank it down, and excused himself to go to the bathroom.

"Akhenaten after him did the same thing," Father Joseph said. "He just picked a different principle with which to associate himself, the sun."

Claire laid her head on the bag containing the Marvin.

Lucy gave Mort a glance that told him to listen. Mort tried, in vain, to pass that glance onto Todd, who was nodding asleep.

Father Joseph continued, "He didn't make himself the god, of course. He did what they all do. He picked a principle he pretended to have control over, the sun. That's what they do. They pick out a principle and call it their god. Then they show you how only they control the way to understanding that principle."

Mort picked up the ammonite and set it on his lap. "But this ammonite here, this is life, out of the grasp of kings and gods. This ancient creature, his religion is mathematics. He grows in size according to the Fibonacci sequence. And his life code, his life god, is held forever in stone."

Father Joseph stood and stretched. "Mort, remember that people were using mathematics to make themselves into gods before all this happened, before you fell asleep. You couldn't do anything without hearing the word 'algorithm,' like it was a new religious doctrine. It was another way of having power over people. Trust me, I know. I'm a computer scientist. I went from being priest of the one true God to being priest of a new religion. And we coder-priests were losing control of our algorithm-gods before all this happened."

The door to the conference room opened wide.

Father Joseph continued, "Mathematics was not enough to make our little ammonite live forever. Life is wise and will let die whatever does not fully resemble God."

"That's a relief," Todd said, yawning.

Huntsman stood in the doorway and scanned the conference room. "You all made it. That's good." She very slightly shrugged her shoulders and let her hands fall at her hips. "Pack your bags. We're all in this together now."

***

Todd leaned carefully over the abyss. Only a metal traffic barricade, not screwed into the concrete head of the borehole, separated him from a four-million-foot vertical drop. The Russians had drilled most of the way through the Earth's mantle, and they were about to show the OSS how they had done it. A metal gantry spanned the ten-foot opening and its concrete staging area. From the center of the gantry hung what looked like an old nuclear warhead outfitted with studded belts. Over the din of tractors and workmen barking at each other, Todd could barely make out Huntsman's voice asking questions of their host and lead engineer, Mikhail, in fluent Russian.

She nodded at something and turned to Mort, Todd, White Wolf, Claire, and Lucy, all huddled together; Father Joseph had said he was not in a position to whisk himself away at a moment's notice and would join them as soon as he could. "He assures us it's perfectly safe to stare down the hole as the bomb goes off. The nuclear blast will occur about eight hundred miles down and won't send any debris our way."

Mort pulled his chin into his neck. White Wolf grumbled something. Todd looked down at Sir Bear, whom he held on a leash.

Mikhail whistled at the men making noise, and when they quieted, he nodded to Huntsman.

She translated for him: "We began this project on land after failures drilling through the seabed. Unseen complications. Chinese are still at it. We drilled a borehole about twenty centimeters wide, like at Kora Superdeep, and arrived much deeper, much faster. After a few years, we reached the edge of the lithosphere, two hundred kilometers deep from here, well into the mantle. And then it was voilà. Asthenosphere opened up like sponge."

Huntsman began to take on a Slavic accent. "So then we think, 'We have big open cavities like you find at Yellowstone, only bigger, why not use them to dump rock?' We used ever-bigger drill heads, and debris fell into the cavities. We would fit a man down there.

"We lowered men on cables—no one gave us your hover technology, or it wasn't ready yet, world will never know—and ran into same problem. Men go crazy at Moho, boundary between crust and mantle. So we think, 'Why not a bigger hole?' But the cavities filled up with debris. So then we think, "Why not blast through cavity walls? See how deep the rabbit hole goes? We have plenty of old warheads stockpiled, more than we said we had.'"

Mikhail laughed. Huntsman waited.

"We're even now with hover tech. The only Cold War we fight now is with nine-year winter. It is good to be here now, before winter sweeps across Siberia again. It has been long summer, easy winters. Anyway, success with nuclear bombs, and after thirteen years of drilling and blasting, here we are, near edge of mantle, which is thinner now because of inversion, just over two thousand kilometers thick. If there is way to hell, it will definitely be through Russia.

"Only one problem with our blasting. Something happens with our calculations, wrong timing, smaller blast, like the material is not as fissile as it is on surface. But we have plotted this, and we can see curve, gradual, but getting steeper. This goes with theory that space-time go slower, smaller, out there on the outside of the planet."

Huntsman gave Mikhail a curious glance, and the two exchanged a few words in Russian.

Mikhail continued in English, "Yes, theoretical outside of planet. So now, without further ado, please enjoy your first nuclear blast. We named this one Melania, in honor of your daughter, Mr. Wolf."

Huntsman turned to White Wolf. "Your niece, he means."

White Wolf nodded solemnly.

Mikhail shouted orders in Russian. An alarm blared. Men scurried over the muddy ground. Mort knelt down to reassure Sir Bear. A more pleasant ding took over for the buzzing alarm, emanating from a panel that showed a countdown. When it reached zero, the warhead dropped silently.

Twenty heads bobbed over the side of the barricade all at once. Todd could see, for a minute or so, the thrust of the tiny jets strapped to the side of the missile, straightening its course. When the missile disappeared into the darkness, Todd could sense the Russian heads turning away and looked up.

"It will be several minutes before the bomb reaches its target," Huntsman said. "Mikhail is saying that even though there is less atmosphere, that the missile should fall faster, there is less gravity, as there is less mass the deeper, the farther out they go. It will slow down after a while."

Todd raised his hand. "Does that mean that, at a certain point, the missiles will stop falling, that they won't be able to dig anymore?"

Huntsman asked Mikhail and returned his answer. "Based on their calculations, the missiles should have enough momentum from their free fall to shoot past the gravity well all the way back up the depth of the core."

Todd looked around the site, waiting to be told to look down again. Mort had taken Sir Bear sniffing around. Huntsman was conversing with her peers. White Wolf appeared, after a few minutes, with a tray of coffee in his hands. A worker stopped him, pulled a bottle out of his vest, waited for White Wolf to shrug, and poured clear liquid into each cup.

"*Caffè corretto, come Italianski,*" said the man. "Sambuca. *Vashe zdorov'ye.*"

"*Vashti nivzeha,*" Todd replied, raising his cup.

Huntsman smiled at him.

A few minutes later, Todd watched with the others as

the nuclear warhead reached its target. A small blue light shined briefly.

He found Mort and said, "Are we really the only two people on Earth who can do this?"

Mort put his hand on Todd's shoulder. "I have a hunch about something. Come, take a look with me."

***

Todd sat between Mort and White Wolf at the dining-slash-conference table in one of the OSS mobile offices that had flown to Siberia, moving a marked scrap of paper over a paper map to measure the precise distance he and Mort had traveled across the United States together.

"One thousand three hundred and thirty-one miles," Todd said. "Give or take."

"Yep," Mort said, looking at a diagram that Mikhail had drawn for him. "Almost exactly."

"Well, I'll be," White Wolf said.

The three men sat back.

Huntsman walked in through the door. "What's with all the serious faces?"

Todd stuck out his chin and said, "As it turns out, Dr. Huntsman, Mort and I traveled alone together across the country the exact number of miles it will take for us to reach the other side of the mantle, thirteen hundred miles according to Mikhail's new estimates of its being stretched a little thinner in the inversion."

She pulled her head back.

White Wolf said, "Don't tell me that after all this time, you don't believe a little in divine providence."

Huntsman clasped her hands at her waist. "I believe I

will be happy to see you both make it down that far. All of us will. And I'll be even more glad when you come back." She nodded awkwardly and walked to her berth.

37

A week passed, and then another. Mikhail's team had developed a routine with the arrival of the Americans: nuclear blasts in the morning, careful measurement by probe in the afternoon. They had so far dug to six-point-nine million feet below the surface. The Russians had installed a series of magnets along the upper tenth of the borehole to slow the warheads' descent and to send Claire's Marvin probes back up. These were working. Soon, the dervish itself, unoccupied and operated remotely, began descending and ascending what Mort had called the Highway to Hell.

This morning, it was Mort and Todd's turn to ride that highway, and to a depth that only an American working in inches and feet would find symbolic—the lower boundary of the lithosphere, 666,000 feet down.

"That's two hundred and three thousand meters, Todd, if it makes you feel any better."

They were sitting in one of the dervishes they had brought, doing pre-flight prep.

"It does not. Why can't the Marvins just do this once they break all the way through?"

"Because of the way the cavities open up past the lithosphere," Mort said. "Too many variables to find the narrow borehole on their bounce back from the great beyond. We, sir, can steer our way back from hell."

"And if we go crazy?"

"We won't. That's proven."

"And if we make monsters?"

"We will fight them this time," Mort said. "Come on. Let's do warmups. Read my mind: what am I thinking?"

"You're thinking that in a few minutes, when we're falling at four thousand miles per hour and your stomach is in your heart, you'll be sorry you had *syrniki* for breakfast."

"It's only two minutes down to mark."

"And two hours back up," Todd said. "If Mikhail's magnets even catch us."

"We've sent the dervish down twenty times already."

Mikhail knocked on the glass.

Mort gave the thumbs-up sign. He steered the dervish into the borehole and, once on a straight trajectory, let it drop. As soon as the darkness enveloped them, the lidar map came through clearly on the heads-up display. Claire's probes had shown every crease in the rock all the way down. The physical path to Earth's core, now its theorized outer edge, was clear. All Mort and Todd had to do was not go crazy, and the way would be safe for the rest of mankind.

Two hours and three minutes later, the dervish re-emerged into daylight. When the capsule opened, Mort could see his own physical state reflected on the fearful faces of the Russian team: clammy, pale skin erupting in sweat. His arms flailed to unbuckle his belt and tight legs teetered over the edge of the dervish. As he raced for the office trailer, Huntsman called out to him.

"What's your status?" she asked.

"*Syrniki.*"

***

The party was in full swing. White Wolf, surrounded by a few men, was telling tales. They had presented him earlier with the hide of a Tundra wolf, white with a faint ruddy hue running along the back, and demanded in exchange stories of his adventures in the American West.

Mikhail was chatting with Huntsman, who looked distracted.

Todd was dancing with Claire to K-pop, and Mort was glad for this. She had been the most open and friendly with Todd. Todd could build a bridge for Mort with Claire, who had continued to be courteous and distant with him. Todd had admitted, in his words, that she had "maybe a sort of Greta Garbo thing going on," but Mort did not know the reference, and watching old movies, or any pre-ecliptic movies at all, did not seem to be a thing people did anymore.

Mort approached Huntsman, who seemed only too glad to be rid of Mikhail for the moment. "I have a question in the realm of psychology," he asked.

"I'm all ears," Huntsman said.

"Claire…."

Huntsman smiled.

"Anyway, slaying a dragon doesn't seem to be enough to capture her attention, you know? She has people she likes and people she doesn't like."

"If that's the case, ask yourself what the members of each group have in common."

Mort built two lists in his mind. "I can see what her father, White Wolf, and Todd have in common for her, but I don't know what I have in common with Lucy."

"You're about to find out," Huntsman said.

Mort turned to see Lucy approaching.

"Professor X," Lucy said, nodding to Huntsman.

"Mrs. MacDuff," Huntsman said, grinned at Mort, and walked away.

Mort, for all of his forty-one years, still found himself unable to decipher nuances of tone and was not sure if Huntsman and Lucy were teasing each other or him.

"You spent some time in Antarctica," Lucy said to Mort.

"Yep. Doing work on lichens. You?"

"I'm a volcanologist, as you know. Not much to see in icy old Antarctica, but my future husband was leading a group, and I had to make sure he stayed faithful."

"How does a girl ensure that her boyfriend won't cheat?"

She chuckled. "He wasn't my boyfriend yet." She studied Mort in a way he could not understand. "Come on. Let's have a drink, show these Siberian huskies how we stay warm down in Antarctica."

Mort followed her to the bar, where Lucy grabbed the bottle of vodka and poured two shots.

"Cheers," she said and swallowed.

Mort smiled and looked for Claire. "I'm sorry to hear about your husband Declan's death. And about your missing son. What was his name?"

"His name is Hudson. Present tense."

Mort nodded.

"Do you know what microchimerism is?" she said.

"Of course. Cells from one individual end up in another, usually passed on from fetus to mother. It can help the host fight off diseases."

"It's also a tracking device for a certain kind of mother. My son's not gone. Not from this world anyway."

Mort caught himself studying Lucy's tall, slender frame. She was the same age as Huntsman, but years of wind and ice had worn her down. "It also occurs in twins," he said. "It's well-known in cattle. It can actually render a female more masculine and infertile, what they call a freemartin. Anyway...." Mort rubbed his belly. "Um, so maybe you can tell me why Claire wants nothing to do with me."

"Oh, that's easy," Lucy said.

While she poured two more shots, Mort scrolled through his mental list of obvious physical, mental, and moral defects.

"You're one of us," Lucy said.

Mort did get this. "And she's not."

"Not just that," Lucy said. "She was. When she was a kid. All kinds of premonitions. Her dad subjected her to all the weirdest tests Huntsman could concoct. But that's just stuff kids do. They see all kinds of things adults don't. They're all a little schizo. She thinks you're something she should be but can never be. Hence the unicorn. You know the Wilkes Land Crater?" she asked and took her shot.

That was the biggest non-sequitur Mort had heard in a long time. He took his shot and winced. "No. What's that?"

"At the time of the Permian-Triassic, there's a major impact on the exact other side of Earth from where we are now, or, at least, as the continents were back then. Some suggest that's what caused the traps we're standing on. A comet or asteroid hits on the other side of the Earth, seismic waves bounce and intensify right here at the antipode. Boom."

"So what you're saying is...what are you saying?"

"That's something, then, isn't it? That both of us end up on the other side of the world from where we started." She poked his chest. "And where we stopped. I know your story, PhD-candidate Sowinski. It's no accident that you're here. It's as if Mother Earth herself knows you, wants you to trace her wounds from beginning to end."

At talk of Mother Earth, Mort began scanning the party behind Lucy. "Do all you people have to talk this way?" he began to say but lost his focus. Claire was walking out the door, hand in hand with a Russian engineer.

Mort's stomach turned, and he set down his shot glass. His belly shut tight, trembling with rage.

The light in the room dimmed then flashed into darkness. Something like a wind blew outward from or around Mort's abdomen. All was quiet. No music played. Suddenly, he found himself back in the party, where all eyes fixed on him. Some stared in wonder. Lucy's eyes burned with warm, understanding welcome.

Before Mort could find a word, Huntsman stomped over. Her dark eyes scanned him up and down, looking for something.

Mikhail walked over. He brushed past Mort and felt the wall behind him. Mort saw that the wall bulged inward. Mikhail said something in Russian, and Huntsman motioned for him to stop, that it was alright, whatever had happened.

"By the look of things," Lucy said, "I would say that was your first." She rubbed his arm.

Huntsman brought her hands to her face and neck in exasperation. "Is this the first manifestation?" she asked. "Todd...where's Todd?"

"I, uh...what happened?" Mort said.

Mikhail stood up and started yelling at Huntsman, who ignored him. Mikhail spread his arms wide to make his point, and he accidentally hit Mort with his hand. Mort barely felt this and looked at Mikhail, who pulled back both hands in surrender.

"I think I just blacked out a little, that's all," Mort said. "Long day. Too many shots."

Lucy leaned in and spoke softly in his ear. "You blacked us all out for a second. Nearly blew the wall of the trailer out, too."

"In," Mikhail said. "Blew it in."

Lucy poured more shots.

Huntsman tried to grab the bottle. "I think we need to sort out what just happened with Mr. Sowinski here."

"And I think Mort needs to take the edge off," Lucy said, adding with her eyes, *before this happens again.* "Come on, Mort. It's time to relax now."

Mort swallowed a shot of vodka. When his arm fell from his face, he saw Todd coming over. Everyone at the party was still staring at him.

"Mort, are you alright?" Todd said.

Mort put his hand on Todd's shoulder. "Yes, my friend. All is well. Why do you ask?"

Lucy poured two more shots.

***

In the morning, Mort sat on the wooden steps of his trailer, leaning against the railing. His mouth hung open. Each of Sir Bear's incessant barks from inside sent lightning crashing inside his skull. He heard Todd trying to shush the dog. White Wolf sat down next to him on the steps.

"I saw the whole thing," White Wolf said.

Mort nodded weakly.

"As far as I know, they were only going outside to smoke clove cigarettes. Claire is not that kind of woman."

Mort attempted to swallow.

"But you made your rage into something else, something very dangerous. Men would love that kind of power, especially when they're angry and jealous."

Mort pulled his head from the wooden railing and looked at the old man. He was holding the wolf skin the men had given him, rolled up, with the jawless head facing outward.

"Huntsman thinks you need weeks or months to learn to use this. It could come in handy. I'm not so sure. It might be something just for the moment you're in."

Mort retched a little, but the feeling passed.

"No, I actually argued with Doris about this, and Lucy agreed with me. The time for you is now. But I'll say no more."

"Black Mare," Mort said.

"What about her?"

Mort winced. "I think she gave it to me."

"Hm. Well, that's between you two. Or you can tell me later. What's with you and my nieces anyway?"

"Why does Claire call you Uncle Billy?"

White Wolf shrugged. "I'm an old man who's not her father. Helped raise her. Come on. Up and at 'em."

Mort took White Wolf's extended hand and stood. "What now?"

"I have a special remedy for you. Put the wolf skin on."

The wolf's upper teeth dug into Mort's skull.

"Now we run," White Wolf said. "Sweat it out. Best cure for a hangover."

White Wolf started a short-step jog in the mud, chanting some ancient Crow magic.

Mort followed for a few seconds, collapsed onto all fours, and vomited.

38

Todd did not know whose idea it was to visit the North Pole, and after a flash of touristic excitement, the place lost its wonder for him. The Russians needed some time to finish their blasting through the mantle, so Huntsman and White Wolf were taking Mort and Todd on a world tour. Mort was about to break. He had said something about running naked around the North Pole, and it was all he could do to convince Huntsman that this had been a practice among Antarctic researchers. Todd watched him instead stare blankly into the fire he had made.

White Wolf was taking some deranged pleasure in their excursion. He lay like an angel in the snow, making remarks about how, in this position, he could mark the six corners of the Earth with his members. Todd did not know if he was being lewd or mystical.

Sir Bear, at the first bite of Arctic air on his nose, had been smarter than to venture outside. The driver was warming the hover discs.

"At least it's not windy," Todd said.

"Hm?" Mort said.

"Never mind." Todd turned to Huntsman, who was setting up a camera. "Where exactly are we, again?"

"Norway," she said without looking up. "Near the old Saltfjellet–Svartisen National Park. The new North Pole. For today anyway. It will be .05 degrees to the east tomorrow."

Todd turned up from the fire to gaze at the stars. "And why are we here, again?"

"One of the regulations for requisitioning equipment for travel like this is to take certain measurements at different points on the Earth. We'll have to do at least twenty-five hours of time-lapse photography of the sky, and this is an opportune day of the year to do it. We'll also measure ground temperature, local gravity, the magnetic field, cosmic rays, and so on. We don't have satellites to do this for us anymore."

"And why is that, again?"

"Come here, Theodore," White Wolf said.

Todd trudged over the snow-whipped ice and stood over the old man. White Wolf gestured for him to lie down. He obeyed. Shivers came more quickly lying still, and he instinctively brushed an angel shape across the ice.

As he did this, a field of stars filled his vision. The faint orange light of the fire occasionally lapped into view, but even when he turned his head left, right, and down, those new constellations were inescapable. The ice was a dim gray. Just above the snowy skullcap of the Earth, a band of black wrapped the horizon.

"If you're so miserable out here, why not go back inside?" White Wolf asked.

"It's not miserable, just cold. It is negative eighty degrees Kelvin or whatever. And it's only slightly warmer in the bus."

"You'd rather be miserable out here than alone in there. Look up, then. Do you know what you're seeing?"

"I get it," Todd said. "The mathematical warping of our view of space around the Earth has reconfigured the stars. They're all jumbled up."

"Maybe," the old man said. "Or, just maybe, we have a top-down view on the whole universe."

A brief wind sliced Todd's face, masking his grimace.

"That's what these pictures we're taking are for, Theodore. To map the stars we see against the stars we know. I bet these are all new." White Wolf brushed the sky with his hand. "I bet, or I believe, that past those stars is the other side of Earth itself. It's not just an optical illusion. It is a new reality. The Earth has really turned inside out."

"Look, I'm not a scientist like the rest of you, but I know enough to say that it's physically impossible. You can't fit the entire universe inside the Earth, not even with your idea of Hyperborean space."

"Hyperbolic space."

"Whatever. You can't drop a snowball from the North Pole to the South Pole."

"Not directly through the infinity of space, no. But at an angle...." White Wolf leaned on his side to face Todd. "Anyway, what I mean is, I believe that because of you, Theodore. What you've seen."

Todd turned to face the old man, who was acting younger with each new word he spoke. "I saw emptiness and death inside the Earth. And now you people want to send me through to the other side, poke my head out like a turtle."

"Or up," came Huntsman's voice. She lay down next to Todd. "Behind us, beneath the ice, beneath what you've already seen, is 'up there' at a certain point. Once you get there, everything we see above will become within."

"Within what, Dr. Huntsman?" Todd asked. "This doesn't sound like you. You always seem so measured, to have the answers already."

"No, Mr. Farkas. That's not my role. I'm not a discoverer. But it is my job to measure what we discover. And, if necessary, to put a fence around it."

"So you need me and Mort to put in the first fence post. Against what? The 'outer darkness, where there will be wailing and grinding of teeth'?"

Huntsman said nothing.

Todd continued, "But who has the power to turn the Earth inside out? If it's aliens with that kind of technology, what chance do we have? If it's God, why go against it?"

"Let's put it this way," White Wolf said. "Whether it is God or something else, we have to deal with what is within our reach. This other has, so far, met us on a scale we can face."

"This is my life, then," Todd said. "To go burrowing into caves like Huck Finn. It figures. If maybe I had a Crow name, I could face all this."

"Hm," White Wolf said. "Let me think about that."

Huntsman lay on her side to face him. With White Wolf still doing the same, Todd felt for a moment like a baby on his parents' bed. The constellations spun slowly above him, a mobile hanging over its crib.

***

A week later, Mort sat with Father Joseph at a lakeside in Iran, eating lunch.

They had left Norway after a day of photography and field measurements and passed over an empty London covered in snow unscarred by human tracks. Much of the North Sea and all of the English Channel had become a muddy waste. Paris had looked like little more than a snow globe encircling the Eiffel Tower. They had turned eastward just south of the Alps, the new Arctic Circle, as entering Saharan airspace would have required piles of paperwork adorned in stamps and seals. They had rested comfortably in Rome for a few days, where Father Joseph had joined them. Since then, Mort had confided in the priest the story of his life to the present.

"You're not going to find a place in Claire's heart by coming here," Father Joseph said. "She's never had any connection to Iran."

Mort studied his falafel sandwich for a moment while he scanned his brain for why Claire's father would have said this and gave up. "Why would she have a connection here?"

"Through her mother. Claire's half-Persian, you know."

Mort had felt real joy only a few times in his life, and now was one of them.

"I did not know that," he said. "I wanted to come here because of a travel poster we had growing up. I always felt a connection, something familiar."

Mort had often felt his joy leave when his brain took

over, which told him now that the only reason he had liked Claire was because she looked like the woman in the travel poster. Knowing her only as Cici, she had been an escape for him when out in the Secure Zone. His attraction to her, even after their awkward moment at the cathedral, had been built on that. His brain told him to turn off his attraction as false, but all that would leave him was joy.

"You'll get yourself twisted up inside, searching for signs," Father Joseph said. "And even more so if you arrange your life around desire for a woman. Trust me on this."

Excess sauce dripped out of Mort's wrap and onto his hands. "I thought that was the way, the romantic thing."

While Mort licked his fingers, Father Joseph said, "You've got to be your own man first. Fight for your own life, and she'll see you can fight for hers. That's the old knight on horseback, right? He's proven himself in battle before winning the woman."

"I thought I did that with the *Dakotaraptor*."

"And she broke her arm at the same time, on that stupid unicorn. You can see a string of providential events at work here, Mort: Cass Ridge, Wall Drug, your childhood travel poster, to say nothing of her work with her uncle Danny and aunt Cynthia bringing you two together. Your paths are joined, at least for the moment. But you have a friend now in Todd, and your path is more certain. Finish out that path first. The way things look to me, so much of this has to do with each of you setting out on a better path than the one this life first put you on. Don't neglect him, ever. Here. A poem comes to me about that, about the two of you, where you come from."

Father Joseph held his head back, closed his eyes, and said,

"So that you could satisfy a momentary lust
You asked us all to sacrifice a thousand years of trust

"Or maybe those lines are about something else completely," the priest continued.

***

When they arrived at the borehole site after another week of touring central Asia, Mikhail ran out to greet the OSS mobile office as it landed.

He stormed onto the bus, bringing with him the stench of cigarettes. Huntsman tried speaking to him, but he held up his hand.

"I want to try English for good news," Mikhail said. He thought for a moment. "Our light does not reach us."

"Our light does not reach us?" Huntsman asked. She then asked in Russian.

Mikhail replied in English, "Our laser does not bounce back. No light. Last explosion goes all the way through. Big hole."

Huntsman spoke again in Russian. Todd looked at Mort, White Wolf, and Father Joseph, who seemed to be straining to understand. Huntsman crossed her arms and turned to the men.

"Mikhail is saying that their recent blasting has opened up a cavity with no detectable wall behind it."

"Above it," Todd said.

Huntsman lowered her eyelids. "Yes, or above it. They

have no reflection from any of the light sources they have shot at it. They think they have gone all the way now."

Mort opened his hands and said, "All the way to where?"

"Beyond mantle," Mikhail said. "To void, emptiness. To everything. Or nothing."

39

"How does this happen?" Todd said. He stared over the metal barricade into the borehole, a month since his return from Europe and Mikhail's announcement of success. They would not steer the dervish into the borehole themselves this time. Mikhail's people had installed a metal cone to the bottom to make the machine more aerodynamic for their fall. Air jets would straighten their descent. If they needed to steer, they could jettison the cone and turn on the dervish's hover carpets.

"How does what happen?" Mort seemed much more serene than Todd remembered him ever being.

"That we're here, in a hovering gumball machine, hanging like cowboys from a noose in an old western, about to drop thirteen hundred miles into a Jules Verne novel, you and I, who woke up from a thirty-year coma just a few months ago."

Mort sighed. "The way I see it, what other path was there to take? Water flows to its lowest point and carves an even deeper channel along the way. Life flourishes in those valleys, along those river banks."

"You sound like White Wolf now. Maybe we're just

characters in someone else's dream. Look at me, wearing a spacesuit."

Mort pulled the thick white fabric of Todd's spacesuit, cut into a combination of wetsuit and coveralls. Black patches at the shoulders, knees, and elbows and attachments for life-support systems made him look like a cow. "No. This is real."

"What do you think is even down there?"

"Rocks. Maybe tardigrades, I don't know. Maybe we'll discover a silicon-based lifeform. Most of the crust is silicon and oxygen. If such a creature existed, it would poop out silicon dioxide, you know, sand."

"Nothing a high-fiber diet couldn't fix. Maybe God did poop out the planets."

Mort laughed. "I'm glad we can make jokes. What *are* we doing?"

"Using the Earth like a swing set. Falling all the way down, falling back up again. Twenty minutes each way, more if we have to thrust."

"Twenty minutes to go thirteen hundred miles. What took us two weeks before."

Todd watched Claire, Lucy, and Huntsman walk out of the trailer together. "Don't look now, but here comes your fan club."

Mort smirked and tried not to look. "They're not my fan club. Not a single one of them."

"No, but they are when they're together."

"They can hear us."

"Not with all the workers screaming at each other."

"They're not my fan club."

Mikhail silenced the workers then looked at Mort, who signaled a ready sign. Various speeches and well-wishes were made. Todd hugged Sir Bear then shook hands with Huntsman and White Wolf.

White Wolf would not let go of Todd's hand. "I've got a name for you, Theodore."

Todd felt his whole body swelling outward to make room for this newly imparted dignity.

"Thornapple."

Todd checked his laugh against the stern cut of the old man's face.

"Thornapple," Todd said. "Thank you. That's actually a river in Michigan near where Jake, Jr., has a pretend farm but where he really just drinks and sleeps."

White Wolf patted Todd on the shoulders and whispered, "Present tense?"

Todd's face burned, and he did not know if he was angry, embarrassed, or simply sad for having overlooked the other obvious place Jake could have gone, a place they had likely flown right over.

"I know," White Wolf said. "He's not there, either. We looked. But you, keep your eyes open to the obvious from now on."

Todd sat in the dervish and saw Huntsman approach Mort.

"By the way, Mr. Sowinski," Huntsman said, "I just want to say thank you."

"For what?"

She smiled and kissed him on the cheek. "I am sixty-one years old."

White Wolf's face fell open. Claire knit her brow. Lucy smirked. Father Joseph waved his hand in blessing.

Mort, the color of borscht, stumbled into the capsule. Todd looked up to heaven.

Perched on a far beam of the gantry, Todd saw an owl staring at one or both of the men. One of the engineers pulled a lever, and cables pulled the capsule across the beam to the center of the borehole. Once stopped at the center, the capsule continued to sway back and forth, leaving Todd alternating views of an infinite abyss and the taiga treetops. The owl kept its eyes fixed on them.

Todd turned and checked his spear, for which the Russians had rigged a holder behind Mort's seat. Mort's was behind Todd. All was secure. "Space suits and spears," Todd said. "And still no toilet. Definitely dreamland."

They made checks and double checks of the equipment. Mort pulled down the glass dome of the canopy.

"Is this thing recording?" Mort said. "Testing."

The words appeared on the heads-up display.

He smirked and said, "And not a day over forty."

Todd had not heard the countdown pinging. They plunged into darkness.

***

"Approaching terminal velocity," Mort said.

Todd looked at the screen, which read 17,757 kilometers per hour. He was glad for the darkness, that he could not see the walls of the empty magma chambers undulating toward and away from him. Hitting any of them would mean instant death. Claire's probes had made this same journey many times already; so had the dervish, unmanned.

342

They were following her map, falling to the many minute adjustments of the air jets Mikhail had installed. The sound of those jets was the only thing breaking the silence between Mort's updates. Twelve more minutes.

"We're at the gravity well," Mort recorded. "We can already feel the difference as we press into the seats. Can you confirm this, Todd?"

"I can confirm that my spine is slowly being crushed."

"I affirm Todd's mental status as healthy."

"Sir Bear didn't seem too concerned up there."

"He doesn't know what's going on."

"He has a doggy sense," Todd said. "Dogs know when something's wrong."

"You never had a dog before. Now you know dogs?"

"I know Sir Bear."

"I'll take that as a good sign, then. I'll take the help of animals now."

"Oh? First animals, next you'll be asking for God's help."

Mort sighed. "It's not that I don't believe in God."

"Stop right there," Todd said, raising his finger. "Whatever you say next is only because a certain someone's father is a priest."

"Atmospheric pressure is at point-zero-one atm but slowly increasing. Huh."

Todd lips curled upward at his double victory. "Is that unexpected?"

"Claire's probes did not record that. Increasing air pressure will give us more drag and slow us down. Why is it increasing?"

"Didn't they say there's gas in rock?"

"More in the crust than in the mantle. Alright, well, we have full battery. Plenty of thrust. No problemo."

Todd swiped through the atmosphere menu. "Water vapor present. What does that mean?"

Mort tapped his way through the screen then sighed. "We're not projected to pop above the lower surface. We have two choices. One, we thrust before we zero out our velocity so that we can catch a glimpse of the lower surface and actually make this mission worthwhile. Two, we don't, and we let ourselves fall back upward, maximizing our battery for a safe landing."

Todd gazed at the canopy, which had become a mirror in the darkness. He had come so far with Mort, and they had not made one choice for safety on their overland journey except to stay where surrounded by water. He jerked his head forward. There was water all around them; Earth was giving them safe passage. "Let's press on. We're going to be alright. The magnets in the lithosphere segment can always grab us."

The air soon thickened into a fog that slid upward across the canopy, slowing the machine more than all of Earth's mass above them would have done. Once they slowed to three hundred miles per hour, the highest speed at which they could operate the dervish's whirling carpet, Mort tapped his way through the control screen. "Ready for reverse pivot?"

"Ready," Todd said.

The capsule swung head over heels. Todd's intestines took their time. Mort looked dizzy. Todd took the controls.

"I'm alright," Mort said.

"Just like in Toledo. Let me do this. Your blood has farther to go than mine."

Todd turned on the dervish's propulsion system and released the bottom cone. They were on their own power.

Three minutes later, the two men emerged above the lower surface of the Earth's mantle. They could see this only on lidar imaging at first until they broke free of the pool of fog that blanketed the area around the borehole. The water on the canopy froze.

"We are at eight hundred feet above the surface of the mantle," Mort recorded. "Visibility is zero. A fog surrounded us as we came within a few hundred miles of the surface. Todd, is the dervish actually working? The carpet must be frozen. Give us a spin, but don't take us away from the hole."

Todd pressed the pedals to yaw the machine. "That's a negative."

"Damn. What about another reverse pivot?"

"Um," Todd said, thumbing the accelerator. "Maybe not? I've got no power, no GrEV's. The dervish is dead. We're frozen in this vector or whatever."

Mort pulled his head back. "No one saw fog. No one saw what humid air would do. But we knew it from our trip to the North Pole. Frozen carpets don't work."

"No, they don't," Todd said. "We've got the air jets, though."

"We've only got enough in them to make an emergency landing."

Todd's lips fell heavy with defeat. "I think that's our only option now." He straightened in his seat. "No. What am I saying? Claire will send a probe. We'll be here. The Russians can then send men after us. We have another dervish with us."

Mort nodded. "Okay."

Todd thrust against their upward momentum with the air jets, and an alarm sounded. Mort silenced it. Todd tried steering back to the opening three thousand feet below them. Mort took his controls to help. Without a word, the two men steered with near-perfect synchronicity. They stared at the target in the lidar screen. In the silence, Todd heard only the rustle of fabric and the cracking of ice below him. The ice on the canopy dissolved. Todd glanced out.

"Oh my God," Todd said.

Mort looked out. Todd heard what he was thinking.

Some occult light shined on the scene. Pillars of ice rose thousands of feet from the floor of the mantle, which resembled a sponge of gray rock, though parts glowed red. The pool of fog below them clung with spindly arms to the pillars of ice, and Todd did not know which one fed which. From a thousand miles above the mantle, Todd wondered where the metal core of the Earth had gone.

"Me, too," Mort said. "But more concerning is that." He pointed to his left then turned the machine with the air jets to center his curiosity.

It took Todd a moment, but he could see faint blue light on the surface of the mantle forming a swirling pattern. "Maybe it's ice." He heard Mort's question in his mind. "Not without military backup," Todd said. "Let's just land this thing in a safe space."

"You're right."

Todd aimed for what Mort had targeted on the lidar

map, a flat-looking swath of rock that rose just above where fog was lapping at the base of an ice pillar. Mort was right: ice was shelter and water. With just the slightest bump, Todd landed the capsule.

"This is Mortimer Sowinski reporting. We are thirty minutes into our journey. Theodore Farkas and I have just landed on the lower surface of the Earth's mantle. Our capsule has had a malfunction. We may have just enough in our air jets to skim the surface to the borehole, which is now...sixty miles away. Our plan of action is to remain here, emitting signal, until a probe is dropped to locate us. We have ninety percent battery life, enough to keep us warm for twelve hours. Temperature outside is...wait, can that be right? Negative five Celsius? That's practically balmy. Down in Antarctica—"

"Mort," Todd said.

"What?"

"I don't know." Todd craned his neck, studying what he could see through the canopy. Some tiny seed in his brain signaled danger. This was broad danger, the fear of looking into the woods at night. "Maybe it's nothing. But...maybe we're not alone."

Mort scanned the horizon then played with the lidar map. "Todd, can you back us into this crevice in the ice column?"

"Won't that limit what we can see, who can see us?"

"We have line of sight on the borehole." Mort turned down the temperature inside the capsule. "I don't want anything else seeing us." He dimmed the lights on the control panel.

From the darkness of their capsule, Todd watched the new world outside slowly come into view. Massive trunks of ice soared upward into a pitch-black sky, clinging to an unending sponge of rock where it did not glow dimly red, their roots no doubt fed by the falling oceans of the Earth's surface. Todd reached behind Mort and pulled out his spear. Mort did the same.

De luto faecis

Mikhail was screaming at the engineers. Huntsman was yelling at Mikhail. Father Joseph was pleading with Huntsman to calm down. Lucy was leaning over the railing, mouthing something.

Sir Bear sat on the concrete apron surrounding the borehole, looking downward with Lucy. It had been three hours since they had lost contact with Mortimer and Theodore. This was the third or fourth wave of emotions the team had ridden since then. White Wolf did not wait for the next lull and squatted down next to Sir Bear. What attracted White Wolf was not the absence of concern on the dog's face, which he thought such an intuitive creature might otherwise express, but his pose, fierce and unflappable, in the manner of a watchman.

"What do you know, boy?" White Wolf asked, stroking Sir Bear's neck and shoulder. "Hm?"

Sir Bear did not acknowledge White Wolf.

Father Joseph walked over to Claire, who was thrusting another probe at an engineer.

White Wolf stood up and looked at Huntsman. "Doris, Doris," he said, trying to calm her.

She turned. He had never seen such helplessness in her eyes. "We should have given them more training. Covered every scenario," she said.

He held her arms. "Doris, listen. They know that machine as well as anyone else. No one saw the water vapor coming or could have." He looked at Claire, who was walking over. "Not even you, Claire. Come on. We'll get nowhere with panic."

"My probes are sending gibberish," Claire said. "And they're not even returning. The fog is absorbing their momentum like a net. All I can think is that the dervish froze and that they lost maneuverability."

Mikhail barked, "Yes, that is what I'm sure happened."

Lucy ran her hands across her belly.

That's not the way you saved them in Boulder, White Wolf thought.

***

Todd sat in the capsule leaning on his spear. He did not know how long they had been waiting in silence. He looked at the control panel. "Has the clock stopped?"

"Looks that way," Mort said. "Maybe it froze. No, that makes no sense. It's the computer's clock, and the computer's working fine. Slow but fine."

Todd pulled out his father's pocket watch. "But here it says twelve hours. Look."

Mort knit his brow. "So the computer is slow."

Todd could not complete the thought in his head and said it aloud. "What if…you remember how Mikhail showed us what the nukes did, how there seemed to be a time dilation closer to the core? Like they couldn't release enough energy on time?"

"But your mechanical clock is reading just fine. It does feel like twelve hours have passed."

Todd sighed and stared out. "I should stand up for a second." He stood bent over, stretching his legs. "Huh."

"What?"

"I don't have to pee."

"Good."

"And I'm not hungry."

"Even better."

"Mort...."

"I hear you."

Todd sat down. "How can a person sleep for thirty years with no life support? And how can Doris Huntsman and William DeSoto and Lucy MacDuff age thirty years without really aging? But clocks keep ticking as if time was going on normally. What's the difference, Mort? You're the scientist."

Mort shrugged. "There are two ways of doing this. One, we look at each phenomenon separately. Two, we ask what they all have in common, and that includes the resurrection of extinct species. So what does it take to raise a species? Or an animal at all?"

"Sex and food, right?"

"Energy and the transfer of energy. Your wind-up pocket watch works on the transfer of mechanical energy. But this computer, on the conversion of chemical energy into electricity. Aging is a chemical process, so is digestion. That's what got our friend so annoyed on Devils Tower. You remember? 'You are shit, and to shit you shall return.' We're not dying fast enough for him. And the Earth can make things live with much less chemical and electrical energy than it used to. So, alright, if we're now closer to the edge of hyperbolic space, where distances are shorter, this new sort of chemical efficiency is even greater."

"We're in the fountain of youth, Mort. Just look at it." Todd stared into the hellish darkness. A thought pierced his belly. "Or 'Where the worm dieth not.'"

Mort breathed in deeply and out again.

"Yes, Mort."

"I never thought of it as a physical place."

"Nor did I. But it was called the 'outer darkness.' Now that image makes sense to me. Here it is. I heard my pastor preach once on the difference in time between heaven and hell. Heaven is eternity, where there is no time, just one big moment with God. Hell is where time drags on forever. My God, Mort. Here we are. Welcome to hell."

"What do we do about it, then?"

"For now, we wait, I guess." A laugh burst out. "We have all the time in the world."

Mort pulled his head back.

Todd leaned his face against the shaft of his spear.

***

White Wolf stared upward at the starry Siberian sky. It had been three days since they had lost contact with Mortimer and Theodore. Their capsule only had eleven hours of life support left, even with energy-saving measures. The light in Mikhail's trailer was on; he and Huntsman were preparing a rescue mission. Another dervish would go down, equipped with more powerful air jets, perhaps even a rocket engine. It would not work. They would have to blast through the ice closing up the hole at Mort and Todd's end. And they might be blasting right where the two men were whom they were trying to save.

Some of the Russian workers, to vent their frustration, had built a small house for Sir Bear. The dog had not left his post. He had only growled at anyone who attempted to move him.

White Wolf walked over. "Sir Bear, listen. Let's speak wolf to wolf here. Tell me what you know. Tell me what I should do."

Sir Bear did not turn his head or otherwise acknowledge the old man.

White Wolf stood up and began pacing around the compound when he slipped backward on the mud. He lay on the ground for a moment and brought his hands to his face. The mud was cold, almost frozen, this late October night. White Wolf rolled over onto all fours and caught Sir Bear's black eyes reflecting what stars they could in his direction. The old man pawed the mud. He felt it ooze between his fingers.

He went into his trailer and looked in the bathroom mirror. There was not much to say to himself. Lola had already said it. Without washing the mud off his hands and face, he removed his clothes, keeping on only his underwear. He fetched the wolf skin that the Russians had given him, along with a belt, and walked outside.

White Wolf lay his wolf skin on the step of his trailer. Kneeling on the ground, he rubbed mud over his torso, arms, legs, and face. He shaped wolf's ears out of the chilly mud and stuck them to his head. Sir Bear watched all this, turning his head to follow the wolf skin up from the step to the old man's back. The wolf's skull held firmly on his head. The belt wrapped the rest tightly around his waist.

The man-wolf knelt on all fours and showed himself to Sir Bear. Sir Bear sniffed then woofed. The mud-wolf crawled to the edge of the borehole. He could hop over the barricade. But that was not what mud would do. He removed the barricade. On all fours, he peered over the edge of the borehole.

White Wolf set one muddy palm to the inside of the neck rimming the borehole. He pressed downward, testing the grip of his flat hand against the smooth concrete. It did not budge. He removed his other hand from the concrete pad above, and with one quick breath, he set that second hand to the inside of the concrete neck. It held his weight. Only his knees and toes fixed him to the concrete pad, to the Earth's surface, to the rules of an ordered world. He had flaunted those rules so many times in his life, from his youth until recently. He ignored the number taunting him from the unseen, the distance he would fall. He remembered his first run. He let fear flame into fire. A bee's nest burst inside his belly, an ancient syllable echoed outward, and the man set his foot against the neck of a thousand-mile serpent and crawled downward into darkness.

41

Mort tapped and swiped his way through the console menus. Nothing had changed in the past twenty-four hours except that Todd's humming had gone from annoying to innocuous. Battery still read ninety percent, though they had been running the heat, sending out laser signal, and occasionally scanning the near horizon with their headlights. The dervish was not tall enough to stand up in, and it was not that Mort's muscles were aching; he only wanted to change up his posture. Leaning forward on his spear was no longer enough to break the boredom of leaning back in his seat. Neither man had grown sleepy or hungry.

"She's not going to let us stay put, is she?" Mort asked.

"Who?"

"Mother Earth, or whatever."

"We're totally safe here."

"We're at a standstill here. It's like when we were at your house."

Todd heaved a long sigh.

"We could have stayed there forever," Mort said. "But we would never have found anyone, and they would never have found us." Mort leaned his head back and closed his eyes.

"Unless we had built a fire."

Mort's head jerked forward. "Hey. That's it."

"What are we going to build a fire with?"

"No. The radio. This thing does have a working radio."

"I'd love to hear what Hell FM has got playing."

Mort tapped his way to the radio function and scanned automatically through the frequencies. After a minute of screech and static, the radio paused, picking up on something like a pattern. "Todd?"

"I hear it."

Hau...antikoaren ahotsa...ekartzen dizuna.

"Are those words?" Todd said.

Mort's heart began to pound against his ears.

"That's not Russian, is it?" Todd said.

Hau da Atlan...ahotsa, atzoko...biharko musikarik ederrena ekartzen....

"Please give me a scientific explanation for this," Todd said.

"I have none," Mort said. "Radio signals do not penetrate this far into the Earth. This signal must be coming from up here, out here, wherever we are."

...musikarik....

"That's the word 'music,' right?" Todd said.

"But I don't hear music."

...Atlantikoaren....

"That's the word 'Atlantic,' right?" Mort said.

"And we're nowhere near the Atlantic."

The speaking stopped. Mort and Todd waited several minutes and scanned other frequencies, but the words did not return. "See, just a fluke," Mort said.

Bat ikusten dut.

"There it is again," Mort said.

"Sh," Todd said. He had turned his ear toward the canopy window and began putting his hand over the speaker on the console.

Bi ikusten ditut.

Mort turned off the radio.

Zer egiten dugu.

Mort's heartbeat echoed off the inside of his skull. He swallowed, sending his collected breath shooting through his nose. "Todd?" he whispered.

"I feel it, too."

Mort haltingly turned his head to face outward. With the lights in the capsule, he could not see past the window. The lidar map showed it. An amorphous mass ambled upward toward them. Mort pulled his fingers from the spear and reached forward. From within his darkened cave, shielded by ice on three sides, he waited. His eyes widened to the darkness. The figure crept closer and grew wider. He did not want to take his eyes off the lidar screen, but Todd called his attention upward.

The sky above them had a ceiling. What Mort could make out were long, thin strands of silver glowing red and blue where they touched. If this was the outer core, it had become an inverted ball of yarn.

Or a radio, he heard Todd think.

Or an electromagnet, Mort thought back.

Both men, in unison, pulled down the visors of their helmets.

The approaching monster split in two. It was two men,

two sets of orange lines on the lidar screen, two silhouettes walking stiffly up the road of rock, faintly lit by the distant blue glow they had seen from above. A few feet from the dervish, they stopped. The fear Mort had felt before was not here. This enemy had a form. Mort turned on the headlights. These were humanoids.

***

Five minutes passed. No one spoke. The air jets were nearly empty. They could not simply fly away. He handed the line of his communications tether to Todd.

"We can't wait like this forever," Mort said.

"We won't last long outside in these suits."

"We only have to last long enough to stab these things."

Todd pulled his right foot back, ready to strike with his spear. Mort untethered and pulled up the canopy. The humanoids stepped back.

Their voices echoed inside his suit. *Behia erditzen ari da. Bi txahal ateratzen dira. Hiru behi orain.*

Mort stood and looked down at the machines. One of the humanoids looked up at him while the other kept its eyes on Todd. Mort, his limbs bursting with some new power, stepped out of the capsule. Todd did the same. Mort crouched with his spear pointed at his foe. It was courage that kept his heart rate low, or perhaps some other organ told him there was no danger at all.

Txahalek ibiltzen ikasten dute, the machines said. *Lagundu behar al diegu. Ez dira behar bezala ibiliko laguntzen badugu. Ez txahalak, gizonak. Ez txahalak, gizonak. Ez txahalak, gizonak.*

A third humanoid arrived. Mort felt his internal battle

engine turn on. There was no subtle twitch in the robot's leathery face that told Mort this one was better trained or more intelligent. It was this machine's more gracious footfall. It was a quicker turn of its head from left to right. It was some code woven into the nucleus of his every cell that told Mort this machine was smarter. It had learned to kill.

Horrela hiltzen dugu.

It stepped forward while it drew something from its belt.

By the time Mort saw the blade in its hand, his own spear was in its chest. So was Todd's. The humanoid fell to its knees. Its tongue glowed orange. Its eyes had burst.

Mort withdrew his spear. This steel trowel on a bamboo shaft had once severed the spinal cord of a prehistoric raptor and had now taken life from a murder machine. What would, in another world, have dug a hole to plant rhododendrons glowed bright blue and copper with some strange life it derived from death.

A kernel in Mort's brain reminded him where he was, sucked air into his lungs, and turned him to face the other machines. His heart raced. They stood still and silent. Todd reached down for the blade in one of the dead humanoid's hands and gave it to Mort. *Obsidian*, Mort thought. The other blade was the same. If this mechanical body dissolved into dust and only this obsidian remained, hell's archaeologist would never know anything but a man had once been here.

One of the remaining humanoids looked at the dead one and fell to its knees as if in imitation.

Todd looked at Mort. He knew what Todd wanted to do and nodded.

After leaning his spear against the capsule, Todd tried to pull up the kneeling humanoid. It did not budge. Todd knelt in front of it then raised one knee. The machine mirrored his move. Todd stood, and so did the humanoid. Todd clapped, and the machine walked forward. Todd stepped quickly backward and thrust his finger into the air. The machine man stopped short.

Mort attached the communications tether on his suit to Todd's. "It looks like we have an army of robots to train," he said.

***

Todd looked past the two humanoids toward a vast sea of fog that glowed blue from somewhere within, likely from the large, blue object they had seen when they first shot out of the borehole. The road of rock that led from their broken-down dervish back to the borehole disappeared, a few miles away and below, into that fog.

"It's sixty miles, Todd," Mort said. "The same distance from Detroit to Toledo."

"And nothing but our own two feet to get us there."

"Maybe these things can carry us."

"Let's not get too close and personal yet," Todd said. "If they're up here, they've got, like, a secret base or something."

"Which means that there are more of them," Mort said, "more of them eager to kill like this one. Hey, let's pretend like we're their prisoners."

Todd looked up at the sky, the ball of silver yarn that was probably the Earth's core. "I'm not sure that's untrue, that we're prisoners."

The two humanoids stood still.

"It's a two-day walk," Mort said.

"We've got everything we need in these suits," Todd said. "Protein bars, sacs of water. And, look, maybe we get by like we have been, not needing food or sleep."

"It's a big risk and an uphill walk if we're wrong."

"It's a risk just to stay here. We don't need momma cougar to tell us that."

Mort scanned the horizon, which was violet where the bright blue clouds below him blended with the glowing red rock of the mantle. "No, we don't."

Todd handed Mort his spear, clapped at the humanoids, and pointed down the dark road. With the machines marching in front of them, Mort and Todd began their walk.

***

Within a few hours, Mort and Todd reached the fog line. It was here that the humanoids began to look less like men and more like machines, making short, quick steps over the wet, slippery rock. Todd found himself, and then Mort, imitating them.

The world did not glow bright blue as Todd had expected, but dark, and he and Mort saw the road by the lidar map displayed in their helmets. Or Todd imagined that Mort was navigating the broader scene. Todd was simply following the shape of the humanoid in front of him. As he waded through the fog, Todd wondered if this was what a baby saw in the womb.

"We are headed for the borehole, right?" Todd said.

"Straight for it, by the map."

"And we're assuming these machines know we want to go there?"

"I am not assuming that. We'll break loose when we need to."

Near the end of a full day's journey of thirty miles, which Todd hardly felt had passed, they came out below the fog line onto drier rock, under a brighter sky, and atop a curious landscape. The blue object they had seen was some kind of spiral shape miles in diameter. It lit up the sky the way a city does at night.

"Maybe that's their city," Todd said. He could hear the end of Mort's spear as it tapped the ground with each step.

"Actually, yeah. That makes sense."

"Mort, how do you get readings in the helmet? About the air, I mean."

Mort handed Todd his spear and tapped the panel on his sleeve. "You're right. There is some air down here. I bet these clouds above us are trapping some warmth, drawing gas out of the rock. It doesn't look breathable, though."

"Would maybe the humanoids be making a place for humans to live, you think?"

"I don't know, Todd. Who knows about any of this?"

Todd held his flashlight to his great-grandfather's pocket watch, which he had tied to the shaft of his spear. "I know it's been ten hours and I'm not tired."

As the seconds ticked away into the oblivion around them, and as the hours forgot to remind their bodies of hunger and fatigue, the swirling blue city began to drift toward the edge of Todd's field of vision. It was not near the borehole.

"It looks like it's about twenty miles to our right," Mort said. "Same as our distance to the borehole now."

"We should maybe check it out, though, right? We have nothing but time and energy."

"But no way to get there from here. The road falls off pretty steeply. It's like we're walking on a sponge, between the big air holes."

***

Mort stood at the edge of the borehole ten hours later. He and Todd had circled it three times, looking for a way down the crater that Mikhail's last blast had caused. No indication of an easy descent shined in the dim blue light of the distant city or the orange lines of their lidar map. The humanoids made no move, either.

"Um," Mort said.

"Um is right," Todd said.

"Well, maybe you were right. Maybe that city is our way out."

***

Mort lay flat atop a shallow rise of mantle rock, looking out toward the vast spiral that housed some form of life. Todd lay next to him. The humanoids, in imitation, did the same on either side of the two men.

"Spies like us," Mort said. "I wonder if they know what they're seeing."

"What are we seeing, Mort?"

The city filled his field of vision. According to the lidar data, it was about two miles wide. It was built as one long tube of rough glass or ice that spiraled outward from a dark center. From this distance, each irregular facet of the glistening surface glowed like a bright blue star.

"Like a galaxy," Todd said, completing Mort's thought.

"With something moving around inside."

Mort watched. He had been used to staring at lichens for minutes at a time, knowing they took months to grow to any dimension. There was an overall movement inside this spiral city toward the dark center. He looked over at Todd, who was mouthing what he took to be prayers.

"God telling you anything?" Mort said.

Todd turned his head slowly. "I think He already did."

"And what's that?"

"It's time to go down there."

***

An hour later, Mort, Todd, and the two humanoids stood within arm's reach of the outermost wall of the city. That wall arched upward for a few hundred feet, a dim blue glow dissolving against the steely gray sky. But it was bright blue within, where the inside of the icy vault came down again.

"It looks like daylight in there," Mort said.

"It looks like people in there."

Mort and Todd pressed their helmets against a flat facet of the ice wall. The humanoids copied this. Mort pulled back to measure the miles of open country he saw inside, filled with roads, farms, and villages crawling with cars and people, against the vaulted segment of spiral he was leaning on, only a few hundred feet in width on the outside.

"This must be where the rest of humanity went," Mort said. "I bet there's a thousand other alien cities just like this out here." Mort pulled away and looked at Todd. "They're all gradually moving toward that dark center. We have to save them."

"Maybe they're better off in here than in our world, you know?"

"Todd, look around you. This is hell."

Todd's head jerked back. "What did you say?"

"This is hell, the outer darkness, as you called it."

Todd put his hands on his hips. He turned toward the borehole, twenty miles behind them. "No, this is not hell. Maybe not yet anyway."

"What makes you so sure?"

Todd faced Mort. "I know what hell is. It's making myself into too many things for other people. It's...." Todd seemed to choke up, but Mort could not hear that through the communications tether. "Hell is the insatiable desire for what I can never have. And this is not it. No, Mortimer, I know what this is. Come on."

Mort and the two humanoids followed Todd around the edge of the city until they came to the outer end of the spiral shape, a flat wall of ice that filled in the tall, vaulted shape that spiraled inward from there.

"What are you thinking, Todd?"

Before Todd could answer, one of the metal strands that lined the sky broke off and lowered toward them like the end of a ball of yarn. The end of that slinking sliver of nickel-iron core traced the edge of the city, and the first image that came to Mort's mind was that of the male *Camarasaurus* sniffing his mate's head. There was no head at the end of this metal serpent, though, only a diamond shape like that at the point of a nail.

The sliver hovered over one of the humanoids. The diamond-shaped end opened. The sliver pressed downward and engorged the humanoid.

"Um," Todd said.

"Um is right," Mort said. "We go now."

Mort and Todd had only walked a few feet before Mort turned and saw the serpent swallow the second humanoid. The two bodies of the humanoids bulged outward in the serpent's throat, and it turned to face the entrance to the city. The tip glowed red and melted through the ice. It expelled the humanoids inside the icy walls, which quickly closed up again.

Mort turned to keep walking, and the communications tether tugged back at him. "Todd, come on."

Todd had stopped and turned around again with his hand on the communications tether. Mort tugged, and Todd faced forward.

The two men walked quickly toward the borehole at the same pace at which they had escaped the wooly rhinos in downtown Detroit. Todd had his lidar map on in rear-vision mode and was telling Mort that the snake was slowly gaining on them, slithering up the path they were taking.

It was six hours of brisk walking, little talking, and Mort's heart beating through his suit against the empty air. He felt his fear burn like a living fire. He was going to live, and he was going to make Todd live. With the edge of the borehole's crater in sight, he let a smile break across his tense jaw.

Mort tripped over something. It was one of Claire's probes. A red light was on, indicating the probe was in sleep mode. He turned it on, and it shot out of his hands on a jet of air, eventually disappearing into the borehole. "That'll help us." As Mort stood up, he saw the slithering sliver of metal raise its faceless diamond head over Todd.

Todd looked up at it.

"Todd!"

Todd kept looking.

"Todd, I know you were thinking of going into that city. But that is not how you are going in."

"Go, Mort."

"Without you? Go where?"

"Go now."

Todd disconnected the tether. He raised his arms above his head.

Mort heard words from Todd's mind:

Wake, Theodore, wake from summer
Wake to winter's chill
Live to wake a world in slumber
Watch over them, still

Before Mort could make sense of this, he saw the serpent open its jaws and swallow Todd.

The light left Mort's eyes.

***

Mort came to on his back. He was at the bottom of the crater. What he had done to the trailer on the surface when he had seen Claire with another man he had done here at the sight of Todd in a serpent's mouth. Some engine of anger had turned within him and broken through the crater's edge.

He stood and slipped. The ground was shifting beneath

his feet and grinding against itself. Mort looked around the crater, which was filled with a coiled serpent of metal. That serpent's head was poised to penetrate the borehole. Mort found his spear at his feet. Another of Claire's probes was nearby. He picked up his spear and walked to the probe. The serpent was about to enter the hole.

Mort thrust his spear between two grinding coils of the serpent. The metal monster began to glow blue and red. The blank diamond head pointed itself at him. Mort grabbed Claire's probe and, while he ran across the metal coils toward the borehole, felt for the power button. At the edge, probe between his outstretched hands, he leapt.

The air jets soon turned on. Mort fell downward, back to the surface. The chambers through which he passed grew smaller, and he fell faster until the lidar map in his helmet display became a dizzying jumble. He held on to the probe.

The rear-vision map showed the serpent's diamond head slowly gaining on him.

At the gravity well, he slowed to a near stop. The air jets on the bowling-ball-sized probe were not meant to carry a man upward.

Mort felt mud seep into his suit. He thought this was simple sadness, what it felt like to be prey in the moistened mouth of a monster. The mud seemed to be sucking him upward, but he might already be in the mouth of the serpent. He smelled wet dog hair and lost consciousness.

***

Mort woke up to something pinching his hand. The hand through which his spear had once splintered now felt like it was being clamped by two rows of teeth. Whoever's jaws these were tugged at his arm.

His helmet came off, and thin mud spilled outward.

He could not breathe.

Two hands grabbed his shoulders, and a sharp electric jolt caused every muscle and sinew in his body to twitch. His lungs expelled the mud inside them.

"Mort," a voice said.

Someone had pulled him up to his knees.

"Wash the mud off your eyes, Mortimer." It was a woman's voice.

Someone dipped his hands in a bucket of water. Mort washed.

The first thing he saw was Sir Bear sniffing at his face. The dog gave a woof of approval.

Father Joseph was towering above him, arms crossed at his chest.

Lucy squatted in front of him and rubbed her thumb across his cheek like he was her child.

Mort's eyes dashed left and right. He saw a row of trailers, the taiga treetops, and an owl perched on the metal gantry above him.

42

Mort sat in the Hall of Watchers on one of the basalt benches surrounding President Palmer's sleeping body. It was night in St. Louis, and beyond the dim torchlight, Mort could see a few stars shining through the glass skylight. Lucy, Father Joseph, and Claire sat across from him. Huntsman sat on one side of him. Vice President Philips sat on the other.

"It is an incredible story," Philips said. "No, that's mistaken for me to say. It would have been incredible, beyond belief, if you hadn't returned with all your data. I have to say, and maybe I shouldn't, that when your body cam showed Mr. Farkas being swallowed whole, I...." Philips's eyes grew misty. "But if he was so certain...."

"*Is* so certain," Mort said. "Present tense."

Lucy gave the slightest grin.

Philips said, "Then it means that, among all those people you saw down there, there is hope for my son, Tyne. Hope for the millions, the billions."

Huntsman leaned back a little. Mort had heard her analysis. There was no way any number of small spiral cities like that could be housing seven billion people, not as Mort and Todd had measured it. And Father Joseph had a very different idea about where most people had gone because he had sent them there. Mort looked back up at the stars.

Mort continued, "I can't convey to you the confidence I saw in him in that last moment. And besides, White Wolf gave him a name, Thornapple."

Philips's eyes asked Mort to explain.

"It's a plant," Mort said. "And that plant is also called 'devil's snare.'"

Philips seemed to shiver ever so slightly. "Where is Mr. DeSoto?"

No one answered. Claire tucked her head in toward her father. Mort had made the painful choice to share his hypothesis about White Wolf with everyone. Huntsman had waved her hand as if to brush off this theory, but her glistening eyes had said otherwise. The man had made himself into something else, even something less, to save Mort. What that mud would become now, no one could say.

"Well," Philips continued, "I know these little encounters of ours always bored him."

Claire stood up, straightened her dress, and excused herself. She walked directly to Mort, weakly stretched out her hand toward him, and said, "I'm sorry you also lost someone in all this." She turned on her heels and whisked herself out of the room.

Mort, after savoring her scent, looked up helplessly at Father Joseph. Mort caught Lucy's glance, though, and another slight grin.

"You've been right about everything, Doris," Philips said. "You put together your Wepwawet group when you saw all this happening, before anyone else could see it. You sent your people down into the depths of hell because you believed we'd find something there, and we did."

"I was only right because I listened to Billy," Huntsman said.

Mort leaned back to let the two talk.

"And now he's gone," Huntsman continued.

Philips began to say something but stopped.

Words Mort never would have said before, especially in the presence of the vice president, took life within him. "Well, Dr. Huntsman, what are your instincts, then? What do we do next?"

Huntsman turned to face Philips, glanced upward at the glass roof, and said, "We go up."

***

Heads of wild grass hung heavy under fresh Montana snow. Mort kicked his boots against the wooden deck, waiting for Marigold to answer the door.

Her leaden eyes held him at the threshold.

"Hi there, Mrs. DeSoto," Mort said.

"Hello, Mortimer."

She did not make any motion to welcome him inside.

Mort ran his hand across his head and accidentally took off the woolen cap warming him. "I guess I just wanted to say I'm sorry about Billy, you know? I, uh...."

"He became what he needed to be. That is what he has always done to save others. What he is now, I don't know, but he is a human soul. He is alive."

Mort crossed his arms and looked down. "In any case, our work has taken a different turn. I don't know what I'm supposed to be now. I thought...if you maybe needed some help around here, I could set up some gardens. I've also gotten pretty good with horses, too. I am, after all, an adopted member. You could even give me a Crow name."

Marigold reached a hand out from her blanket and rubbed Mort's cheek. "I've got a lot of grandchildren around here already, Mortimer." She patted his cheek. "You, walk ahead into the world Billy's opened up for you. Fight for what you're being given. Become the man you need to be to win your woman."

She almost smiled and slammed the door, on which a Christmas wreath bounced.

Mort turned around and looked into the light gray sky, at the pine trees in the distance, and down the gravel path.

The door opened behind him. He turned around again.

"One more thing," Marigold said, "about your so-called 'powers.' Don't forget one thing, maybe the most important thing: you made the devil show his face, and more than once." She nodded and gently closed the door.

Mort breathed in long and huffed. *Todd, you there? Come in, Todd.*

A pair of wolves howled in the distance.

Mort closed his eyes, felt the world bending wide around him, and opened them again. With Sir Bear at his heels, he walked down the gravel path toward the waiting car.

***

ACKNOWLEDGEMENTS

I would like thank my family for their enthusiastic support of this project, especially my parents, Tom and Jan. Indeed, all who have read the prequel, *Under a Darkening Moon*, in print or online—friends, colleagues, and three parish families—have nourished my hope that the Hyperbolia Series will be successful. Once again, Danielle Dyal of Bookfox has continued to share her own enthusiasm for this series, along with her masterful editorial care at the developmental and copy-editing stages. Any faults, defects, or infelicities in the representation of the surreality I propose in these pages remain my own.

Living in this surreal world are characters coming out of very real situations, and with regard to the life of William DeSoto White Wolf and Marigold in particular, growing up in and around Crow country, I listened, as best I could, to the voices speaking through the following volumes:

Linderman, Frank B. *Plenty-Coups: Chief of the Crows*. New Edition. Lincoln, NE: University of Nebraska Press, 2002.

———. *Pretty-Shield: Medicine Woman of the Crows*. New York: Harper Perennial, 2021.

Lowie, Robert H. *The Crow Indians*. Lincoln, NE: University of Nebraska Press, 2004.

McLeary, Timothy P. *The Stars We Know: Crow Indian Astronomy & Lifeways*. Second Edition. Long Grove, IL: Waveland Press, 2012.

Medicine Crow, Joseph. *From the Heart of the Crow Country: the Crow Indians' Own Stories*. Lincoln, NE: University of Nebraska Press, 2000.

Medicine Crow, Joseph and Martin, Linda. *Brave Wolf and the Thunderbird*. New York, London: Abbeville Press, 1998.

Additionally, I had frequent recourse to the Crow Dictionary Online by the Crow Language Consortium, at dictionary.crowlanguage.org.

Any misrepresentations of Crow/Apsáaloke culture are unintentional.

INTO A HEARKENING SKY

HYPERBOLIA, BOOK THREE

1

A sagging spiral of razor wire sliced the bare blue sky. Lance Corporal Hudson Bridgewater MacDuff was an hour into his watch at the eastern gate of New Norfolk Section A-III, which encompassed one hundred and sixty acres of Quonset huts and 3D-printed, concrete houses planted on Mammoth Tooth Hill, a muddy mound of the recently exposed continental shelf. Old worlders, the people of his mother's generation, had once found a mammoth tooth here, on this knuckle of a hill within a finger of land pointing from the continental slope toward the abyssal plain. The archaeologists of her generation had somehow found that tooth when the mud, into which Hudson was slowly sinking, had been covered by the steel-gray sea.

Hudson could find no reason for the razor wire. The only thing that was imprisoning the residents of this outpost on the ocean's new edge was a pioneering sense of reward for their efforts. In other words, the gambler's paradox. Specters, on the rare occasion that they did emerge directly from the Atlantic Ocean, never climbed the Faraday fence that surrounded the town. They simply tore into it as violently as they tore into living things, bursting like flowers in brief blossoms of color and light before decaying into the primordial chaos from which they had emerged.

"If you pull back any farther, another head's going to grow out of that Adam's apple," Benny said. Lance Corporal Hector Benitez was often on watch with Hudson. His company was the only thing that made it bearable.

Hudson tried to swallow, but the angle of his neck would not allow it, and he turned his eyes back toward the ocean, where he was supposed to be watching, anyway.

"What are you staring at up there?" Benny said.

"It helps me see. I always sense the specters coming before I actually see them."

"This is a no-woo-woo zone. Put your head down. You're gonna get us in trouble."

Benny had brought Hudson into this trouble in the first place. They had graduated a few months ago from Norfolk Canyon High School. It was not a high school like Hudson had heard about from the old worlders, with classrooms and bells and backpacks, but one with a few hours of daily tutoring from whatever non-essential personnel the Navy could scrape off its ships. Hudson's mother, Lucy, taught Earth science. Only the best and brightest went on to college these days. Benny was not one of them, at least not when it came to books and tests. Hudson might have been. He might have done better on the college entrance exams if he had not been studying with Benny, who had never had any real hope of passing, but who had aspired toward college so he could go to flight school and live like the guys in *Top Gun*. Instead, Hudson and Benny were serving in the Virginia Naval Militia, a once-independent organization now fully funded and controlled by the US Navy.

The USS *Dwight D. Eisenhower* and much of Carrier Strike Group 2, out to sea during the Great Eclipse nineteen years ago, were currently serving as a base at the mouth of the Chesapeake River while engineers built a series of locks from old Norfolk to the coast. Sea level had fallen nearly six hundred feet—four hundred during the Eclipse itself and ten feet per year since then. The fleet in Norfolk waited behind the only set of locks they had built so far, ninety miles away, before the James River met the Chesapeake. That shallow river had found its way to sea through Norfolk Canyon, the canyon it had carved during the last ice age before the seas had risen and the same canyon that, for the past ten years, the MacDuffs had called home.

Benny bent over to wipe a spot of mud off his boots and said, "You gonna retake the exams?"

Hudson hammered the end of his long Dreamcaster rifle into the ground. "Maybe."

"Don't do that," Benny said. "You're gonna set it off again."

Benny was right, but it was hard to take somebody with permanent dimples seriously. Hudson looked at the midnight-blue tip of his Dreamcaster's devonium bayonet through its metallic cage. He tried to catch glints of copper color in the mid-morning sun.

"What do you mean, 'maybe'?" Benny continued. "All you have to do is tell them you're Lucy MacDuff's son. College is a done deal."

Hudson looked out toward the sea. "My mother is Lucy

MacDuff, which means I have to make sure my little brother, Owen, is fed and clothed for the next few years."

When Hudson looked at Benny again, Benny turned away.

"You're just bored," Benny said. "The old worlders always complain that the apocalypse is way more boring than they thought it would be."

"Well, maybe it's not the apocalypse then. In the real apocalypse, we wouldn't have to wait so long," Hudson said.

"Wait for what? Death? Not all of us stop aging."

"My mom's not one of the un-aging ones. She's not like Father Joseph."

"You sound like you're dying already."

Hudson looked out at the world available to him: a muddy continental shelf that always smelled like rotting seaweed and a steel-blue ocean that sent out agents of death at irregular intervals.

A garden trolley rounded the hill leading from the shore in electric silence. Benny's dimples deepened. Hudson would let him handle this one.

Benny stood his short, stocky frame squarely in front of the open gate, feet slightly spread, chest high, shoulders back, and Dreamcaster planted vertically before him in both hands. When the garden trolley drew near, he raised the palm of his right hand, forcing it to stop. Two young women they both knew, with looks of resignation on their faces, sat in the cab. Benny gave Hudson a slight smirk, inviting him to take his post in front of the trolley.

"Alright," Benny said with playacted severity. "What have we here?"

The woman driving, Hazel, sighed and said, "You know what it is, Benny."

Benny, pretending to inspect the front fender of the miniature truck, jerked his head back in feigned outrage. "That's Lance Corporal Benitez, ma'am."

Hazel sighed again. "Whatever, Lance Corporal Benitez. It's exactly what you think it is. Baskets of shellfish."

"I'm afraid we're going to have to take a look inside," Benny said. He walked along Hazel's side of the car and sniffed a little.

Hudson knew, and would never say, that Hazel wore perfume only on days she would have to pass through the gates on Benny's shift. Hudson looked at Hope in the passenger seat. When she finally returned his gaze, he lifted his eyebrows. Hope jerked her head to the side. Hudson could never figure out what about him had always repulsed her.

Benny tried to lift the tarp off a woven basket, but Hazel had tied it too tightly. He set his spear against the side of the truck and lifted the basket to see where she had knotted it. Seeing this, she released the brake ever so slightly and slammed it again, sending the Dreamcaster to the ground.

"Whoa there, young lady!" Benny almost shouted.

"Oops. Sor-ry," Hazel sang.

"You could have set that weapon off. You would have made Lance Corporal MacDuff here into a phantom. And he's skinny enough as it is. What's in this basket, anyway? You said shellfish. These are clams."

Hazel, recovering from the real danger of almost having blasted Hudson, replied, "Clams are shellfish, Lance Corporal Benitez."

"Sir is fine, ma'am."

"Okay, Lance Corporal Benitez, sir."

"Alright then. But we have a problem. Clams are clearly mollusks."

The same Benny who could not pass a test to save his life was recalling details from bio 1 four years ago. Hudson looked at Hope to try to share some sympathy for Hazel, but Hope was drilling her eyes through the fence to her right. Sometimes she was friendly with Hudson, sometimes not. Hudson never knew which version of Hope he was going to find.

Hazel sighed a third time. "What is the difference, Sir Benny?"

Benny leaned his hip against the front of the truck. "Alright. I'm going to let you go, just this once. But no more claiming that clams are shellfish." He slapped the fender of the trolley twice and turned to let them pass. The two men watched the truck turn a corner inside the drab city streets. Benny gazed a little longer.

"Why don't you just have a normal date with her?" Hudson asked.

"With who?" Benny feigned surprise.

"With who? Are you kidding?"

"I don't know what you're talking about," Benny said and walked away from the gate.

"Do it," Hudson said, "so I can have a shot with Hope."

Benny did not answer. Instead, he made sucking sounds with his boots in the mud.

Hudson craned his neck backward again. Beyond the blue veil of the sky was an abyss more impenetrable than the

deep ocean. Before he could will it, his head jerked forward again, toward the sea. "Close the gates."

Closing the gates automatically sent the alarm to Marines on the watchtower. Hudson waited with Benny behind the closed gates while confirmation came of spectral emergence. Hudson could already see a slinking worm of bent light crawling over the hill on nearly the same path Hazel and Hope had taken. The alarm blared in bursts of three. This was a fast mover.

It took six more seconds for the specter to find the Faraday fence, and when it did, its bright burst faded quickly, leaving a smell of burnt wool and a humanoid lurching toward the fence.

"It's one of the dumb ones," Benny said. "He's gonna fry himself on the fence."

"Let him," Hudson said but put up his hand anyway. The humanoid kept walking toward the gate.

Benny put up his hand. The humanoid stopped.

"How is it he obeys you?" Hudson said.

Four Marines arrived, roped the machine-man, and carried it away without a struggle.

"I possess a certain *je ne sais quoi*," Benny said. "Meaning I'm at more of his intellectual level."

"I'm not far ahead of you, Benny. I got a B-minus in Earth science. The class my mother teaches."

"Yeah, how do you not get an A in your mom's class, anyway?"

"I guess we both assumed the knowledge would come automatically from living together."

Lucy was always saying that the words "Earth science"

had become an oxymoron. The receding sea should have been revealing more of the Earth, but with every foot it fell, humankind could fathom less and less about what lay underneath. Above, one thing was certain: no known science would bring a human body beyond the moonshock, the hard barrier between the Earth and the rest of the universe. The only thing the moonshock let pass was light. Hudson had once heard his friend Claire say that a photon never experienced time. The eight-minute journey it took from the sun to the Earth was felt instantaneously by the photon. Photons were the happy children of this universe, asleep at a party, waking up for the brief moment when they were passed from one set of arms to another, when they turned from light into heat.

Hudson looked down and saw Benny leaning against a concrete pillar, eyes closed, mouth agape. Benny was not suddenly bored. As much as the man had wanted excitement in his life, coming down from an event like this spectral emergence was more than his central nervous system would allow.

Benny barely opened his eyes and said, "That thing was right behind Hazel."

It almost got us, too, Hudson thought. He drew a spiral in the mud with his boot while he waited for the command to reopen the gate. He could retake the college exam and go where Benny and these people could not—into the sky, away from this place. When someone invented a way through the moonshock, he would go there. But the higher he went, the more useless and alone he would be, like the razor wire on this fence.